∽ OF GODS AND MONSTERS ∽

BOOK 1

THE DREAMMASTERS

A Paranormal Women's Fiction Novel

KD PRYOR

PRYORITIES PUBLISHING, LLC

To my husband...for everything

Chapter One

"We're so very sorry for your loss." The man's large hand engulfed mine, his kind eyes soft with compassion. "Such a tragedy." He paused, pulled my hand closer, and leaned in. "Still no suspects?"

A hush fell over the mourners behind this man, and the ones closest seemed to lean in with him. Every head cocked, and every ear perked up as they waited for my reply.

I shook my head and stifled a gasp, hoping my smile was still intact even as pain splintered my body. Many people had asked veiled versions of the same question, as if bringing up the mystery surrounding Mom's death was allowed. But it wasn't, and I was sick of the assumption.

I glanced around the large reception room of Mountain View Inn. My mother's inn. She'd lived, worked, raised a family, and died in this stately old home built in the 1850s by a retired sea captain. In this room, she'd greeted guests and checked them in. Now, the space was filled with people she'd touched during her lifetime, all come to mourn her loss.

The line of guests waiting to share their condolences had winnowed to fewer than twenty, and the rest of the mourners had clustered in navy wingback chairs around the crackling fire to the right of the entrance, or at the bar, situated across the wide expanse of shining hardwood flooring. Their subdued chatter mingled with the quiet music from the speaker system. We could be at a cocktail party, except for the profusion of black attire and the mantle of grief that hung over the room. I took a deep breath, eyeing the bar, and considered getting a glass of water to soothe my sore throat.

"The police are still investigating," said my husband, Trevor, from beside me, his voice sharp. "And this isn't the time."

I knew what killed my mother. It was a monster in a dream. I couldn't explain that to the police, to my husband, or to her friends and clientele watching me with undisguised curiosity. They wouldn't believe me.

I released a pent-up breath, my fingers searching for his. He gave my hand a squeeze and let me go. I wished he hadn't, but I knew not to reach for him again. Trevor was averse to public displays of affection.

"Yes, of course," the man murmured, his eyes downcast. His face wasn't familiar. Many of the faces in the crowd weren't, and I assumed they were past visitors to the inn my mom had run for forty years, like the man whose fleshy hand still clung to mine.

I wanted to pull away. I'd barely begun to accept that Mom was gone, barely processed all that had happened on the night of her death. Discussing her with folks who'd only known her as their hostess set my teeth on edge. She'd been my best friend and my mother, and while I knew they meant well, I wished they'd go away and leave me to tend to my shattered heart alone.

"Thank you for coming," I said, hoarse after a day of saying the words to the two hundred guests who'd come to celebrate Mom's life. Tears burned in the back of my throat, and I swallowed with difficulty. It seemed like such a farce, this claim of celebration, after her life had been extinguished only two weeks earlier.

"Mary was a lovely woman." The man's wife took his place, grasping my hand in her dry, bony fingers. "I just can't believe she's gone. She was so young." Her eyes gleamed, and she opened her mouth, about to speak again.

"Yes, she was," I said, hoping to forestall any more painful conversation, feeling her fragile bones within my hand, wondering how difficult it would be to snap one if she persisted.

The woman grunted and pulled at her hand, and I realized I'd tightened my grasp. I released her with a tiny smile. "So sorry," I murmured. I had to get a grip.

She hurried after her husband toward the bar, shooting me a quick, alarmed look before turning and accepting a glass of wine. I sighed and rubbed the bones at the bridge of my nose. She had been right about one thing. Mom had been a young sixty-three. She'd called the inn her fountain of youth. Running Mountain View Inn had kept her busy after Dad's unexpected death right before my sixteenth birthday, and she hadn't stopped, not even for vacations, until the cancer sapped her strength. Up until her diagnosis and treatment, she'd been at the helm, answering calls, interfacing with guests, and managing the team she'd hired to keep the place going. At one time I'd been part of that team, filling in where she needed me during summer vacations and the winter holiday season, until I'd graduated from high school and headed off to college.

This place where I grew up contained so many memories, with its tongue-and-groove ceiling and widow's walk perched at the peak of the house. Sunlight gleamed through stained-glass porthole windows next to the double front door. Our village was in the center of New Hampshire, miles from the coast, not the obvious spot for a house built to resemble a ship. But when I was a child, snug in my attic bedroom, I'd pretended I was on a magnificent vessel in the middle of the sea, safe from any harm. And on dark, stormy nights, when rain slammed the old clapboard and hammered like a million nails peppering the windows, and I was tucked up in my bed, the illusion was complete.

I loved this place almost as much as Mom had, and now I had to figure out what to do with it. And much more quickly than anticipated, because Mom had been improving. Her doctor had even used the word *remission*. I'd been with her, in the office, where she reached out to me, a smile spreading across her face, grasping my hands at his pronouncement. "See, Aisling. It's going to be fine."

I'd believed in Mom's vision of healing, had dreamed of the day when her strength returned, along with her stubbornness and her boundless energy. The weight of peremptory grief had lifted from my shoulders as I shared the news with my husband and grown children. Days later, Mom was dead.

I bit back a sob, shoved away the horrific images trying to crowd my brain from the night Mom died, and offered my hand to the next mourner, a woman wearing a solemn black dress and a sober expression. Her hands were sweaty.

"Such a tragedy," she said. Her husband nodded next to her, his jowls wiggling. "Hugh and I will miss seeing her next summer. And being here, at the inn." The woman watched me, still grasping my fingers in hers, her penciled eyebrows a deep-black bow above faded blue eyes that hinted at the other question several of Mom's repeat visitors had asked. Would I keep the inn open? I evaded this question just as I had the questions about Mom's death.

My head thrummed, the pressure building behind my eyes. I swallowed, forcing back the burned coffee trying to escape up and out of my throat, pressing my stomach with my hand to stave off nausea, praying I could avoid vomiting until the guests had all left. I wanted this day to be over.

"Thanks so much for coming." It was all the answer I could manage.

Another couple took their place. More followed. I passed them on to Trevor, who had a knack for easy conversation and winning smiles. He was a lawyer, an actor trained to sway a jury with a seamless performance. Today, I appreciated his acumen and was grateful for his support. He'd been absent most of the past week since Mom's death, citing urgent issues at work, scheduled appointments he couldn't miss. Leaving me on my own to make decisions about burying my mother. I pushed away the twinge of irritation that tightened my jaw. At least he was here now, and I wished I could disappear.

Finally, the line ended.

My shoulders slumped, and I propped my limp body against a wing-back chair next to me. My face hurt after a day of forced smiling. My hand was sticky from the touch of pressing hands.

"Good crowd." Trevor stretched his arms over his head. "Lots of people loved Mary."

"Yes." My voice was raspy. Grief stuck in my throat, burning in my chest.

Trevor circled my shoulders with the briefest of hugs. "Things will get better." He released me and waved to a couple across the room. I followed his gaze to where his law partners, Michelle and Gary Randal, stood by the drinks table. He glanced at me. "I could use a beer. You want anything, Ash?"

Did I want anything? Mom to be alive. The dream that haunted me to be just that—a terrible dream, a harkening back to the nightmares of my childhood and the visit to my mom's family home in Ireland. But the dream had been more. It had been real.

"Ash?" His voice was soft, and I longed to sink into his arms, longed to feel his chin resting on the top of my head, his heartbeat a calming vibration beneath my cheek. I couldn't pinpoint when our former intimacy had vanished, but I knew my husband wouldn't appreciate such a show of affection here and now. He waited, his brows pinched, half turned from me, poised to move.

"White wine," I whispered, praying my stomach would agree with my decision. "If you don't mind."

"You got it." He patted my arm and headed across the polished wood floor to the other side of the room, his voice booming a greeting to his friends as if he were at a bar association meeting and not a funeral. But that was Trevor—loud, gregarious, and able to get away with it. Everyone loved my husband.

"Aisling?" My best friend, Beverly, stood by my side, her green eyes searching my face. I hadn't heard her, but, then, Beverly moved like a gentle stream, her flowing grace a nod to her peaceful nature and training as a yoga teacher. "Can I get you anything? You're very pale."

She touched my hand, her fingers on my wrist, reminding me of the nurse at Mom's doctor's office checking her pulse. I wondered what my vital signs would be, given that my body was hollow, cold, dead inside. I shifted, forcing her to drop my hand.

"Thanks, Bev. I just wish everyone would leave." I squeezed my eyes shut and rubbed my temples. The funeral had been at ten o'clock. It had to be after two. "It's been a long day."

"Quite a few have left."

"Yes." I surveyed the room, my eyes landing on my twins, Catrina and Conall, dark-haired and dark-eyed like me, sitting in the large bay window at the front of the lobby. I smiled as I watched them with their friends, a group of young people they'd grown up with. They all thought themselves very adult at nineteen. But even though their childhood features had sharpened as they'd matured, I could still glimpse the soft, round faces of the children they'd once been.

Tomorrow, Trevor would take the kids back to campus. They'd been here a week, since Mom passed, had helped me plan when Trevor wasn't available. Conall laughed, sounding so much like his father, and my heart twisted. I missed the old days, when they were young and close by. When Trevor was home more often. But things changed and life moved on. And I needed time to grieve alone.

"So many people asked me about Mary's death."

I looked at Beverly, had forgotten she stood beside me. "Yes, they just can't help themselves." I heard the acid in my tone, but I was beyond caring.

Her eyes clouded, her fingers twisting, and I sensed she wanted to hug me. I was glad she didn't. Beverly sighed before she spoke, her voice soft. "Still nothing from the police, then?"

I closed my eyes, remembering the morning Margaret, the manager of the inn, had called to tell me Mom was dead. Beverly had come with me, had seen the blood covering Mom's sheets from the fatal slashing injury to her throat and the deep gash in her side. I knew where the wounds came from, but I wasn't ready to tell Beverly a hulking shadow wielding a sword had killed my mother in a dream and then followed her spirit from the horror of her nightmare, one I'd shared, back to the reality of our world.

"The fucker was too careful," Trevor said. He'd returned in time to hear Beverly's comment. He handed me a glass of wine. I shuddered at his tone and choice of words, especially on this day. But Trevor didn't notice my reaction. He seldom did. I ran a hand over my eyes as my husband continued. "The buffoons from the village can't handle this type of investigation. They've never dealt with a murder." He took a deep swallow of his beer. "They've finally called in the murder squad from Manchester, and the new lead detective let us in on a bit of the postmortem report. Obviously, something sharp caused the wound, but the report shows the weapon wasn't a knife. It had a long blade."

I shivered. "Like a sword." I whispered the words, unable to suppress the picture of the sword in my dream, glinting in a downward arc to pierce my mother's flesh. I hadn't told Trevor about the dream. I'd tried to tell him about my unusual dreams when we met, but he'd scoffed, told me I was too sensitive and refused to hear any more about it.

"Right," Trevor snorted, scowling. "Something like a sword. Which is odd in itself. Who carries a sword around?" He laughed. I cringed. "That's all they've got, though," Trevor continued. "No fingerprints. Only the large footprints indicating there could have been two of them involved."

I flinched as if he'd slapped me. Trevor shook his head, swigging his beer.

"I know it hurts, Aisling, but it's what happened. You can't hide from the truth." He turned to Beverly. "The big question still is why. There was nothing missing from the inn, and Mary didn't have any enemies." He swept his arm over the room. "Look at the people who showed up today. They loved her." He took another gulp of his beer. "I've got friends in the Public Defender's office who tell me the police are stymied. They might never solve this thing."

He nodded at Bev and me as if his considered opinion settled the matter, then swaggered off, back to Michelle and Gary and his other life, the law life, where I didn't fit.

Bev and I stood in silence, and I wondered if she was thinking what an ass my husband was, because that was what was running through my mind.

Bev cleared her throat. "Let me know if you need anything. I can help you sort through Mary's things."

The tears in her eyes moved me, and I softened and drew her into a hug. "You've been wonderful." I whispered the words, thankful to have another person who grieved as I did. I pulled away, wiping tears of my own. "Thank you."

"I'm here, Aisling." She squeezed my arms. "I can take time from the shop. Call me."

"I will."

Beverly squeezed my arm and turned away. I watched her walk across the large foyer and touch her husband Pete's arm. He took her hand, and they headed to the door. I was holding back on Beverly, and she sensed it. But my nightmares had vanished years ago. I didn't want them back, didn't know how to explain what I'd seen the night Mom died, and wasn't sure I wanted to share it with anyone.

Margaret came toward me, efficiency in motion despite her grief. The staff had wanted to host the reception here to say good-bye to Mary Fitzgerald O'Leary. They'd all worn the crisp white shirt and pleated navy pants Mom had chosen as the uniform. Mom had worn the same every day of her work life.

"We're ready to clean up, if that's alright with you." She surveyed my face, her forehead furrowing. "I know you're planning to stay tonight, but maybe you should go home. I'll watch over the place if you want to be with your family. And I'll be here tomorrow to help you." Margaret lived on-site, the only live-in employee other than my mother.

"I'll stay, but you don't have to worry about me. I just want to be close to her." I shrugged. "I don't know what else to do." I blinked back tears, wishing Mom was here to talk to. But she was gone. I was alone.

Margaret touched my shoulder, nodding. "Let me know if you need anything."

"Thank you, Margaret." I sighed, rolling my shoulders.

No one stopped me as I headed across the foyer and outside to the sweeping front porch, the white of the railings catching the lingering late-afternoon sun. Catrina and Conall had disappeared, and I wanted to find them, hug them, tell them I loved them one more time before they headed across town to our family home with their father.

Leaning against the painted railing, I inhaled the scent of crisping leaves and fading blooms, the unmistakable smell of approaching autumn. The sun was low, the afternoon slipping into dusk, which came earlier by the day as October neared.

I saw the kids in the distance, sitting with their friends in a circle under the old oak tree. Mom always claimed the tree sealed her decision to purchase the inn, reminding her of her home in Ireland.

I shivered.

Ireland. Where the dreams began.

CHAPTER TWO

I had a plan. But I needed everyone to leave.

After the last hug good-bye, I headed to my mom's apartment. She'd created the three rooms from an old sitting room, laundry room, and toilet. Dad had shared the space until his death years ago. My bedroom and bath were at the very top of the house, under the sloped eaves of the attic. I took a shaky breath, remembering all the talks we'd had, tucked upstairs, far away from the rest of the house. I hadn't been able to face the room of my youth since Mom's death.

Family photos lined the long hallway. My parents' wedding photos, followed by my baby pictures. The school photos that featured my toothless smiles I hated, but Mom insisted deserved wall space. Then the picture showing Dad and me sledding the long hill at the front of the house and landing in holly bushes, saved from the prickles by our winter gear. There was my first car, a baby-blue hatchback that Dad helped me find and loaned me the money to buy. He'd died a month before I earned my license. The pictures of Mom and me on our own followed. High school, college, my wedding, the birth of my children. Milestones without my father. I still missed him. And, now, my mother was gone. They were now together. Everyone said it. The thought didn't comfort me. I was too alone without them.

At the end of the hall, I paused before one large, framed photograph of a bonfire. A dozen guests sat on wooden benches surrounding the flames, the dark outside of the circle casting shadows, creating the spooky atmosphere many of Mom's guests anticipated, even craved.

Her inn might have been in the heart of New England, drawing leaf peepers in the fall and skiers in the winter, but the most popular activity on the inn's busy calendar happened in late October, when Mom celebrated her Irish roots and the ancient Irish new year by inviting her guests to join the festivities. Crowds flocked to join in her celebration of Samhain, which she explained was pronounced *Sowen*, her Irish accent identifying the land of her birth.

Samhain occurred on November first, but Mom had the celebration and bonfire around the oak tree in the front of the house on the eve of Samhain, or Halloween, a spooky time that fit well into all that Samhain encompassed. She'd explain, her lilting voice full of mystery, how this was a liminal time, when the veil between the spirit world and the world of the living was thin and easily traversed. She'd tell how Halloween evolved from the ancient Irish festival of Samhain. She'd invite the guests to leave gifts around the tree of cream, honey, fresh bread, and chocolate for the fairy folk and spirits. And she'd weave a magical web of terror and joy with her fairy stories and myths about spirits walking the land.

On this particular Samhain celebration, she'd honored me.

"Aisling will be leaving us before the next Samhain, heading to college." Mom hugged me as I'd ducked my head, embarrassed at the attention. "I'll miss you, my darling girl."

My name was the other way Mom had pulled Ireland into our lives. Aisling was the Irish spelling for Ashling, and the name meant dream or vision. Which was a little too coincidental on this day of her funeral, given what I knew about her death.

In Mom's cozy sitting room, I lit the wood laid in the hearth. In the peaceful blue bedroom, I pulled off the black dress I'd had to buy in a hurry and flung the garment to the floor. I'd donate it, along with any of Mom's clothes I could bear to give away.

I pulled on sweats and a warm, fuzzy sweater, and padded to the galley kitchen. Margaret had loaded the full-size refrigerator with food, but I wasn't hungry. I did, however, pour another glass of crisp white wine and take a long sip.

In the sitting room, I sank into Mom's favorite velvet armchair next to the snapping fire and released a deep sigh, as though I'd held the breath inside all day and only now was it safe to release. Tension seeped from my shoulders, and I leaned my head back and closed my eyes, happy to let go of all thoughts for a moment.

Before long, images from the dream infiltrated my repose, and I didn't shove them away. I needed them, needed to see once more. So, I let them run like a bad movie, a horror flick I'd usually switch off before the first slasher scene.

Mom's voice cried out, calling to me, pulling me into the stormy center of a spiraling vortex. "Aisling."

Wind and rain buffeted me as I dropped, a force against my body. I landed on sharp rock, the odor of dirt, fetid water, and decay filling my nostrils. Loose bits of dirt pelted me. Stinging drops of water dampened my clothes and skin. I crawled forward, cutting my hands on pointed stones, focused on finding my mother. It was too real. The memories made my pulse race.

Fear for Mom pulled me forward through pitch dark until I teetered on the edge of a cliff, peering through turbid fog. Walls of rough stone surrounded me, water painting the surface a glossy green. Beyond the precipitous drop was the sound of falling water. Through the murky dark, I saw Mom clinging to a ledge of spiny black rock, a man hanging on next to her.

The man was familiar. Not his face, which I couldn't really see, but the essence of his presence. I knew him from my old dreams. The same way I knew this place. I'd been here before, but not since I was a teenager, when the nightmares that had plagued me for so long stopped coming.

"Mom." Dizzy, I stared down at the unforgiving rock beneath me. How could I save my mother?

"You can't save me, Aisling," Mom hollered up at me. "You must save yourself."

"Where are we?" I shouted, gripping the rock. "I can't leave you here." But even as I spoke, the scene faded. "Don't go." I screamed until my throat was raw, my voice hoarse. "Mom."

"Lorcan," Mom yelled, grasping the arm of the man next to her as her voice weakened. "The Underworld." I could barely see her, almost not hear her. "Not safe."

I leaned over, darkness eclipsing the shadows below. "Mom."

Something leapt through the inky dark and lightning crackled, a splinter of light illuminating my mother and the man next to her. His dark eyes burned in his narrow face.

"Go," he yelled at me, his voice a deep rumble. "Get out of here."

A shadow rose behind the rocks and a mighty roar rent the air, dissipating bits of the murky fog to reveal the hideous face of a monster. Eyes bulged from its round face, and sharp teeth winked in its open mouth. The beast raised a massive arm, and metal glinted in the sparks of electricity. A sword? Or a claw? I couldn't tell.

I jumped back, heart pounding. "Mom, behind you."

She turned as the blade flashed in a downward arc and sliced into her flesh. I watched, unable to move, as a gush of red spurted from her neck.

The monster wasn't done. It raised its arm and struck again, this time penetrating the side of Mom's body.

"Mom," I screamed, my head pounding, pulse throbbing, as I searched for her face. "Mom." But she was gone.

My phone had woken me at six the next morning. I'd reached for it, pausing to stare at my bloody hands in shock. The phone rang again, and I pulled it to me to answer, shivering in my damp nightclothes, heart racing as if I knew what was coming.

It was Margaret. From the inn.

My mother was dead.

I surveyed the room and the damage I'd inflicted upon my mother's tidy space as I searched for answers. Answers about the dream and any mention of the man called Lorcan.

I'd scoured her bookshelves, combed through her drawers, and dug into old trunks until I'd found what I was looking for at the top of a stepladder. Her journals. And one journal in particular.

She'd hidden them well, tucked into a six-inch-deep compartment concealed within the top of an antique bookshelf. I'd never known the old cabinet had a secret hidey-hole, and Mom had never shared its existence. But she'd made use of it. Her slim leather journals were stacked by date and protected by the heavy wooden lid. It took some doing to hold the lid open and fish the books out. I'd resorted to dropping the volumes to the floor, relieved when no one had come to investigate the racket I was making. But the specific book I was looking for—an old leather volume with a picture of a woman and two swans tooled on the front, the one I remembered Mom using to record my dreams—wasn't there.

The journals I'd found contained notes about the inn, entries about our family life, and details about my progress in school, but a few entries scattered within the pages pertained to my dreams, as if her thoughts had demanded immediate expression and she hadn't taken time to fetch her special leather journal. I picked up a journal I'd left on the side table next to the chair and opened it to an early entry detailing my dreams. I'd been just seven when the dreams began. I blamed it on Ireland. After all, they started there.

Despite all my efforts, Aisling still has the dreams. I've taught her the mantra to close off the separate part of her brain from where these dreams originate, but still they infiltrate her sleep, although they aren't as terrifying. It might help if my daughter could remember specific details, but she is young and the dreams fade. This is for the best. What she remembers is bad enough. Shadows. Flashing lights. Growls and snarls. What Aisling calls monsters. Mother and I speak about other methods to mitigate the dreams, and I assure her Aisling wears the protective swan pendant. I know this is all related to Geraldine. She opened abilities Aisling isn't ready to understand. What I cannot fathom is the dark nature of the dreams.

I'd watched my mom write notes after every one of my dreams. She'd never shared her thoughts, but I could see her worry in the way she rubbed her hands, the deep crease in her brow as she contemplated me. I wondered if I was defective, like my favorite doll who'd lost a leg. But when I asked Mom, her brow would clear and she'd scooped me into her arms, assuring me I was perfect, and I wasn't to worry about my dreams.

Most of the few entries I discovered were similar. A few had more details. Halloween had been a bad time for me, when the dreams had taken on a corporeal feeling, like the one on the night Mom died. The monsters had been more vivid, the shadows less murky, and I'd seen claws and fur. Hot breath seemed to burn down my back when I'd fled. The man Mom had called Lorcan had been there every time, but he'd never been able to help. In fact, I forgot him until the next dream, so I'd never shared his existence with Mom.

I studied the entry once more, lingering over one name. Geraldine. My aunt. Mom's younger sister.

I'd met Geraldine and my grandmother once, years ago, at my grandfather Fitzgerald's funeral when I was seven. It was the one time Mom had gone home in all the years she'd lived in the States. Aunt Geraldine had taken an interest in me when everyone else had been focused on my grandfather's death. She'd even taken me to her attic hideaway and shown me old books and shiny crystals. When Mom found us, her body shook in fury and she declared we'd never return. I never understood why. Mom had never shared her suspicions about Geraldine and my dreams.

A stack of sympathy cards rested on the side table, and I picked up the top one, examining the return address.

Fionnuala Fitzgerald. Old Oak Manor. Galway, Ireland.

Granny had sent this note and flowers. Not enough, in my estimation, to commemorate the life of her eldest child. But she claimed physical impairment kept her away. A badly broken leg that hadn't properly healed. My aunt Geraldine had no such excuse. I picked up Geraldine's note. Short, curt, to the point.

I wasn't disposed to cordial feelings toward either of my only relatives on Mom's side. But I could put anger aside for answers. And I needed answers about the dream.

I'd found Granny's phone number in Mom's ancient address book. I'd called her once, a brief call to let her know of my mother's death. Geraldine wasn't listed as a contact in the book or Mom's phone.

It was nine thirty in the evening in Galway. and Granny was old, over eighty. But I punched in the numbers anyway. Answers took priority.

The phone rang. Five times. On the sixth ring, I sighed, about to disconnect. Tomorrow would have to suffice.

Then the line clicked. Someone cleared their throat, took a deep breath, spoke in a croaky voice. "Hello."

The voice was old, weary. It had to be her. But she'd sounded brighter, stronger, so different only a few days ago, before she'd learned of Mom's death. I wanted to speak, but my mouth opened, then closed.

"Hello." A tapping came over the line, as if she was poking the phone, checking if it was working. "Is anyone there?"

I'd started this. I had to speak. "Granny?" My voice cracked on the word.

The tapping on the other end stopped. "Aisling?" There was a sharp intake of breath. "Is that you, child?"

I cleared my throat, forced my trembling hands to hold the phone steady. "Yes. Hello." I paused. What did I say to a grandmother I didn't know and had spoken to only once in thirty-seven years? "It's Aisling. I needed to speak to you."

There was a rustle, a sniff. "Her funeral was today." Granny's breath hitched, her voice quavered, and I knew she was crying.

"Yes." I paused. "The day was beautiful. Mom would have loved it." My voice trailed off, not adding the unspoken words. *If she'd been alive.*

Granny swallowed. "How are you coping, child? I wanted to come. My damned leg." She paused. "I know it sounds weak, pathetic. My daughter is dead, and I wasn't there. I'm so sorry, Aisling. So very sorry. I've missed Mary. And you. So much." She choked out a sob.

I bowed my head, unable to speak, wiping tears from my cheeks. When I had my voice, I responded. "Why didn't you ever come? Why didn't you call me?"

Granny moaned, as if I'd injured her. "I wanted to. I didn't know if you'd care to speak to me. It's been so long." She sniffed again. "I did what Mary asked, but I hated every minute, every day and year I wasn't part of your life. Didn't get to see you, know you, be with you and Mary."

I took a deep breath, letting the words flow over me, sink in. I didn't forgive Granny for the years of silence, but the sincerity in her voice blunted the edge of my anger. "Why did Mom ask you to stay away? Was it because of something Geraldine did? Was it because of my dreams?"

Granny's voice sharpened, and I could imagine her sitting up straighter. "Where did you get the idea it was about your aunt?"

"I found Mom's journals. She wrote about my dreams. She mentioned her sister."

"Oh." She cleared her throat. "She told me you didn't have the dreams anymore." A combination of fear and curiosity laced her words. "Are they back?"

I didn't answer at first, processing. The dreams frightened Granny as much as they'd terrified my mother. I heard it in her voice. What I'd never known is why my dreams, in particular, were so bad. Other kids I knew had nightmares. But Mom thought mine were worse, dangerous. Almost as if they'd had a power. She'd even accused me of manipulating situations in high school to my advantage with my dreams. I hadn't meant to, but sometimes my dreams seemed to correlate to changes. That was one explanation for how I'd ended up with Trevor.

We'd been a year apart in college. He was a TA, leading exam reviews and offering help with homework. He was handsome, charismatic. I went to every review session, gloried in his nearness when he'd help me with clunky math equations. He didn't know me after the sessions ended, ignored me when we passed on campus. But I was determined. He was the man I wanted. I told Beverly. She told me to give it up. He was taken. But I didn't listen. I daydreamed. I drew pictures. I even wrote a story in my journal about us being together. And that night I dreamed of him, that he loved me. A day later, he asked me out.

I'd claimed it was the law of attraction, a theory Beverly had explored when she discovered yoga. My friend had shaken her head, but I'd maintained my story. Until the other dreams, after the kids came. But all my dreams paled compared to the one the night Mom died.

I sighed. Only Mom's dream mattered here. No need to tell Granny the rest of it.

"I had a dream. A bad one." My stomach clenched at the thought of telling her. "The night Mom died."

Granny gasped. "Like when you were younger?"

"Mom told you. She wrote that in her journals."

"Yes." She paused. "She kept me apprised. Do you still wear the pendant I gave you?"

The silver swan had hung around my neck from the time I visited Ireland when Granny presented the gift until I was close to eighteen and the worst of the dreams subsided. I hadn't thought to put it on now. I'd even considered giving it to Catrina, but Mom had vetoed the idea when I suggested it.

"Your granny gave it to you," Mom had told me. "It's a special gift, a talisman. Always keep it, Aisling." She'd clasped my hands, her eyes solemn, pleading. "You might need it."

I hadn't needed it in years. Just as I hadn't needed the mantra Mom insisted I repeat every night before sleep—*I will not slip around the bend, past the place where normal dreams end.* But it was somewhere, in a jewelry box. "I have it."

"But you don't wear it." She paused. "Or say the mantra Mary taught you."

"The worst dreams ended years ago. I couldn't predict there'd be another one the night of Mom's death."

"Perhaps you should wear the pendant for now."

"The dream with Mom wasn't like the other ones. It was almost real. In fact, I was wet in the morning, like I'd been in a storm."

Silence hit me like a wall. Had Granny hung up?

"Are you there? Granny?"

"Tell me the dream, Aisling." Her voice was low, raspy. "Every detail."

I clenched my teeth, dreading the retelling, but willing, if she had answers. If Granny could explain Mom's injuries. Could tell me who the man was with Mom. I began.

When my voice faltered to a stop, Granny spoke, the first hint of her presence since I'd begun.

"Mary was killed in the dream." I could almost see her eyes close and the tears seep out. I could hear her snuffling breaths.

"She was," I said softly. "I don't understand how it happened. I don't understand how I got there, but I had blood on my hands and dirt on my pajamas. How can that be? How does a dream like the one Mom had even work?" Panic rushed through me, clogging my throat until I had to stop, cough, and take a breath. Granny remained silent aside from a deep sigh, and I wondered if she thought I was crazy. I had to make her understand how desperate I was for answers. "I saw her wounds the next day. In her room. In her bed. The police are investigating her death. I saw what happened to her, but I can't speak up. The police will think I'm nuts if I tell them what I know. Because murder doesn't happen in a dream. Not in my world."

We sat in silence for what felt like an eternity but was nearer to three minutes. Finally, Granny spoke.

"There's so much you don't understand, child." Granny paused, as if gathering her thoughts. "Mary went too far when she denied you the truth of your heritage. She should have explained."

"But she didn't," I said, holding in my frustration. "And you don't seem inclined to do so either."

"You deserve an explanation," Granny said, her voice stronger, as if she'd made a decision. "But this is not a conversation to be held over the phone and separated by an ocean. You must visit." She spoke as if this was a foregone conclusion. "Things have changed since Mary left." She spoke more to herself than to me. "Old animosities have been put to rest. We must all move forward."

"What animosity?"

Granny seemed not to have heard my question. "I would so love to see you again, child. Introduce you to your heritage and get to know each other."

I took a deep breath. She wasn't going to give me the answers I sought unless I went to her. But was that such a bad thought? I had the time. Trevor was always busy. In truth, I doubted he'd miss me. Maybe a trip to Ireland was the break I needed after Mom's death. And I wanted to understand what was so different about her dreams and mine.

"Yes," I said. "I'll speak to my husband and plan a trip to visit. Maybe after the holidays."

"No, child." Granny's voice was sharp. "Come now. We need to further explore Mary's dream. This isn't something that should wait."

I bristled and took a breath. "Let me check my schedule and get back to you." Another long silence followed. I sensed my answer disappointed her, but I wasn't about to be pushed into a decision. I stifled a yawn, hesitating to even mention the man after all we'd discussed. He seemed unimportant compared to the damage done to my mother by the forces of the dream. But something compelled me to ask.

"There was one last thing."

"The monsters didn't hurt you." Her voice was sharp.

"No. It was a name. Of the man I saw with her. She seemed to know him. It's probably not important, not now that she's gone."

"What's the name, Aisling?" Granny's weary voice asked the question, and I knew it was time to let her rest.

"I'm sorry. I know it's late for you."

"It's fine, child. Tell me."

I sighed. "She called him Lorcan."

Granny cried out at the name, as though the sound of it broke her.

"Granny. Do you know this guy? He was with Mom. Was he her friend?"

When she'd gathered herself, Granny spoke again.

"You must come to me, Aisling. It's the only way. We must find Lorcan."

Chapter Three

"Of course, I can't go." I wasn't sure if I believed my words. All I'd been thinking about since the call with Granny was a potential trip to Ireland. But it seemed selfish to go on vacation so soon after Mom's death. I pulled out an armload of dresses buried in the back of Mom's closet, grimacing at one with a frilly collar. "No way Mom ever wore this thing." I dropped it on the growing pile of donation items.

"Why can't you go?" Beverly had come by a few hours ago to check on me and stayed for lunch. Afterward, when I announced I was cleaning out Mom's closet, she offered to help, and for the first time since Mom's death I was happy for the company, my heart lighter than it had been in weeks. Bev held up a gold lamé sheath dress, her eyebrows raised, a faint smile on her lips. "What about this one?"

"I think she wore it once, years ago. To a fundraiser." I walked over and touched the slinky fabric, the hint of Mom's favorite violet perfume lingering in the weave. Part of me wanted to gather the fabric close, as if hugging the dress could take the place of hugging Mom. Grief, heavy and hot, washed over me as images from the dream filled my mind.

"Aisling?" Bev's voice was gentle. She touched my hand.

I pushed away the disturbing memories. "Is this stuff even in style any longer?" I swallowed back tears and forced a laugh, hoping to recapture the prior lighter mood.

"I hope not." Bev scrutinized me, as if assuring herself I wasn't about to collapse from grief and dropped the dress on the pile. Her tone lightened. "Why can't you go to Ireland? And explain one more time why you didn't tell me before today about the dream the night your mom died." She took a shaky inhale and rubbed her collarbones, as if gathering the words before speaking. "The dream when you watched a monster kill her."

I pressed my hands to my lips, my cheeks hot. "I was muddling through, Bev." My voice was a raspy whisper, and I sank onto Mom's bed, fingering the ivory silk duvet. Mom loved little luxuries. I was very much her daughter in that respect. "I didn't mean to push you away. I just didn't have the words."

She sat next to me. "You're better now, though." She reached over and clasped my hand in her warm fingers. I returned the pressure. "At least you can speak about it."

I smiled. "Yes. You must have read my mind when you decided to visit this morning. Now that the funeral's over, I needed to tell someone. You're my closest friend." I shrugged. "My weird dreams disappeared years ago. And this one sounds unbelievable. I knew Trevor wouldn't understand. The nightmares stopped before we got together." I sighed. "I'm just glad he was out of town the night it happened."

Beverly frowned. "A meeting in Boston, right?"

"Yeah. He stayed over when it ran late." I picked up another frock, this one plaid with a wide patent-leather belt. I bit my lip, unable to visualize Mom in this thing, and looked at Bev. She shook her head. A definite no. Dropping it onto the growing heap of discarded items, I continued. "Before, when I was young, the dreams felt real." I ran my finger along the slippery patent belt, watching my friend in order to catch her immediate reaction to my next words. "But the dream the night Mom died was real."

She cocked her head, a frown creasing her forehead. "Real how?"

Her eyes didn't condemn or dismiss me. But she looked skeptical. Should I continue when I knew how fantastic the entire thing sounded? But Beverly was the only person I knew who might accept my story, and I needed someone close to me to hear it. I cleared my throat. "I was soaked when the phone woke me. My hands were bleeding where the rocks cut them." I looked at my palms, the cuts nearly healed from where the sharp black rock had abraded my flesh, and looked back at Bev, my heart pounding. "I was there, in the dream." My eyes filled with tears, and I dropped my hands to my lap. "I should have saved her."

Beverly wrapped an arm around my shoulders. "Aisling, you can't save someone in a dream. It seemed real. But it couldn't have been."

"Then how do you explain the wetness? How can you rationalize the blood on my hands? And what about the man? Lorcan. Granny said we needed to find him. I don't understand what that means."

Beverly's eyes widened, but she said nothing.

"Maybe I should go. Maybe it's the only way I'll get answers." I rubbed my tired eyes. "How would I explain a trip to the kids? They need me after Mom's death."

"Your kids are fine. Tell them you need a break. They'll survive. Probably won't even notice you're gone."

"That's helpful." I frowned, annoyed that she was right. I wanted my kids to need me more than they did.

"You know what I mean."

"I do." I nodded, my mood lifting. "You're right. They have friends, activities." I paused, my voice slowing. "It's me who feels alone, lost. Mom was my touchstone. I don't know where I belong anymore, Bev. Even Trevor's acting oddly." The lightness had vanished, leaving my limbs heavy and cold.

"Pete said the same. About Trevor. How he hadn't seen him in months, not even for a quick lunch." She frowned. "The four of us haven't had dinner since last spring."

"He's never here. It's always work." My voice dropped, and I looked away. "He belongs to the law firm more than he does to me. I don't know where I fit into his life any longer. Or if I even do." Trevor's face floated in my mind, and I squeezed my eyes shut, refusing to voice the niggling worry that kept me awake at night. Was there another woman? I shook away the consideration. I didn't want to ask him, didn't have the emotional bandwidth to deal with anything else at the moment. I needed a break.

Beverly squeezed my hand. "Take some time for you, Aisling." It was as if she'd read my mind.

"Maybe you're right." I stood and stretched, stifling a groan, reminding myself I was only forty-five. "Come with me. I'm sick of ugly dresses and cleaning out closets. I want to show you something. And I want a glass of wine."

Late-afternoon dusk had darkened the sitting room, and I switched on a table lamp and added a log to the smoldering fire, which released a wave of pungent wood smoke and a spate of fiery sparks that popped against the grate.

I grabbed the chilled wine and a marble cooler, and we settled in the cushy sitting-room chairs, glasses in hand, the fire crackling behind us.

"Take a look at this." I extracted one of Mom's journals from a pile on the table between us. "After I turned seventeen, Mom considered sending me to Ireland for some kind of training." I handed her the volume. "I never knew."

"It's a journal." Beverly turned to me, wide-eyed. "I can't read your mother's journal."

"I've been reading them. She wrote about the inn, mostly. But there are a few entries about me and the dreams. She had another, a leather journal dedicated to my dreams, but I can't find that one. Still, the entries I have found are interesting. She noted dates when the dreams occurred and what I saw. Nothing to explain what she was afraid of. There were some entries about Dad and how much she missed him after he died. She didn't mention my dreams again after they stopped." Still, she watched me, hesitating. "It's okay. Just this one entry." I tapped the page.

Beverly watched me a moment longer, nodded, and bent her head to the page. I knew the words, had read and reread them countless times, wondering at its meaning.

Now that Aisling is seventeen, Mother has asked me to send her to Ireland for Dreammaster training. The dreams Aisling had for so many years, the ones related to our ancestry, are rare now. The mantra Mother and I taught her quelled the worst of the effects. But Mother insists the training would be beneficial. She's convinced Aisling needs to understand her heritage, especially since she's read the Dreammaster Pledge—thanks to my interfering sister. But I can't let her go. Geraldine's antics on our last visit haunt me. Even though my sister lives in Dublin now, I still don't trust her. No guarantee from Mother will convince me that Aisling is safe around Geraldine. There's also my selfish need to keep Aisling close. Now that Matthew's gone, I can't image life without her nearby. And I can't leave my business for the time training would take.

"What does it mean?" Beverly's voice was hushed as she handed me back the journal. "What's a Dreammaster?"

I shook my head. "I don't know. And I don't remember reading a pledge with my aunt. Although she showed me several books when we were there for Grandfather's funeral."

We stared at each other, Beverly breaking the silence. "There's more to your dreams. I always said so. Your dreams have some sort of weird power." Her eyes drilled into mine. "Now's the time to find out what that power is."

"I think you may be right." Nerves jangled in the pit of my belly. "Trevor's gone the next two weeks. Back-to-back business trips. I'll tell him when he's back." I clinked my glass to Bev's. "I need a vacation." My eyes widened. "And you should come with me. We'd have fun."

"You know I'd love nothing more than to travel to Ireland with you." She rested her head against the cushion, her voice taking on a magical tone. "The green. The hills. The ocean. It's lovely. Ireland's magic." She looked up at me, eyes sparkling. "Your dreams are magic, Aisling. I can't believe I didn't see it before." She bounced in her chair. "You're part of the magic of Ireland. This is your journey, not mine." She paused. "And I'll visit you there one day."

"I live here, remember?" I chuckled at her stubborn expression. "Trevor won't relocate to Ireland. And I'm not magic, just a woman with weird dreams, that's all."

"There's more to your dreams. I can predict the future, and I feel yours in my bones." She pulled the wine bottle from the marble chiller, poured us refills, and clinked her glass to mine. "To your journey home."

CHAPTER FOUR

"**I**'m glad you're home, Daughter." Mother sat back in her chair, watching Geraldine from the other end of the long dining table. "Thank you for coming to dinner. I've missed you."

"I've enjoyed the evening." Geraldine patted her lips and replaced her napkin on her lap, feigning nonchalance as she watched her mother, considering the older woman's mood.

She hadn't lied. The evening had been nice, and the dinner was delicious. The salmon cooked to tender perfection had melted in her mouth, accompanied by small roasted potatoes, soft and fragrant with butter and rosemary. Geraldine sipped the burgundy wine, fingering the cut crystal stem. But as lovely as this visit had been, something in her mother's demeanor hinted at discord lurking beneath the surface of their shared conversation, as though she had planned a surprise and was waiting for the cake and balloons. But neither of them was celebrating a birthday, and even if they had been, they didn't like fuss. Or cake.

Mother steepled her fingers, tapping the tips, her eyes narrowed. Geraldine's stomach clenched as if she was guilty of something, and she berated herself for behaving like a child waiting to be punished, when she was a grown woman who'd done nothing wrong. She'd been gone for two weeks. Busy with business across the country. Whatever Mother's problem was, it had nothing to do with her. She sat back in her seat and smiled at her mother. She wouldn't ask. She'd force Mother to speak.

Mother sighed and dropped her hands to her lap. "You've forgotten."

Geraldine frowned, scanning her memory for whatever it was her mother thought she ought to remember. "Forgotten what?" Mother watched. Geraldine bit back the lick of anger. "Just tell me, Mother. You've been in a state since I arrived, and I've no idea why."

"Mary's funeral was two weeks ago." Mother's eyes welled, and she dabbed away the tears before they could escape down her cheeks. "Your own sister dead and gone, and you forgot."

Damn. Mary had been gone from Ireland so long she barely considered her sister any longer. Mother was correct. Mary's death hadn't affected Geraldine in any meaningful way. But she should have remembered. Should have said something comforting when she knew Mother was grieving.

"I apologize." She kept her voice soft. "I thought of Mary on the day. I should have said something, called."

"You were busy." Mother swallowed, twisting the handkerchief she always had tucked into a pocket. "You're always busy." She looked away.

Geraldine bristled at the implication, her shoulders tensing. Being busy was what had led to her success. And Mother had always been her biggest supporter. Years ago, that hadn't been true. She'd been rebellious, angry, certain her mother loved Mary more. But once Mary had left Ireland, she'd had Mother to herself. And they'd grown close.

Geraldine released her shoulders and rose, walking around the table to kneel at her mother's side. "I'm so sorry. I know you've missed her." She clasped her mother's frail hand, so different from the strong fingers that had soothed her to sleep when she was younger. "I got carried away at work." She leaned her head against her mother's arm, closing her eyes when Mother ran a hand over her hair.

After a moment, Geraldine rose and sat in the chair next to her mother. "We're all that's left, you and me." She sighed. "The last of our Dreammaster line. It's a shame to know our legacy will be consigned to history." She smiled at her mother. "But at least we have each other."

"There is Aisling." Mother's voice was soft, a quiet reprimand laced into her words. Her eyes challenged Geraldine to respond, seeming to dare her to argue.

The muscles in her neck tensed as she bit back her initial response. She'd not considered her niece, but her sister's child had hardly been a family fixture. "Of course, there's Aisling." Geraldine forced her lips into a smile, reminding herself that Mother was grieving, and this maudlin focus on Mary and her offspring would soon pass. "But Aisling isn't a Dreammaster, is she? She's shown no interest in her heritage, and, after so long, I doubt she'll care."

"But her ancestry has touched Aisling." Mother's nose flared delicately, and she huffed. "Thanks to your interference."

Geraldine gripped the arm of her chair and took a deep breath. "That was years ago. A folly, I acknowledge. And I'm sorry for what I did. But how can actions of thirty-eight years ago be relevant now?"

Her mother sat forward, watching Geraldine, her blue eyes shifting to the beady black of the Dreammasters. "She had dreams because of your actions. Dreams only Dreammasters can have."

Cold filled her. "Mary told you the dreams had stopped."

"They had. Until the night her mother died."

Geraldine struggled to swallow. "Tell me," she said in a hoarse voice.

Mother leaned back in her seat, her chin high, her eyes cool. "Aisling witnessed a dream Mary had on the night of her death." She paused. "*Witnessed* is not a strong enough word. Mary must have drawn Aisling into a dream, and Aisling watched as her mother was injured. Mary died because of the injuries."

Geraldine licked her lips, struggling for control. "That's not possible," she said. "Aisling imagined it." Geraldine's thoughts whirred as she considered her mother's words. "Mary didn't finish training as a Dreammaster, and Aisling's never trained."

"Training wasn't always part of the Dreammaster tradition. Many generations ago, if you were born a Dreammaster, you either dreamed and lived or dreamed and died."

"Still, neither Mary nor Aisling could have accomplished such a feat."

"And yet it happened. Otherwise, Aisling wouldn't have awakened wet from the rain and the splashing water she encountered in the dream. Sharp rock wouldn't have cut her hands if she'd been a mere witness." Her mother sat forward, her hands gripping the table. "That's not the worst, however. What concerns me more is what she saw when she was with Mary."

Geraldine shrugged, wishing she could escape, could take a moment to figure out how this claim could be true. "Tell me."

"She saw lightning. Heard storms. Smelled dirt and decay, as if something had died. And she saw something metal, maybe a sword or claw, slicing into Mary's throat and side."

Geraldine's mouth was dry. "That's not a typical Dreammaster dream."

"No. It is not." Mother watched her. "In fact, it's not a dream any honorable Dreammaster would engage in. The Dreamscape isn't a frightening place." She took her time before speaking again. "There's only one part of the Otherworld that is purported to be so savage. A place no Dreammaster may venture."

Geraldine lost feeling in her limbs, and her voice shook when she spoke. "Mary would never have dared to enter the Underworld. Every Dreammaster knows such a thing is forbidden."

Mother nodded. "I'm aware of the rules, Daughter." She took a breath. "There's more."

Geraldine sat still, waiting.

"Mary wasn't alone. A man was with her."

Geraldine released a breath she hadn't been aware she was holding. "Probably her husband. He must have met her on the other side. I can understand how this would have upset Aisling, but it's not a reason for hysteria."

"It wasn't Matthew. Aisling recognized the man from her childhood dreams. The dreams that started after you showed her the pledge and activated her powers." Mother's eyebrows rose. "She said she'd never been able to see him clearly, but she knew the essence of him."

"She's mistaken." Cold sweat slid down her back. "Dreams are nebulous things, and even our clients don't always remember every detail."

"Aisling sounded certain. Mary knew the man as well. She said his name."

"Who?" Her raspy voice caught in her throat. "Who did she say it was?" But she already knew before Mother answered.

"Lorcan." Mother's eyes held hers.

"Lorcan." Geraldine whispered his name, pictured him as he'd been the last time she'd seen him. Her heartbeat thrummed in her ears, and she almost missed her mother's next words.

"Yes, Lorcan. Aisling saw her mother with Lorcan." Geraldine looked up to find her mother watching, her eyes narrow slits. "Perhaps you can tell me, Daughter, how Lorcan ended up in the Underworld?"

Chapter Five

My mind wandered as I set the patio table for dinner that night, coming to rest on my one trip to Ireland and my aunt Geraldine. Aunt Geraldine had talked about magic as if it existed in the world, the same way Beverly had spoken of magic and my dreams, although I couldn't remember exactly what she'd said. In fact, magic was more of a feeling Geraldine exuded, and being around her had been unsettling and yet exciting.

I stopped, knife in hand, as a recollection from my short time with my aunt surfaced. Geraldine had read me a story from an old book of fairy tales, and after, when I examined the cover, I imagined the illustrated swans had come to life. I lifted the book to show my aunt the swimming swans, when one of them had scratched me. Or so I'd thought. I frowned. It was a crazy thought, though it had seemed real. I squinted at the tiny scar on the back of my right hand where I'd been certain the swan had pecked me, touching the spot and recalling the searing pain of the cut. Geraldine had pointed to the frayed binding on the old book as the cause of my injury, an explanation that made more sense. That was the first night I'd had the recurring dream and seen the man. Now I knew his name was Lorcan.

Magic. And dreams. What did it all mean? A shiver snuck up my spine.

The sun slid behind a cloud, and I trembled in the sudden cool, wrapping my arms around my body, shutting out the old memories I'd buried. Leaves rustled in the forest, and goose bumps popped along my arms as I searched the darkening woods, reluctant to name what I was looking for as I scanned the dusk for a hulking shape that didn't belong. My imagination had been working overtime since the night of Mom's death, seeing monsters in every shadow, but there was nothing to fear in my forest.

The screen door slapped against the house, and I screamed as I spun around. The knife I was holding clattered to the ground.

"Hi. I didn't mean to startle you." Trevor stood on the steps, a beer in his hand, a sheepish smile on his face. "I came home a little early."

Closing my eyes, I leaned on the table, a hand pressed to my chest, as if that would stop my galloping heartbeats. I took a steadying breath and picked up the knife before looking up at my husband. "How was your trip?"

"Good." He was already turning away. "Want a glass of wine while you cook? I could open a bottle."

"There's a white in the refrigerator."

"You got it." The door slapped closed behind him.

We ate outside, mostly in silence. Trevor grilled the juicy chicken thighs I'd marinated. The scent of charcoal lingered—the only way to grill, according to my husband—mingling with the aroma of the cheesy potatoes I'd made because they were his favorites, a way to welcome him home after his week away on business.

"I called my granny."

Trevor paused and looked at me. "Why, when the old girl has never been in touch?"

"I don't know. I was missing Mom. It was good to speak to my grandmother."

"Great." He nodded and continued eating.

"She invited me to Ireland."

This time his eyebrows rose. "That'd be interesting."

I leaned back in my seat, crossing my arms over my stomach. "Why?"

He looked back up. "You haven't traveled on your own much."

I held his eyes. "I'd be fine."

He shrugged. "Super. You should go."

I bit my lower lip. "You'd be alright without me?" I paused. "It'd only be a week or so." I wanted him to say he'd miss me too much to let me go. He didn't.

"Yeah, I'd be fine." He cleared his throat as though he had more to say but then thought better of it.

"How's dinner? I made it for you." I reached over and touched his hand.

"Thanks." His smile was brief before he bowed his head and sighed. When he looked up, he continued eating, but his smile had disappeared, taking with it our conversation.

"Everything okay, Trev?" I covered his hand with mine. He looked at our joined hands before pulling away. His rejection stung, and I picked up my wineglass and took a sip, hoping the alcohol would calm my nerves. "How was your trip? You never said." I was babbling and couldn't stop. "Maybe I could go with you next time. Or you could come with me to Ireland." *Please agree with me. Don't let it be something else.*

Finally, Trevor looked at me, his eyes sad. He sighed, then dropped his head as if bowing to pray before he looked back up. The heat fled from my body at his expression.

"I think you should go to Ireland, Aisling. It would be good for you, get you away from here for a while." He sighed and looked away. "But I won't be going on a trip with you."

"Trevor?" My heart pounded against my ribs. "What is it?"

"This is hard, Aisling." He cleared his throat and looked at me. "But the truth is, I want a divorce."

My heart stopped. I couldn't take a breath.

"Ash, did you hear me?"

I shook my head, wrapping my arms around myself.

"Aisling, say something, will you?" Trevor thumped his glass of beer on the table and sighed, running his hand through his hair. "You must know things haven't been working."

"Really?" The word came out as a croak, and I cleared my throat. I couldn't feel my body. I raised my hands to my face, pressed cold fingers against my numb cheeks, assuring myself that I was here, in my body, and wasn't hovering overhead, watching this scene play out at my patio table. I'd known something wasn't right. But I hadn't wanted it to be this.

"There's someone else. Melissa, the intern. You met her at the office party." His voice droned on as I thought back to the willowy Melissa. "And we're moving in together."

"What?" My mouth gaped open. "You can't be serious. She's barely older than our kids." He was serious. I saw it in his eyes, in the resolute set of his shoulders.

"I'm leaving. Tonight." He leaned closer. "I'm sorry, Aisling. I truly am. I waited to tell you, wanted to give you time after your mom died. But I'm ready to start over with someone new."

I struggled to make my brain work. "Four weeks." I spoke through frozen lips. "You gave me four weeks to get over Mom's death."

"Yeah." He looked away.

"And you never said anything. Never told me." I couldn't cry, couldn't get tears past the river of ice in my veins. "What about the kids?"

"I'll tell them next weekend when we meet for lunch. I wanted to speak to you first." He paused, watching me. "Will you be okay?"

"What?" I pushed out of my chair, walked from the table and back, running my hands through my hair. I stopped in front of him. "Did you ask if I'd be okay?" I lashed at him. Hot blood pumped through my chilled veins.

"Don't get nuts on me, Ash." He got up and pushed past me into the house. I followed, watching as he opened the refrigerator door and grabbed another beer.

"Don't get nuts." My voice rose, anger thankfully replacing numbness. "What am I supposed to do, you asshole? Be nice and wish you well?"

"You can get as mad as you want, but it won't change my mind." Trevor sat at the kitchen table, his voice low and reasonable. I wanted to hit him just for that.

"How long have you had this planned?" I kept my voice low too, even as I wanted to scream. "You've never said a word or suggested we were in trouble."

"Long enough," he said, pouring the beer into his glass. Not looking at me. "The kids are fine. You will be too."

"How long do you think the kids will be fine when you tell them?" I walked to him and leaned in. "Stop drinking beer and look at me."

"I'm not one of the kids, Ash. I don't have to do what you say. You need to stop being such a mom. You need to get a life."

I straightened; words of defense caught in my throat. He swigged the last of his beer and stood.

"We'll talk this out with our lawyers next week. I'm using someone from the firm. You'll need to find an attorney not related to my practice.

Conflict of interest and all. Don't worry. You and the kids will be taken care of." He started to turn.

"No." I slammed my hand on the table. "You stay right here. We need to finish this." I was working hard not to throw up. Maybe numb had been better.

"Sorry, but you don't have a say any longer. It's over." He walked away, leaving me like he'd leave the remains of a mediocre dinner on a restaurant table.

I followed him to the front door, my hand reaching in front of him to barricade it before he could pull it open. "How can you do this to your family? Throw away twenty-five years? I don't understand, Trevor. I really don't."

He turned back to me, his face stony. "I think it's best we speak through our attorneys from here on out. I'm sorry you're being unreasonable. I'd hoped we could have a rational discussion."

"Rational discussion." My breath was ragged. "This isn't rational, this leaving. You've given me no warning, are walking out, destroying our family ..." I clutched my stomach, gulped down bile.

"Good-bye, Ash." He turned to the door.

"Trevor," I started, then threw up on his pant legs.

"Jesus, Aisling," He looked at the mess I'd made with angry eyes, then took a deep breath. "Bring me a towel." I did as he asked, but I didn't offer to clean it up. He'd brought this on himself. He could deal with the mess.

He wiped up the vomit in silence, the sour stench a disgusting blend with the woodsy scent of cleaner. He was careful to avoid contact as he walked past me to the laundry room. I bit my lips and swiped away tears when he wasn't looking. Back at the front door, he paused. "Aisling," he started, then he stopped and shook his head. "You'll hear from me." He stepped onto the porch. "And don't worry about my things. I've got a bag with what I need." He jogged down the three steps to the brick sidewalk.

I caught the door before it closed. "Trevor, don't do this." I stepped onto the front porch. "We can work this out." My empty stomach ached, and I pressed a hand to it to stop the rumbling. "How could you break up our family?"

"Aisling, it's over."

I shook my head, powerless to stop the tears from streaking down my cheeks. "Come back inside and let's talk. Please." I blew out a breath. *Stay calm.*

"I've said all I have to say, Ash. I wish you well, but we're through. Have been for a while now. You couldn't see it or didn't want to."

Was he right? "Why didn't you say anything? Give us a chance?"

He sighed, shook his head. "I don't love you anymore, Ash. Haven't in a long time, in fact."

I closed my eyes to block the words, but they hit my body all the same, daggers piercing me even though the wounds weren't visible or bleeding. My body heated, my face flushed, and rage bubbled up and out.

"How dare you say that?" I walked down the first step, legs trembling.

"How dare you leave me for some girl?" Second step down.

"You'll realize your mistake and come back. By then, I might not want you anymore."

He laughed at that, fueling my anger.

A few more steps. "You don't deserve me." I stood in front of him, muscles quivering, heart racing. "I could kill you, you bastard." Pulling my arm back, gathering my strength, I hauled off and smacked him.

For a heartbeat only his eyes moved, and then he raised a hand to where a welt had begun to swell on his cheek, red and angry. His eyes narrowed, and I backed away. He didn't move toward me, didn't say a word, as he climbed into the car.

My legs buckled, and I bent over, hands on my knees as I gasped for breath. I rose when Trevor started the car and watched as twenty-five years of my life sped away.

CHAPTER SIX

Geraldine, Friday, October 13, Ireland

"Why are you asking me, Mother?" Geraldine's hands balled into fists.

"I'd think that was obvious, Daughter." She sat tall, her tone imperious. "The last time the boy was seen was on October thirty-first, the eve of Samhain, forty-six years ago. On that same night, unbeknown to me, you and Mary decided to try a dream without permission." Mother's voice rose as she spoke. "Samhain is a liminal time, as you know, when the boundaries between realms are thin. It's easier to make mistakes, especially for two Dreamkeepers in the beginning of their training." She let her words hang in the air.

Geraldine would not look away. It was what Mother wanted, and she refused to back down from the veiled accusation. "You're implying that I somehow sent Lorcan into the Underworld." She squared her shoulders.

"Lorcan was nowhere near Galway when he disappeared. He was with his friends in Dublin. They said he'd nipped into the loo and didn't come back."

"His physical location isn't relevant to the dream. You know that. You and Mary dreamed, and the boy disappeared. And then he appears for the first time in years with your sister in the Underworld."

Geraldine watched her mother for a moment, then stood and strode around the table. She stopped in front of the large windows, wrapping her arms around her body to quell the trembling in her limbs, and gazed out into the night. A circle of light from a fixture over the front door provided a pool of illumination that stopped before the end of the courtyard drive. Beyond the property, more lights from neighboring houses fractured the darkness. Geraldine studied her reflection in the glass, noting the tension lines on her forehead. Behind her, Mother shifted in her seat, her eyes trained on Geraldine's back.

Heat flushed through Geraldine. How dare her mother assume the worst about her rather than assign blame to Mary? Since Mary left, Geraldine had believed her mother was hers and loved her best. Now she knew the truth. It was as it always had been. Mary was the perfect daughter and could do no wrong. Geraldine's stomach burned, and a wave of nausea nearly made her choke as she pictured her sister. She watched her own lips twist in the wavy glass of the window. She was glad Mary was dead. Now, she had to dispel her mother's suspicions concerning Lorcan. To do so, she must remain calm. Geraldine took a deep breath, exhaled, and pivoted around.

"Mary and I had no idea what we were doing that night. I wanted to practice dreaming, and I asked her to practice with me. But we achieved nothing."

"Both of you claimed a strong force came at you. You both lost consciousness. Maybe that force was the entrance to the Underworld."

Geraldine wanted to pound on something, and she blew out a forceful breath, willing herself to relax. "I can't remember what happened. It was years ago. Besides, it makes no sense. Getting into the Underworld is forbidden and would be more difficult than two novices could manage even if they tried. Which we did not." She resumed her seat. "Why have you focused on this as the answer to Mary's dream?"

"What Mary said to Aisling in the dream. The noise, the commotion. The wetness and the smells. Aisling heard snarls and growls. And saw a sword or a claw. She wasn't sure. But where else would there be a claw? There aren't clawed creatures in the Otherworld."

"Aisling wasn't sure it was a claw." She waited until mother shook her head. "The old myths are full of swordplay. Our ancestors defended themselves with swords. The god Nuada's sword is legendary."

"Her dream was real. Aisling was there. And what happened to you and Mary was real. You were both incapacitated within a dream."

Geraldine snorted. "You didn't suggest any of this at the time. So why now?"

"I had no reason to suspect the two of you had breached this boundary. Mary's appearance with Lorcan and her assertion he's in the Underworld changed all that." Mother paused, her face flushed. "It's all that makes sense."

Geraldine closed her eyes, taking a moment to formulate her answer. She reminded herself to be logical and calm. Mother was in a stew of anger and grief. What she needed was careful handling until Geraldine had time to think through her mother's revelations. Heat flushed her body. Lorcan. Alive. It didn't seem possible after so many years. She forced her tense shoulders to relax and kept her voice soft but firm. "Mary hadn't dreamed in years. Unless she'd been lying about her Dreammaster status."

"No. She didn't use her Dreammaster powers." Mother was definite. "But she had a brain tumor."

Geraldine flinched. She hadn't known what type of cancer had killed her sister. "That's rare, for Dreammasters."

"But not unheard of. And it might have opened the Dreammaster part of her brain to dreaming."

"All of this sounds far-fetched." She stifled a yawn. "I'm worn out, Mother, and I need to sleep. I have several meetings tomorrow in preparation for the acquisition on the first. Could we speak about this later?"

Mother slapped the table. "Aisling must come to us in order to save Lorcan."

Geraldine's breath caught. "Why? She has no idea what we do, who we are. How can Aisling help, even if we do decide to attempt to rescue Lorcan?"

"The dreamer must finish her dream, Daughter, unless she can't. Mary is dead. Aisling's the closest connection to Mary, and therefore she must dream in her mother's stead."

"I was there, forty-six years ago. When Mary started the original dream." Geraldine pressed her fingertips to her temples, as if she could push away her mother's words and the emotions they evoked. She'd put the past behind her, buried her long-ago love for Lorcan when he'd betrayed her and then disappeared. She didn't want to face the feelings tumbling through her body, making her stomach roll and her heart pound. Geraldine could barely swallow past the dry lump in her throat as she considered Mary's daughter. She most certainly didn't want Aisling in Ireland as a visual reminder of how her sister had ruined her life all those years ago. Mother had to be made to see reason.

She looked up. "I was with Mary in the dream, making me a closer connection. I'm the logical choice to finish the dream, and you don't have to import me to Ireland. Plus, I'm a trained Dreammaster." She nodded. "Let's speak tomorrow or the day after. We'll figure out how to go forward."

"Aisling is Mary's daughter. She watched her mother die." Her mother choked back a sob and thumped her cane. "There's nothing to figure out, Daughter. Aisling's presence is necessary to save Lorcan. I don't deny that you should be with her as she dreams to save him. But she must come." She took a breath. "I think you ought to call Aisling. Convince her to visit. Samhain is less than three weeks away."

Aisling

I watched Trevor's taillights flash red at the end of our street before turning and disappearing into the deepening night.

Swaying, I stumbled backward, landing on the corner of a brick step. The slice of pain was satisfying, better than the numbness that had overtaken me. Trevor was gone. First Mom. Now my husband. I was alone.

I sat on the step, arms wrapped around my trembling knees, staring into the stand of trees that separated our property from the road. I dropped my forehead and rocked back and forth, moaning softly. Fall night sounds—the drop of an acorn, the scurry of rodents in the leaves—kept me company as I considered my plight. What was I going to do? Save my marriage was the obvious answer. The only answer. Because I wasn't the only person involved. The happiness of my kids was at stake as well. I unwound my arms and rested my elbows on my thighs with a sigh, wondering why I felt such resistance at the thought. But I knew why. I was sick of making things right in the family. I'd had it with being flexible and compliant.

A wave of heat washed over me, and I fisted my hands, my nails scoring my flesh. Trevor left me. He hadn't given us a chance to save our marriage. He didn't care how his actions impacted our family. So why did I think I had to chase after him? He said he didn't love me. Fine. Let him explain the mess he'd created to his kids. They would be hurt, sad our family unit was broken, but that didn't make it my responsibility to get the asshole back. In fact, I ought to adopt his attitude and let him go. I straightened my fingers and rolled my shoulders down my back. No one would blame me. I hadn't made this happen. My short burst of confidence shattered. Or had I? Had I been a bad wife? Was I unlovable? My shoulders rounded, and I leaned my head in my hands. Too many thoughts fought in my head, pulling me in different directions. What was the answer?

Beverly would know. I sat up, rubbing my chilly hands on my jeans. She'd have suggestions, better solutions than I'd come up with. I'd call her tomorrow, not tonight. She'd had enough of my problems over the last week. And maybe I needed to try to figure this out for myself first.

I pushed up, my behind cold and legs stiff, and trudged into the house, turning to lock the glass screen door. Headlights swept up the street, an engine roared, and my gut tightened. Was it my husband? Had he come to his senses?

The car continued past the house, and I released a sigh. It was for the best. I didn't want to see him, not tonight. Tonight, I had to decide my next steps. And if he could leave, put himself first, maybe it was time I did similarly.

I stood in the hall, the acrid stench of vomit stinging my nostrils. I'd spray air freshener. Tomorrow. Tonight, I wanted to escape. Grabbing a sweater, I poured a full glass of wine and headed to the back patio.

The remnants of our dinner remained. I cleared the plates, dumping everything into the kitchen sink. Back outside, I slid into a chair and tucked my feet underneath me.

Breathing in the citrus aroma of the chardonnay, I sipped, savoring the tang of acidity as I wondered why I wasn't crying. That's what women did when their man left. My tears had dried up, leaving my body hollow. What did I want?

I considered what about my life I wanted to change and what I wanted to keep the same. Being a mom and a wife had always been my top priorities. But my kids didn't need me like they used to. And Trevor didn't want me any longer. Pain clutched in my gut, and I bit back a sob. What I most valued was gone, and I didn't know what to do next.

I pushed the wine away and dropped my head on my arms, allowing the tears, now back in force, to flow. Memories fueled my grief: the day I married Trevor, the day the twins were born, the birthdays, anniversaries, and holidays celebrated in this house. Grief stroked me with clammy fingers, stoking my tears until my body was empty and my heart was frozen. I reached out a hand, patting the top of the table until I found a loose napkin, and blew my nose.

Cried out for the moment, I slowly lifted my throbbing head. Rubbing my raw eyes, I wondered how I'd allowed this to happen. I'd become a caricature of a real person, a woman focused on the roles of devoted wife and mother to the exclusion of anything else. I'd worked at the library, mingled with the authors who gave readings and recommended books to the patrons. But the job had been a way to fill my days, and it no longer fulfilled me, if it ever had. Rather than be surrounded by books, I'd wanted to write them. I'd wanted to go to graduate school, my goal to earn a master's in fine arts, but Trevor had talked me out of it, until, eventually, only motherhood and marriage defined me. Now, both of those roles were gone. I hiccupped and swallowed back the acid burn of wine in my throat. I'd been a fool.

"Well, hell." I took a ragged breath and ran a hand through my tangled hair. "I'm an idiot."

The chair scraped the bricks as I pushed away from the table and paced around the perimeter of the patio, my teeth grinding. How had I allowed this to happen?

I picked up my glass on my next circuit, considering my marriage, wondering where we'd gone off track. Two years ago, right about the time the kids left for college, Trevor had started traveling more. A year ago, Melissa had come on board as the intern at Trevor's law firm. My face heated as I considered the possibility that the affair been going on all that time. How could I have been so naïve?

I breathed in the cool fall air, letting the touch of the gentle breeze soothe me, even as my thoughts continued to whirl in my head. He'd chosen another woman. I wanted to hurt him for his betrayal, make him ache as badly as I did. At least I'd smacked him. But that wasn't enough.

"Shit." I sank back into my seat. He'd made our marriage into a midlife stereotype. Horny middle-aged man hooking up with a younger woman at work. The thought suffused my body with heat, and I wanted to smack his other cheek. Why had he done this? He could have said something to me, discussed his dissatisfaction. Instead, he fell in love, or more likely lust, with his trophy girlfriend. I ground my teeth until they squeaked at the thought of them together. He'd said he'd stopped loving me, so I shouldn't want him back. But I hadn't stopped loving him. I sat up straight, breath held. Had I?

I considered my husband, his still handsome face, his sparkling blue eyes. He'd been the one. I thought it would be forever. Shouldn't I be sadder? More depressed? I closed my eyes, rubbing my fingers over the lids as I yawned. All of that would come. The truth of it all was just sinking in.

The phone rang, vibrating in the middle of the wrought-iron table like a large electronic bee. I didn't want to speak to anyone, and I picked it up to silence the ringer. The number across the screen stopped me.

This wasn't a local number. I recognized the prefix. This call was from Ireland.

A frisson of energy sparked through me. Ireland. I wanted to go to Ireland. That was something I did want to do. Granny had invited me.

I could escape for a week or two. Maybe travel first class. On Trevor's credit card. A smile spread over my face.

The phone rang for a second time. I frowned. This wasn't Granny's number. The last four digits were wrong. I bit my lip as I stared at the phone. It was five hours ahead there. After one in the morning. My heart pounded. Had something happened to Granny? Damn. And right when I'd decided I did want to visit her.

On the third ring, I reasoned that no one in Ireland would call me about my grandmother's status. I'd only spoken to the woman once in thirty-seven years. But that raised the question—who from Ireland might be calling me?

On the fourth ring, I answered. "Hello." The word was a croak. I cleared my throat.

"Aisling?" A woman's voice, tired but alert, greeted me. "This is your aunt, Geraldine."

"Aunt Geraldine." I searched my mind for something to say. Maybe I'd had too much wine. Maybe I needed another glass. "Wow. Are you okay?"

"Yes." She paused, sounding confused. "Thank you for asking."

"Sorry, it's just late there. Is Granny well?"

"She's fine." Her tone changed, her voice clipped. "We need to speak. About the dream with your mother."

Very businesslike, as though ignoring any familial connection. Fine. I didn't know Geraldine. But I didn't have to speak with her this evening either.

"I'm glad your mother is well." The breeze picked up, and I stood. Time to go inside. "But I don't feel like rehashing Mom's dream tonight. It's been a crappy evening. Maybe it would be better to speak tomorrow."

"I'm very busy tomorrow, Aisling. And this matter cannot wait."

I closed the back door and locked it, taking my time before replying. "Granny and I spoke. I told her what happened. I take it you've spoken to her."

"Yes, I have." She inhaled sharply. "I wanted to let you know that I can handle anything that needs to be done from here. There's no need for you to upend your life and travel to Galway."

My shoulders slumped. This wasn't what I'd expected. Something about her voice caused my head to pound. I sank onto the couch and leaned back against the cushions.

"Granny asked me to come to Ireland." I paused, suddenly filled with a desperate need to escape my life. My fingers gripped the phone. My aunt couldn't do this to me. "As it happens, I'd like to visit. There's so much I don't understand, so much Mom didn't tell me." At the thought of Mom, my throat clogged. I missed her. I needed her. Maybe going to Galway would make her feel closer. "In fact, this is a good time for me to plan a trip."

"Be that as it may, I'm better prepared and positioned to find Lorcan. If he is in the Underworld, as your mother suggested, I can more easily get him out."

I sat up, my headache forgotten. The urgency of my need to go to Ireland propelled me to my feet. I wanted to learn. And I didn't want to be here. "Mom wrote about my dreams. She said I read some kind of pledge because of you." Geraldine hissed. I pushed on. "She was upset, but I want to know what it means. You could show me, teach me about my dreams. Then I could help Mom and her friend." I had no idea how I'd do that, what it might entail, but I'd figure that out later.

"He was my friend too." Her low voice was filled with pain. "I lost Lorcan too."

I paused. "I apologize. I didn't know."

She sighed. "I'm the one who's sorry. Lorcan was friends with Mary and me. We both cared for him."

There was something there, beneath the surface of her words. "I see." My curiosity was piqued, increasing my determination to go to Ireland. "I still think I could be useful. And I need to get away."

To my dismay, tears welled in my eyes. I blinked, sending the tears cascading down my cheeks. I sniffed, working to hold back a sob, but it broke free. "I'm sorry." I sank back onto the couch and reached for a tissue. "Like I said, bad night."

"What happened?" Her tone softened. "Are you missing Mary?" She paused. "I'm very sorry for her death."

I wiped my eyes, turned from the phone, and blew my nose. "That's part of it." I wasn't going to say anything, tell this woman I didn't know about Trevor, but it spilled out, as if someone had pulled the plug in a bath releasing the water. "My husband left me earlier this evening." I moaned. "I thought I was okay, but I'm not." I pulled the phone from my ear and sobbed. Maybe it was the fact of another person witnessing my anguish, but whatever it was, I let loose.

"Sorry," I said, when I could speak.

"It's okay, Aisling." My aunt's quiet voice, a lot like Mom's, was soothing. "When you're ready, you could tell me about it. What's his name?"

"Trevor. And there's not much to tell. All of it's very cliché." I hiccupped. "He's involved with a younger woman."

Aunt Geraldine snorted. "Trevor doesn't sound like he's worth your effort or affection."

I giggled, another semi-hysterical reaction. "He isn't. In fact, he's an ass. Has been for a long time." My lip trembled. "But he was my ass."

"Still, do you want someone like that back in your life?" Her voice hardened. "Men who hurt women deserve to be hurt themselves."

Her voice was cold, and I wondered if she was angry at me or at men in general or both.

"I don't know if I want him back. But I need a break. That's part of my reason for coming to Ireland. I need to escape my life. And I want to understand the dream with Mom. I've never had a dream like that. But I have had dreams that changed things. Small things." I thought of Trevor and our courtship. "Maybe I need to learn to control them a little better."

Geraldine didn't say anything, but I could hear her breathing.

"Geraldine." I was about to tell her not to worry about it. That, if she insisted, I wouldn't come, even though I wanted to. But she interrupted me.

"You should come." Her voice sounded as surprised as I felt. "Yes." She exhaled. "Maybe having you here would be beneficial. I'll find time to train you. We'll discuss your mother's dream. And my mother would love to see you."

My pulse raced. I was going to do something for myself. And maybe discover the truth about my family as well. "Are you sure?"

"Yes. I'm sure. Be here by October twenty-sixth. That will give us time to train before Samhain. It's the best time, the only time, to save Lorcan." She paused. "You do know about the ancient Celtic New Year?"

"Yes. November first. Mom told me about it." I swallowed the lump forming in my throat. "I'll be there on the 26th. Thank you, Aunt Geraldine."

"Don't thank me, Aisling." She paused. "Come ready to learn. The lessons won't be easy."

Chapter Seven

Aisling, October 13, New Hampshire

I was headfirst in free fall, rushing through thick, inky blackness. I had to stop my momentum, but there was nothing to grab, no way to halt my tumble, and as my body accelerated, I gasped for breath. I may have screamed, but there was no one to hear me. My hands and legs pumped to stop my progress, like a swimmer fighting against a riptide.

And then everything slowed, and I hovered above choppy water roiling in the storm of my mind waiting to engulf me in spiky-gray waves. I watched the tempest below, anticipating the plunge, breathing in bursts, terrified of drowning.

A boat appeared, rollicking over the turbulent water, my lifeline if I could reach it. I stretched my arm toward safety until I could almost touch the boat. But it was out of reach, and my fingers scraped at the wooden sides but found no purchase. My breath hitched, and my teeth clenched as I tried again while the boat bobbed, still out of reach and moving further away, carried on the ocean waves and growing smaller. I was stuck where I was, immobilized by an unseen force that pressed against me, halting my progress, my limbs heavy and cemented still.

"Aisling."

Someone was calling me. Was it my mom? Were we back in the same dream as before, all noise and fog and turbulent water?

"I'm here. Mom, is that you?" An elusive shadow whipped by the hint of a face, the sense of familiarity. "Don't go. Help me." I reached out, trying to fly, to catch up, but the presence was just beyond reach, taunting.

"Let it go, Aisling." The voice was different. "Let me go."

Trevor? He couldn't leave me here. "I'm here, Trevor. I can't move. Don't go. Help me, please." The last word was a plea ending in a sob.

My body released, and I fell hard, like a hunk of granite zooming toward the ground, my hands waving, clutching at nothing. Finally, I landed. I was in a garden, and everything was in sepia tones, like an old photograph. Brown ivy covered a wrought-iron trellis, and brown roses waved in a gentle wind that rearranged my curls and brushed against a shadowy brick wall. A garden bench sat beneath tall trees, the white blossoms of one of them providing the only pop of color. This garden was familiar, and I turned in a circle, head back as I craned to see the top of the tall stone house next to it.

I had to find Trevor. I ran into the house through an open doorway, finding myself upstairs at the end of a long hall. I ran along the hall, passing more doors than I could count, heading for the stairs, which stretched further and further into the distance. And there, standing under a dimly lit bulb at the top of the staircase, was Trevor, his arms around a woman. I saw blond hair, heard a tinkling laugh, watched as he kissed her. My stomach heaved.

"Trevor. How could you do this to me?" Again, I ran toward him. He laughed and turned away, touching her, stroking her hair, ignoring me. I made no progress in my pursuit, no matter how fast I tore along the hall. Sobs caught in my throat as my legs raced to reach him. I tripped, scrambled to my feet, and tripped again, finally reduced to crawling on the rough carpet toward the couple.

"I don't want you with me." Trevor laughed, his face red and contorted. He kissed the woman, and I screamed. They vanished in the sound of it.

Where had they gone? I'd find him. He couldn't do this to me. I'd given him everything, and he was taking it all away. I stood, running to every door and throwing them open. Trevor wasn't in any of the rooms. I kept going down the hallway, closing in on the stairs.

"Aisling." Trevor yelled for me, his voice hot and demanding. "You can't stop me."

I dropped to the ground with a whimper. "No." I sobbed the word. "No. I'll never let you go."

"You will." Trevor stood at the staircase, towering over me, his arm raised, hand flat and ready to slap. "I'm done with you. I don't love you."

"No." Suddenly on my feet, I confronted him, rose taller than him, and glared down at him. He raised his hands to shield himself, his eyes wide with fear. I grinned but felt no joy, only satisfaction. It was about time.

I lunged, hands outstretched, and shoved. Trevor roared, his hands flailing as he tumbled backward down the wooden stairs. He somersaulted, an uncoordinated gymnast, his limbs thumping with each strike of flesh on wood, the side of his head banging into the unyielding metal railing on the offbeat. His scream accompanied his descent, rising and falling with every body blow.

He landed, bloodied and unmoving, at the bottom, his legs jackknifed at an unnatural angle.

"Aisling, what have you done?" A woman's voice. From nowhere and everywhere. I whipped around, dizzy with the effort, but saw no one. My heart rate quickened. The voice was like Mom's. She'd understand.

"He deserved it. He hurt me."

I floated over Trevor, moving further away as all of it faded until the dream was less than a memory and more of an impression.

I turned, struggling with sheets that were twisted around my legs, and blinked into the darkness of my bedroom. Kicking free, I moved to the center of the bed where the sheets were cooler, then I stretched, rolled, and yawned, clutching at whispers of my dream, which teased me before slipping away.

"Trevor," I murmured before drifting back to sleep.

October 14

I awoke and reached for my phone moments before it rang, as if I knew what was coming. My hands trembled as my ringtone played, an unknown number flashing across the screen. Six thirty in the morning, too early for good news. On the second ring, my heart began to race as my finger hovered over the button. Had something happened to the kids? On the third ring, I answered, even though a deep part of me didn't want to hear whatever it was the caller had to say.

"Hello." My voice was curt, my palms sweaty. I listened to the dispassionate voice on the other end and answered the questions the woman asked me, my stomach clenching. "Yes, I'm Aisling Doyle. Yes, my husband is Trevor Doyle." Memories of the night before filled my head, and all the warmth drained from my body. He'd left me. Walked out. I glanced at the empty space in the bed next to me, feeling as vacant and cold as it looked. "Who is this?" I heard the harsh accusation in my tone, as if this woman was somehow at fault for the abdication of my husband.

I softened my voice. "He isn't here right now."

"Mrs. Doyle, we need you to come to the New Hampshire Medical Center as soon as possible." She was curt, giving nothing away.

My breath caught, and I couldn't take a full inhalation. "What for?" I managed. "What's happened?"

"Your husband suffered a fall in the early hours of this morning and was brought into the emergency room via ambulance."

"Trevor's there?" She'd said *fall*, and a wisp of my dream flashed behind my eyes. My breath came in pants. "Is he okay?" I had to calm down, or my heart would jump out of my chest.

"We need you to come in, Mrs. Doyle. It would be best if you could have a friend or family member accompany you."

"Is he okay?" I asked again as I scrambled out of bed while holding the phone, heading to the closet for clothes. "Is he awake?"

"I'm sorry, Mrs. Doyle, but I'm afraid your husband is dead. We need you to come in as soon as you can to identify him."

"What? Dead?"

I collapsed onto the floor of my closet, the phone pressed to my ear, my pulse thrumming like a jackhammer, drowning out all other sounds. The voice on the other end of the line kept talking, but I couldn't hear what she was saying. All I could hear was a different voice, one in my head, repeating three words: *Trevor is dead. Trevor is dead. Trevor is dead.*

"I'll be there." I hung up, not even sure if the woman had finished speaking. My body was stiff, my brain in a fog except for technicolor flashes of my dream. I squeezed my eyes closed, unable to stop visions of Trevor tumbling as his head banged into the unforgiving wood and collided hard with metal. After I pushed him. I pulled my knees to my chest, whimpering. But that was only a dream. How could Trevor be dead? Why wasn't I crying? Why couldn't I move?

I sat that way, still and stiff, for several minutes, working to process the call I'd received. I'd have to go to campus to tell the kids, and a sharp pain stabbed my chest at the thought of their reactions. This would devastate them.

The phone may have rung again, but the sound was distant, drowned out by the blood rushing through my ears. Finally, I looked down and saw I'd missed two calls. I ignored them and pressed Beverly's name, hoping she was awake. Praying she'd answer.

"Aisling?" I heard her voice, a note of alarm in it, but I couldn't say anything. "Aisling, are you there?" I heard Pete in the background. Beverly's husband was speaking to her. Mine never would again say my name. I whimpered. "Aisling, I hear you. What's wrong? Are you sick?" Beverly's words rushed out, one on top of the other.

I started to cry then and couldn't stop, couldn't speak.

"She's crying, Pete." Her voice was muffled as she turned to speak to him. Then she turned back, loud and clear. "Aisling, I'm coming over."

"We're coming over," Pete said, his voice a grumble in the back-ground.

I'd left my closet by the time Bev and Pete arrived. When I opened the door, Bev drew me into her arms. She kept her arm around me as she walked me to the kitchen and sat me down on a chair at the kitchen table. "Tell me," Beverly coaxed, her voice gentle. "What's happened?"

"Trevor walked out last night." I took a shaky breath, gripping Beverly's hand. "He said he was divorcing me."

"Oh, sweetie, I'm so sorry." Beverly's voice shook, and she pulled me to her. "Why didn't you call me?"

"I didn't want to bother you." I buried my head in her shoulder and bit my lips, but I couldn't suppress a sob. "He left me for Melissa. The intern."

Pete gripped my shoulder. "We're here for you, Aisling. Tell us what we can do."

I pulled away, shaking my head. "Nothing. There's nothing anyone can do." I knew my voice was verging on hysterical. "My aunt Geraldine called. I'd decided to go to Ireland." I'd forgotten the call until now. I shook my head. "I was going to get away. Then I fell asleep." I gripped Beverly's arms hard. Her eyes widened. "But I can't go, Beverly, because he's dead."

"What?" Pete's question shot from him. "Trevor's dead?"

"The hospital just called. They said he had a fall. I need to get there." And then the sobs started. I held on to Beverly, and Pete's arms surrounded both of us until the worst of it subsided. For the moment.

"We'll go with you," Pete said. "And you can come and stay with us while everything gets sorted."

"I can't do that," I said, hiccupping.

"We'll figure it out later," Bev said. "Right now, let's get you dressed, and we'll go."

"I did dress." But when I looked down at myself, I saw my pajamas. "But I thought I did."

"It's okay. You're in shock." Beverly guided me out of the kitchen and to my room. She helped me change, told me to brush my teeth, and waited while I peed. When I emerged from the bathroom, tears leaking down my freshly washed face, she held out her arms and comforted me.

"One minute," I said, before we left the room.

On my dresser, I rummaged through my jewelry box until I found the swan pendant. I rubbed my hand over the smooth silver, tarnished now from lack of use. Granny had said to wear it. Mom had called it a talisman. I needed it today, even if it was only a reminder of my mother.

As I fastened the clasp, a pulsating heat from the swan spread into my heart. Placing a hand over the pendant, I closed my eyes and inhaled the long-forgotten peace and protection the swan had afforded me when she'd awakened me from the worst of my dreams as a child.

"Come on, Aisling." Beverly held out a hand, her eyes soft and her voice gentle.

Taking her hand, I followed her from my room, flashes of Trevor falling down the stairs still playing in my mind. Would my friend be so gentle, so understanding, if she'd been in my dream and seen me push my husband down a staircase? Beverly had always insisted my dreams had power. Was she right? Had that power manifested in an ugly way last night?

Chapter Eight

"The nurse will take you and your daughter back, Mrs. Doyle." The woman at the front desk spoke in a kind voice.

"My daughter?" I spun around, heart racing as I skimmed the faces in the waiting room. How had the kids found out? "Where is she? Where's Catrina?"

"There's a young gal over there who followed your husband in. I thought she was your daughter." I followed the nurse's pointing finger and froze.

Melissa, her blond hair hanging lank and her eyes red-rimmed, watched us. I'd looked over her, not recognizing the sexy blonde from the law firm without makeup and business attire. I turned back and leaned against the desk, lightheaded and nauseated. She'd gotten here before me, had probably been with my husband when he died. It should have been me.

"She's not our daughter, no." My jaw tensed. "She's not a relative."

The woman's eyebrow quirked. "Do you know who she is?"

My face felt hot. I didn't want to answer. But, then, I hadn't created this situation. "She was one of my husband's work colleagues." My voice was faint, tired.

The woman nodded, her lips compressed into an unforgiving line. "I understand, Mrs. Doyle. Don't you worry, dear. After you identify your husband, I'll put you in a quiet room where you can speak to the doctor uninterrupted." She patted my hand.

"Can my friend come with me?" I asked. Beverly nodded beside me. Pete had waited outside.

"Of course, dear." The woman smiled at Beverly. "Why don't you follow me?"

I turned from the desk and saw Melissa standing, still watching, her eyes pleading, as if asking me to take her along. I stared at her, the blood pounding in my ears, then slowly shook my head. Melissa sank into the seat, her lips trembling. Satisfaction spread through me, filling me with a feverish heat. She didn't deserve to see him. She wasn't his wife. My eyes narrowed, and I almost smiled when her eyes widened and filled with pain. I held her gaze in mine a moment longer before turning away to follow the nurse, Beverly's hand under my elbow.

Trevor's body was in the hospital mortuary. I hesitated at the wide double doors, cold and shivery, knowing I didn't want to go inside.

"It's okay," Beverly whispered. "I'm here."

"Just in here, Mrs. Doyle." The mortuary attendant opened the door and ushered us into a room where a sheet-draped table stood. I blinked back tears and pressed my hand to my mouth, fighting the urge to gag. I knew what was under the sheet. And the pungent chemical odor of the room didn't help settle my stomach. My throat clenched. Beverly put her arm around my shoulders.

"Tell me when you're ready, Mrs. Doyle." The attendant stood back as I looked around the room at everything and anything besides the covered form of my dead husband.

"Was he dead when he got to the hospital?"

"No ma'am. He died soon after the EMTs brought him in." The attendant spoke in an impersonal tone, as if that might take the sting out of his words. I swallowed and looked away.

"How did he die?" Beverly asked.

"The EMT's report stated he tripped and fell down a staircase."

"No." I gasped, my stomach clenching.

"Aisling?" Beverly hugged me closer. "Are you okay?"

I shrugged, and she loosened her grip. "What caused his death?" I whispered the words, picturing the falling Trevor from my dream, the way his head slammed against wood, the way his body sprawled at an odd angle when he hit the bottom of the staircase. "Did he hit his head, or ..." I stopped, the words caught in my throat.

The man checked a file, looked back at us. "Are you sure you want to hear this, ma'am?"

"Tell me."

He sighed before speaking. "It appears your husband suffered a traumatic head injury. A witness said he tripped and fell. There will be an autopsy to rule out any contributing factors, including heart attack or external forces, that might have caused his fall."

"Oh no." I bent over, hands on my thighs, trying to catch my breath. Beverly rubbed my back.

"I'm sorry, ma'am." He sounded sorry.

I straightened and nodded at him. "It's okay." I looked away, stuffing my hands in the pockets of the lightweight jacket Beverly had insisted I bring. She'd been right. It was cold in here. My fingers were numb. "Where did it happen? You said there was a witness." My voice was barely audible. I didn't want to know. But I had to.

The man reviewed his notes again, staring at the page before raising his head. He started to speak, stopped, then tried again. "He was at a private home. An apartment in a complex in Manchester."

I swayed, and Bev grabbed my hand. He must have been at Melissa's house. "When did it happen?"

Again, he paused, and when he spoke, I had to lean in to hear. "Emergency services received the call at three forty-three in the morning."

I gulped and looked away. Trevor had been with Melissa in the middle of the night. Sharing her bed, like he'd once shared mine. A rock as hard as New Hampshire granite filled my belly, and I wanted to hurt Trevor the way he'd hurt me. Which was crazy. He was already dead.

"Are you ready, Mrs. Doyle?" The voice of the attendant broke into my thoughts.

Was I ready? I closed my eyes, took a breath, and opened them.

"It's okay, Aisling," Beverly said. "This is just a formality. And then you can go home."

I nodded, biting my lips, my feelings oscillating between trepidation and rage. When I spoke, my voice was harsh. "Yeah. Let's get it done."

When he pulled back the sheet to reveal Trevor's face and neck, my breath caught. The man I'd been married to for twenty-five years, a guy so colorful, so loud and funny, so alive that he'd always been the life of our family, had been reduced to a cold, pale, unnaturally still body. I walked closer and touched his face. Abrasions, maybe from where he'd hit as he fell, darkened his skin.

"He feels strange. Rubbery. Cold."

Beverly squeezed my arm.

The attendant turned away, giving us privacy, and I ran my hand over his cheek, touching the place where I'd slapped him before he drove away the night before, seeing the bruise that had already started to form.

"I'm sorry, Trevor," I whispered.

"This must have been where he hit his head," Beverly said in a hushed voice.

My head snapped up.

"Where?" I rounded the table and looked where she pointed, recognizing the wound on the side of his head from the dream the night before. "No." Dizziness hit, and my legs buckled. I grabbed the side of the gurney as Beverly took hold of my arm.

"Ma'am." The attendant rushed to my side. "Sit here." He pulled me to a chair and produced a paper cup filled with water. "It's shocking to see. You're not the first to get woozy."

I sipped as I stared at the purplish-black bruise and accompanying swelling. I'd seen this injury. In my dream. I had to say something. Confess I'd killed him. But who would believe me when I confessed to murder via dream?

"What do I do?" I moaned, rocking back and forth in the chair.

"Aisling." Beverly leaned close to me.

I didn't answer, couldn't form words. The full force of my dream came flooding back to me now, cementing my mounting doubts that it had been a dream at all.

"It was me." I gripped her hand. "My fault."

"Hush, Aisling." Beverly patted my back. "It's the shock, sweetie."

"I pushed him." I gripped her hand, whispering hoarsely.

She leaned forward, squeezing my hand as she whispered in my ear. "Stop it, Aisling. Trevor wasn't even home last night. His fall had nothing to do with you."

"Is everything okay, Mrs. Doyle?" The attendant had turned and was now standing across from us, his brow creased in concern.

"She's fine. It's hard to see him like this." Beverly tugged at my hand. "I think it's time we left, don't you, sweetie?"

"Listen to me," I insisted. "Please."

Beverly shook her head, leading me toward the door. The attendant looked from me to Beverly, as if he'd like to question us but wasn't sure what to ask.

"It's the shock," Beverly said, and his face cleared.

"Of course." He nodded as he covered Trevor. "You'll see him again at the funeral home if you wish." He watched us, and I could tell he wanted us to leave.

In the hall, I leaned against a wall, breathing deeply. "I saw it. I really did. I thought it was a dream, but it wasn't."

"Aisling, I don't know what you saw, but you need to pull yourself together." Beverly squeezed my shoulder, her voice gentle but firm in the way I would have spoken to Catrina had she been here. "We need to find Pete and get you home."

"Beverly, listen to me." I took her arm, desperate for her to understand. "I pushed Trevor down a set of stairs last night. In a dream."

Beverly took a deep breath. "I understand you've had some bad dreams in the last couple of weeks, Aisling. But I don't believe you caused Trevor's death, no matter what you say you saw. You couldn't kill anyone." She smiled, nodding at me to understand and agree. "Sometimes a dream is only a dream."

"I saw the head injury last night. The one on his temple."

"You imagined it, Aisling." She pried me away from the wall. "Let's get you some food."

"Beverly, you don't understand."

"I do, sweetie. I understand that the last twelve hours have been awful, and your reaction is normal after a shock like you've suffered."

"No, Beverly." I clutched her arm. "You said it yourself. My dreams have some kind of weird power." I took a deep breath, my voice shaking. "What if you're right? I could be dangerous—I saw the evidence of it this morning. What if I killed Trevor, pushed him to his death in a dream?"

Beverly smiled, a small, sad upturn of her lips, and pulled me into a hug. "You didn't kill Trevor," she said softly. "You're in shock. Let's get you home."

I let her lead me through the hospital, wishing with every step that I had her confidence. All I knew was that I needed answers about the power of my dreams. With Mom dead, there was only one place to turn for those answers, and the realization stole my breath. I had to go to Ireland. Even after Trevor's death—especially because of his death—I had to know the truth. Before I did something else awful in my dreams.

CHAPTER NINE

B y the time we found Pete waiting at the car, my body was trembling uncontrollably. His eyes widened when he saw me. "Where are we going?" he asked. "To our place? Or to ..." He let the words trail off.

"Let's get Aisling into the car, and then we can discuss it?" Beverly ushered me into the backseat and closed the door. I heard the murmur of their voices beyond the closed windows, but I didn't focus on their words. I didn't care. Trevor was dead. Because of me.

I wrapped my arms around my shaking body, my mind saturated with the pale, cold image of my dead husband and the purple bruise at his temple. I took a shuddering breath and leaned my head against the window, wishing I could unsee the wound. I barely noticed when Beverly and Pete joined me in the car.

Fabric rustled, and a hand touched my knee. I sighed, keeping my eyes closed. The seat in front of me creaked as Beverly shifted. "Maybe our house would be best." Beverly spoke softly, whether to Pete or to me, I wasn't sure.

"No." I lifted my heavy head. "I want to go home."

Beverly turned, her eyes wide. I returned her gaze. I had to go to my house, the place filled with family memories of where Trevor and I had raised our family. Where he'd left me. "I need to be there." The words were a whisper, and as much as I longed for escape from the stark reality of this day, I also longed for the comfort of home.

"I think I understand," she said.

"Beverly," Pete started in an undertone. I heard the surprise in his voice. "Is that wise? And what about the kids?"

I sighed, each breath heavy and painful. "I have to tell them in person." My throat tightened as I fought a fresh onslaught of tears. My heart was heavy, cumbersome inside my body, as if an anchor had been tied to it and was pulling it toward my stomach. I imagined their shock and grief and knew I had to be there to hold them.

"Of course. We'll take you," Beverly said. She reached back and took my hand, her fingers warm on my freezer-cold flesh. "Nothing's going to change in the next hour or so. Let the twins sleep a little longer while Aisling takes some time to prepare."

My lips trembled as I considered my next moves. Whatever I did, my life from this moment forward was irrevocably changed, and I didn't feel capable of handling that right now. What would I say to the twins? And Trevor's parents? They'd doted on their only child. They'd come to approve of me. I tolerated their biannual visits. But they adored the twins, which was what mattered most. I struggled for breath, knowing I'd have to come up with the words to tell them Trevor was gone.

Pete drove us back to my house in silence, and I sensed he wasn't happy with this turn of events. He parked on the circle drive in front of the house where the night before Trevor had pulled away for the last time. I stared at the yellow, red, and orange leaves falling from the trees overhead. The sun shone, illuminating the perfection of the fall day, making me want to scream. The universe had blackened overnight, become a cold, dark place, and yet nature hadn't received the message. Instead, autumn, in all its vibrance, was in full swing. Trevor's favorite time of year. And he'd miss it. I clenched my teeth, took another shaky breath, and unbuckled my seat belt. Leaning over, I touched Pete on the shoulder.

"Thank you," I whispered.

He reached back and covered my hand with his. "Anytime, Aisling." He squeezed. "Call me when you're ready to head to campus."

I nodded and stepped out of the car. I was about to follow Beverly up the brick walkway when a rustling in the trees fronting my house stopped me. I glanced over my shoulder. Shadows had appeared, hanging like thunderclouds over this part of my yard, blocking the sun and chilling the air. I'd seen shadows or imagined them since the dream when Mom died. But, today, they were closer, more real, like inky warnings on the periphery of the yard where grass met forest. I shivered and pulled my jacket closer around me, watching as the shadows flitted between the trees, not quite substantial, not something I could see—more a wispy thought hiding just out of reach. Orbs of light flickered, dancing and winking within the forest like eyeballs blinking.

When a branch dropped, landing close to Pete's car, I flinched, but Pete didn't notice. He sat in his car, unconcerned, fiddling with his phone. I frowned, tremors of unease running up my spine, and glanced to where Beverly stood on the brick walkway. She was looking at me, but her eyes were vacant and her body still.

"Bev," I called. She didn't answer. "Beverly, can you hear me?" My voice rose as panic filled me. Again, Beverly didn't or couldn't answer. What was going on? It was as if time had stopped. I wanted to run to her, but my feet held fast to the ground, my legs like tree trunks rooted into the earth.

I bit back a cry, took a shuddering breath, and looked back into the trees between my house and the street. Was that a figure standing just beyond the drive? And another one behind the first? Were there more? As if in answer, the shadows swayed back and forth, to and fro. Four blinking lights accompanied the waving movements, along with a low rumble of sound, like a soft growl.

My heart thumped up my throat and threatened to pound out of my body. My breath came in rapid gasps. What was I seeing? Whatever was hiding in the shadows had never come this close. I closed my eyes, willed myself to take a breath before I passed out, and pushed back at the fear. "Calm down," I told myself. "It's not real. Calm down." I unclenched my balled fists, feeling where my fingernails had scored my flesh. As I took deeper breaths, a spark of energy rose from my feet to the top of my head, and my swan pendant pulsed. I touched the heated silver, confused. The charm had never throbbed before. What did it mean?

When the rumbling intensified, I opened my eyes and stared into the undulating blackness. "Go away." My voice trembled as I spoke. "You have no place here. Leave now." My arms hung at my sides, my open palms hot and tingling and emitting a thrumming power I couldn't explain.

As I watched, sparks of deep green appeared within the energy flowing from my hands, and pricks of light, like a sparking electrical wire, struck the shadows. I heard a low, hoarse groan and in moments the shadows dissipated, the blinking orbs vanishing along with the darkness. I examined my cooling hands, but they looked the same. When I glanced back where the shadows had been, the sun broke through, dissipating the remaining darkness to illuminate the forest, rays of light streaming through branches and pooling on the leaf-strewn ground. I breathed in, waiting, watching, not trusting what I had seen, was now seeing. Had I been hallucinating? Had any of it been real? Or was this part of another dream?

I closed my eyes again, praying that I'd wake up in a moment and Trevor would still be alive. He'd call me and tell me he'd made a mistake, that he didn't want to be with Melissa, that they had nothing in common and he wanted our family to stay together. When my phone rang, it almost convinced me I was right, and I dug into my pocket, fumbling to grab the phone, but the ringing stopped before I found it.

The din of the ringtone broke the earlier spell, and Beverly spoke as if nothing had happened. "Come on, Aisling. Let's get you inside." She smiled and held out her hand, unaware she'd been as immovable as stone only moments earlier.

I looked at the car, noticing that Pete was watching me as well, a frown on his face. If I didn't move, he'd probably insist Beverly and I get back in the car and go to their house. I nodded at him, hoping to reassure him I was fine when I wasn't at all sure that was the case. I tested my legs, relieved to find that they could move and my feet were steady beneath me. I shuffled over to the front walkway like an old woman, taking it slowly in case my legs locked up again. Beverly had my keys, and she opened the front door and gestured for me to go ahead of her into the house. I gave her a searching look as I passed, and she smiled. How had she missed the shadows? Not heard the rumbling?

I took a deep breath and stepped over the threshold, pausing in the front hall where I'd vomited the night before, my stomach threatening a repeat performance as I stood there, remembering my rage, the hateful words I'd hurled at Trevor.

"Aisling?" Beverly touched my arm.

"I puked. Right here. After he told me he was leaving me for Melissa." I squeezed my eyes shut, hoping I could block the memory, knowing it was a futile effort.

"Oh, Aisling, I'm so sorry." She scooted closer, but I wrapped my arms around my middle and shrank away.

I walked to the screen door and peered outside. Pete had gone. "I followed Trevor outside to where Pete was parked just now. I told him I wouldn't want him back even if he asked. That I hated him. That I wished he were dead." I turned back to my friend. "My final memories of my marriage and my husband. And, of course, I'll always remember killing him in my dream."

"Aisling, you didn't kill Trevor. Dreams can't kill people." There was a pleading tone in her voice, as if she was trying to reason with a stubborn child. "You're exhausted, emotionally shattered."

"I wish I was as certain as you."

We regarded each other for a moment longer, and I almost asked about the shadows in the front yard. But Beverly had obviously not seen that either, and I didn't want to share another crazy thing only I had seen and further shake her belief in me. Instead, I shook my head, broke eye contact, and headed toward my bedroom. "I need a shower."

After my shower, I found Beverly in the kitchen.

"I made eggs and coffee," she said, wiping her hands on her favorite of my aprons, a vintage blue with white with yellow flowers and ruffles. Usually seeing her in the apron made me smile. This morning I only sighed and reached for a mug.

"I told Pete to pick us up at nine to head to campus." She checked her watch. "That gives us thirty minutes." She placed a plate of scrambled eggs in front of me and handed me a fork before sitting. She took a bite while I stared at my plate, poking the eggs with my fork, wishing they didn't smell so eggy.

"You ought to eat." She put her fork down, watching me.

I took a deep breath and sipped my coffee. My stomach was a knot of pain, clenched so tightly I was sure I couldn't digest anything solid, would throw it back up if I tried. I sipped coffee again, happy for the scalding bitterness as it slid down my throat.

"Do you feel better?" Beverly asked, hesitating. "After your shower?"

Placing the mug on the granite countertop, I traced the swirls of cream and black running through the smooth stone before looking up into the face of my dearest friend, considering how I could make her understand the words I was about to say, the conclusion I'd come to as the hot water sluiced over my body in the shower. I took a deep breath.

"I have to go to Ireland."

Beverly sat back, saying nothing, fiddling with the paper napkin in her lap as she watched me.

I hurried to explain before she verbalized the doubt I saw in her gaze. "First was the dream on the night Mom died." I shook my head at the memory, the pain of my mother's death still an acute ache in my heart. "When I saw the monster stab her," I whispered.

She watched me, her eyes wide. "Maybe"—she paused—"maybe it was only an intruder. Not a monster in a dream." Her voice was hesitant.

"No." I shook my head. "I told you. I was there, wet and dirty in the dream, when she was stabbed." I sipped my coffee. "And then there was last night."

Beverly shook her head. "You weren't in the dream last night, were you?"

"I don't think so." I released a pent-up breath. The two dreams were similar yet different, something I couldn't explain. "I don't know. The dream was vivid, but it felt different from the dream with Mom. Except when I clearly saw myself pushing Trevor." I paused, eyes closed, considering. "I didn't feel Trevor, though, when I pushed him." I shook my head. "But it all happened like the mortuary assistant said. So, I must have been there, right?"

Beverly sighed. "It's like I said earlier. You had a bad dream." She covered my hand with hers. "Your husband had just left. And the dream with your mom, her death, happened only four weeks ago. I don't know how you're handling it all as well as you are."

I squeezed her hand before pulling away. Leaning my elbows on the counter, I watched her. "Bev, you can't have it both ways." I touched her hand, hoping to soften my words with a lowered voice. "When it suits you, I have some sort of magical ability related to my dreams. When it's uncomfortable and I might have done something horrible, you dismiss it all." I shifted in my seat. "You know the shadows I keep seeing?"

"You're exhausted."

"I saw the shadows again when we pulled into the driveway this morning." Her eyes widened, but she said nothing. "I think it's the monster who killed Mom. I think it followed me here, and another one came along. There were four eyes blinking in the forest. I made it go away with my hands." I lifted my hands, showing her my palms, as if that was proof. "If a monster, or monsters, can escape from a dream, I could have entered one and killed Trevor." I squeezed her hand. "I have to find out. Tell me you understand."

"I do, yes." She nodded, running her hands over her face. "But I don't want you to go over there and announce to your Irish relations that you killed your husband when you don't know that you did." She slapped the granite. "You can't kill with a dream, Aisling."

"Why not? I had some pretty weird dreams over the years. A few were vivid, lifelike. What if dreams can kill?" I bit my lip, hesitating a moment. "I can't think of any other way to find out the answer except to go to Ireland and ask."

"Dreams can't kill." Bev's mouth set in a stubborn line.

"I have to know, Beverly." I whispered the words. "And Mom never explained about my dreams." I gulped. "But she was frightened of them." Tears threatened. Again. "I can't live with myself until I learn the truth."

We stared at each other for a long time until the coffee went cold in my cup and our eggs congealed on our plates. After a few minutes, she nodded.

"You're right." Her wide eyes watched me. "You have some kind of power, but I still don't believe you're capable of killing."

"But ..."

She held up her hand, and I stopped. "I'll accept that danger could lurk within a dream, but only if the person dreaming intends to cause harm."

"I wanted him dead." I stated it matter-of-factly, hating the cold that penetrated my body at my words. Could I have wanted Trevor dead badly enough to cause his death?

"You were angry. But I don't believe you really wanted to kill Trevor. If that was all it took, people would be dying every night in droves."

"Unless there's something about *my* dreams that makes them more powerful. Something Mom knew but never told me."

Beverly tapped her fingers on the granite. "You've got a special gift, and you need to understand it." She nodded. "You need to go to Ireland." She sipped her coffee. "And we need a new pot of coffee." She stood, picking up our cups. "But how are you going to explain a trip to Ireland now?"

"I'm not sure, but I'll figure it out. I do need your help." I'd thought this through as I dressed. "You and Pete."

"What can we do?"

"Be here for the kids. Cover for me while I'm gone. Because I have to get to Ireland by October twenty-sixth."

She watched me, stone still but for her blinking eyes. "But that's less than two weeks from now. And there's the funeral to plan, all the arrangements."

"I just went through it with Mom." I rubbed my eyes, my very bones weary at the thought of what lay ahead. "I know the drill. And being busy helps."

"You have to grieve." She pulled a bag of coffee from the cupboard.

"I will. After I know the truth." I sat back, sighing. "My aunt Geraldine called me last night. After Trevor had left. Did I tell you that?"

"Yes." She paused, coffee heaped on a scoop, and shook her head. "It seems odd that she'd call you on the night your husband dies. She's never called you before, has she?"

"Not once." I bit my lips. "But Granny told her I'd called. She was nice. She said Lorcan was her friend as well as Mom's. She didn't want me to come to Ireland at first. But I told her I wanted to learn, to find out about my dreams. And then I told her Trevor had left." I sank my head in my hands. "I can't believe I told a woman I don't know about my husband leaving me." I looked up at Beverly. "She said something about Trevor not being worth my effort or affection. Last night, I agreed with her. Today, I just wish Trevor was still alive." I pushed away memories of last night's dream.

"I know."

"Anyway, Geraldine said to be in Ireland by the twenty-sixth so we could train, whatever that entails, before Samhain."

"Samhain." Wrinkling her forehead, Beverly considered. "Your granny said the same. To be there before the Celtic New Year."

I sighed, smiling for the first time that morning, thankful my friend loved ancient Irish festivals as much as she loved Sanskrit chants. I didn't have to explain about the Celtic New Year to Beverly.

"Yes. I know Samhain is considered a liminal time, and in the pagan belief system the spirits came from the Otherworld to visit on the eve of the new year, October thirty-first. Hence Halloween, and the modern trend of trick-or-treating. I don't know what it has to do with dreams, but I'll find out." I frowned. "I hate to leave the kids so soon."

"Pete and I will watch over them. They can stay with us as long as they need."

"I hope they'll want to go back to campus, where classes and friends might distract them."

"Whatever they need and want, we'll take care of it."

My eyes filled with tears, and I swallowed, unable to speak for a moment. "Thank you." I choked out the words. "I don't know what I'd do—"

Beverly hugged me. "You only have to ask." She sat back down.

"I'll only be gone about a week. I have to know the truth." My heart skipped a beat as I saw my hands push Trevor, saw his battered body splayed at the bottom of the staircase in my dream. What if I didn't like the truth once I found it?

Chapter Ten

Tommy, October 16

Tommy lifted his head to the sky and breathed in the cool, damp air. The sun had graced Galway with its presence this early morning after a night of lashing rain, heating his face and bumping the temperature up a few degrees. He strode briskly, impervious to the puddles in his waterproof wellies, his hands tucked into the pockets of his waxed cotton jacket.

Nuala would be in the garden awaiting his arrival, ready to hand him her list of gardening chores scrawled in her spidery hand on her personalized ivory stationary as she had every season for the forty-six years he'd lived in Galway and tended to her garden. Tommy had given her a small notebook for her list years ago, not wanting her to waste the expensive paper she ordered from a local printer. She'd smiled, thanked him, and passed the notebook on to her housekeeper, Maeve, for grocery lists and meal planning. The memory brought a smile to his lips.

He checked his watch—nearly eight. He'd best hurry.

A rook soared overhead and settled on the branch of an ash, rustling the autumn red leaves and sending drops of water onto Tommy's head. Tommy paused, swiped a hand over his hair, and met the eyes of the rook, which sat, unimpressed with Tommy, the leaves of the tree a vibrant backdrop for his black feathers. The rook opened its beak and cawed, and the raspy sound was answered. Another rook flapped to the ash and perched. Tommy moved in time to avoid another soaking and hurried on his way.

He knew these two birds, knew they'd follow him to Nuala's house. The pair identified him with his friend, Fergus Hennessy, who had a natural affinity for all winged beings. They also loved Nuala's garden and spent much of their time in the old oak standing in the middle of her lawn.

A quarter of a kilometer later, Tommy turned onto the driveway leading to the house, which was still hidden by the burnished gold leaves of the chestnut trees lining the drive. Tommy came face-to-face with the three-story stone manor home as he rounded the final gentle bend, and from here he spied Nuala. She was dressed as he was, in gardening pants and a waterproof coat, her feet ensconced in rubber wellies. She carried a basket and secateurs and was clipping the last of the roses from the bushes lining the rear brick wall.

He paused a moment to watch her. The sun glinted off the drawing room windows facing the gardens, shining through the autumn leaves of the old oak tree, a giant specimen planted over two hundred years earlier by Gerard's ancestors. From the oak came the name of the house—Old Oak Manor. The rooks that had stalked him settled in the upper branches of the old oak, a prime spot in the center of the garden from which to watch and admonish the humans. For now, they watched in silence, and Tommy lost himself in memories.

When he'd arrived in Galway over four decades earlier—in search of a Fomorian, an enemy of Tommy's people and of the Irish, who had escaped from the Underworld realm into Ireland—Nuala Fitzgerald and her husband, Gerard, had welcomed him, given him a place to live, and nursed him through physical and emotional wounds. They and their two daughters had become his family in Galway, and he'd do anything for any of them—but now, only Nuala and her younger daughter, Geraldine, remained.

They'd lost Gerard—husband, father, friend—thirty-eight years ago, and his passing still caused an ache in Tommy's chest. Gerard had been his first contract, his first friend, in Ireland. He missed him, the smell of his pipe tobacco, the way his eyes shone as he spoke, how he listened without blinking or interruption to what Tommy said. He'd been more of a father to Tommy than had his own father, King Finvarra of the Otherworld, the ruler of the Sídh Cnoc Meadha.

Mary Fitzgerald, the older daughter, had left Ireland two months after Tommy arrived, but he'd met her, liked her, and had seen her once since, at Gerard's funeral. She'd brought her daughter, Aisling, who had been seven at the time. Mary was dead now as well, killed in her bed only weeks before by an intruder. The murder had shocked her family and the small New England village where she'd lived.

Tommy's jaw tightened as he remembered Nuala's reaction to the news of her daughter's death. He'd been here when she'd received the call from Aisling. Nuala's bright smile of surprise at hearing her granddaughter's voice had turned to an open-mouthed expression of horror as Aisling had relayed the news. He'd caught her as she'd stumbled toward her chair in the golden bright sitting room, helping her to sit as tears poured in rivulets over her icy, pale cheeks.

Tommy blinked back tears, remembering the frosty barrier Nuala had erected the first few days following the news, as if she couldn't bear to allow anyone to see her pain. She'd just recovered from a badly broken leg. Her doctor had advised against travel, even though Tommy had offered to accompany her. Nuala had said no, it was better she stay away. It was what Mary had wanted. To keep her Irish life removed from her life in America. She'd left for a reason, after all. But the decision had destroyed a piece of Nuala as surely as the blade that pierced Mary's body had ended her daughter's life.

Tommy had checked on her daily, a silent offering of support, until the ice had broken and Nuala had allowed him in. He'd held her as she ranted at the universe. And he'd stayed close ever since. Nuala needed him. She'd turned to Tommy rather than her younger daughter, Geraldine. There'd been animosity between the sisters Tommy had never fully understood, and Geraldine had never cared to explain even during their brief four-year marriage. Geraldine feigned sadness at the news of Mary's death, but even Tommy could tell that she was acting a part for the benefit of her mother.

Nuala paused in her pruning, back still to him, and dropped her arms to her sides as her shoulders slumped. Her head bowed and her shoulders shook, a slight movement barely discernible beneath her coat. His heart caught. The grief came upon her suddenly, he knew, and he headed toward her. As he made his way across the damp grass, still green in the temperate mid-October climate of Ireland, she turned, spotted him, and swiped a hand across her eyes. When she looked up, she smiled.

Tommy returned the smile and waved. "I see you beat me to it," he said, reaching her side. "You weren't supposed to start without me."

"I figured you were sleeping in again," she bantered back. "But I've got the list, just waiting for you." She clutched the crisp paper in long, elegant fingers. The page waved in the breeze.

He groaned and then grinned at the familiar repartee. They'd played this pantomime over every year since his arrival. He took stock of his friend, noting her red eyes and the new lines of grief etched into her forehead. He paused, eyes narrowing, gaze never wavering. Because there was something more, something new. Her deep-blue eyes held a shadow he'd not seen before.

"Here it is," she said, handing him the note. "I wrote it out last night. Almost forgot this year." She chuckled, but the sound wasn't cheerful, and the set of her mouth warned him something was wrong.

"What happened?" He took the page but didn't spare it a glance. He tilted his head, waiting.

Nuala leaned into the cane she now carried, the one Tommy had carved years earlier for Gerard and topped with a silver swan, as if holding herself upright was too much. As if she'd given up. His heart pounded a staccato rhythm against his chest, and he gritted his teeth to keep from asking more. He'd learned long ago that Nuala wouldn't speak when pressed.

She shook her head and closed her eyes. Her once long honey-blond hair, now short and white, brushed softly at her chin. She opened her mouth once, twice, started to speak, and swallowed her words. He couldn't remain silent.

"Nuala, what is it?" His fingers clenched, crumpling the thick paper he held. He shoved the note in his pocket and reached over to her. "It can't be that bad." He kept his voice soft, hoping to soothe her.

She chuckled, and the chuckle turned to a groan as she bent forward to rest her chin on her hands clasped atop the cane, as if praying for the right words. "You've no idea, Tommy. And I've no right to keep the truth from you, although I wish I could. I don't want to lose our friendship."

He felt as if an arctic wind had pierced his skin and frozen his insides. He ran a hand over his hair, hoping to hide the trembling of his fingers. What had upset his friend?

"Nuala, you can never lose my friendship. I thought you knew the truth of that."

She swallowed, and the skin of her neck pulled tight. She looked up at him. "I suppose you didn't meet with Geraldine during your stay last week in Dublin."

Tommy frowned until his forehead crinkled. Why would she ask such a thing? Nuala knew he and Geraldine maintained a respectful, even friendly relationship. But they were no longer close. The circumstances of their marriage and subsequent divorce had driven a wedge between them, a distance that he doubted could ever be bridged.

"We did not see each other. Geraldine was working. I was checking on Eilish's house and her grandparents' farm." And there was the familiar tug at his heart, the pain dulled after the passage of so many years and yet never fully absent. The house belonged to Eilish Sheehy, his soulmate and one true love, who had disappeared almost as soon as they'd met. She'd had her reasons, and he'd understood at the time. But after a forty-six-year absence, he wondered if the threat she'd run from was worth the lifetime apart. He'd searched for her so many times over the years, just as he'd searched for the Fomorian enemy he'd come to Ireland to find and vanquish. He'd found neither the woman he loved nor the monster he sought. But still he kept on, despite the lack of leads and the knowledge that either, or both, could be dead. Although, in his heart, he believed both were still living. "Why do you ask?"

Instead of answering, she changed the subject. "I received a call two weeks ago. Another from Aisling." Her voice dropped so low he had to bend closer to hear. "She called after Mary's funeral." Nuala's lips trembled, and she pressed them into a thin line.

"Ah, Nuala. 'Twas kind of her to be in touch that day." Tommy wrapped his arms around her shoulders and pulled her close. But Nuala shrugged out of his embrace and took a step away. "Nuala?" A cold stone of fear lodged in his gut. "What is it?"

"She told me more about her mother's death." She looked up at him, her eyes swimming with tears. "The first time, all she'd said was Mary was murdered in her bed. But according to Aisling, it wasn't as simple as that." She took a shaky breath. "Mary had a brain tumor. I'd learned that only after she died."

"Yes, you told me." His throat was dry, and he wondered what was coming next.

"Yes. Well, Mary had a dream that night." Nuala paused. "A Dreammaster dream."

"But her training was incomplete."

"Geraldine said the same when I told her. But, as I reminded my daughter, Dreammasters are born with the inherent ability to dream in the tradition of the goddess Caer Ibormeith. Training didn't happen formally in centuries past. Mary wouldn't know every aspect of her powers unless she'd studied or been taught, but she had the powers nonetheless. I wonder if the brain tumor somehow enhanced Mary's abilities. Because, on that night, she managed to pull Aisling into a terrifying dream with her."

Tommy realized he was holding his breath. He took a deep inhalation. "And?"

"They ended up in the Underworld."

Tommy felt the stone in his stomach drop to his toes. "What?" The word shot from him. "How?"

"I can't explain how, but what happened next is what matters." Nuala pressed herself up, straightening into her full five-foot-three-inch height, her shoulders back as if she was steeling herself for battle. "Mary was with a man, clinging to a rock in the middle of raging water. Aisling watched a monster, a Fomorian, attack and kill her mother. But before Mary died, she identified the man to Aisling."

She looked at him, caught his eyes in the bleak, desperate gaze of hers.

"Who was it?" He could barely speak past the lump in his throat, and he knew he didn't want to know.

"It was Mary's fiancée, the man who disappeared forty-six years ago." Her voice was hoarse. "It was Lorcan."

Thunder rumbled, a timely punctuation to Nuala's announcement, and before he could question her further or begin to process for himself the full import of her words, the heavens opened.

"They were both incapacitated by a dream that night," Nuala whispered, dripping onto the slate tile surrounding the fireplace in the sitting room and staring into the flames of the earthy-scented turf fire burning in the hearth. She'd resisted coming inside, as if the elemental nature of the storm soothed her in some way. But when the rain pelted them, hitting their skin like pins and needles thrown by an angry seamstress from the purple-blue sky, he'd tugged at her elbow, and she'd capitulated.

"Sit, Nuala," Tommy said. "And we can talk." She seemed not to hear him, and her body swayed from side to side in time to some secret music. The back of his neck tingled, and he rubbed the spot as questions batted around in his brain like an errant metal ball in a pinball machine. What meaning did Nuala ascribe to Lorcan's presence in the Underworld? And how did it impact him?

"Sit, Nuala," Tommy said. "I'll ask Maeve for tea." She walked to her favorite chair, sat, and smoothed her wet hair from her cheeks. "I'll grab a towel as well."

"Coffee," Nuala said. "No tea."

She shrugged into her seat, leaned her head back, and closed her eyes. Tommy watched for a moment as his friend clasped her white-knuckled fingers into a tight knot. Maeve believed coffee was bad for Nuala. Tommy didn't feel like fighting with either woman, but for Nuala's sake, he'd brave Maeve's wrath.

"I'll be back."

"Yes," Nuala said.

When Tommy returned, towels in hand, Nuala was sitting as she had been. He walked to her and offered her the towel. She glanced up, her eyes red and weepy, and accepted it from his hands.

Tommy sat on the couch next to her, rubbing his hair, waiting for her to explain. When she'd blotted her hair and face dry, she leaned her head back and sighed.

"I don't understand, Nuala." He kept his tone neutral. "You say *they* were incapacitated by a dream. Are you referring to Mary and Aisling and the dream of the night Mary died?"

Maeve bustled into the room at that moment, placed a round tray on the low table between them, and gathered the towels. "You two are still soaked to the skin." She tsked. "You both should change before you catch your death. I can find something dry for you, Tommy. One of Gerard's old sweaters."

"I'm fine, Maeve," Tommy said in a tight voice.

"Nonsense," she replied, her tone curt. "I'll be back shortly."

"Nuala," Tommy said, once Maeve was gone.

"Do as she says," Nuala said. "And we'll talk once Maeve's satisfied. Otherwise, the woman will never leave us be."

Tommy poured tea for himself and handed a cup of coffee to Nuala. She sipped and sighed.

Maeve returned, helped Nuala change into a dry sweater, and handed a gray wool sweater of Gerard's to Tommy. He breathed in the faint lingering aroma of tobacco, the essence of Gerard still woven into the wool, as he pulled the sweater over his head.

Maeve collected the damp clothes, looked between them, sniffed, and stomped from the room. Tommy tightened his grip on the teacup and cleared his throat. Whatever was coming, he wanted to hear it.

"Go back to the beginning, Nuala. Tell me everything."

Nuala looked at him, deep sadness and regret in her eyes. "It was Samhain. Forty-six years ago. The girls started a dream that night."

"Samhain," he whispered, his mind thrown back to the event that had brought him to Ireland. "The same Samhain when the Fomorian arrived in Galway."

"Yes," Nuala murmured. "And you followed a week later, sent by your father to find the monster." She rubbed her forehead and dropped her head in her hands. "Gerard and I didn't know about a Fomorian entering Ireland, and you didn't tell us who you were seeking at first." She looked up at him. "I never put the two events together. Until now."

Buzzing filled Tommy's head as if a hive of bees had taken up residence in his brain. Tingles spread through his body and he stumbled from the couch, nearly dropping his teacup in his haste to move. He paced the room, searching for words, his tongue heavy in his mouth.

"Are you suggesting ..." His voice trailed off. The thought was impossible. He tried again. "But the girls couldn't dream on their own. They weren't fully trained." He stopped, staring at her, willing her to agree. To tell him whatever she thought had happened hadn't. And life could go back to the way it was a moment ago, before she'd correlated the dream of two inexperienced Dreammasters in training with the arrival of a monster from the Underworld.

"No." Her voice was a sigh, filled with exhaustion and something more. "The dream was against all the Dreammaster rules. They were both in training, still Dreamkeepers. Geraldine just turned seventeen a month earlier, and Mary celebrated her eighteenth birthday in June. She'd only been training a year. What they did was wrong." She closed her eyes and continued. "I reported the dream to the Dreammaster council. The tribunal was convened. They suspended the girls' training for six months." She looked back at Tommy. "But I never suspected the dream was anything more than ill-advised folly. They would have had to create a rift, open a portal, done something beyond just entering the Dreamscape for Lorcan to have gone into the Underworld. Or for a monster to come out." She shook her head. "But how? The girls were so young, so inexperienced."

He paused in front of the bank of three windows forming a wide floor-to-ceiling bay, staring with unseeing eyes into the garden, his hands clenched at his sides, his breath condensing on a cold pane of glass. He should have been told. And they'd kept this from him. Heat filled his limbs, and he pivoted to face his friend. "Tell me everything, Nuala." His harsh voice demanded the truth. "What, exactly, did they do?"

"All I know is what they told me." Nuala sighed, her usually bright eyes hazy. She swallowed, leaned forward, and gripped the arms of her chair. "Mary started the dream because Geraldine begged her to practice. I had a client, and I didn't know the girls had headed to the attic together. But I should have known they were up to something. They were actually getting along, whispering and giggling, falling silent as soon as Gerard or I came near." She clenched her teeth together, the force of it tightening her jaw.

"What happened?" Tommy's pulse raced, and he crossed his arms over his chest, as if the action could keep his heart from pushing through bone and skin.

"They said a force came at them as they entered the Dreamscape, and both claimed to have lost consciousness. This isn't something that happens, Tommy." She spoke in an anguished tone, begging him to understand. "I've never encountered a force like that in the Dreamscape. It's a peaceful place. Dreammasters act in a peaceful, loving way."

"Yes," he murmured. Dreammasters were peaceful, and their use of the Dreamscape, a part of the Otherworld, was predicated upon the assumption that any dreams conducted would only be for good. But it didn't explain what had happened to Mary and Geraldine. However, what Nuala told him did tally with something his father told him regarding that long-ago Samhain night.

"There's something I didn't tell you, Nuala," Tommy said. "Something my father told me before I came here. Something related to what you just shared." But he had told someone. Someone who should have made the connections. Someone who had remained silent for many years. At the thought, heat rushed through him. He banked the anger. For now.

Nuala watched him, her lips trembling. Her voice was shaky when she spoke. "Tell me, Tommy."

"On that Samhain forty-six years ago, Father sensed a disturbance at the boundary between the Otherworld and the Underworld. Father and one of his men went to investigate, and they encountered one of the Fair Folk living nearby. He told Father he'd seen a portal open and watched a monster come through. A violent wind had knocked the man over, causing him to lose consciousness. When he awakened, he still sensed the potent essence of the Fomorian. Father was convinced that the boundaries between the worlds had been breached, and the treaties governing interactions between the realms had been broken. He sent me to find the monster."

They stared at each other for several heartbeats until Nuala shifted further into her seat and leaned her head back as if her neck could no longer support the weight.

He watched her, his mind working, pulling at old memories. He wanted to scream, to punch something, to go back forty-six years, taking into account this new information as he searched for the Fomorian. But the past was gone. He had to focus on now. On what this news meant in the present.

"Remind me what happened to Lorcan."

Nuala sighed. "On that same night, Lorcan Byrne disappeared from a pub in Dublin. His friends had no idea where he'd gotten to. Some suggested he ran off because he was frightened of fatherhood. Others said he might have been kidnapped, killed, his body buried too well to be discovered." She shivered and wrapped her arms around her middle. "But what if that wasn't what happened? What if the force the girls encountered in the Otherworld that incapacitated them was actually the opening of a portal into the Underworld? Your monster came through to Ireland. And Lorcan Byrne was somehow transported into the Underworld, where he's been stuck all this time."

He paced the perimeter of the room, his breathing ragged, his mind in a whirl. Finally, he stopped in front of Nuala. "If I'd known about this all those years ago—" He stopped. What would he have done? His father had already been aware of the Fomorian's passage from the Otherworld into Ireland. But no one had known Lorcan Byrne had somehow found his way into the Underworld. No one until the night of Mary's death.

"It's a disaster," Nuala said, her eyes brimming with tears. "Mary left because of it, her heart broken. Although, she never believed Lorcan had deserted her. She knew there was more to his disappearance. Geraldine went to university in Dublin. You were forced to leave your home to come here. And, still, the Fomorian eludes all your efforts and the efforts of your team to locate him and send him back."

Something Nuala said caught Tommy's attention. He resumed his seat on the couch next to her. "Do you think Mary knew what happened and didn't want to say anything?"

"No." Nuala nearly shouted. "Absolutely not. She loved him. She would have said something. I would have done anything to find the man and bring him home had I known."

Tommy reached over to capture her hand, keeping his voice gentle as he asked the hardest question. "Then how did she know to go there that last night? She must have suspected he might be there."

Nuala squeezed his hand. "I wondered that as well." Her chin trembled, and tears welled in her eyes. "She was in pain because of the cancer. On strong medications. Perhaps the combination opened the unique dreaming part of her mind, allowing her to see things she otherwise couldn't."

Tommy wondered if Nuala was correct. Or if there was another explanation. One that made his body burn.

"What about Geraldine?" he asked softly. "Could she have known?"

Nuala clenched her teeth, and he watched the battling expressions of disbelief, fear, and grief cross her face.

"I asked her at dinner the other night. After she'd returned from Dublin." She swallowed, her eyes searching Tommy's. "She said no. I want to believe her."

Tommy thought back to the first year of his marriage to Geraldine. Before her father had died. When it seemed like life was brighter, that perhaps he'd found a way to breathe again after losing Eilish. When he'd told Geraldine the story that prompted his arrival in Ireland. The story about the Fomorian coming into the Otherworld on Samhain that night long ago. He struggled to take a breath as he remembered her wide-eyed look of innocence and interest. Her voice as she encouraged him to continue his search. All the while, never sharing that on that same night she'd begged her sister to dream with her, and they'd both been hit by a force that caused them to lose consciousness. Why had she said nothing?

"I have to go," Tommy said, working to keep the anger from his voice. He released her hand and rose to his feet. Outside, the rain had stopped, but a glance at the dark sky through the windows warned of more to come.

"Where are you going?" Nuala reached for his hand. "What are you going to do?"

"What I would have done forty-six years ago had anyone told me of this dream." He paused at the threshold between the sitting room and the front hall and turned to face Nuala. "I'm going to question a possible witness about the arrival of the Fomorian into the Otherworld." He took a jagged breath. "Geraldine has some explaining to do."

Chapter Eleven

The walk into downtown Galway did nothing to abate the anger simmering below the smile Tommy had pasted on his face. He waved to acquaintances as he passed and turned down an offer to join a group of friends for breakfast as he hurried on. The closer he came to Milligan's, the flagship store in his old friend Mel Milligan's retail empire, the more tense the muscles in his shoulders became, and he forced himself to breathe, to relax, knowing that to appear angry when he spoke to Geraldine would be to his detriment. Her face would freeze into a tight smile that set his teeth on edge, and any possibility of hearing the truth would vanish.

He arrived at the store, a handsome brick two-story establishment with display windows flanking the double glass front doors. Milligan's employees were busy in the front windows adjusting clothing displays to the left of the front doors and arranging food from the kitchen and specialty food department to the right.

Geraldine served as vice president and head of marketing for the Milligan's corporation. She was an early riser, always had been, and Tommy knew she'd already be in her office, probably in a meeting he was happy to interrupt.

He pulled on the door handle, but the doors didn't budge. Bollocks. What time was it? He hadn't thought to check.

Glancing at his watch, he saw he was twenty minutes early for the prompt ten o'clock opening time. He could wait, stroll about, head across the pedestrian area to Violet's Cafe and grab a tea, but the jittery energy in his limbs compelled him to find a way in now. He turned, heading for the side of the building, when the front door whisked open and a voice called his name.

"Tommy, what can I do for you?"

Tommy turned to see Torin, Mel's older son, standing in the front door. The lad was handsome, as was his father, although Torin's eyes were a bright blue where his father's were gray, shifting to black when he was angry or amused. Torin's hair was still the black Mel's had been in his youth, although, at forty-four, a few strands of silver shone through.

"Is everything okay?" Torin asked.

Tommy walked to him, fighting back the need to push past and race to Geraldine's office. He tempered his voice and his expression. He hoped. "I need to speak with Geraldine. It's to do with her mother?"

Torin's eyes widened. "Oh no. Has something happened to Mrs. Fitzgerald?"

"I'm sorry, Torin. But I need to speak with Geraldine."

Torin nodded and stepped back. "Of course. Come in." He waved Tommy through the doors and locked them behind them. "I'll take you to her now."

Walking into Milligan's was like entering a different country, a land of imagination, decadence, and luxury. The entire first level of the store was devoted to the sale of high-end retail goods. Tommy had been in

Milligan's hundreds of times, usually to meet Mel. Other times to shop for special occasions, although the prices were generally out of his league.

Glass cases filled with opulent body products greeted him, and the blended fragrances of expensive perfumes assaulted his nostrils. He sniffed, trying hard not to sneeze. He glanced toward the jewelry section to his right, the displays showcasing stunning jewelry, much of it sourced from local artists.

Tommy followed the rapid click of Torin's black Oxford leather dress shoes as they struck the marble flooring. Torin, like his father, dressed impeccably. Today, he sported charcoal wool trousers and a casual navy blazer.

Lights were flickering on across the space, illuminating the balls of crystal hung like a series of spacecraft from the chandeliers dotting the ceiling. The effect was an artful blending of the modern with the old-world brick-walled charm of the building.

"Stairs or elevator?" Torin asked as they approached the sweeping staircase to the second level and executive offices.

"Stairs are fine, Torin. Thank you."

Torin led the way up the curving staircase, the plush ivory carpet muffling their footsteps. At the top, he turned right, and Tommy followed him down the hall leading from the broad landing to the executive suite of offices. Torin stopped at Geraldine's door and knocked, opening the door without waiting for a reply and interrupting Geraldine mid-sentence.

"What is it, Torin?" Geraldine snapped.

Tommy shifted enough to see into the office. Geraldine sat behind her sleek wooden desk stained in a deep black, a sheaf of papers in her hands. He glimpsed another person facing Geraldine across her desk, but Torin's shoulder obscured the person's features.

"It's Tommy Kennedy. Something to do with your mother."

Geraldine's lips compressed, her eyes narrowed, and a look of irritation passed over her features. Until she spied Tommy and relaxed her stern expression.

"Tommy, come in. Is Mother okay?" Her words welcomed him. Her cold tone did not.

Tommy didn't care if Geraldine was perturbed. When Torin moved, Tommy strode into the office, reminding himself to remain calm, until he spied the back of the woman facing Geraldine. Waves of shiny coppery hair fell past her shoulders. That feature alone was enough to stop Tommy's heart and still his feet as he stared, the breath caught in his throat. Eilish had hair this exact shade, and he remembered how her silky tresses felt beneath his fingers.

"Tommy." Geraldine's sharp voice brought him back.

Tommy coughed, gave himself a mental shake, and looked away from the woman who appeared to be putting papers in a folder. He trained his eyes on Geraldine, reminding himself that many women other than Eilish had coppery-red hair.

"Good morning, Geraldine." He worked to keep his tone neutral. "We need to speak." He let the words hang in the air for a moment, noting the darkening of her eyes. Did he imagine it, or had she expected his visit?

Geraldine sat back in her chair, steepling her fingers, watching him. He returned her stare. He'd never understood why she wasted her pointed glare on him. It had never been effective. She sighed, dropping her hands in her lap. "Fine. Eileen, we'll continue this later. Make the calls we discussed."

"Yes, Ms. Fitzgerald." The woman rose and turned to face Tommy. Again he froze, stopped by the resemblance of this woman to the love of his past.

He was staring. He knew it. But he couldn't look away. It was Eilish Sheehy. His Eilish. With her pale, creamy skin and her almond-shaped aquamarine eyes. He gulped, almost choked, and cleared his throat, finally looking away from the startled blue of the woman's eyes. He blinked and reminded himself to breathe. This woman, Eileen, bore a striking resemblance to Eilish. But his Eilish would now be in her sixties. If she was still living. Eileen was no older than her mid-forties. Possibly younger.

"Hello." Eileen nodded at him and scooted past, and Tommy couldn't blame her for the nervous glance she cast him.

"This is Eileen Ryan," Geraldine said curtly. "My new assistant."

"Eileen," Tommy said, about to offer his hand. But Eileen retreated through the office door, almost as if she didn't want him to touch her.

"You can go now, Torin."

"Thanks for bringing me up, Torin," Tommy said.

"Of course." Torin nodded and backed out of the office, pulling the door closed behind him.

Tommy took a moment, still reeling from the sight of Eileen. But he was wasting time when he needed to speak with Geraldine. Doppelgangers existed. That was what this was. Or his memory was faulty. He'd last seen Eilish forty-six years before. He touched the place at his heart where her memory still rested and took a deep breath. Everything of significance in his life seemed to have happened forty-six years ago. Where had the intervening years gone? Had his life been so empty since that nothing else mattered?

"I don't have all day, Tommy," Geraldine said. "So out with it. Why are you here?"

Tommy ignored the demand in her voice and instead wandered her office, pausing at the tall black vases in the far corner, continuing to the double windows spreading across the width of the space and looking over the front of Milligan's at the pedestrian area of downtown Galway. Finally, he stopped in front of her desk and watched her for a moment, gathering his thoughts.

"For goodness' sakes," Geraldine said, exasperation and anger mixing and coloring her words. "You look like you did when we were married and I'd disappointed you."

"What have you done, Geraldine?" he asked, his voice low but demanding.

Geraldine pursed her lips, pushed her chair back from her desk, and crossed her hands in her lap. "You spoke to my mother, didn't you? She told you about speaking to Aisling. About Mary's dream the night she died and Lorcan. And then she tied it to the dream Mary and I began on that Samhain." She rubbed the top of her eyebrows with long fingers. "So, now, after Mother's veiled accusations, you've come to accuse me of somehow opening a portal into the Underworld and sending poor Lorcan to his doom." She steepled her fingers, the blue of her eyes like hard marble. "I can't even believe the two people closest to me think me capable of something so cruel."

"You used your Dreammaster gifts for cruel purposes during our marriage when you dreamed in order to bring pain or harm to someone." He took a step closer, never breaking eye contact. "You dreamed this way on more than one occasion, in contravention of the Dreammaster pledge you swore to uphold, based on the sole accusations of your clients against the men who'd spurned them." He rested his hands on the back of the chair vacated by Eileen. "Why is it such a stretch to imagine you'd want to punish Lorcan and you sister for falling in love by sending him away?"

"I was very young when we were married, Tommy." She spoke in a condescending tone, as if her youth had excused her actions. "I made mistakes. I should never have conducted dreams as I did. The tribunal punished me and kept me from dreaming until I proved I was trustworthy. I could then continue my Dreammaster practice. And I've not broken faith with my sisters since."

"How did Lorcan Byrne get into the Underworld?" He gripped the chair.

Geraldine rose and walked around her desk. She stopped behind him, forcing him to turn and face her. She fisted her hands on her hips.

"Tommy, this isn't worthy of you or of our friendship. I've admitted to my wrongdoing as a Dreammaster. But you're accusing me of doing something at seventeen that I had no way of understanding. I'd barely begun to train. How would I have known how to open a portal into the Underworld and transport a person through? I don't even know if such a thing is possible. It's certainly not covered in Dreammaster training." She crossed her arms over her stomach and glanced away, as if she couldn't bear to meet his eyes.

She was being evasive. His hackles rose, and he leaned closer. "What are you hiding, Geraldine? What did you do?"

She looked back at him, her eyes stricken, her face pale. "Tommy, why are you accusing me? What about Mary?"

"Why would Mary send her fiancée into the Underworld?"

Geraldine dropped her arms and sucked in a breath, her eyes wild with pain. "Why would I send the man I loved into a horrible place like the Underworld?"

"You were infatuated, Geraldine. But you knew Lorcan chose Mary. He met her first, and he intended to stay with her, marry her. They were in love. They were about to have a child together."

"How do you know Lorcan still felt that way about Mary? How do you know he hadn't fallen in love with me and hadn't had the heart to tell Mary yet? Or maybe he told her and that was why she banished him to the Underworld." She leaned in, her eyes blazing. "Because he loved me. There was a connection between us no one will ever understand. But it was real." She pulled back, standing tall, breathing in rapid bursts.

Tommy shook his head, and she opened her mouth. He forestalled whatever protest she was about to launch. "I don't believe you. I never heard this version of the story. And you didn't seem to care about Lorcan's disappearance all those years ago, when you deliberately provoked your sister, who was suffering his loss." He remembered Geraldine's childish behavior one afternoon when he'd joined the family for lunch. She'd taunted Mary, accused her of trapping Lorcan, and flounced from the dining room after reducing her sister to tears. Nuala had mentioned a rivalry between the girls for Lorcan's affections. But he'd assumed it was a youthful infatuation on Geraldine's part. She'd never once proclaimed her love for Lorcan to Tommy.

"I had no reason to want him gone. I wanted to be with him. It broke my heart. And no one cared that I was heartbroken."

"You never said a word of this to me."

"Why would I say something to you? I barely knew you. And you were on Mary's side. Everyone was on Mary's side. No one considered that my dear, sweet, wonderful sister got pregnant to trap Lorcan so he couldn't be with me." Her voice dripped with hate. "Look how quickly she married when she arrived in New Hampshire. It didn't take her a year to trap another unsuspecting male with her innocent act."

"Mary wouldn't have tried to trap Lorcan. I don't believe that for a moment." He thought of the gentle young woman he'd known, her utter despair at the thought of raising a child without the man she loved, and her final decision, when it seemed he'd never come back, to leave the country of her birth in order to escape memories and start again. "As to Matthew O'Leary, from what Nuala told me, Mary resisted his proposal. But he persisted. They had a happy marriage. He was a good father to Aisling."

"As I said, evidence Mary didn't truly love Lorcan."

"She was on her own, Geraldine. Everyone had given up hope of finding Lorcan alive."

"Believe what you will." She sniffed and rubbed the space between her collarbones. "I only wish you could believe me when I tell you I'm the one who suffered when Lorcan disappeared."

Tommy listened to her words, but he struggled to believe her. "You never mentioned Lorcan during our marriage."

"Why would I mention lingering feelings for a man who'd disappeared? You were my husband. I had no desire to cause you pain. Most days I pushed the old memories away." She looked at him with tear-filled eyes. "I still push back at those memories and try to banish the old feelings. I wanted to be happy with you, Tommy. But I wasn't." She patted her heart. "I've never found another love like I felt for Lorcan. I doubt I ever will. And I'm sorry because those feelings hindered my ability to be a good wife to you. You deserved more from me. I deserved more from you, as well. Because you never seemed happy with me or our marriage." She plucked a tissue from a box on her desk and dabbed her eyes.

He watched her display, unsure whether to believe her words. "We married too quickly," he said, not wanting to rehash their marriage. Wanting to close that part of their conversation. "You weren't who I thought you were, Geraldine. You should have told me about your feelings for Lorcan." He paused, considering that he hadn't mentioned Eilish to her. He too had been trying to forget, had hoped to find happiness. "And maybe I wasn't who you thought I was."

She stepped to him. "I don't want to fight, Tommy. But you hurt me with your doubts. You scarcely knew my sister. You were married to me. You should believe me, not rely on a faulty memory you have of Mary. She was grieving, and I'm sorry for that. But I didn't cause Lorcan to disappear."

"I told you about my father's experience on that night. How he was sure a Fomorian had come through the Otherworld and passed into Ireland. Yet you never said a word about your dream with Mary. Why?"

"I didn't think about it, Tommy. And what would it have mattered if I had? Mary and I were unconscious. We didn't see what happened. If anything did, in fact, happen in the Dreamscape Mary created."

"We're back to my question. How did Lorcan end up in the Underworld?"

Her eyes blazed. "Why do you suppose it was down to Mary and me? Have you or my mother ever considered that another Dreammaster might have been operating in the Dreamscape that night and opened the portal?"

She walked around her desk but didn't resume her seat. He followed her movements, considering her words. She was right. Another Dreammaster could have entered the Dreamscape with bad intentions. A more skilled Dreammaster would have had a better chance of success.

"If you're so worried," Geraldine said, "ask the Dreammaster Tribunal to review the dreams on that night forty-six years ago. Dreammaster activity is tracked. There are records, even though the actual dreams are private. You can find out for yourself that Mary and I did nothing to harm Lorcan or cause a rift between boundaries."

"Can that even be done, given the promise of privacy?" Tommy rubbed his chin. He'd not heard of such a thing happening, but then, he wasn't a Dreammaster.

"The tribunal cannot force a Dreammaster to allow access to her dreams. But if there is a question about a dream, the Dreammaster will acquiesce to the request in order to clear her name."

"Mary was the Dreammaster who started the dream."

"Yes," Geraldine said.

"She's dead. She can't agree to the review."

"True," Geraldine acknowledged.

"So, you've suggested something that cannot happen?"

"If it were up to me, I'd show you the dream. I can't do that, however. It was Mary's dream. It has died with her."

Tommy walked to her desk and leaned over, closing in on Geraldine, happy to see her discomfort. "So, you suggested a solution you knew wasn't workable. Why? To prove to me your willingness to help me. But it doesn't help." He straightened, running his hands over his head. "If I'd known Lorcan was there all those years ago, maybe my father could have had the man rescued. But it's been so long, I'm not sure what we can do. The Fomorian king will laugh at us if we ask, deny a human man is trapped within the Underworld."

"The Fomorian king denied that one of his subjects left the Underworld and made his way to Ireland when your father asked," Geraldine said. "He'd never have admitted holding a human man captive, even if you'd asked the day after Samhain." She shook her head. "Whether you learned about my dream with Mary then or now, doesn't matter. It changes nothing." She leaned close to him, and he caught a whiff of her perfume mixed with perspiration. Geraldine didn't perspire. Unless she was worried. "We didn't know where Lorcan was back then. We do now. And that is not something we could have learned just because Mary and I encountered a force in a dream. The bigger question is, what are we going to do about Lorcan?"

Tommy met her eyes. "What do you suggest?"

"I've spoken with Aisling."

"So has Nuala. She said Aisling called to tell her about the dream."

"She did. But I wanted to hear my niece's voice and find out what it was she wanted. Mother invited her to Galway. She believes only Aisling can save Lorcan if saving him is possible." She paused and looked down at her hands. When she looked up again, her eyes were determined. "I invited Aisling here as well. I wasn't certain it was a good idea at first. But after speaking with her, I believe she could be helpful."

"You can't expect her to make a strong enough connection with Lorcan in the Underworld to bring him out within a dream. She's never trained as a Dreammaster." Tommy drew back, his pulse pounding in his temple.

"I can train her. We'll see how she does. But I'll be with her. If her connection is shaky, I can bolster her link to Lorcan. I can guide her if she gets into trouble, and once she's made the connection, I can take over and bring Lorcan out myself, if need be." She watched him. "I don't want to lose anyone else, Tommy. Aisling is family. I want to find him for her as much as for myself. If he came back …" She straightened, rubbing her arms, a tentative smile on her face. "If I could save him, we could have a second chance."

"A second chance?" Tommy took a step back. "After all this time?" He shook his head, his arms tingling at his sides. If she felt so strongly and had for forty-six years, how had she hidden it so well during their marriage? Or had he been oblivious to signals, ignored the signs? He thought again of his own dishonesty. He'd hidden his feelings for Eilish.

"I love him, Tommy." Geraldine spoke softly. "I think I always will." She took a step, as if she intended to come toward him.

"But does he love you?" He paused, watching her face pale. "Who knows what Lorcan feels after so long away from home, trapped in a violent land like the Underworld? He might not even remember you."

She gasped, stopping at the corner of her desk.

"How could you say something so cruel?"

Tommy sighed and crossed his arms over his midsection. "But it is something you have to consider. If anyone can rescue the man, that is. I fear Lorcan is stuck in the Underworld."

Geraldine's lips trembled. "You must hate me, Tommy, to speak to me as you are."

Tommy sighed, weary of Geraldine and their conversation. There was nothing left for them to say but plenty left for him to ponder. "I don't hate you. But I now realize how ill-suited we were. We should never have married, Geraldine. We lived a lie for four years."

Geraldine's eyes blazed, and Tommy sensed another angry onslaught about to commence, when a knock on her office door interrupted them. As if she didn't hear, Geraldine barged ahead.

"Are you jealous of a man I knew so long ago?"

Tommy stiffened, about to deny her accusation, when she continued. "Lorcan was the love of my life."

"So you've said." He spoke through stiff lips.

Her eyes narrowed, and she rounded the desk and stood before him. "I've hurt you. You are jealous." She reached out and touched his hand. "Let it go, Tommy. Let me go."

"What a ridiculous thing to say," Tommy spluttered, when the office door opened, and a man spoke.

"Sorry to interrupt." Mel Milligan's deep voice, laced with hesitation, brought an end to Tommy's defense.

Tommy swiveled to face his closest friend. He'd met Mel when they both arrived in Galway, and they'd remained friends even after Mel had moved to Dublin for work. Tommy had been thrilled when, twenty years earlier, Mel and his family had relocated to Galway so Mel could run the local branch of what once was Osheen's Department Store after Henry Osheen had promoted him to CEO of the company.

"Everything okay?" Mel asked, looking from Geraldine to Tommy. "Should I leave?" He glanced at his watch. "It's just that our meeting with Shane Morris and his attorneys starts in twenty minutes. We had a few things to discuss beforehand."

Tommy swallowed his irritation and smiled at his friend. He'd missed Mel, who'd been traveling for work the last two weeks, but his inter-ruption was inconvenient. Especially after Geraldine's last ridiculous remarks, which he'd not had a chance to refute.

"Everything's fine," Tommy said with a force he didn't intend. He softened his tone. "We've finished our discussion." Tommy checked his own watch. "And I've got to get back to Nuala and her garden." He glanced back at Geraldine, who stood with her shoulders back and a haughty look in her eyes. His hackles rose. She believed her assertion that he was envious of Lorcan, which was absurd. He opened his mouth to set her straight, when she smiled, as if she knew what he was about to do and wouldn't believe him, regardless. He closed his mouth, pressing his lips together. Fine. He knew the truth. That was what mattered.

He turned back to Mel. "I'll be off, then."

Mel stepped back as Tommy approached the door. Mel clapped Tommy on the shoulder as he passed. "Let's meet up for a pint and dinner soon," Mel said. His face brightened. "How about tonight? We can catch up. I'll fill you in on Rory and Neassa. She sends her love, by the way." Mel lowered his voice. "And you can tell me what Geraldine said to make your eyes burn and your face flush."

Tommy chuckled, though he felt no humor at the remarks. "I'll meet you at your pub at seven. And I'd love to hear about your trip and your family." He deliberately didn't mention Geraldine, and Mel got the hint.

"As you wish, my friend. I'll see you later." He stepped into the office as Tommy stepped out. "Geraldine," Mel started, "let's go over the marketing campaign planned for after the acquisition one last time. We have a couple of minutes, and I have a question ..." Mel's voice faded as the door closed behind him.

Tommy turned to leave when he noticed Eileen and Torin watching him from across the hall. He paused, returning their stare for a moment as he absorbed the energy emanating from the duo. On the one hand, he sensed lust, and a look at Torin's flushed face confirmed his suspicion. Would the lad never learn? He had a lovely wife and a new daughter, but Torin was known for his philandering. Tommy quirked a brow and Eileen scooted away from Torin, as if she suddenly realized the boss's son was standing too close.

Eileen returned his gaze, her direct eyes appraising, as if she wanted to ask him something. Eilish had watched him in the same way, as if she saw into his soul. His heart wrenched at the thought of her, and he looked away from Eileen. Perhaps her scrutiny had to do with his conversation with Geraldine, and his gut tightened at the thought they'd heard Geraldine's claim he was still pining for her. He wanted to refute the assertion, but to say anything would only make him look foolish. The moment passed, and she glanced away.

Tommy cleared his throat. "Thank you again, Torin, for letting me in." He nodded at Eileen. "It was a pleasure to meet you, Eileen. I hope you enjoy your position with Geraldine."

At the mention of Geraldine's name, Eileen straightened, assuming the professional posture from earlier.

"Thank you." She looked at Torin. "I need to check that everything is in order in the conference room." She headed down the hall past Geraldine's office and around a corner.

"I'll take you back down, shall I?" Torin asked.

"No need, lad. I can find my way." He nodded at Torin and headed for the staircase, feeling the younger man's eyes on his back until he began his descent.

Chapter Twelve

Geraldine, Sunday, October 22

On Sunday afternoon, Geraldine walked to her childhood home from her sleek penthouse apartment with its pale marble floors and full-length sliders overlooking Galway Bay. She carried a small leather satchel over her shoulder. The morning rain had burned off, and the colors of Galway—from the brightly painted front doors of houses she passed to the green of the grass to the sparkling blue of the sea—shone in the sun. She paused a moment, her eyes focused on a group of a dozen or more mute swans gliding over the water, her mind elsewhere.

Aisling arrived on Thursday. Despite the loss of her husband, she had insisted on coming to train and to assist in saving Lorcan. Geraldine had expected her niece to cancel her trip upon learning of Trevor's demise. But the woman had backbone and determination, two things Geraldine hadn't expected from her sister's daughter. Mary had been such a sad sap. Weak. Sniveling. And afraid of everything. Especially her Dreammaster powers. She'd been terrified of Aisling understanding the powers. Geraldine smiled, a chill satisfaction spreading through her limbs. Mary might have run from her heritage, but Geraldine would step in where her sister failed. Aisling would understand everything by the time her visit to Ireland came to an end.

Her eyes narrowed as she recalled Aisling's determination to take the bus from the airport into Galway. Geraldine had offered to pick the woman up at the airport, but in a galling display of American independence, her niece had refused, claiming a need to center herself before meeting her family. Geraldine snorted as she gripped the rails of the bridge over the Corrib River, which flowed from Lough Corrib through Galway and into the bay. She had her work cut out for her, but she appreciated a challenge. She'd allowed her niece her way on this one matter, knowing that once training started, she'd be in full power and full control.

Geraldine squared her shoulders and resumed her walk, her back straight, her steps firm. She'd taken a rare day away from the office and spent the morning planning for her niece's trip. With so much to teach her, they'd need to commence training on day one. The pace would be rigorous, and Geraldine needed to be nearby. So, she'd decided to stay at Mother's in her old bedroom for the week of Aisling's visit.

At the thought of her childhood bedroom, she stifled a shudder. She hadn't been up there for years. She didn't want to return now. But being even a twenty-minute walk away was too far, given the dire nature of their situation. She had to monitor all that Aisling learned and did. Even her interactions with Mother, as much as that would be possible. So, staying at Old Oak Manor was mandatory. She'd have a poke around her old room and make a list of things she'd need for her stay. After that, she had another stop to make before the left the house. Up to the attic. But she'd need to ensure Mother was occupied first.

Mother and her dearest friend Bernadette O'Shea were seated under the oak tree in the garden. Geraldine saw them before they saw her, and she paused, shielded by the tall chestnut, the final in a line of sentinels lining the drive, and gathered herself. She took a breath, patted her chest, composed her thoughts, and banished any notion circling her brain about entering her attic dreaming space. Mother didn't want her in the attic and would protest if she sensed Geraldine's intention to visit her old haunt. Geraldine didn't want to have that fight and could usually circumvent Mother's intuition. But Bernadette was a different issue. The old woman didn't like Geraldine and, worse yet, seemed to read her mind, as if Geraldine was broadcasting every thought out loud.

Smile in place and thoughts under control, Geraldine stepped from the protection of the chestnut and headed to the garden.

"Good afternoon, Mother." She stopped at the bench and bent to kiss her mother's cheek. "Hello, Bernadette. It's been a while since we met."

Bernadette's dark-brown eyes met Geraldine's and the woman nodded, as if she knew something. "Geraldine." Her throaty voice made her name sound like an accusation. "It has been some time. My Emer's excited about assisting you to train Aisling."

Her breath stopped in her throat, and she stared from Bernadette to Mother and back. What did Bernadette mean about her granddaughter, Emer Sullivan, assisting? Her eyes shifted to Mother, who was watching her with raised brows. Geraldine's fingers clenched. What had Mother done?

"I suggested Emer assist you with training." Mother tilted her head, as if waiting for an objection. "She's nearer in age to Aisling. I thought they might be friends. And Aisling will need as much support as possible, given her recent losses."

"I'm still surprised she's coming," Bernadette said. "After the death of her husband."

"She insisted," Mother said. She smiled at Geraldine. "You don't mind, do you, Daughter? If you aren't available, Aisling can call on Emer to answer questions."

"I see." Her nails scored her palms, and her words stuck in her throat. Aisling could consult her grandmother. She didn't need Emer. But Geraldine said none of this. Which was for the best. She didn't wish to provoke a fight.

"With my leg still so painful, I don't plan to enter the Mist or the Dreamscape with you during training. Especially not once you get into the advanced levels. And I believe Aisling will benefit from learning from more than one trainer."

Geraldine was practiced in keeping a cool countenance, and she held in her scathing retorts. Mother was waiting for a reaction. She knew Geraldine understood what this was about. Mother wanted someone to watch her as she trained Aisling. She still believed Geraldine had something to do with Lorcan's disappearance. Geraldine drew a deep breath and relaxed her fingers. Soon, Mother would understand her mistake. But, for now, Geraldine would make Emer feel welcome. After all, she wasn't as experienced or as powerful. Even with Emer tagging along, Geraldine would be the one in control.

"As you wish, Mother." Geraldine allowed a small smile to cross her lips. Just enough to allow Mother to think she accepted her plans. "I thought I'd look through my room in preparation for Aisling's visit. I'm still planning to stay here if that won't be an inconvenience."

"It's your home, Daughter." Mother smiled. "I'd be glad to have you here."

"How's work, Geraldine?" Bernadette's brown eyes locked on hers. "And Mel Milligan? How's he? Still buying up all of Ireland?"

Geraldine opened her mouth, ready to defend Mel and his business ventures. Bernadette's spreading smile had her clamping her lips closed. The woman was a menace, always poking at Geraldine, making snide comments about Mel, as if she suspected him of something nefarious rather than being the savvy businessman he was.

Geraldine held Bernadette's eyes a moment longer before answering. "My job makes me happy. Milligan's is doing quite well, as is Mr. Milligan." She smiled. "If that's all, I'll head inside." She turned and headed toward the house, Bernadette's throaty laugh following her.

"Stop back to say good-bye before you go," her mother called.

Geraldine waved in acknowledgement but didn't turn. All she wanted was to escape the two old women. Especially Bernadette and her probing eyes.

Inside, Geraldine greeted Maeve and made her way upstairs. She headed down the hall past her mother's room and turned left to reach her door. Here, she paused, put her hand on the knob, and closed her eyes. Taking a deep breath, she stepped into her childhood room.

The fragrance of vanilla and lilies of the valley assaulted her first. Her favorite scent as a young woman, she'd dab the cologne behind her ears and feel so grown up. No doubt every remaining piece of clothing in her closet smelled the same.

Memories of growing up within these walls overwhelmed her. She took in the dim interior—the mahogany four-poster bed against the far wall, the wide mirror above the matching dresser reflecting the bed back on itself; the trunk under the window overlooking the backyard where she'd stored her treasures: the two upholstered chairs on either side of the Connemara green marble fireplace. She'd chosen the pale yellow of the walls and the floral print wallpaper when she was twelve. Mother had been on a redecorating spree.

She took another step, and a third, until she stood in the center of the room. She'd played with Mary here, her sister creating families with dolls, the flowery yellow and green carpet becoming the lawn of a house made from old boxes and adorned with bits of fabric. Mary loved make-believe, while Geraldine preferred reality and hard, cold facts, even at a young age. What a shame that her sister had been older and, therefore, the first to reach the age of initiation into the Dreammaster sisterhood. If the roles had been reversed, Geraldine was certain none of the current mess would have ever occurred.

At the bed, Geraldine dropped the small satchel, releasing a plume of dust into the air, the scent filling her nostrils. The dirt tickled her nose and she frowned. Maeve would have to air out the room.

Stopping at the large windows overlooking the back garden framed in draperies matching the carpet, she watched Tommy, who was pushing a wheelbarrow filled with mulch and the fertilizer he tucked around the plants before winter. Geraldine leaned her head against the wavy pane of glass, feeling a tug at her heart when she heard a snippet of his signature straggling whistle. Tommy had been in her life for as long as Mary had been out of it. She hadn't loved her sister. Had she loved Tommy? Not as she should have. And no longer in a romantic sense at all, although they'd had fun for a short time. Before he'd turned on her.

Her eyes narrowed. He still didn't trust her, even after all these years and the way she'd turned her life around. She'd followed the rules. She'd done as she was supposed to. And despite that, Mother and Tommy immediately suspected she'd had something to do with Lorcan's disappearance. She thought back to the dance over forty-six years ago when she'd met the dashing, dark-eyed Lorcan Byrne. Her vision blurred as Lorcan's face filled her mind, his laughter ringing in her ears even now. He'd set her pulse thrumming, had stolen her heart as well as her breath, and then he was gone.

She squared her shoulders, knowing what she had to do. Being sentimental would only hinder training, and Aisling had important lessons to learn before Samhain.

Geraldine turned from the window and headed into the bathroom, pulling open cabinets and drawers, taking stock of what personal items were here. The aroma of lavender wafted up from a drawer where an old bar of soap still resided. She tossed out jars of outdated creams and lotions and a half-full atomizer of her youthful fragrance, still ruminating on the past. Tommy hadn't understood her need to dream in her own way. He was too comfortable, refusing to resist the status quo, and while he'd sympathized with the plight of the women she'd sought to help, women who had been terrorized and abused by men, he'd disapproved of her methods, as had the Dreammaster Council. Everyone around her had insisted on mind-numbing conformity and subservience to outdated rules that hindered progress. Her jaw clenched thinking of it even now, and she slammed the drawer shut as she forced her teeth to stop grinding. The rules, coupled with the refusal of her husband and those in power to listen to her reasoning, had spelled the ruination of their union, and she'd left Tommy before their fourth wedding anniversary, heading back to Dublin, seeking the support of university friends and a new career path.

Geraldine gazed at herself in the mirror, sighing at the hints of passing time. She was still stylish, attractive despite the white in her hair and the wrinkles around her eyes. She touched her skin, still soft even after sixty-three years of living. She frowned, the wrinkles emphasized, and she slapped her hand on the vanity. But she'd compromised for too long. She'd had no choice but to give up on her ideas for modernizing the Dreammaster structure and regulations in the past, and the fact still stuck in her throat like a bit of dry food. She had power now, and she would wield it to her advantage. When the time was right, she'd present the Dreammaster Tribunal with a new and egregious crime. This time they would listen. She smiled at her reflection and raised her chin high, shivers of impending success rippling up her spine.

Geraldine hummed under her breath as she made a quick inventory of the personal items she'd need. After a rummage of her closets, she sent a text to her assistant, Eileen, with a list of what she would require for an extended stay at Old Oak Manor. Finished, she headed for the door and her next task, grabbing her leather satchel on the way.

At the threshold, she surveyed the room once more, wishing she didn't have to leave her chic, sleek apartment, all done in grays and blacks with few frills and no dust. She sighed. There was no choice. It was only a few days. A small sacrifice to ensure success. Knowing she'd done what she had to, and that Eileen had the matter in hand, Geraldine closed the door, pausing for a moment to listen. She heard nothing to indicate Mother and Bernadette had come inside, and why would they while the sun still shone? Reassured, she headed to the attic staircase.

Passing through the attic doorway, she pulled it closed behind her and flipped a switch. Dim light made shadows of the steps rising upward. She climbed, releasing her hold on the gritty, dust-coated banister that left her fingers covered in a sooty fuzz. No one had been up to the attic in years, probably not since she'd moved out of the house. She sneezed, the combination of damp and dirt tickling her nostrils.

Geraldine paused at the top of the stairs, surveying the space spread out before her. Bright sunlight filtered through windows that rattled when the wind gusted. Thankfully, the autumn breeze was mild today. Sheets covered old furniture interspersed with trunks and stacked boxes.

Walking past the graveyard of discarded things, she headed for a closed door at the end of the attic, swiping at cobwebs as she went. Opening the door was like an assault, memories hitting her from every direction. She pushed back against the tide and walked into the room. Her Dreaming Space. The place she'd practiced and done her first dreams, oh, so long ago. With a snap of her fingers, she started a fire in the hearth, coughing at the initial burn-off of old, dirt-covered turf. The bulb in this room glowed brighter when she turned it on, and she circled the perimeter, refamiliarizing herself with the space after the long absence.

She didn't have time for a full inventory or a thorough clean. For now, she made do with an old feather duster, a nearly empty bottle of lemon oil, and a rag, clearing away the worst of the accumulated grime from the hearth, the side table, and the long dark wood table at the back of the room. After dropping her satchel in a chair, she shook out two wool throws, closing her eyes as dust flew, and then folded them. Next, she picked up a crystal swan from the middle of the hearth and stroked the sparkling surface, whispering words, establishing her intention. The swan nodded, the light of the fire dancing off its gleaming, faceted surface, the throb of its energy mingling with the hum of power radiating from Geraldine, and she closed her eyes as the energy swelled to surround her. Opening her eyes, Geraldine stroked the swan upon her glossy head and replaced her on the hearth. She rubbed her hands together, her body alive and aware, ready for the next step.

Geraldine carried the satchel to the refectory table, then withdrew two books. The larger one belonged to her mother, but Geraldine had borrowed it from Nuala's Dreaming Space earlier in the week for review. She'd need it later, after Aisling's arrival. Mother hadn't entered her dreaming space since she'd broken her leg. She'd never know the book was missing. The second, smaller book was Geraldine's, and she considered it a priceless treasure. She cradled it in her hands as if it were a holy relic. This book would be the link between her and Aisling. Hopefully, once Aisling saw this book, held this book herself, and read the words within, she'd understand and accept her powers, making training easier.

After placing the book on the table, Geraldine withdrew one more item from the depths of her bag. Holding the slim glass tube up to the light, Geraldine regarded the liquid within, smiling. The liquid shimmered and pulsed against the glass.

Pulling the smaller book close to her, Geraldine placed her finger on the painted leather, her touch awakening the three illustrated swans on the cover. The swans began to swim, the lake beneath them rippling, and Geraldine watched for a moment, mesmerized at the symmetry of their movements. She drew a breath, smiling. All was going as planned.

Picking up the vial again, Geraldine swirled the liquid within, watching as a rainbow of chartreuse, blood-red, and black whirled and eddied, each color slipping in and between the other. Satisfied, she uncorked the vial, watching as a mist escaped and dived toward the swimming swans. One swan stopped, beady eyes watching the trailing mist as it drew closer and opened its beak at the mist's touch.

She had memorized the words necessary to activate the spell and began her recitation, watching as the potion flowed from the vial into the swan.

"From vial to swan, I now release you
Potion powerful, intention pure,
From swan to woman with one peck true,
Flow swiftly through veins the purpose sure.
Upend emotions hidden inside,
Obscure revelations that hinder progress,
Bolster only what assists our side,
Assuring her dreams result in our success."

When the vial was empty, the swan beak closed. "Thank you," Geraldine said, and the swan bowed its regal head. Geraldine waited until it had joined its companions, swimming in circles in the lake upon the book's cover, before again touching the book. The swans stilled, mere pictures once more. She picked it up, soaking in the energy emanating from the volume, her hands shaking as she thought ahead to the night to come. She placed both books on the round table between the chairs and surveyed the room a final time.

"Yes." She nodded, murmuring to herself. "Ready."

Chapter Thirteen

I slipped into Galway on the early morning bus from the Shannon Airport with murder on my mind. For the last ten days, my brain had spun in a dizzying wheel around one central question: Could murder be committed via dream, and, if provoked, could I do such a thing?

I'd pushed away my dark thoughts during the daylight hours after Trevor's death when I comforted Catrina and Conall or planned their father's funeral. When Trevor's parents arrived, I listened and cried with them as they repeated oft-told stories of their son. By day's end, my body ached, each bone saturated with a deep, penetrating weariness, and I yearned for sleep. But it was nightfall I dreaded the most. Alone with my thoughts, my belly on fire and my legs twitchy with the need to move, my body denied me the release of slumber. I'd writhe as if in pain on the soft cotton sheets, thinking about nothing else but my possible culpability in my husband's death.

Despite it all, I'd forged ahead, skimming makeup over my pasty skin, plastering a smile on my face even as my throat choked back hot tears, determined to barrel through and deal with the particulars of Trevor's will and the dissolution of his partnership interest in the law firm he'd help to found.

Finally, on the Sunday nine days after his death, my in-laws left. Later that day, I'd taken Catrina and Conall back to campus, where a circle of friends had greeted them. Beverly would pick them up Friday afternoon for the weekend. They protested my trip and stopped speaking to me for a day. But we'd reconciled. Sort of. Although, the empty, haunted look in their eyes would travel with me, as would the soul-certain feeling that I was letting them down.

When I returned home from campus, I found my suitcase in the basement, and, with a pounding heart, I packed for my trip to Ireland.

Beverly and Pete drove me to Boston late Wednesday afternoon to catch my evening flight. I sat in the backseat, watching the forests of New Hampshire make way for the increased traffic and urban sprawl of Boston. Dying sunlight glinted off Boston Harbor as we crossed the bridge before the tunnel that led to Logan Airport. I was about to embark on my first solo international adventure. Shivers of excitement filled my belly. Would I have done this if not for the dreams? If Trevor was still alive?

At the departure terminal, as Pete took my bags out of the back of their SUV, Beverly had pulled me to her. I hugged her tightly. "Thank you, Bev, for everything."

"Always, my friend." She pulled away and met my eyes. "The kids will be fine." I nodded. "You be safe and keep me posted." She paused. "And don't forget who you are, Aisling. You are a wonderful mother, the best of friends, and a good person." All that was missing was a renewed declaration that I wasn't a killer, but as Pete wasn't aware of my conundrum, the words were unspoken.

"Here you go, Aisling," Pete said, offering me my backpack followed by the handle of my roller bag. "Good luck."

"Call when you get there," Beverly said as I pulled away.

I nodded, shrugged the backpack over my shoulders, and wheeled my bag to the terminal entrance. When I had glanced back a last time, they were gone.

And now I was on a bus in Ireland, making my way to Galway. I checked my watch. Ten minutes to eight in the morning here. Five hours earlier in New Hampshire, meaning everyone at home would be asleep, and I didn't have to make any phone calls or take care of anything. Not for a bit, anyway.

I closed my eyes and opened them again, unable to shut down the whirring thoughts pounding against my temples. My hands trembled, and I twisted my fingers into a knot, pulling until my knuckles were white. Was it possible my soul was as dark as the charcoal mess of clouds spreading overhead, as turbulent as the unsettled atmosphere that had attacked the plane I arrived on as it fought its way to the ground? I had to know the answers, and the only people who could provide them were here, in Ireland.

I sighed, leaning my head against the bus window, not focused on the view outside like a typical tourist, although it was hard not to admire the green of everything that predominated the landscape, despite the lashing rain. My finger traced the rivulets of water sliding beyond my nose, slipping down the pane of glass in squiggly streaks. The bus entered a large roundabout where a sign welcomed us to Galway. Rows of apartments rose from the wet green land beyond the highway, and multiple billboards advertised local businesses.

I sucked in my breath, my skin tingling. I was here. Where Mom was born. If only she'd come with me. I'd asked several times to visit her home. I'd seen the yearning in her eyes but also the fear. I sighed. Mom had always said no, it wasn't safe, but she never explained why. By the time of her cancer diagnosis, I'd stopped asking. And then, she was dead, and it was too late.

The closer the bus got to the station, the faster my pulse raced and the harder it was for me to draw a breath. I forced my hands to unclench and focused on releasing the tension from my jaw by surveying the view beyond the bus.

Outside, the rain poured, and clouds hung dark and low. The sea appeared as taller buildings made way for residential neighborhoods, the water a deep blue, tossed by the wind, waves white-tipped. I sighed, leaning my head against the window, mesmerized by the distant movement.

My head smacked the window with a *thunk* when the bus scaled a speed hump and dropped to the other side. I glared up at the driver, a young man with acne, oily hair, and an expression that warned against engaging him in conversation. He'd ignored the passengers as we boarded, his only greeting a mumbled statement that we'd arrive at the Galway station by fifteen minutes past eight. The bus swayed yet again, and I checked my seat belt. *If* we arrived.

He caught my eye in the massive rearview mirror above his head, his features suddenly distorted and grotesque in the reflection. I sucked in my breath, and the swan pendant around my neck began throbbing as energy radiated down my arms. The swan had been a barometer of my inner turmoil since Trevor's death, although I didn't understand how a piece of silver understood my moods. I remembered the warmth from childhood, but I was sure the pendant hadn't thrummed with energy. Granny had given it to me for protection. Did that mean it was magical? My logical brain scoffed at such a notion. But I couldn't deny the warmth spreading across my chest and throughout my body.

The bus driver watched me, his eyes—antisocial slits before—now bulbous orbs of indeterminate color, wide and pulsing with malevolence, blinking like the orbs in the forest around my house. His body had filled out, and muscles bulged under his thin jacket. He raised a hand and flexed long, thick fingers sporting talons rather than nails. I blinked and closed my eyes, praying it was a hallucination.

I looked again and stifled a moan. The creature snarled, a quick show of spiky teeth, and I pressed back, glancing around to see if anyone else had noticed the monster up front. The man across from me was focused on his phone. The woman behind me was chattering inanely to someone called Donald. The young couple in front of me slept.

I closed my eyes again, praying the illusion would have vanished when I opened them, telling myself it was jet lag. My brain playing tricks. Everything would be fine.

But when I looked again, the monster still watched me. I wanted to yell at him to pay attention to the road, a ridiculous impulse, and he grinned as if he could read my thoughts, then winked, not a friendly gesture but more of a warning to keep an eye out—he knew who I was.

I shivered, wondering if I ought to alert the other passengers, when the creature blinked, and the horror disappeared. The driver looked away, stifling a yawn, once again the boorish young man marking time driving a bus.

What had just happened? I rubbed my hands over my face, resting my elbows on the backpack in my lap, willing the bus to move faster. I needed to get to Granny. She'd know. She'd have the answers. And, once I knew the truth, I'd go home. Until then, I was on a mission, and nothing, no matter how freaky, would deter me.

Traffic picked up the closer we drew to downtown. At a stoplight, I noticed a cheery bed-and-breakfast, white with red shutters, on a rise across the street. Ah, normalcy. What I'd give to be staying in that sort of place, rather than making my way to the dreary stone home of my mother's mother. I'd only seen the place once, years ago, but the abundance of gray—gray stone, gray skies, the gray features of my relatives—stuck in my brain. All gray except for Granny's beady black eyes, and they'd been the worst. She'd seen everything, had Granny Nuala. I'd been uncomfortable in her presence and refused to be alone in a room with her, certain that no matter how well I was behaving, she'd discover a flaw in my seven-year-old character.

The loudspeaker crackled, startling me to attention as the bus turned into a large, covered parking garage.

"Pulling into Galway Station. Be sure to take all your belongings. I'll be unloading the bags curbside."

My bag was the last to be pulled from the stowage area under the bus, and I fidgeted, my stomach churning, as I waited, watching all the other passengers walk away, leaving me alone with the driver. He set the bag at his feet and gazed up at me, challenging me to come closer. I gulped but met his gaze, flinching inwardly when his eyes bulged from murky blue to a puke brown. His lips twisted in a grimace, dark, oppressive energy radiating off his body. Keeping my eyes on his, I walked to my bag, reached out a shaky hand, extended the handle, and pulled. The bag stuck. I sucked in a moan, desperate to escape this monster, yet determined not to show my fear. I stiffened my spine and pulled again. The beast growled, a low rumble in his throat, a warped laugh.

My eyes narrowed even as my heart beat a staccato rhythm against my chest. "Let it go." I punched out each word with force, my pendant pulsing with power, hot energy thrumming through my body. "Now."

He quirked his eyebrows, and my bag released. He laughed, a low growl of amusement, when I stumbled and lost my grip, knocking the case to the ground. I reached for the bag, but the driver got there first, setting it upright and holding the handle out to me. His pale lips twisted into a caricature of a smile as he waited.

Energy, stronger than before, flowed from my heart to the pulsing swan and down into my fingers, each tip hot and tingly. I didn't understand the power, but somehow I knew to use it, and I returned his smile as I took the handle of my bag, my heated fingers touching his icy ones. He yelped and jerked away, shaking his smoking red-tipped fingers.

My eyes widened. I looked down at my hands, my fingertips pulsating with heat. I'd done that. Satisfaction washed over me, and I smiled at the thought.

"What the hell." The driver took a step back, holding his hand, his eyes slits, surprise and anger radiating from him. "Be careful, Dreamer," he snarled.

My eyes narrowed, and I yanked the handle away. "Leave me alone."

I hurried through the bus station and toward the exit to the street beyond. What had just happened? I pressed my fingertips to my cheek, each tip warming the skin where it touched. I'd felt the energy since Mom's death, but this heat was new, as was the ability to cause direct bodily harm, and the thought made me queasy. I wasn't a mean person. I didn't want to hurt other people. Trevor's face flashed in my mind, his death a refutation of all I believed about myself. I had so many questions. I tugged on my bag, ready to get to my grandmother's house.

Outside the train station, a biting wind lent teeth to the pelting rain, whipping straight through my water-and-windproof jacket. Even my fingers cooled as I pulled my hood over my head and hitched my backpack over my shoulders. Perfect. Wonderful. Mom had always said Galway was the rainiest spot in Ireland, and the city was making good on her words. None of the other passengers appeared to notice the weather as they hurried across the street and dispersed into downtown. I tugged my suitcase. Nothing for it but to join the fray.

A cacophony of horns warned me moments before disaster, and I jumped out of the way just in time as a wave of shiny, wet vehicles swept past, numerous headlights capturing my graceless fall onto the corner of the sidewalk behind.

"Damn," I muttered, pushing back onto the curb. My butt screamed where the sidewalk cut into flesh. I'd have a bruise by the afternoon. Pushing off the pavement, I teetered on wobbly legs, when a steadying hand gripped my left arm. Warmth spread down my arm and throughout my body, dispelling the chill of moments before.

"Are you hurt?" The voice was deep, the accent lyrical, and I turned to stare into moss-green eyes flecked with gold. My breath caught in my throat, and my stomach hollowed as if I'd been punched.

I'd read of this reaction in books and scoffed at the overblown romanticism, not believing for a moment that instant attraction could bowl a person over. But this man, and the butterflies circling in my belly, proved me wrong. He must have been near my age, and when he smiled, a deep dimple appeared in his right cheek. Faint wrinkles added depth to his startling eyes, which were fixed on mine. I broke eye contact, then looked back. His eyes flickered, and his expression suggested he knew what I was thinking. I swallowed, suddenly self-conscious. What on earth was the matter with me?

I gulped. "I don't think so," I said, looking away as my cheeks heated. I brushed my hands over my trembling legs. "Only my pride." I looked up and smiled. He smiled back, the smile reaching from his full lips to his sparkling eyes. "Thank—"

"She's fine, she is," a younger woman said briskly and without sympathy, her blue eyes skimming over me, her bow-shaped mouth pursed in a way that told me she found me and my predicament distasteful. "'Tis best if you look to the right before you cross, dearie, or you'll be getting knocked flat every time you step out. We drive on the left over here." She smiled without warmth, reached for her companion's arm, and pulled him away, crossing the street before I could reply.

How strange. Mouth open, boots soaked, I watched the pair until they vanished, not turning down a street or into a shop but disappearing before my eyes. I touched the swan, wondering about magic.

Too much. I grabbed my suitcase that had landed in a puddle near a storm drain, yanked it close, took a deep breath. Everything. All of it. Too much. I snorted. What a welcome to the land of my mother's birth. Beasts on the bus. A couple that appears and vanishes. My own fingers operating as weapons. Maybe I was mad. Or maybe it was real. Taken together, it was almost a sign, but not quite enough to make me run. Not after I'd come this far.

Looking to the right this time, I crossed the street, arriving at the pedestrian area of downtown Galway a few minutes later. The rain had subsided, and despite the early hour people bustled through town. My hands were numb with cold where I'd been gripping my bag. I needed to shift my luggage, and I needed a jolt of caffeine before arriving on Granny's doorstep. A pale-purple awning shimmered through the gray of the day, protecting the wide, outdoor service window of a café. The enticing aroma of coffee and baked goods beckoned to me.

"Hiya," said a smiling woman at the window, her violet eyes a match for the awning over her head. "What'll you be having?"

"Latte, please," I said, blowing on my white fingertips and rubbing my hands together. My internal heater must only work around monsters.

"You've got it," she said, calling out the order to the barista. "That's three euro fifty."

"Just a moment." I scrounged in my backpack for my wallet, happy I'd stopped at an airport kiosk for euros. "Here." I handed her a five euro note.

"Grand." She accepted the cash and offered me change. "Where're you from, then?"

"New Hampshire." She looked at me, wrinkling her forehead as she processed the unfamiliar state name. "Near Boston."

"Ah." She nodded, eyes gleaming. "I'd love to visit Boston. 'Tis supposed to be a grand city, it is."

"Yes, it's nice." I accepted the hot cup, grateful as the warmth spread to my fingers. I sniffed, sighing in appreciation. "Thanks very much." I paused. "I'm heading to this address." I showed her my phone. "Am I going the right way?"

She looked up from my phone, holding my eyes in her unblinking gaze. As impossible as that seemed, I was powerless to look away. She studied me, her glance flickering to the silver swan at my throat, her fingers lightly tapping my hand. Finally, she looked back up at me, her glowing eyes deepening to purple. "Yes, and it's time," she whispered, gripping my hand in hers.

"Excuse me?" A jolt of electricity surged up my arm at her touch. "Who are you?"

She smiled and released me. "I'm Violet. Owner, baker, and chief barista of Violet's Café." She grinned and tapped the map on my phone with a lilac-tipped fingernail. "That's a lovely part of town, that is. I take it you know folks in Galway, then?" She looked up, watching me as if she already knew the answer.

"Family." I nodded. She waited, eyes eager, but I offered nothing more. She pointed to the map on my phone.

"Keep following Shop Street to Quay Street until you cross the river past Galway Bay. Then you'll veer right and eventually turn here." She pointed at a place on the map. "Keep going, and you'll end up where you're heading."

"Thank you." I grabbed my bag handle, disconcerted by this woman and her interest.

"Have a brilliant time with your family, now," she said, turning to help the next customer in line as I moved away. "And, Aisling?"

Her voice stopped me, and I glanced back, startled. Had I said my name?

"I'm here if you need me."

Chapter Fourteen

I stopped to sip my fragrant coffee, taking a moment to process my arrival in Galway as the sun peeked from behind the dark clouds. Already, I'd encountered a monster and hurt it with a power I didn't understand, watched a handsome man and his companion disappear, and spoken with a woman who seemed to know me although we'd never met. Ireland was shaping up to be as mysterious as my mother had always claimed, and the thought raised the hair on the back of my neck. All of this, and I hadn't even made it to my grandmother's house or asked a single question about my dreams. I sipped again, but the coffee didn't alleviate the sudden dryness in my mouth. I should go get it over with. Find out the worst. But I couldn't make my feet move toward my destination.

In the large shop across the broad pedestrian walkway, the lights came on as if mimicking the sun, the illumination starting at the back and spreading like the coming dawn of a new day to reach the double front windows on either side of the entrance. Milligan's. Curious, and aware that I was delaying the inevitable, I crossed, taking care not to slip on the shiny, wet cobblestones. Standing under the store awning, I examined the displays inside.

Pumpkins, ghosts, and ghouls peeked from between mannequins dressed in fall colors and situated around a long table displaying autumn-themed tableware and colorful kitchen accessories. On the opposite side of the entrance doors, old wood and rustic furnishings highlighted the specialty food sold inside. An employee arranged scones, pies, cheeses, and smoked meats on black and orange platters. My mouth watered, and my stomach rumbled. If only I could wander through the store, sit and have breakfast, maybe find gifts for my kids.

I closed my eyes, drawing a deep breath, hoping to settle my system. I didn't want to ask the hard questions, and I knew why. But even if I was a murderer, wasn't it was better to know than to hide from the truth?

"The food is grand," said a slow, deep voice from behind me. My eyes blinked open. I hadn't heard the man approach, but there he was, reflected over my left shoulder, his black hair longer than most of the men I'd seen, his face clean-shaven, jaw chiseled, full lips smiling. He was handsome and sure of it. Almost too handsome and too self-assured.

My swan pendant pulsed, and I turned and took a step away, pretending to adjust the handle of my suitcase. "I'm sure it is," I said. "And if I wasn't in such a hurry, I'd try it."

He smiled, deep dimples appearing in each cheek, his blue eyes the color of the ocean on a sunny day. "I'd be happy to show you the food court when you have the time. I know all the best bits." His eyes roved over me, making my skin crawl.

"I should be on my way." I started to turn, but he spoke as if he hadn't heard me.

"You're visiting, then." He touched my shoulder and I flinched, turning back to face him.

"Yes." I indicated my suitcase. He watched me, waiting, reminding me of a predator about to pounce. I frowned. "I'll be going now. I'm here to see family."

He beamed. "I thought as much. We've been expecting you."

My frown deepened, and I gripped my suitcase handle, ready to pull away. This man was odd. Stalker odd. "What do you mean?"

But the man ignored me and held out his hand. "Let me be the first to welcome you to Ireland. I'm Torin. Torin Milligan."

I eyed him, not releasing my bag. The warning thrum of my pendant turned into a staccato beat against my skin. I didn't want to shake his hand. Still, he waited. Stifling a sigh, I relented and unhooked my fingers from the bag handle, then placed my hand in his as his last name plunked into place. "Milligan?" My eyes widened. "As in Milligan's, the store we're standing in front of?"

"Guilty." He nodded, thrusting out his chest. "Been in my family for years. As the eldest son, I'll inherit it all someday." I pulled, but he continued to hold my hand in his sweaty palm. "My father, my brother, and I have been fortunate to expand our operation. Our store in Galway"—he gestured at the storefront— "is not our largest outlet, but it's home."

"Great." Still, he held my hand. "I'll stop in sometime." His possession was uncomfortable, as if he was laying claim to me, which was a ridiculous thought. "But this morning I have business to attend to." I offered a silver of a smile and tugged my hand.

"But you can't go yet." His eyes locked on mine, holding me in his gaze. I frowned, not interested in an early-morning flirtation with a strange man. What I did want was my hand back.

Heat rose in me, a power that thrummed through my veins. "Let me go, Torin. Now." I'd had my fill of strange men this morning. "You may be nice, but I don't know you and I'm not interested."

At that, Torin chuckled, the deep sound rolling from him, his eyes flashing blue sparks, his shoulders shaking as if I had made the funniest joke he'd heard. His lips parted to reveal large front teeth, the fatal flaw that spoiled his outer veneer of handsomeness.

The power in my fingertips sparked, crackling like a live electrical wire, and Torin screeched and dropped my hand. "What did you do?" He whimpered as he examined his blistering palm. His blue eyes burned with anger when he looked back at me. "You burned me."

I wiped my hand on my pants and backed away. "You wouldn't let me go." I stood tall, staring into his eyes. "When a woman says to let her go, you let her go."

"I think the lady put you in your place, Torin." A deep, resonant voice announced the arrival of a tall, older man with thick black hair, although the white at his temples hinted at what time had in store.

"She thought I was on the prowl and she was my target." He scowled. "I'm a happily married man. And you're too old for me."

My eyes widened. "You wouldn't let go of me. And I can only guess what 'on the prowl' means. Lovely euphemism, by the way." I looked him up and down. "Being married doesn't ensure a man is faithful. Given the way you acted, I'd guess you're not." I ignored the age barb. He might have been a couple of years younger, but I wouldn't give him the satisfaction of showing I cared about his words.

A few pedestrians gave us curious glances as they walked by. "She has a point," the older man said. "And you'd do well to listen."

"She's lying." Torin's face flushed. "She was holding me." The older man shook his head and turned to me.

"You'd be Aisling, then."

I frowned, eyes narrowing. "How did you know my name?"

"Your aunt Geraldine is the vice president of marketing for the Milligan's corporation. She asked me to watch for your arrival." His smile was as smooth and modulated as his voice, but neither reassured me—not when I looked into his gray eyes, almost white when the sun shone directly in his face. I shivered. "I'm Meallàn Milligan," he said, not noticing my reaction. "Mel to my friends. And I hope you'll consider me a friend. I also hope you'll forgive my son's behavior." Mel bowed. "He's often undone by beauty."

I swallowed, knowing a line of crap when I heard it. I wasn't beautiful. Not even my husband had called me beautiful. Not in years. Considering his affair, I supposed he'd stopped noticing me or caring enough to comment. But I knew myself, knew I was a normal-looking forty-five-year-old woman with brown curly hair touched with a strand or two of silver and prone to wave in ways I couldn't control. My skin was clear, but wrinkles hyphenated the outer edges of my deep-brown eyes. I wasn't tall or short. I was average. My swan pendant pulsed, as if disagreeing, and the power flooded my system. I smiled. Well, maybe a little more than average.

Mel smiled back, thinking my smile was for him. "Welcome to Ireland, Aisling."

He reached out, and my instinct was to hide my hands behind my back, sensing this man was no better than his son, for all his suave airs. But he'd taken my side against his son. I clasped his hand and wished I could pull away as soon as his skin touched mine. Crawling sensations swept over my fingers and around my hand, snaking up my forearm. Power surged down my arm, fighting the creeping sting of his touch, and he gasped and yanked away, his strange eyes widening and darkening, reminding me of a dingy fog. I shoved my hand in my jacket pocket.

"Interesting," Mel said, his voice low, his eyes narrowed. He pulled a handkerchief from the breast pocket of his suit and wiped his hands. "How did you learn to do that?"

"It's time for me to go." I tugged my bag closer and hitched my backpack over both shoulders. I would not discuss a power I didn't understand with this man.

"Enjoy your reunion, Aisling." His eyes narrowed, and I shivered under his dirty-gray scrutiny. "It was an unexpected pleasure meeting you."

Torin glared at me but kept his mouth closed as he followed his father into the store.

Blowing out a breath, I merged into pedestrian traffic, which had picked up. The encounter with the Milligans had slowed my progress, and I hurried over the uneven cobblestones, yanking my bag over ruts, wishing I could stop and explore the colorful storefronts I passed. I'd come back before I left, look for presents, and stop for lunch. Take a few hours to be a tourist.

A busker was setting up on the sidewalk, an open guitar case at his feet and a large wooly dog sprawled out next to his stool. The man's curly hair fluttered in the breeze, and his lilting voice, as he spoke to a passerby, sounded familiar. As I drew nearer, he looked up, and I recognized him as the man who'd helped me up after my tumble to the curb less than an hour before.

"Hiya," he said, his green eyes flashing. I slowed to a stop, captured by his musical voice and amiable smile.

"Hi," I said. The shaggy dog rose and pressed his damp nose into my hand. I bent to pet him. "What a sweet boy. Is he yours?"

The man grinned, fine lines crinkling around his eyes. "Nah. The scruffy beast belongs to the shop owner across the way." He nodded toward a small shop opposite where he sat. "I'm fine if he wants to hang out. He attracts listeners." He watched me as his long fingers deftly plucked and tuned his guitar. "And women with velvet-brown eyes when I'm lucky." His voice was soft, yet I heard every word.

I swallowed, caught in his gaze like a tongue-tied schoolgirl. I had to say something, but I'd lost the power of speech. *Get it together, Aisling. It's a guy.* A guy I'd never see again.

I took an unsteady breath, watching him, wondering why this man discombobulated me the way he did. I needed to say something or leave. I cleared my throat. "I think we've met before. I'm Aisling."

"Aisling," he said, his deep voice a low rumble sending shivers through me. "I'd be Fergus." He held out his hand, and after a moment's hesitation I took it and gasped. Despite the heat in my fingers, our skin didn't burn upon contact, though his touch sizzled, sending tingles through me. I looked from our joined palms to his face, catching his golden-green eyes in mine. His lips parted, and a flush rose up his neck to his cheeks. My heart pounded as the ripples of awareness intensified until I wondered if I'd become a human firework and my hair was standing on end emitting fiery sparks.

"Aisling," he said again as he released my hand, his fingers trailing across my palm, his eyes never leaving my face. I was cold without his touch, and I shoved my hand in my pocket. "Have you avoided traffic in the last"—he checked his watch— "forty minutes?" His grin returned, and I smiled back.

"Yes. So far, so good. Although, I'll have a fair-sized bruise by tomorrow." I swallowed a chuckle, undone by his stare. "Thank you. For saving me. And thank your friend as well." Mention of the woman broke the spell, and he looked away as my mood deflated like the shattering of an iridescent soap bubble. Of course, she was his wife or girlfriend or something. And why in the hell did I care, anyway?

"Emer will be glad to know you're fine." He plucked a note on his guitar.

"So, you play." I wanted to sink into the pavement at my inane comment, but something about him kept me rooted to the spot.

He smiled, as if he could read my thoughts. "I do my best. Sing a bit as well, I do." He strummed a chord. "You ought to stop by later, have a listen. I'm not too bad, if I do say so."

"Maybe." I glanced at my watch, noting it was later than I'd told Granny I'd arrive. "I should go. It was nice to see you again."

"And you, Aisling." He looked as if he wanted to say something else, but he only nodded and turned his attention back to his guitar. I walked on, sorry to leave him, knowing I'd never see him again.

"Aisling." I stopped and turned at the sound of his voice. "Be careful. Nothing is quite what it seems."

I wanted to go back and ask him what he meant, but he looked away. I watched a moment longer until another woman stopped to speak to him. Biting my lower lip, I turned and walked on, ignoring the hollow sensation in my belly and the pain in the middle of my chest, although Fergus's eyes haunted my steps.

The pedestrian area narrowed, pubs and restaurants lining both sides. Flowers were still blooming in many spots, spilling from hanging baskets. The aroma of coffee mingled with hints of cinnamon, vanilla, and yeasty bread wafted up the street, but the thought of food was no longer appealing.

I paused in the middle of a bridge spanning a rushing river that spilled into a calm expanse of blue. If the map on my phone was to be trusted, I faced Galway Bay, and the water rushing toward the sea was the Corrib River. Gulls called to one another as they circled in the early-morning air. The salty scent of the sea filled my nostrils.

As I made my way over the last of the bridge, a burst of sun broke free of the clouds, illuminating two swans resting on the riverbank. I stopped and leaned against the rail, fingering the silver swan at my neck. The swans watched me with beady black eyes, and my pendant pulsed. Tension released from my shoulders.

Several blocks past the bridge, I turned onto a residential street. I was getting closer, and my stomach clenched at the thought of meeting my mother's family again after so long. I hadn't a clue how I was going to bring up Trevor's death, but I'd promised Beverly I wouldn't start with discussions of murder. "Ease into it, Aisling," she had advised. While I wanted answers, this morning I agreed with her counsel. I'd take it slow, get to know my mother's family first.

A stretch of larger houses with extensive front gardens behind iron gates sparked my memory. I'd walked here before, Mom's warm hand holding mine. I blinked, pain constricting my heart, wishing Mom was with me.

At the next traffic light, I crossed and started uphill. Parked cars lined the street, narrowing the lane until, to my eye, no more than one vehicle at a time could pass through, although a line of traffic on each side proved me wrong. Beyond the cars, a row of narrow houses with brightly painted front doors stood side by side, a series of conjoined masonry and brick.

Past the row of houses the road widened, and individual homes stood behind stone walls with driveways and gates. My map said I'd arrived, and I halted, panting and sweaty in my jacket with my bag hanging off my back. I needed to get in shape.

I turned in a circle, blowing out a breath as I took in the street, the lovely homes, the emerald green of the grass. Nothing looked familiar, but I'd been seven when I was last here. The phone indicated I was in the right spot, and when I completed my circuit, I saw the signboard I'd missed, affixed to a brick pillar.

Old Oak Manor.

Chapter Fifteen

Geraldine, October 26

Geraldine checked her watch. Almost nine. Aisling should have arrived by now.

"Relax, Daughter. She'll be here."

Geraldine wrinkled her nose as Mother added cream to her cup of coffee. Geraldine hated coffee. It tasted horrible. And she'd often told Mother how unhealthy it was. But her mother disagreed and insisted on drinking the odious beverage. The very smell and sight of the concoction disgusted her. As did her mother's obvious disregard for Geraldine's opinion.

"She should be here." Geraldine stood, teacup in hand, and walked around the room, the action alleviating the twitchiness in her limbs. What was taking the woman so long? Surely, she wasn't sightseeing. This was hardly the time for such a frivolous activity.

Her pacing space was limited in the cozy yellow sitting room her mother preferred. Geraldine had suggested greeting Aisling in the formal reception room. Mother had disagreed, and, as with all things, Mother had her way. As Geraldine passed the floor-to-ceiling windows looking into the side garden, movement from outside caused her to stop.

Her breath huffed out, and she spun around and headed to the side table, where she slammed her teacup onto the matching saucer. Tea sloshed from her cup, but she didn't stop to wipe up the spill. Damn the infernal man. He had no business being here. She straightened her deep-gold blazer and centered the sparkling citrine resting at the base of her throat. It was time he stopped taking liberties. This wasn't his home. She headed to the doorway into the front hall.

"What is the matter now?" Mother asked, her voice sharp. She shifted in her seat, and Geraldine felt eyes on her back. "Where are you going?"

Geraldine paused in the doorway. "Tommy is in the garden." She stared at her mother, challenging her to defend Tommy.

"Tommy's often in the garden." Mother watched her as if she didn't understand Geraldine's irritation. "He's here at the house most days of the week, for one reason or another." She leaned back. "He likes to check in. It's reassuring to have him so close."

Geraldine stifled a retort at her mother's obvious ploy to make her feel guilty for not stopping by more often. "Good for Tommy," she said. "But he doesn't have any cause to be here this morning."

"He most certainly does," her mother said, rising to face Geraldine. "Mary's death and Aisling's visit are tied directly to Tommy's arrival in Ireland. He has as much reason to want to speak with Aisling as we do. However, I imagine he simply wants to extend his welcome this morning." Her eyes narrowed. "But don't think for a moment that you can keep Tommy from Aisling. He will have his own questions, and he has every right to ask them."

"Not this morning," Geraldine said, knowing her voice was shrill. "This is family time. And I don't want her bullied."

Her mother's eyes widened, and she had the audacity to look affronted. "Tommy is no bully. If anything, I believe you should remind yourself to remain calm, Geraldine."

She pressed her lips together. "Thank you so much, Mother, for your faith in me."

Her mother dropped her head and sighed. When she looked up, her eyes were calm and steady. "I meant no offense. But you approach things from a business mindset, grilling others for the answers you demand. You cannot approach your niece in that way. She's lost her mother and her husband in the space of a few weeks. We will not add to her sorrow." She paused. "At least not today."

Geraldine gripped the doorframe. Mother was going to throw up roadblocks to their success. "She's going to have to be told about her connection to Lorcan. That and her Dreammaster powers are the main reasons she's here."

"Aisling is here at my invitation because she is a part of this family." Mother's eyes filled. "I've missed my granddaughter. I want to know her better." She sniffed. "We will proceed with abundant caution and care," she said, steel in her voice. "As we've already discussed."

"Fine. But I don't want Tommy here. Not now. He can speak with her later."

Without waiting for Mother to answer, Geraldine strode down the long front hallway and out the front door.

She didn't pause until she stood a foot from Tommy, her shoulders thrown back and her chin high. This was her home, not his, and her stomach burned at the way he assumed his presence was wanted. Of course, it was her mother's fault for welcoming the man. Geraldine swallowed the bitter taste of betrayal on her tongue as she recalled how Mother had always taken his side, even when he instigated divorce proceedings. Usually, she could let her mother's breach of faith go, but not this morning. Especially not when she thought back to his questioning of ten days ago, and the way he assumed, as did Mother, that she had somehow sent Lorcan into the Underworld.

Tommy had heard her approach and turned. His eyes narrowed and filled with suspicion.

"Good morning, Geraldine," Tommy said without warmth, as if he knew what she was about to say.

"I don't know why you're here," she said, dispensing with the niceties. "But I want you to leave. This reunion is for Mother, Aisling, and me. We need this time as a family to become reacquainted."

Tommy folded his arms across his chest and regarded her with cool eyes. "What are you afraid of, Geraldine?"

She looked away from his stare and berated herself, knowing she'd given him ammunition to challenge her. She was sure of it when she met his narrowed eyes. "This has nothing to do with fear, Tommy. This has to do with family. And you are not family. Not any longer." She spoke with deliberation and enjoyed the anger and hurt that flashed across his face.

"You're hiding something, Geraldine." He held her gaze a moment longer, before turning his attention to the oak tree towering over their heads. "The leaves are nearly all brown." He plucked a golden leaf and twisted the stem in his fingers. "I won't allow you to shut me out, Geraldine. Finding and saving Lorcan matters as much to me as it does to you. Lorcan may well hold the key to discovering and returning the monster I've sought for forty-six years." He dropped the leaf to the ground. "I will say my hellos to Aisling and be on my way. For now."

She spluttered, her hands fisted, and the man had the gall to smile. "Don't do that."

"Fine." He pressed his lips a straight, tight line. "I won't smile. But I'll say this. Don't you undermine Aisling's life and her relationship with her mother."

Heat rushed through her, and she pressed her hands to her sides. "Aisling's reaction to the truth is not down to me. I didn't run away and never come home. Mary did."

"Mary left because she was heartbroken. She needed support, and you offered her nothing but contempt. And when she did come back, you showed her disrespect when you shared with Aisling things about her heritage Mary had chosen not to reveal."

"Mary should have—"

"Perhaps she should," Tommy growled. "But you're not Aisling's mother. You had no right." He leaned closer. "Just as you have no right to barrel in and present Mary in a bad light to her daughter. Explain it all, Geraldine. The truth will be difficult for Aisling. But you can make it bearable if you so choose."

"What about my truth? My broken heart?" She clutched at her chest and leaned in until they were inches apart. "You neglect to consider my pain."

"Your pain is old. Hers is new and raw." His nostrils flared. "Proceed with care."

Fury was a fire boiling her blood, and Geraldine wanted to strike out, to hurt Tommy, to make him disappear. Instead, she turned on her heel and headed for the house. She didn't have to listen to him any longer. He wasn't her husband. He was nothing.

She could feel his eyes following her. She didn't care. Let him stay and greet Aisling. What could it hurt? He'd hardly see the woman after this morning. Geraldine took a deep breath, willing her heart rate to slow. She was in control. She smiled, almost laughed, but held it in. Tommy had no idea of her plans. And she had no intention of enlightening him.

Chapter Sixteen

Aisling

The house rose as I'd remembered—tall, imposing, and very much a part of its surroundings, grounded in the earth of Ireland. I shivered, a cold sensation creeping along my spine as I gazed at the windows, dark in the cloud-shaded early morning. Were they watching me, warning me away? I shook off the fanciful feeling as a breeze shifted the clouds, uncovering the shining sun. Beams of light danced off glassy surfaces, transforming what was forbidding into glimmering welcome.

I raised my head to the sun with a sigh, taking a moment to release the tension fluttering in my belly as the sun warmed my limbs.

"The weather is changeable, it is." A male voice broke into my meditation, and when I raised my lids, I looked into the bright-blue eyes of an older man standing nearby.

I hadn't noticed him as I approached the house, and my initial reaction was to shift away, even though he kept a respectful distance. He was tall, over six feet, and his thick blond hair was generously sprinkled with white. Something about his presence was soothing, and I stayed still, watching him, wondering why he seemed familiar.

He watched me as well, and he smiled at my scrutiny. "Hello, Aisling. I'm Tommy. Tommy Kennedy." He paused. "You won't remember me," he said, "but I met you when you were a wee lass come for your grandfather's funeral." His lips took a quick downward turn at the mention of my grandfather, but a moment later his wide smile was back in place. "And now you're back and fully grown." He nodded and held out his hand. "It's lovely to meet you again."

I placed my hand in his and the feeling of calm intensified, allowing my memory to kick in. "You showed me the garden." I bit my lips. He'd rescued me from my mother's anger and my grandmother's worry after Geraldine had shown me the attic. He'd been kind back then as well. "We were sitting on a wooden bench under a tree when Mom found me."

"Correct you are lass." He offered an easy smile, and I wondered if he too remembered my mother's anxious expression and shaky hands when she pulled me into her arms. "The bench and the old oak tree are still there."

He nodded and my gaze followed, spying the wooden bench in the center of the rambling garden under the spreading branches of a tree much larger than the one I remembered. Grass, as green as springtime back home, was a velvety backdrop for lush bushes and shrubs, a few of them still flowering, although fall had burnished the trees and leaves scattered the ground. The smell of recent rain, wet and clean, permeated the air. Beyond the garden wall, more houses of a similar age and stature stood sentinel, silently watching my arrival from a distance.

"What do you think?" He followed my gaze. "Is it like you remembered?"

"Sort of." I turned back to Tommy. "The tree's bigger." I tilted my head, bits of memories flooding back. "You were married to my aunt. Geraldine."

"You've an excellent memory, lass. We'd been married a year when her father died." His eyes clouded and he looked away, pulled a handkerchief from his pocket, and rubbed perspiration from his forehead. When he spoke again, his smile was back, but it hadn't quite reached his eyes. "We aren't married any longer." He tucked the square of fabric away.

"Ah." I nodded. His tone lacked the warmth of a moment ago, and I wondered if mentioning Geraldine had upset him. My look must have given me away.

"Nothing for you to worry about, lass. All for the best. And we're still friends." His expression was forced, and I wondered what he wasn't saying. "'Twas years ago. And I'm still a permanent fixture around here. The resident gardener and herbalist, when either need arises. As such, I see your granny most days."

"Tommy," a feminine voice, deep and commanding, drew our attention, and Tommy and I turned to watch as a tall woman approached, her strides purposeful.

"And here's Geraldine now," Tommy said under his breath. I glanced at him, still sensing an undercurrent of unease.

"Why didn't you tell me she was here?" Geraldine said with an edge in her voice, shooting Tommy an irritated glance before stopping in front of me.

"Calm yourself, Geraldine." Irritation laced his words. He tempered his tone with a smile at me. "Aisling's just arrived. We'd barely exchanged pleasantries."

I returned his smile. Geraldine didn't spare him a glance but focused her attention on me. "Aisling, *fáilte*," she said, smiling. "I'm your aunt Geraldine." Her voice was soft, clipped, almost businesslike, as if she couldn't decide how to address me, and I was surprised at her lack of accent. It was as if my aunt had schooled herself to sound less Irish. Her eyes, the same blue as my mother's, met mine. My heart hammered against my ribs and my mouth went dry, stealing my words. Aunt Geraldine looked like my mom, only taller and less approachable. Even her hairstyle was similar, but shorter and sleeker—deep-brown curls laced with white. I swallowed, willing myself to remain impassive, even while the sight of my aunt acutely drove home the loss of my mother.

"Hello, Aunt Geraldine, and thank you." My words were true, and yet they felt forced as I faced the fixed expression of my aunt. She stood erect, like a general, without any of the warmth Tommy exuded. As far as I could tell, she was nothing like my mother. I gave myself a mental shake. It was too early to make assumptions. After all, she had encouraged me to visit.

Geraldine placed her hands on my shoulders, her eyes searching mine. I resisted the urge to squirm under her intense scrutiny. "You've been through so much in the past few weeks. Mother and I were very sorry to hear about the death of your husband." She squeezed my shoulders. "I hope being here is restful, even though we have much to accomplish."

My throat tightened, and I swallowed. "I'm glad to be here. I need to understand."

"And you will." She placed her arm around my shoulders. "But, right now, relax and take time to adjust."

"She's right, lass," Tommy said. "The jet lag can get you."

I nodded, stifling a yawn. "I'm sure I'll sleep well tonight."

"If you'll give me your bags," Tommy said, "I'll take your things up to your room."

"Thanks." I shrugged the backpack from my shoulders and handed it to Tommy, noticing he'd already grabbed the handle of my roller case.

"Thank you, Tommy," Geraldine said. "You're free to go after delivering her suitcases." She gave a dismissive nod. "And now, Aisling, my mother is waiting to greet you." She gestured to the front of the house and I turned, spying an elderly woman standing there, watching.

Granny Nuala. My throat tightened, the heat of my pendant intensifying, as if it too recognized the woman who'd gifted it to me. I stepped away from Geraldine's hold and focused on my grandmother.

Granny Nuala hadn't been in touch, hadn't seen me since I was seven. She'd even missed her daughter's funeral. She deserved no outpouring of emotion from me. And, yet, seeing her, being so close to my mother's mother, was potent.

A wave of dizziness swept over me, and I swayed. Tommy steadied me, keeping hold of my arm as I wobbled. I rubbed my forehead, breathing deeply, wishing the tilted world would right itself.

"Aisling?" Geraldine's voice penetrated the rushing of blood in my ears. "Are you well?"

"Yes." I nodded, sucking in a breath. "I'm fine."

Steadier now, I took a tentative step toward Granny, steeling myself to remain detached. I'd come to understand my dreams, to get answers to my questions. Nothing more. And, yet, my heart pounded with each step.

"Go on, lass," Tommy prodded, his voice kind. "She's overjoyed to see ya, she is."

Granny stood on the stoop before the red-painted front door, leaning on a silver-headed cane. That red of the door and Granny's vivid purple shawl stood in vibrant contrast to the monochromatic stone facade of her home. Her hair was pure white, cut short, curls framing her small face. Her piercing blue eyes watched my every step.

Blue eyes? I stopped. For so long I'd imagined her stooped with beady black eyes like the sharp-voiced crows I remembered from my only visit. There was one even now perched in the branches of the tallest tree in the garden, watching as I approached. Or had I imagined her eyes as black, mixed Granny up with the crows in my fear of them both? Could I trust my childhood remembrances?

Granny stepped off the front stoop, leaning on the cane. I took another step. She'd aged. But it had been thirty-eight years. She'd grown old, and I'd grown up.

I continued toward her. Granny was small like my mother had been, and suddenly Mom was there with me, her spirit slipping next to me as I continued forward. Was Ireland playing tricks on my imagination? Or was exhaustion making me wacky? Either way, whether real or imagined, the sense of Mom was comforting.

I stopped in front of her, noticing the tears in her eyes, surprised at the unexpected tears gathering in my own, the catch of my breath in the fullness of my chest. This was my family.

Emotions swirled within me, from grief, to anger, to fear at what I might learn on this trip, but I pushed them away for now as I faced my grandmother. I missed Mom despite her faults and the truth she'd withheld about my heritage, and I'd been so alone since her death.

"Aisling." Granny's small hand reached out to clasp mine. Her grip was firm, her voice strong. "How good it is to have you home, child, with your family."

I wanted to deny any belonging, any idea that this was my home, but a growing warmth, beginning where my palm joined Granny's, was spreading up my arm. The power flowed through my body, relaxing me, and I blinked, not sure what I'd been about to say, what argument I'd been about to make. Instead, I smiled, knowing whatever it was would keep. And here and now, as I gazed into the eyes of my grandmother, I was happy that I'd come to Ireland.

"You have questions," Granny said, her penetrating eyes searching mine. I nodded.

"So many strange things have happened since Mom died—even here, since I've arrived." I'd come for answers. But now, standing before her, my questions stuck in my throat, the words like burrowing creatures unwilling to face the light.

"Yes. You've had an eventful journey." Granny kept my hand in hers as she searched my face. Could she know, see all that had happened? "There's turmoil and fear churning in you, child." She cocked her head. "Why do you doubt yourself as you do?"

"Because nothing makes any sense any longer. Nothing feels safe." I swallowed. "I need you to explain the truth about my dreams. Mom never did."

"Mary was wrong to keep your heritage from you," Geraldine said, joining us. "But to be fair, she had her reasons."

Granny squeezed my hand. "It was an awful time. Mary did what she thought was best. You were always her priority, Aisling. Everything she did was done to give you the best life she could."

"Yes," Geraldine said, an edge to her voice. "But when she knew she was dying, she should have told Aisling everything. Lies don't keep anyone safe."

"Mom didn't lie to me." The words tumbled from my trembling lips, and I pulled my hand from Granny's. "She didn't explain my dreams. But she never lied."

Geraldine watched me, not taking back her words. She reached over and placed a hand on my shoulder. "Why don't we head inside? Breakfast is ready if you're interested. And then, we can talk."

My stomach churned at the mention of food, and I knew I couldn't eat. Not until I understood what Geraldine meant.

"The sky's about to open, ladies." Tommy's voice interrupted us. "Get inside with you, before you're soaked."

"I believe you're correct," Geraldine said, offering her arm to Granny and leading her to the front door.

I waited to follow, watching as Granny navigated the step, using her cane as leverage. Tommy stood next to me, holding my bags.

"If you've some free time, you should pop around to my house for a visit," he said, his tone light and his face relaxed again. Did the change have to do with Geraldine heading inside? Or was I being fanciful? It was difficult to know, seeing as I'd just encountered these people for the first time since I was seven

"Do you live close by?" I asked, pushing away my musings. The relationship between my aunt and her ex-husband was none of my business.

"Indeed, I do. My house is up the street." He pointed in the direction. "Nothing as grand as Old Oak Manor, mind, but I love it all the same. It's red brick with a matching neighbor beyond. If Mrs. O'Malley answers the door—and you'll know it's her, for she wears a flowered housedress every day and I don't—you've gone one house too far."

He beamed, amused at himself, and I chuckled, envisioning Mrs. O'Malley in her dress. "What does she wear in winter?"

"Same dress, bless her soul. I think she must have a closetful. But she adds a sweater on top and warm slippers." He grinned at my laughter. "Now, I've a workshop in the back garden where I make odds and ends out of wood. You're welcome anytime. Listen for the whine of a wood saw, and you'll know you've found me." He glanced toward the door, then back at me. "I'd love an update about your mother. Mary was a lovely girl. 'Tis a shame she left so soon after I arrived. But it's obvious she was a caring mother." He patted my arm, his fingers warm. "I can tell she raised a fine daughter."

I blinked back tears. "I don't know about that, but I know she was a great mom." I swallowed hard. "Thank you, Tommy."

"Here you go, lass." Tommy handed me a clean folded handkerchief.

"Oh no, I can't."

"Of course, you can. I have loads." He pressed the fabric into my hands as Geraldine appeared at the door. I dabbed at my eyes and shoved the handkerchief in my jacket pocket.

"I've settled Mother in the sitting room." She focused on Tommy, a brow arched. "Will I see you this evening for the art opening?"

He stiffened but nodded. "Of course. Shall I pick you up here, then?"

"I'm heading to the office later. Mel and I have work to do this afternoon in preparation for a big event scheduled for the first of November." She paused. "I invited Mel to join us this evening. I hope you don't mind. He needs a break from the stress of the week. Why don't you meet us at the office, and we'll stop for a drink beforehand."

"Grand," Tommy said. "I've not seen the man since we met for dinner ten days back." He grinned with pleasure, his eyes shining.

"Mel Milligan?" I asked, tamping down a feeling of revulsion as I remembered the touch of his hand.

"Aye," Tommy said, his tone enthusiastic. "The man's my closest friend." He nodded at Geraldine. "Geraldine's the head of marketing for his fine company."

"Yes. I met him and his son this morning. He was very welcoming." I plastered a big smile on my face and hoped my cheerful voice was convincing.

"Why don't you join us this evening?" Tommy suggested.

"I've a feeling Aisling might need a rest later," Geraldine said.

"You're correct. I don't imagine I'll be up past nine, if I make it that long. And I won't be fit company past five. Probably won't be able to speak in complete sentences." I grinned. "But thank you for asking."

Dark clouds scooted across the sky, and Tommy glanced up. "I'll take these up, but I'd best put away a few tools first." He placed my suitcase and backpack in the foyer and, with a wink, headed for the garden, whistling under his breath.

I watched, wishing I could follow Tommy, sink my hands into the soil of Ireland rather than face my aunt. Why did she think Mom had lied to me? I had a sense that she didn't like my mother much, and I remembered Mom's assertion that she and her sister hadn't been close.

If that was the case, why had Geraldine encouraged me to visit? And how much support would she offer after I confessed my fears about my dreams? I shuddered at the direction of my thoughts, wondering for the first time at the wisdom of my decision to visit Galway.

Chapter Seventeen

Shadows of the past wrapped around me like a shroud as I stepped inside Old Oak Manor, paused at the threshold, and gazed down the long hall. I hunched inside my jacket, arms around my waist, as long-ago phantoms enveloped me.

The last time I'd stood in this hallway, I'd been surrounded by a sea of trousered legs and shiny nylons pushing me along like an insignificant twig caught in their undertow. No one had noticed me, all of them too busy scurrying around and piling roasted meat, boiled potatoes, and sharp cheese on plates while offering sympathy to Granny and her daughters. The pungent smells had choked me and led to a lifelong aversion to anything boiled.

I'd covered my ears to drown out the incessant chatter swirling overhead, wishing I could find my mother. But she was lost to me, buried somewhere in the crowd, and my isolation was my fault. I'd run from her when she'd insisted I accompany her into the living room, where

Grandfather's coffin rested, the tip of his waxy nose visible over the lip of the long brown box.

Trapped in a forest of grown-ups who smelled of perspiration, cologne, and cigarette smoke, I'd pushed into the dining room and tried to crawl under the long table, but I'd snagged a bit of the lace-edged cloth, almost upending a plate of sandwiches. A man's calloused hands had pulled me out. A loud woman wearing a monstrous black hat and resembling a witch had dispatched him to find my mother. I'd screamed and wriggled out of her pinching grasp, my heart pounding as I ran.

My heart pounded now at the memory, and I shivered, determined to walk down the empty hall without looking into either room. I took a breath and stepped further into the house. The cigarette smell was gone, replaced by the lingering aroma of yeast and sugar, a whiff of brewed coffee, and the musty odor of old wet that had permeated upholstery and soaked into wood.

With slow steps, I advanced along the hall as snatches of forgotten memories returned. The ticking of the old grandfather clock still counted the seconds. The same red and black tiles covered the floor. I paused outside the sitting room. I'd stepped on a toy car here as I'd run from the black hat, slipping and cutting my knee on a broken piece of plastic. The boy rolling the car had yelled at me, his green eyes drilling into mine, his curly red hair bobbing over his forehead, and I'd wanted to strike at him. But Mom had found me then, lifted me up, and taken me upstairs.

I looked ahead and tensed. There they were. The stairs. Leading to the room I'd shared with Mom. Where my childhood nightmares had begun. I swallowed hard, pressing my hand into the middle of my belly, and looked away from the stairs. I'd face that later. I smoothed my hands over my rumpled clothes, pulled my shoulders back, and entered the sitting room.

"Here she is," Granny said. "Fill a plate, Aisling. Airplane food is horrendous. Not that I've traveled in years. These old legs just won't let me sit still that long. Our housekeeper, Maeve, has been busy in the kitchen, and we have currant scones, a quiche with sausage and cheese, and a bowl of lovely fresh fruit. Not to mention the best butter in the county, courtesy of a local farm."

"Thanks." I glanced around the cozy lemon-yellow room lined with bookcases littered with pictures and knickknacks. Full-length windows offered a view into the garden. A fire crackled in the hearth, the earthy scent of burning turf rising to my nostrils. I remembered this smell from my trip with Mom. "Are these family photos?"

The thought of food sent my stomach into a spin. I bypassed the table and stopped in front of a grouping of photos, some on shelves and others hung on the wall behind.

"They are," Granny said. "You'll find several of Mary when she was young. She was a lovely girl." Granny's voice caught.

My eyes roamed over the pictures until I found a close-up of Mom standing in the garden beyond this room, her curly brown hair waving around her face, her smile reaching her eyes. She'd been beautiful, but I'd known that, had seen the few pictures she'd brought with her from Ireland. She'd still been beautiful, her eyes just as lively and loving, even when the cancer had sapped her strength.

"How old was she?" I held up the picture for Granny to see.

"Bring it over, child." She motioned for me to sit on the couch next to her chair. I handed her the frame and sat.

"This was on her eighteenth birthday." Granny smiled, closing her eyes. "The last birthday before she left home." She looked at me. "We'd had a lovely day. And she had plans that night. Off to a dance at the university."

Geraldine gasped, her face ashen. She dipped her head forward, rubbing her hand across her eyes.

"Geraldine?" Granny's voice was filled with concern.

"Aunt Geraldine?" I leaned toward where she sat across from me. "Are you okay?"

She took a shaky breath and raised her head. "Sorry." She took a moment. "I accompanied Mary to the dance."

I looked from Geraldine to Granny, wondering what had happened.

Granny spoke, her voice soft. "A man accosted Geraldine that evening." She paused. "I shouldn't have mentioned the dance."

"Oh my." I pressed a hand to my heart. "That's horrible."

"It was a long time ago," Geraldine said, wrapping her arms around her middle. "I don't think about it often." She glanced away.

Granny sighed. "Lorcan came to your aunt's rescue. Thankfully, she was physically unharmed." She clicked her tongue. "But she suffered emotional repercussions."

Lorcan. I'd been absorbed in the dream of Trevor, worried about what I might have done. Lorcan had slipped from the forefront of my mind. "Of course." The anguish on my aunt's face was plain to see. "I'm so sorry that happened to you. And how fortunate Lorcan was there. I understand why he's so important to you."

"Thank you, Aisling." Geraldine's haunted eyes met mine. "He was my hero."

"Was Lorcan your beau?" Boyfriend sounded too informal for my aunt, who had resumed her straight-backed posture.

She closed her eyes, as if composing herself before answering. "He was not, although I believe he might have been, if circumstances hadn't kept us apart." Her voice was hoarse, filled with emotion. She had cared deeply for this man.

"What kept you apart?" I kept my eyes on her, my voice soft, remembering times like this with Catrina and the boys who hadn't returned her interest.

"Wouldn't you like some food, Aisling?" Granny asked, startling me. "Or a cup of tea or coffee?"

Granny's voice shifted my attention away from Geraldine when she'd been about to answer. "Um, maybe a cup of coffee, if it's not too much trouble."

"Excellent." She turned to her daughter. "Would you ask Maeve to fix coffee and tea?" She settled back into her seat. "And then we can continue our conversation."

Geraldine's eyes looked like hard blue marble as she watched her mother. "Of course, Mother," she finally answered through stiff lips. "Excuse me, Aisling. I'll be right back."

Geraldine strode from the room, her spine stiff. I looked at my grandmother, wondering if she'd explain what had happened.

"You should eat, Aisling." Granny kept her voice light. "In fact, would you bring me a scone? I was too excited to eat earlier."

I wanted to ask what was going on, why she'd interrupted her daughter, but Granny's eyes had the beady look I remembered from my childhood. Instead, I nodded. "Of course." I rose and walked to the food, my mind buzzing.

I picked up a scone, the buttery aroma mixing with the sweet scent of currants making my stomach rumble. Maybe I was hungry too.

I handed Granny a plate and sat with one of my own. Taking a bite of the flaky pastry, I closed my eyes and sighed. "Your housekeeper is a remarkable cook."

"She'll appreciate hearing that," Granny said. "She taught the girls to cook. I never much cared for messing about in raw food things. I much prefer stirring about the dirt in my garden."

Geraldine entered the room, her face set and cold like stone, carrying a tray with three cups. She handed a cup to her mother, gave one to me, placed one in front of her seat, and put the tray on a table across the room.

"Thank you, Geraldine." Granny smiled as her daughter resumed her seat. Geraldine did not.

I sipped the coffee, watching the interplay between mother and daughter. Something had happened involving Lorcan. I stifled a sigh and steeled myself for whatever was coming. I had to ask. I had to know. I was tired of secrets, sick of no one telling me the truth. I put my cup on the table next to my elbow and cleared my throat.

"Maybe this isn't my place, but I'd like to know what Geraldine was about to say earlier. About Lorcan."

Two sets of eyes watched me. Neither woman spoke.

I rubbed my hands together, shifting in my seat. "I'm sorry if that upsets you, but I'm here because of Mom's dream. She was with this man. Geraldine told me they were all friends, but clearly she cared more deeply for him." I shrugged. "What's the mystery? Did he do something?"

"It was long ago, child," Granny said softly.

"Please, don't deflect." I stood and paced around the room. "We don't know one another yet. But we have to work together if you're going to teach me about my dreams." I looked at Geraldine, who watched me. "If it was a long time ago, then it shouldn't matter all that much now, right?" I returned to my seat and perched on the edge of the couch. "So tell me. Don't lie. Geraldine accused my Mom of lying, and I'll agree she wasn't as truthful as she should have been. Don't the two of you do the same." My mouth was dry, and I was surprised at my audacity, even as my heart raced. "Please, tell me."

"I agree with Aisling, Mother," Geraldine said, her voice sharp.

Granny sighed and bowed her head. "You have to know, child." Her voice was so soft I almost couldn't hear her. "Because the truth does matter." She looked up at me. "And, despite the passing of years, this particular truth is still consequential."

"Something that happened, what, forty-six years ago, matters that much even now?" I folded my hands together, my fingers stiff and cold. "I'm sure I can handle it. And you said I need to know." I looked back at my aunt. "What happened, Aunt Geraldine? What kept you apart from the man you so obviously cared for?"

Geraldine's eyes blazed, and she held me in her gaze.

"Your mother," she whispered.

"My mother?" Dizziness swept through me, and I gripped the arm of the couch.

"She stole him." Geraldine's hollow voice rang through the room. Her pain stabbed me, and I looked away from her unblinking stare.

"How?" I flexed and straightened my fingers, trying to organize my swirling thoughts. "Why would she?" I looked at Granny. "I don't understand. This doesn't sound like Mom."

"Oh, it was like her." Geraldine stood, her hands clenched into fists. "She didn't care if I suffered. As long as she had what she wanted."

I flinched as though she'd struck me. "I'm sorry," I said, my voice choked.

"Enough, Geraldine." Granny shook her head at her daughter. "I know the relationship between Mary and Lorcan hurt you. But you've been stingy with the facts."

"Have I?" Her nostrils flared with every inhale. "Once again, you throw your support to Mary. She was always your favorite." Geraldine strode to the windows overlooking the garden, her back to us, her shoulders trembling.

I started to stand, to go to her. Granny reached over and touched my knee, shaking her head.

"You need to know the full story, Aisling," Granny said, her eyes shadowed. "From a measured viewpoint."

Geraldine sniffed, but she didn't turn around. Granny's eyebrows rose, and she sighed.

"Mary met Lorcan in the spring of her first year at university. They began seeing each other, unbeknownst to me or her father. She was young and naïve and hadn't had a serious suitor. Your grandfather, Gerard, was especially protective." She pinched the bridge of her narrow nose. "Probably why Mary kept this information from us."

I nodded, waiting.

"On her seventeenth birthday, the year before, Mary had begun training to use her dreaming gifts." Granny paused. "Mary never explained about your ancestry, did she, child?"

"The Dreammaster thing?" My head swung to Geraldine at her sharp bark of laughter.

"Being a Dreammaster is a gift." She huffed over her shoulder.

"I meant no disrespect." I spoke to her back, and when she didn't respond, I turned back to Granny. "Mom wrote in her journal about me coming to train when I was seventeen. But Dad had died, and she couldn't leave the inn. She wouldn't allow me to come on my own."

Granny nodded. "Yes. I couldn't convince her." She paused. "We'll explain further about Dreammasters as we train you. A trainee is called a Dreamkeeper, which is what your mother was. She was excelling and soon would have advanced to Dreammaster." Granny smiled, her eyes sad. "She loved life, loved training, loved school." She looked back at me. "Mary was happy. Lorcan multiplied that happiness, and after a few months, it was hard to miss. Gerard and I had guessed there was a young man. She admitted as much and invited him for cake on her birthday so we could meet him."

"His smile lit up the room," Geraldine said, turning to look at me. "When he smiled at me, I tingled."

I frowned. "But he was with my mom when you met him."

Geraldine scowled. "Love isn't convenient. The heart knows."

Granny sniffed. "Lorcan and Mary were a couple, but Lorcan was a flirt. They invited Geraldine to go with them to the university dance, and he was kind enough to dance with Mary's younger sister."

"It was more than that, Mother. You weren't there." She walked to the sofa and leaned over, her fingers pressed into the cushions. "Lorcan saved me from the thug." Her eyes shone. "He was the most handsome man in the room. He danced with me all night." She smiled. "He didn't dance with Mary once after he came to my rescue." She circled the sofa and sank back into her seat. "He knew, just as I did. He even told me, 'Darlin' girl, we could conquer the world.'" She leaned back, dabbing her eyes with a tissue.

"Lorcan watched over you, Geraldine," Granny said, a touch of impatience in her voice. "And he'd been drinking."

Geraldine gasped, her eyes wide. "So, it was the drink, hmm?" She shook her head, her hair shaking. "I don't think so. If that was all, why did he take me for tea only a week later?"

"Because you were Mary's younger sister. And he was a thoughtful young man."

I looked from Geraldine to her mother. "I'm sorry Lorcan hurt you, but I don't understand why you're so angry with my mom, Geraldine." I cringed inwardly at her glare. "She met him first. They were a couple."

"He would have left her had it not been for the unfortunate accident that bound them." Her expression lightened. "He did leave her, in the end. Right after she told him what she'd done."

"What accident?" I frowned. "When did he leave?" This sounded like a case of unrequited love, but I'd give my aunt the benefit of the doubt and at least hear the rest.

Granny took up the story. "Lorcan disappeared on the eve of Samhain, October thirty-first, forty-six years ago. He'd been in Dublin with mates. They'd no idea what happened to him."

"And what had Mom told him that made him leave?" Possibilities crowded my mind—she'd met another man, she'd broken up with him, she'd caught him with another girl—but none of those were accidents. "What could be so bad?"

"She told him she was pregnant." Geraldine watched me, triumph shining from her eyes.

Icy cold flowed over me, locking my limbs, freezing me from the outside in as I watched Geraldine. Not even my lips could move.

Geraldine's lips twisted into a cruel smile. "What do you have to say to that, Aisling? I believe you said your mother always told you the truth."

"That's quite enough, Daughter." Granny thumped her cane. "Mary did what she thought was best under difficult circumstances."

Air whooshed into my lungs, and I found my voice. "Did she lose the baby?" That had to be the answer, and I bit my lip, waiting for Granny to answer, even as a murmur of dread rumbled low in my belly.

"No, child." Granny reached over and touched my hand, her eyes filled with sympathy.

I swallowed. Lorcan had disappeared forty-six years ago. I was forty-five. I pulled my hand from Granny's touch, my lips trembling. "No," I whispered. "She'd have told me." A sob broke free, bringing with it my tears. "No."

I bent over, my head in my hands, forcing myself to take deep breaths. How could she have kept this secret? And what of the man who'd raised me, the one I considered my father? Had Matthew O'Leary known? His face flashed before my eyes—the crinkles around his deep-brown eyes, his brown hair touched with silver when he died far too early. Mom had said I looked like my dad. What dad was she referring to?

"There, child." Granny settled next to me on the couch and placed her hand on my back. "I hadn't wanted to start with this." She sighed as she rubbed my back in a circular motion, the way Mom had when I was young. "I'd hoped we could take time to know one another better before …" Her voice trailed off.

I looked up, wiping away tears with Tommy's handkerchief. "Before you told me the biggest lie of all?" I coughed to clear the lump in my throat. "Did you think that would make this easier?" I wrapped my arms around my body. "I don't understand why she never said anything." I looked at Granny. "Why Dad never said anything." A rock had lodged in my throat, making swallowing painful. "He must have known if Mom was pregnant when she left Ireland. Why would he marry her? Why would she marry him after just losing Lorcan?" Another thought tightened my chest. "Am I really forty-five, or did she lie about that too?"

Granny took a measured breath. "Mary met Matthew almost as soon as she arrived in New Hampshire. Through my cousin, Maude. He was her accountant. Matthew fell in love with Mary when he met her. He wooed her, hoping to convince her to give him a chance to be a husband and father. A few months after her arrival, just before your birth, when there was still no word from Lorcan, she accepted his proposal of marriage. Matthew and Mary married, and she had his name put on the birth certificate. She told you the wedding was earlier, to account for the pregnancy and so she could keep your birthday as it was."

I pressed my hands to my head, as if that would control the spinning of my brain and stop the wave of dizziness threatening to spill me onto the floor. Mom had lied about her life and mine. For so long. "Why didn't she tell me?"

Granny sighed. "Mary planned to tell you Lorcan was your birth father when were seventeen, which was one reason I'd suggested you visit Ireland at that time, to give you distance as you processed the truth." Granny sighed. "She didn't follow through after Matthew died in the car crash. She couldn't bring herself to tell you. She saw it as disloyalty to the man who raised you. But Matthew wanted you to know—Mary admitted as much to me." She shrugged. "Confessing the truth grew more difficult as the years passed."

My insides trembled, and I gripped my sweater to keep the tremors from reaching my hands. I wanted to demand proof, but knew it was a feeble attempt to cling to my fraudulent past. Mom had lied. Matthew wasn't my birth father. I was the child of a man from Mom's past, a hazy vision from my childhood nightmares. I didn't know what to do, where to go, how to process what I'd learned, and I yearned for Beverly's familiar face. Except, I wasn't even certain I could say the words to her. Not yet. Not until I worked free of the seething fire of emotion twisting inside me.

I stood, dragging my hands through my hair, my head spinning. "I've got to get out of here."

"Aisling, child, please sit back down." Granny's slim fingers reached for me.

I sidestepped her grasp and scooted around the couch. "Outside, I think."

"It's raining," Geraldine said, her voice alarmed.

"I don't care." Rain would be better. Wake me up, help me sort through all they'd told me, all my mother hadn't said, and decide what I believed. "I can't breathe."

I bolted from the sitting room and rushed toward the front door, watching the red and black tiles of the hallway floor blur beneath my hurrying feet.

And smacked headfirst into Tommy.

CHAPTER EIGHTEEN

I stumbled, and Tommy caught me before I fell onto the hard tile floor. "Are you okay, lass?"

The soft burr of his voice almost undid me.

"I think so." I couldn't look at him, and as I rubbed the back of my neck, I kept my head bowed and gritted my teeth, determined to keep the endless stream of tears from starting up again. I was sick of crying, even as my head now throbbed as painfully as my heart.

I swayed and Tommy's hands gripped my arms tighter, keeping me upright. "Maybe you ought to sit down for a minute, catch your breath."

I shook my head, sending pain piercing through my skull. "No. I need to move." I tugged my arms from his grasp and backed away, almost tripping over my suitcase.

"I was just taking it upstairs for you." He frowned. "You're deadly pale. Maybe we should call the doctor, make certain you didn't hurt your head worse than we realize."

"No." I closed my eyes and stretched my neck, loosening the tension but not relieving the headache. I leaned against the wall behind me, breathing deeply. "I'll be fine in a moment."

"Aisling. My gracious, what happened?" Geraldine's firm footsteps crossed the hall, then stopped in front of me. I didn't look up. "Tommy?"

"The lass catapulted from the sitting room, and we collided." Tommy paused. "What happened? She seems upset."

Geraldine sighed, and I waited, wondering what she would say. "I said some things." She reached over and squeezed my shoulder. "I am so very sorry, Aisling. I handled that badly. I didn't mean to get into Lorcan right now."

"Lorcan?" Tommy barked the name. "What about Lorcan?"

"I didn't mean it to come out the way it did." She stopped. I looked up and opened my eyes a fraction, noting her pained expression. "I couldn't stop myself." She shrugged, looking away from Tommy's thunderous expression. "I'm sorry." Her voice was devoid of emotion or forcefulness. "I made a mistake."

"You did, Daughter." Granny emphasized her words by attacking the hallway tiles with two thumps of her cane.

I raised my head with care, noting that Granny's expression was similar to Tommy's.

"We'd agreed to take our time. Give the woman a chance to acclimate before discussing her relationship with Lorcan."

"Yes, Mother." Geraldine squeezed her eyes shut for a moment. "I was wrong."

I sighed heavily. "It's done." I pushed away from the wall. "Mom should have told me. Geraldine was right about that. She kept too many things from me." Pain speared my chest at the thought of the lie my parents had told, this vitally important part of my life they'd deemed me unable to handle. Because Dad had been as much to blame as Mom, even though she'd had years after his death to share the truth. But my heart was still beating. Maybe someday I'd understand. Today wasn't that day, however. "I need time to process all of it, though. Some space to think about everything."

Granny nodded. "Tell us how we can make this better."

"Yes," Geraldine said. "Whatever you need, please let me know." Her eyes were sad, begging for forgiveness.

"It's okay, Geraldine." I managed a small smile, even though I still didn't understand her obsession with a man who'd been involved with my mother over forty years ago.

"We can start training, if you'd like." Her face brightened a little at the thought.

"Not right now," I said, shaking my head. "I'm going outside, like I said. I need fresh air."

"Head to the garden, lass," Tommy said as I stepped away from them. "After a rain it's like the air's been scrubbed, fresh and clean." I glanced at him and he nodded, encouraging. "'Tis the best spot to do your thinking."

"The old oak bench is my favorite perch," Granny said, her eyes worried even as she smiled. "Gerard made the bench for me years ago. We used to escape there."

"Great." I stepped past Geraldine, ready to escape. "I'll be there, then. Thanks."

Fresh air helped my headache, and I stretched my arms as I inhaled the scent of wet earth. Birds flitted in and out of trees, shaking the branches and flinging water. I walked through the grass, dampening my trousers and darkening the toes of my leather boots. It was cool here, the breeze bracing. Just what I needed.

At the bench, I ran a hand along the smooth wood, water clinging to my fingers. A large black bird scrambled among the branches overhead, sending sprinkles of water down upon me. I looked up into beady black eyes, and the creature stared back before flapping away. I watched it go. The bird was free, and I wished I could take to the skies and follow, be a bird for a bit rather than me. But I was stuck, feet on the ground, mind filled with a lifetime of deceptions and no way to make sense of them.

"Why, Mom?" Something cracked inside me, growing until pain radiated from my belly up to my heart. My breath quavered, shuddering in and out of me until I caved, bowled over by the weight of it all, sobbing as my fingers pressed into the wood. "Why didn't you talk to me? Why didn't you tell me? What was so wrong with me that you couldn't trust me?"

My knees buckled, and I knelt on the damp ground, resting my head on the back of the bench, my tears mingling with the rainwater.

As my sobs subsided, I became aware of the wet soaking the knees of my jeans. I raised my head, ready to stand, when I noticed the carving on the back of the bench.

A woman and a man, hands entwined, seemed to fly across the wood, the woman's flowing hair streaming around and behind them. Beneath them were two swans facing each other, heads and bodies touching so they formed a heart shape. This was very much like the picture on Mom's journal I'd been unable to find, the only difference between the two the addition of the man. I traced the carvings with a finger, the tip of it growing warm as I outlined the intricate patterns. Heat flowed from my swan pendant, and it pulsed in time with my heart. Peace flowed around me and settled over me, like a fuzzy blanket for my bruised soul. I spread my palm across the carvings, smiling as the energy from the wood mingled with the energy in my hand. I didn't understand the connection, but I accepted it.

"'Tis the goddess Caer Ibormeith and her lover, the god Aengus." Tommy's soft voice brought me to my feet.

I turned, wiping away the bits of grass clinging to my knees. "I didn't hear you." I ran a finger under my eyes, imagining how I must look. Turning, I walked around the bench, not sure what to say to Tommy and wondering why he had followed me, if he had heard my weeping fit. My eyes were sore, my nose stuffy, and I told myself I wouldn't cry anymore today.

"I don't mean to bother you, lass." He walked around from the other side of the bench and dropped two waterproof cushions on the damp seat. "I just thought you might need these. So you don't get wet as the rain itself."

"Thanks." I looked away, not sure what more to say.

"You learned the worst of it today, lass." His voice threatened to crack my resolve. "You're a strong woman, Aisling. This won't break you unless you allow it to."

I looked at him, into the depths of his blue eyes, and almost believed him. "How can you be so sure? I feel like something shattered deep in me, something vital. I don't know if I can fix it."

Tommy took his time to answer, his voice thoughtful. "Maybe, lass, it's not something to be fixed but something to rebuild in a wholly new way."

Hope flickered inside me. "You think it's possible to mend." I thought of everything I'd learned, not only today but over the past few weeks, and the hope fizzed out, leaving me hollow. None of this explained my dreams and what happened to Trevor. "How? How do I mend after all the lies?" I stared at him, praying he had an answer.

Tommy tilted his head, a smile playing on his lips. "I can't tell you the steps, lass. Your heart will guide your course, and I trust you'll find your way." He took a step, two, stopping before me, touching my cheek with his calloused fingers. "You need to believe. To trust yourself."

Chapter Nineteen

Tommy was correct. The essence of the garden soothed me. Birds twittered and warbled, calling to one another as they flitted about. The murmur of the wind whistled through the tree branches. Smoke from a chimney blended with the crisp, sharp tang of autumn leaves that sprinkled from the old tree above me and littered the ground around the bench.

Eyes closed, I let the peace flow into me as I considered Tommy's words. He believed I'd recover, become a better person, like a phoenix rising from the ashes to live again. I wanted to be that brave. But I wasn't sure I could trust myself to accomplish such a lofty goal. I wasn't convinced I could piece my soul together enough to restore feeling to the numbness surrounding my heart.

Raindrops—misty touches of moisture at first, then swiftly becoming fat drops of saturating wet—drove me to my feet to go inside. I paused as I rounded the bench, stopping to examine the carving on the back once more. I'd heard of Caer Ibormeith. Had Mom told me the story? Or was that Aunt Geraldine, when I'd been here as a child?

The rain intensified, yet I stood there, eyes squeezed shut as I tried to force the memory. She was a goddess. That much, Tommy had said. She was the goddess of dreams. My eyes popped open at the memory. Was she related to my dreams?

The wind whipped into a frenzy, sending the rain sideways into my body. Time to get indoors, although I doubted I could get much wetter.

Geraldine greeted me in the vestibule with a large towel. "I've been watching for you." She helped me out of my wet jacket and wrapped the towel around my shoulders, her touch gentle. "How are you feeling, dear?" She picked up a corner of the towel and patted my cheeks. Part of me wanted to pull away, but she looked so like my mother, and I missed Mom despite everything. Mom was the one I would have spoken to about my deepest troubles, but this time she was the cause of them. And she was dead.

I stifled a yawn. "A bit sleepy, to be truthful."

Geraldine smiled and led me down the hall. "Why don't we get you tucked into your room? You can change into dry clothes and take a nap."

"Yes." My eyes drooped at the thought of a bed. "I'd like that."

As we came to the sitting room, Geraldine poked her head inside. "Mother, Aisling's going to head to her room. She's exhausted."

"Excellent plan." Cushions shifted, soon followed by the sound of Granny's cane.

"You don't need to come with us," Geraldine said as Granny joined us in the hallway.

"Nonsense." Granny examined me with narrowed eyes. "You look better, child." She smiled. "Soaked to the bone, but calmer in spirit."

"Yes," I said. "A bit, thank you."

"The old bench always comes through. It's my haven." She nodded before turning and leading the way to the stairs.

"The kitchen's here," Granny said as we passed. "You'll miss lunch, but Maeve will fix you something when you wake up."

"Thanks," I murmured.

Geraldine and I followed Granny up the stairs, our footsteps muffled by the pale-yellow runner.

"My room is here," Granny said at the top of the stairs, indicating a door to our right.

"You're straight down the hall." Geraldine kept a hand under my elbow as if she was afraid I'd collapse.

"Many years ago, Old Oak Manor was an inn," Granny said as we continued down the hall. "Mary loved the idea of running an inn when she was a girl. Used to pester me to reopen the place to visitors." Granny chuckled. "After Gerard's mother passed, I was happy to close the doors to the public. So was he."

"Mom accomplished her goal," I said. "Mountain View Inn is part of our community because of Mom and her dreams." Dreams. I shuddered at the word, forcing myself to shake off the pain thoughts of Mom brought, knowing I'd never actually succeed. "You should have visited."

"Yes." Granny paused, twisting to look at me as she leaned on her cane, her eyes bleak. "I should have." She sniffed and looked away. "I made many mistakes, child. For that, I'm truly sorry."

I swallowed the lump in my throat as we walked on, wondering if things might have been different if my grandmother had been part of our lives. If Mom hadn't run away from her family and her past.

"Here we are." Granny stopped at a tall wooden door and turned the knob.

Breath held, I watched as the door swung open. I knew this room. Remembered the large windows overlooking the garden and the tall four-poster bed. Mom's old room. We'd stayed here all those years ago, when the dreams of my childhood had begun.

"My room is over there." Geraldine pointed down a hall perpendicular to the one leading from the stairs. "I've decided to stay the week you're here, so we can train."

Her words faded to background noise as my eyes focused on the doorway at the end of the hall, past my aunt's room.

"The attic," I whispered. Adrenaline flooded my system, sending my heart pounding into overdrive. "You took me up there, Aunt Geraldine."

"I'm surprised you remember," Geraldine said, her eyebrows raised.

"Mom was angry." My heart pounded as I remembered my mother's flushed face, the look of panic in her eyes when she'd found us.

"She was worried I was bored, Mama," I'd explained, my eyes searching for the warmth I usually found in my mother's face. "She read me a fairy tale and gave me a sweet. But only one, I promise. Look, she showed me her books. The swans on the cover of this one swim. One of them scratched me."

Mom had grabbed the book from me and thrown it at her sister before she grabbed my shoulders and searched my eyes, holding them in the intense blue of her gaze. I watched anger followed by concern followed by confusion flow across her face, one emotion after the other, until she released me. "I can't tell," was all she said. Granny had nodded, worry deepening the creases in her forehead, her eyes a beady black.

"It's her destiny," Geraldine had insisted, pleading with them to understand. "She has to know."

"Not so young." Mom had taken my hand, led me to the stairs. Granny had stayed behind, and I'd heard her voice, harsh, reverberating throughout the attic.

"How could you have been so irresponsible? It's always the same. I can never trust you."

Mom had said something similar to me about not letting me out of her sight and how disappointed she was in me.

Geraldine shifted, and I looked up to find her watching me, her eyes wide and knowing, as if she could read every thought in my head.

"It was a long time ago." Granny patted my arm. "There's no need for you to go to the attic on this trip. In fact, you oughtn't to go up there." Geraldine exhaled, as if about to protest, and Granny's voice hardened. "It's a dusty room filled with disused junk. Best to avoid it altogether."

"That's ridiculous, Mother." Geraldine's tone was placating. "There's no harm in going to the attic if Aisling would like to revisit the place."

"No, Geraldine." She thumped her cane. "I've said all there is to say."

"Fine, Mother." Geraldine sighed, her lips pursed. "I'll be in my room. I may as well change and head into the office." She patted my shoulder. "We'll begin training tomorrow, Aisling." She leaned over and hugged me. "I'm very glad you're here."

"Me too," I said, wondering if that was true. I'd pondered leaving when I was outside on the bench. My life was topsy-turvy, my kids were angry I'd abandoned them, and I wasn't sure how many more revelations I could take about my life. As yet, I hadn't come to any firm conclusion.

"Come, Aisling," Granny said. "Let's get you settled."

I followed Granny into the room, recognizing the blue floral wallpaper from my childhood visit. My swan pendant pulsed, a comforting heat spreading across my chest. I reached to touch it as Granny opened the heavy damask curtains. Weak light spilled in through wavy old windows—a miracle, given the dousing rain pelting the glass. Granny shifted to face me, one hand gripping the back of a small blue upholstered chair under the window.

"Make yourself at home, child. And take time to acclimate." Her eyes zeroed in on my fingers still at my throat, and she smiled. "You're wearing your swan." She nodded. "I'm glad."

"I'd forgotten, put it away when I was older and my childhood dreams petered out." I lowered my hand. "It gets warm and pulses, almost like it knows what I'm feeling."

Granny watched me, and I swore her eyes shifted from blue to beady black. "As was my intention," she said. "She is aligned with you, Aisling.

Pay attention. The swan is your protector. She magnifies and focuses your innate power and warns you of danger."

I shuddered. "What danger?"

"There's magic in your heritage. And where there is magic, there are those who wish to exploit it."

I swallowed, recalling the shadows in my forest, the heat in my hands, the people I'd burned, and all the strange things people had said to me since my arrival—the monster calling me Dreamer, Violet acting as if my arrival had been expected and telling me she was here for me, and Fergus suggesting I be careful because all wasn't as it seemed. I yearned for answers, but I wasn't ready. Not yet. My stomach rolled, and I cringed inwardly, the half of the scone I'd eaten suddenly threatening to come back up. I wrapped my arms around my middle.

Granny frowned. "You must have experienced a wee bit of the power within your dreams, even if unintentionally."

I thought of the things I'd believed had changed because of dreams I'd had and bit my lip, wondering how I ought to respond.

"Ah, I can see you have." She took a breath. "This is what we'll discuss later, if you're up to it. The power of your dreams and where it comes from."

I trembled at the words, thinking of all the questions I had, wondering if I'd still be welcome after I asked about Trevor and his death. Or if they'd ask me to leave. A chill ran down my spine. I wasn't ready to go yet. Even after Geraldine's revelation earlier.

"Okay," I whispered.

Granny walked to me, taking my hand in hers. "I'm so very happy you're here, Aisling, and I have this chance to know you better." She squeezed my hand. "It's like having Mary back, child. I've missed her so very much," Granny whispered, her misty eyes definitely blue.

My heart ached. "I miss her too."

Granny watched me a moment before releasing my hand. "The door in the corner is the closet, and next to that is the bathroom. You'll find what you need in the cupboard, and if there's anything else we can get you, let us know. I imagine you might like a warm shower."

I nodded. "Yes."

"There's an adjoining door between our bathrooms, but you don't have to worry that I'll bother you." She chuckled. "I doubt, after all these years, the old door opens any longer."

"Thank you, Granny." Exhaustion swept over me, and suddenly all I wanted was to be alone, close my aching eyes, and escape into sleep.

She nodded, patting my hand. "Rest well, Aisling. And welcome home."

Chapter Twenty

Waking was like swimming against a strong current. Part of me battled toward consciousness while the other part of me fought to remain asleep as I became aware of the outside world. A bird called outside my window as the wind bellowed, and a tree branch scratched along the glass.

Inside, old pipes banged, followed by the hiss of steam as a radiator turned on. Murmured voices reached me from close by, and a floorboard creaked in the hall. I kept my eyes closed in case someone was coming to check on me.

My stomach rumbled at the scent of roasting meat, and I opened my eyes. I twisted to read the dial of the old-fashioned round-faced clock ticking time away on the bedside table: 2:40. I plopped back onto the pillows. I'd been asleep for three hours and missed lunch. I'd also missed the window of time when I could speak to the kids before class or Beverly before work. Relief washed over me. What would I say anyway? I wasn't ready to share this morning's revelations. I'd barely had time to process them myself. And the kids, still reeling after Trevor's death, weren't ready to hear them. I'd call later. Or tomorrow.

I lingered in bed, considering the morning and the decision I made as I drifted to sleep. I had to stay and learn the truth about my dreams and what it meant to be a Dreammaster. Mom had kept this part of me a secret. She'd been afraid of my dreams, but she'd refused to explain why, and all I could conclude was she thought my dreams were dangerous. Why else would she have taught me a mantra to control the worst of them? I scooted up and crossed my legs. Mom should have told me the truth or sent me to Granny when I was seventeen. She'd owed me that much.

I rubbed my temples, considering my mother. Why hadn't Mom told me about Lorcan? Thinking about Mom's betrayal filled my belly with fire and clogged my throat with words I'd never speak to her. She could have allowed me to be angry with her in person, but she hadn't. The man who'd raised me had been dead since I was sixteen. Nothing she could have said would have made me love Matthew O'Leary less, so why not come clean and explain her past?

Mom had been the one I'd always been able to rely upon, and now I couldn't. I couldn't even ask her if it was true, although I could think of no reason for Granny to lie about my relationship with Lorcan. If I left Ireland, I'd forgo the best opportunity I had to meet my real father, find out what he was like, and sort through my feelings concerning him.

I'd told Geraldine I wanted to help save Lorcan, and I did, even though I didn't know what that meant. Just the thought of that horrible place from Mom's dream made it hard to breathe, and I rubbed a tight, painful spot at the center of my chest. My fear seemed childish, given that Lorcan had been stuck there, on his own, for forty-six years. Whatever rescuing him entailed, I wouldn't be on my own. Geraldine would be with me, helping me. She'd planned to rescue him without me. Now, we could work together, after she'd trained me. That thought calmed my racing pulse, and I relaxed back against the pillows. I could do this. Meet my father. See if we shared any traits, besides our eyes. And then go home, questions answered, duty done, although all that waited for me in New Hampshire was an empty house and kids fast becoming adults.

I forced myself out of bed and dressed in clean clothes, then folded my pajamas and tucked them away in a deep dresser drawer. In the bathroom, I dusted a pinch of blush across my cheeks and swiped a touch of mascara to my lashes. Better. Not quite as pale.

As I neared the stairs, a stout woman with short fuzzy gray hair was stepping out of Granny's door. She narrowed her eyes, put a finger to her lips, and hissed, "Shush." She motioned for me to follow, and I nodded, trotting down the stairs after her bustling form. I presumed this must be the housekeeper.

The woman stopped at the kitchen door and faced me, her eyes steely gray, her hands planted on her generous hips. "I'd be Maeve. Been with your granny for over fifty years, I have. Knew your mother and Geraldine as girls. Even remember you as a wee lass." She looked me over with a sniff. "At least Mary brought you home for the funeral. Couldn't be bothered to come before he died." She pursed her lips. "Or since."

My eyes widened, and I struggled for words, but Maeve continued.

"I got Nuala to sleep, and I don't need you to go waking her."

"Of course," I said, feeling like a naughty child. "I didn't mean to sleep so long."

"She waited for you, she did. Disappointed, she was." Maeve shook her head, as if the concept was one I'd not grasp. "If there's nothing more, I've work to do."

I'd been about to ask for a sandwich, but her expression made me think better of it. "I'll take a walk." I smiled. "If it isn't raining. The weather's hard to predict, isn't it?"

My overture failed. "Do as you please," Maeve snapped, turning to the kitchen. "You cannot wait for clear skies in Galway if you want to get anything done. You'll find umbrellas in the hall tree by the front door."

"Thanks," I said to her back.

"Be back by six thirty. And see that you aren't late," she said as she slapped dough onto the counter and picked up a heavy wooden rolling pin. I shuddered, determined to steer clear.

"I won't be. Thank you. Nice meeting you, Maeve."

She huffed but didn't answer me, and I headed upstairs for my jacket and pocketbook. Outside, the sun shone, though dark clouds hovered on the horizon. No matter. I'd take a walk.

I turned right out of the drive and headed up the hill.

Sun glistened on wet surfaces, making even the blades of grass sparkle in a shimmering green as they blew in the light breeze. The air, while still damp, was fresh, and a salty tang hinted at the nearness of the ocean. Gulls called to one another overhead as they circled. The crows, which I'd come to associate with Ireland since my childhood visit, perched in high tree branches, surveying the land below and issuing *caws* like loudmouthed rulers.

The houses on my route ranged from gated estates to smaller single-family homes, all of them set in lush lawns with plentiful foliage. When I came to a particularly busy intersection, I stopped to allow traffic to clear. As I stepped into the street, a city bus popped over a hill bearing toward me with gusto, and I paused, wasting valuable moments considering whether to step back to the sidewalk or run across the rest of the street.

"Have you never crossed a street before?" asked a deep voice behind me. A firm hand grabbed my elbow and steered me to the other side of the road. On the sidewalk, I stopped next to my rescuer to catch my breath.

"'Tis the second time today I almost witnessed you squashed in traffic."

I looked into Fergus's green eyes, noticing again how the sun picked up sparks of gold within their depths. He smelled good, as if the woods and the ocean had blended and bathed him in their combined essence. I wanted to lean in and sniff. I pulled back instead, feeling my cheeks burn.

"I'd hate to see anything happen to you." His eyes darkened as he said the words, and I caught my breath, trapped in his gaze until he blinked, and the moment vanished.

"What are you doing here?" My words came out more forcefully than I intended, and I shook my head, still grappling with the way his look sent shivers through my limbs. *Get a grip, Aisling.* "I'm sorry. That's not what I meant."

"What did you mean?" he asked, his tone light, his smile teasing. That flustered me even more.

"Th-th-thank you," I stammered. "Thanks for saving me from the bus. It came out of nowhere." Now I was jabbering, but I couldn't make my lips stop moving. "I looked both ways several times, and the road was clear. I swear it was. And just when I stepped into the street, there it was." I took a breath. "The bus." I nodded, sputtering to a stop.

Fergus was grinning, and I shuffled on my feet. What was wrong with me? I was behaving like a teenager instead of a woman recently widowed.

"You're welcome." He paused, and I looked up to find him watching me. "Why are you out and about on your own? I'd have guessed Geraldine would have had plans for your day."

I nodded. "She did." I thought back to the morning's revelations. "But it didn't work out, so she headed back to work. I took a nap, and now I'm on my own."

A passerby jostled into me, and Fergus caught my arm before I stumbled. "Maybe we should move on," he said, laughter dancing in his eyes. "Before you land on the curb again."

"Of course," I said, glancing away. He had places to go, other people in his life, and no reason to spend time with a woman he'd just met. My chest tightened at the thought, but I pushed away the disappointment.

"Care to walk with me a spell?" He smiled when I looked back at him, his brows raised. "I like your company."

My heart danced, a pitter-pat against my chest, and I smiled back. "Yes. I'd like that."

The sidewalk widened enough for us to walk side by side. I glanced at him and found he was watching me. My breath caught in my throat, and I struggled for words.

Birds swooped and flitted above us, hovering near Fergus, chittering in the sea-scented air before darting away, only to return a moment later.

"They like you," I said, gesturing to a pair of bright-blue birds with yellow bellies.

"Blue tits," he said, nodding at the twosome as they winged away. "Cheeky fellows. Always busy." A black bird *caw*ed from the branches of a tree, as if seeking Fergus's attention. He glanced up, blew a whistle through his teeth, and laughed when the large bird screeched again and flapped away. "The rooks issue their proclamations like royalty, they do."

"Rooks." I shivered. "They scared me when I was here a long time ago. Something about their beady eyes."

"Nah, they're good sorts. Very intelligent birds too."

I looked skeptical, and he chuckled. "I'll not try to convince you about my bird friends." He bumped my arm with his, and I smiled. "So, how was it meeting your granny again? I know she was dead pleased you were coming to visit."

"You know her, then?"

He nodded. "Family friends. She was close to my grandmother."

"Ah." How much I didn't know. "It was better than I expected," I said, in answer to his question. "I think she's happy I'm here." I bit my lower lip. "Both she and Geraldine."

"'Tis a good start, then." Fergus nodded to another walker. "Geraldine's a tough one to figure out, and if she's pleased to have you, I'd say your visit is already a success."

"What about Maeve?" I asked, hoping I hadn't breached any boundaries with my question. "It's just ... I think I made her angry when I overslept."

"Maeve's a dragon, she is, always protecting Nuala. She doesn't take to strangers, does Maeve. Not even ones related by blood."

"Good to know." I stretched my legs as far as they'd go to keep pace with Fergus. "She doesn't have to put up with me for long, but I'll be on my best behavior, see if I can make her smile even once before I leave."

"Keep me posted on your progress," he said, and my heart soared a tiny bit at the thought of keeping in touch with him while I was in Galway.

"I'll do that." I paused, catching my breath. "Do you live around here?"

"Not too far," Fergus said. "But I'm heading to Tommy's place. We're working on a project." He gave me a sidelong glance. "You met Tommy, right?"

"I did. He told me he lived near Granny."

"We're almost there." He glanced at me. "Why don't you stop and say hello?"

"No. You're busy, and I'll be in the way."

"Of course, you won't be in the way." He stopped abruptly, and I almost ran into him. "In fact, you can't escape, seeing as we're here and Tommy's spotted you." He nodded, and I turned to see Tommy standing in front of a red-brick house with a bright-red door. A grin spread over his face.

Chapter Twenty-One

"Aisling's joining us," Fergus called as we headed down the short driveway.

Sun glinted off the windows of the house—two bay windows on the lower level, three sash windows upstairs. Something moved in the center upper window, and I saw a large furry face, the hint of bared teeth, and the swish of a tail. Cold swept down my spine, and I shivered. Was it a cat? It seemed too big to be a cat, unless it was some kind of wild thing native to Ireland. I blinked and shook my head, and when I looked back, whatever it was had disappeared. Maybe I'd imagined seeing something up there, the light tricking my eyes. I put it out of my mind when we reached Tommy, and he pulled me into a hug.

"Brilliant," Tommy said. "It's grand you're here, Aisling. Come on in, both of you."

"I rescued her from an oncoming bus," Fergus said as Tommy led us into a small vestibule. "She needs a cup of tea or something stronger."

"A bus?" Tommy frowned.

"I'm fine," I said as we stopped next to him. "Just not accustomed to Galway drivers yet."

"Look right and walk quickly." Tommy nodded with a grin.

Tommy led us through the vestibule lined with hooks for jackets, a stand for umbrellas, and a brass tub filled with wooden sticks of various lengths. I touched the varnished head of a longer walking stick and pulled back, my fingers tingling. I stared at the stick a moment before realizing the men had headed into a door opening off the front foyer. I hurried to follow, peeking into the front room as I passed, noting the rays of the afternoon sun dancing across the large bay windows. Bright rugs covered warm wood floors in the living room and foyer. A carpeted staircase across the hall led to the second level. The smell of a turf fire filled the space with a pleasant tang. Cozy.

I looked up the stairs, wondering if the thing I saw was up there, waiting to pounce. The sound of the men talking shook me out of my silly imaginings. I headed into the kitchen and found the men seated around a long refectory table covered with papers. Tommy shifted a stack of drawings so I could sit. "Fergus here wants to build a bodhran, and we're discussing what wood to use and how deep he wants it to be." Tommy tapped the drawings they'd been examining.

"This is a bodhran," Fergus said, showing me a picture of a traditional handheld Irish drum.

I nodded. "Mom had one hanging in her inn. She brought it from Ireland, and it reminded her of home. Do you play?" I asked Fergus.

"Aye." His eyes twinkled. "Besides the guitar, I play the bodhran, and I even fiddle a bit."

"He's being modest, he is," Tommy said. "Fergus makes magic with his music. The man's gifted—"

"That's enough out of you, Tommy." Fergus shook his head and looked at me. "I dabble, play downtown, as you know, and I'm part of a group that plays in one of the pubs on the weekends. And that's all." He turned back to Tommy, but not before I spied the blush on his cheeks. "Now, you were suggesting ash as the wood for the rim."

"That I was," said Tommy. "We'll use goat skin for the top." He glanced my way. "We won't be but a minute or two longer."

"You have work to do, and I'm interrupting." I pushed back my chair. I'd go to the ocean, find a place to grab lunch. As if on cue, my stomach grumbled.

"Sorry," I mumbled.

"Didn't you eat, lass?" Tommy asked, his eyes wide. "I can't imagine Maeve not feeding you. The woman prides herself on her cooking."

"I took a nap and missed lunch," I mumbled, wishing I could disappear, wishing I could wipe away the sympathy on both their faces.

"And Maeve isn't happy having an interloper," Fergus added, nodding in my direction. "And she considers anyone not Nuala or Geraldine an interloper."

"Even me," Tommy said with a chuckle. "She's warmed up to me over the years, but I'm afraid she never forgave me for divorcing Geraldine." He rose. "Let's get you a sandwich."

"Don't worry about it, Tommy." I stood.

"Nonsense. Sit down." Tommy spoke as he arranged bread, meat, and cheese on the butcher block island in the center of his kitchen. "'Twas a stressful morning. Take a bit of time to relax, because Geraldine won't break once she's started training you."

I started, glancing at Fergus and back to Tommy. Did they both know about dreams and Dreammasters and why I was here?

"I'm sorry, lass," Tommy said, reading my expression. "Finding Lorcan is big news in our small community. Although, Geraldine revealing your relationship to the man was premature."

"She told her?" Fergus exclaimed, his eyes wide.

"Aye." Tommy sighed. "You know Geraldine. Always determined to push ahead and get things done."

"You know about Lorcan? How he's connected to my mother and me?" I asked, my throat suddenly dry as I looked between them. "About what I saw?" I clutched my hands together, feeling exposed and a bit silly. I wondered how many people Granny had shared my dream with. I frowned. The odder thing was, Tommy and Fergus seemed okay with it. "Did Granny tell you?"

"Nuala told me about your dream," Tommy said, his eyes darkening under lowered brows. I shivered at his expression, wondering what about my dream made him angry, when his face cleared. "'Twas good to know what happened to the lad. Though a better question is how he got into the Underworld to begin with."

His voice was low, guttural, as if saying the words hurt him in some way, but I hesitated to ask what he meant by his last observation. I barely knew the man.

"Tommy told me," Fergus added. "It's all been a bit of a shock."

I shook my head and pushed back a stray curl that fell into my eyes. "And, yet, you seem to accept the truth of what I saw. In a dream."

"You're a Dreammaster," Fergus said, his expression confused. "Descended from the goddess Caer Ibormeith. Dreaming is what your kind do, although most are trained beforehand."

I sucked in a breath, remembering the goddess Caer from the garden bench.

"And none would enter the Underworld," Tommy added. "'Tis against the rules." He smiled, softening his words. "But your mother pulled you in. That wasn't your doing."

"So, you both know about Dreammasters, and you don't think it's odd," I whispered, more to myself than to them, as if saying the words again would make them sound less fantastic.

"Of course, we do." Fergus frowned. "Many of us are connected to figures others consider mythological." He rested his forearms on the table. "I'm a Heartseeker, descended from Aengus Og, the god of love.

'Tis why the birds love me. Aengus was a magnet for our winged friends, and he loved them as well. 'Twas said the birds represented the kiss of Aengus and whispered words of love to young lovers. I find they're good messengers." He smiled. "Caer and Aengus were lovers. To this day, Dreammasters and Heartseekers share a deep connection."

"We do?" I breathed, lost in his eyes for a moment. I looked away, taking a breath to center myself, and addressed Tommy. "He was the one carved next to Caer on Granny's bench."

"Aye, and he was," Tommy said. "Fergus, move things please."

Fergus scooted the plans for the bodhran to the other end of the table, and Tommy set a plate of down in front of me.

"Eat," Tommy said, placing a small plate and a glass of water in front of me. "You'll feel better."

Fergus nodded, and both men watched as I picked up a sandwich and took a bite, the savory chicken and crusty bread sticking in my throat when I tried to swallow. They were watching me as if I was a specimen under glass, and I wished I could shrink into a speck of dust and float away. I put down the sandwich and pressed a hand over my eyes. "I'm the last to know," I whispered. "About me. And about Lorcan." I took a sip of water. "It was such a shock."

I looked up, startled when Fergus's fingers closed over my other hand. "Subtlety is not Geraldine's strength." His strong fingers squeezed mine. My heart rate notched up. "And I'd guess you, having just lost your ma and only barely in Ireland, have had a difficult time believing what you heard."

My throat constricted, and I croaked out an answer. "Right." I held my breath, staring at him. "Lorcan disappeared forty-six years ago? You're young to know about him."

"Lorcan is my uncle," Fergus said softly.

"Your uncle?" I said as my stomach lurched. "So, if what Geraldine said is true, we're related." I pulled my hand from under his.

"No, we're not." Fergus said, his eyes glinting, a trace of a smile on his lips. "Lorcan's brother, Barry, is married to my mother's best friend, Ruth. Barry and my father grew up together. That's how Barry met Ruth. Lorcan isn't really my uncle, but he was around so much that I started calling him uncle. Our families have always been close."

"Ah," I said, sifting through the relationships in my head. "How old were you when Lorcan disappeared?"

"I was nearly four." He smiled. "Lorcan wasn't as old as all the other grown-ups. He was only twenty, and he played with me. He'd kick the soccer ball, even play pretend games." Fergus leaned back, lost in memories. "He was grand, he was. Always standing up for me, especially when my cousin Phyllis chased me around calling me her baby or her prince, depending on which imaginary game she was playing." He shuddered. "She was a nightmare, Phyllis was. Still is, in fact. But Lorcan was grand as well as kind. He got Phyllis to leave me be, without hurting her feelings. When the grown-ups were too busy, he would read stories and tell silly jokes to us kids. Lorcan had the best laugh—filled a room, it did."

Fergus focused on me. "You have his eyes. And you bite your lip like he did." I took a shaky breath as he continued. "I remember that especially because he bit through his top lip once when we were playing football, when he tripped. He'd been concentrating so hard. The sight of all the blood scared me, but Lorcan laughed, even though it had to have hurt and told me I was too good for him. He challenged me to a rematch the following week when we were having a family birthday party." His smile faded. "But then he disappeared. We never played that game."

I digested all this, my heart twisting at the thought of a young Fergus missing the uncle he loved. Lorcan didn't deserve to be stuck where he was, far from his family.

"Granny and Geraldine think I can help save him."

"Yes," Tommy said, folding his hands in front of him.

"Geraldine still cares about him, even after all this time."

"She says she does," Tommy agreed, his eyes hardening. He looked away and cleared his throat.

"But she married you."

"Yes. At the time, it seemed the right move for both of us." He paused. "Old feelings are easy to romanticize," Tommy said with care, the expression in his eyes unreadable. "And first love is potent."

"Hmm," I murmured, confused why Geraldine, a seemingly hard-core businesswoman, was still fixated on a man who'd chosen another woman and then disappeared years before.

"His family is thankful to you," Fergus said. "For coming to save him."

"Whoa," I said, suddenly dizzy. "I'm here to help Geraldine. But I don't know how to save Lorcan."

Fergus frowned. "You're connected to him. And your mother started the dream when he was lost. Geraldine can't do it, but she can teach you to dream. You're the only one who can finish the dream. I'm sure you'll be a brilliant Dreammaster." He tilted his head, his eyes wide with concern. "You will try, won't you? Once you've trained."

I took a moment to consider my answer. "No one told me I was the one who had to save him," I said, my voice louder than I intended. Panic fluttered in my chest. "Not by myself." I pushed back from the table with force, causing the chair to wobble. Striding around the table, I paced the room, my legs jerky. I stopped at the far side of the island. "Geraldine was going to do it before I convinced her to let me come. So she must be planning to help me out because she knows I don't understand what Dreammasters are, and I don't know what they do. It's barely a week until Samhain, not nearly enough time." My voice was breathy, and my legs were shaky. I gripped the countertop. "I can't be expected to save anyone."

Fergus's throat moved as he swallowed, and his eyes snapped. "Then why did you come? If you won't even try."

"Calm down, lad," Tommy said to Fergus. "Give Aisling a chance to understand what she's to do." Tommy rose and walked to me, then placed his hands on my shoulders and stared into my eyes. "For now, it's enough to process what you know. Tomorrow, begin working with Geraldine and your grandmother. They'll teach you how to dream as a Dreammaster and what's necessary to get Lorcan out of the Underworld."

My heart beat so hard I was surprised Tommy didn't hear it. "The Underworld." I murmured the words. "It's where I was with Mom on the night she died. But what is it? Where is it, exactly? And how would I even get there?" I licked my lips, my voice unsteady. "It was horrible, terrifying. I don't want to go back. What if I can't get us out? And what about my kids? They just lost their father. They need me."

"Calm down, lass." Tommy gripped my arms with gentle fingers. "You don't have to return to the Underworld. You only have to connect to Lorcan within the Dreamscape, which Geraldine and Nuala will teach you how to do. Your connection will be more difficult because you do have to enter the realm of the Underworld in your dream in order to make a mind connection. It's complicated. In truth, such connections, as ephemeral as they are, are banned. No boundary between the Underworld and the other realms is to be breached. But Nuala has spoken to my father, who is something of an expert in this situation, and they've some notion of how you can make it work." He shrugged. "I'm not a Dreammaster, so I can't fully explain."

"So none of it's allowed," I said, barely able to force out the words through my clenched teeth. My stomach quivered at the thought.

"Don't worry. You'll be fine."

His reassuring words didn't calm my pounding heart, but his peaceful blue eyes soothed me, and I nodded. Until another thought hit me. "But—" I swallowed and nearly choked. Fergus brought me my water.

"I was there with my mother. My body was there. I was wet and bloody. How did that happen if it's not allowed?"

"No one knows," Fergus said. His words didn't inspire me. He continued. "Your mother shouldn't have been there." He spoke softly, his green eyes sympathetic. "That realm has been closed off from the world of the Fair Folk and the humans for thousands of years." He paused, glancing at Tommy. "Until Lorcan disappeared."

"How does that relate?" I asked.

"Lorcan passed through a boundary that had been sealed for centuries," Tommy said. "He shouldn't have been able to get through." His eyes hardened. "We suspect a portal was opened at the time."

I wanted to ask more, but Fergus spoke before I could.

"I'm sorry. I didn't understand why you were reluctant. Now I do. I wouldn't want to enter the Underworld either. It's a dangerous place. Few would make it out alive."

"Mom said it wasn't safe in the dream the night she died. She never said I had to go back there." I looked from Fergus to Tommy. Both nodded at my words.

"She'd never ask such a thing of you, Aisling," Tommy said. "Neither Mary nor Lorcan would want you to risk so much."

"I'm sorry," I mumbled, taking another sip so I no longer had to face them. I was an idiot. Of course, no one wanted me in the Underworld. What a royal mess that would be. All of them would have to come and save me.

"You've nothing to apologize for," Fergus said, touching my arm and sending sparks throughout my body.

"You're grand, lass," Tommy said. "Tomorrow, Nuala and Geraldine will explain the process." He squeezed my shoulders. "You have powers, Aisling. Powers that can be traced back to more than one ancient figure in Irish history. Powers you cannot fathom." He searched my face, nodding. "And you're the person I'm meant to give something very precious to.

I've been waiting, wondering, and now I know. Wait here." He left the room and thudded up the stairs.

I looked at Fergus, and he shrugged and motioned me back to the table. "Maybe you should finish your lunch."

I followed him and resumed my seat, but I couldn't face eating. Instead, I picked up my plate and took it to the counter. Fergus followed.

I washed my dishes. He dried. I glanced at him at one point. He was watching me, a faraway look in his eyes. I sensed he wanted to say something, and I held my breath, waiting.

"I'd forgotten you had kids. Marriage and family." He sighed, looked away, and stacked the last plate in the cupboard overhead. "I can imagine you in the kitchen with your kids, cleaning up or helping with homework." He leaned against the counter. "I missed out on that life." His voice was soft, sad. "I was sorry to hear about the death of your husband." His eyes held mine.

"Thank you," I whispered. I stared into his eyes, unable to look away, my body thrumming. A creak and the sound of footsteps descending from the upper level broke our connection and I looked away. What on earth was wrong with me? He'd offered his condolences on the death of my husband, not asked me for dinner. Or even touched me.

Fergus took a step from me and pressed his hands into the satiny wood of the island. I smoothed my sweater and pressed my hand into my stomach, hoping to quell my jangling nerves.

The footsteps paused and retreated back up the stairs. I released a sigh. What did Tommy have to give me?

"You will help Geraldine save Lorcan, then?" Fergus's voice was low. "He's like family to me. He is family to you." He paused. "He matters to so many people."

"Of course," I said, walking to the island and squeezing his hand where it rested on the wooden surface. "That's why I came here. To learn. And to offer my assistance. I don't want Lorcan lost forever." As

I spoke, I knew my words were true. I was still angry at Mom's betrayal. But I also understood a little. She and Matthew had been great parents. We'd had a wonderful life, the three of us. She hadn't wanted to disrupt my memories or cause either of us pain. Plus, she'd thought Lorcan was missing, probably dead. Keeping it from me was wrong, but it also made a weird sort of sense.

He nodded. "You've every right to be nervous. Especially if you thought we wanted you to go bodily into the Underworld." He chuckled. "Thank the gods and goddesses that's not how things work for Dreammasters. Dreaming in your own Dreamscape is peaceful and safe. At least, that's what my Dreammaster friends tell me." He turned over his hand and threaded his fingers through mine. "You're part of something here, Aisling. Something wonderful. Never forget, there's a group of people who want you to succeed. Your Dreammaster sisters will make sure you're safe and don't get into trouble."

As he said the words, a new thought occurred to me. What if I posed a threat to Lorcan? If my dreams were dangerous, could I be trusted to save him? And could I harm my Dreammaster sisters if I could harm someone in a dream? I had to ask Granny or Geraldine. Tomorrow. I'd get answers tomorrow. Because the last thing I wanted to do was hurt Lorcan or anyone else. "Right," I said, as Tommy's footfalls thumped back down the staircase.

Tommy entered the kitchen and stopped, glancing from the clean table to where we stood at the island.

"Thank you for clearing up." He nodded, smiling. "The place looks great. I ought to have the two of you over for lunch more often." He chuckled at his joke and gestured for us to come back to the table.

Fergus and I sat on either side of Tommy, who sat at the head of the table. He placed two carved boxes on the table, his fingertips lightly touching the glowing, golden wood. "These were gifted to me many years ago by your grandfather, Gerard."

My eyes widened. I'd only seen my grandfather from a distance, his body lying in a coffin. "I never knew him."

Tommy smiled. "He was a special man with many gifts. Gerard's ancestry is similar to Nuala's. He was descended from the Tuatha Dé Danann and inherited the skills of a Druid. He could use words, written and spoken, with magical results. He was also an accomplished woodworker and metalworker, and his creations were as captivating as his words, as you'll see."

I sat back, my eyes widening. "I don't understand."

"And you don't need to for now. Just accept there is more in this universe than we can explain, and that's enough."

His kind blue eyes watched me as I processed what he'd said. I nodded, and he continued.

"My antecedents are similar to yours and Fergus's. As a result, I have certain powers." Tommy leaned back, a faraway look in his eyes. "Gerard was like a father to me. He understood my special gifts."

"Magic keeps coming up," I said softly.

"Do you believe in magic, lass?"

I bit my lips and looked away, thinking of Trevor's dead face, the bus driver turned monster, the power in my fingers.

"Maybe." I looked at my hands twisted together in my lap. "There are things I can't explain in any logical way."

"Stop being logical," Fergus said. I looked over at him, and he smiled. "Accept there's something extra in the universe and see what happens next."

I blew out a breath. I craved control and safety above all else. "I don't know if I can."

Tommy smiled. "'Tis harder for you, Aisling, because you grew up not understanding who you are. Your granny Nuala told me Mary refused to teach you about your heritage and the woman you're descended from. Mary was frightened when she left here, and she had reason to be. But

she denied you an important piece of yourself by denying you the truth."
I was about to speak when he touched my arm. "It's right that you've
come home."

"Home." I let the word dance on my tongue. "Ireland was Mom's
home, but I'm an American girl."

"Maybe." Tommy raised his eyebrows. "Maybe not."

I frowned, uncertain how I felt about the concept of home any longer.

"And Lorcan?" Fergus asked. "He's your family as much as Mary was.
You just don't know him yet."

I stared into Fergus's green eyes and saw the pain and hope circling
there. Lorcan. No one had asked me to save anyone before. When I
thought of the type of person who saved others, the word *courage* came
to mind. I wasn't courageous. I was simply Aisling. But could I be more?

"I want to help him," I said, and my words were true. I wanted Lorcan
freed and back with his family. And I wanted to meet the man from my
dreams, the man who was my father in real life. "But I'm scared I can't.
I'm not that brave. What if I only hurt him in the end?"

"You have support," Fergus said, touching my hand. "You aren't alone
in this."

We were all quiet for a moment.

"I understand feeling alone," Tommy said softly. "I was alone when I
first arrived in Galway, and Gerard and Nuala took me in. They gave me
a home and a family. I was their gardener and surrogate son. Nuala and
I bonded over plants and the medicinal uses of herbs. Gerard taught me
wordsmithing, and we shared a love of woodworking. You, Aisling, are
also family, a part of a very special community. The bond is strong and
cannot be broken. Trust in that bond."

I watched him for a moment, letting his words sink in. Trust wasn't
easy for me, especially not when my mom and my husband had broken
trust with lies. I sighed and nodded. "I'll do my best."

Tommy nodded. "'Tis all I can ask, lass. And it brings me back to the gift I have for you. Gerard gave these to me and asked me to pass along one to the right person. He didn't tell me who that individual might be, but he told me I would know when I met her." He chuckled. "And he did specifically say *her*." He opened both boxes.

Inside, resting on gold crushed velvet, were two identical capped silver fountain pens. A gifted hand had etched tiny people in exquisite detail along the length of both the pens. A wide-trunked tree spread leafy branches over the figures, like a mother wrapping her children in protective arms. Sturdy roots extended connected the lower branches to create a circle.

"Those were my grandfather's?" I said in a hushed voice. Fergus rose to get a closer look.

"Yes." Tommy nodded. "He used his power to forge them. They're called Druid pens. The one who possesses such a pen has the use of words at his or her disposal."

"How do they work?" I asked, curious despite my skepticism.

"Ah, that's the truly magical aspect of these pens, because it's up to the one who possesses the pen to discover how it works for her."

"How does she find out?" I raised my eyes to his.

"I believe she, you, will know." Tommy spoke in a hushed voice, his eyes sparkling. I rubbed my hands over my tingling arms. "Why don't you pick the one that calls to you and see what happens?"

I looked from Tommy to Fergus. Both watched me. I looked back at the pens. I reached out first to the one on the left nearest to me, but I hesitated. Something kept me from touching the pen, as if an unseen force was holding back my fingers. Instead, the pen on the right drew my hand, and when my fingers touched it, it lifted from the box and fitted itself into my fingers.

I gasped, dizziness sweeping over me. Warmth spread through my hand, tingling through my body like a fairy had tipped a jar of magical dust over my head and it was floating down to my feet, covering me in a sparkling blanket. My swan pendant began a slow, even pulse at my throat. I sucked in my breath, my eyes wide. *Magic.*

"Wow." It was all I could manage.

"I knew I was right," Tommy said. "Gerard would be pleased."

"You're glowing," Fergus said, his eyes shining as he watched me.

"Aisling is special." Tommy watched me. "You have gifts from both your grandfather and your grandmother. As you work with the pen, you'll understand the gifts from Gerard. As you work with Geraldine and Nuala, you'll understand what it means to be a Dreammaster."

He reached out, and the other pen floated into his hand. He wrapped his fingers around it. "I'll keep and safeguard the twin of the pen you've chosen. You and I will have a special connection as a result. I'll always be available to you via this connection." He paused, and when he spoke again, his tone was serious. "That you have a Druid pen must remain a secret. No one knows Gerard gave the pens to me. And now, only you, Fergus, and I know where they are."

"Okay," I said, "although I still don't understand how it works."

"But you will," Tommy answered.

CHAPTER TWENTY-TWO

"Anyone home?" a woman's voice called from the front of the house.

"In the kitchen, Emer," Tommy called.

He motioned for me to replace my pen in the box. He did the same. I'd just stuffed the rectangular container in my jacket pocket when the woman appeared in the doorway.

Her gray-blue eyes narrowed at the sight of the three of us sitting around Tommy's kitchen table. I recognized her. She'd been with Fergus this morning when he'd saved me from oncoming traffic outside the bus station. She was impatient when he stopped to help me. And then they both disappeared, which I'd forgotten as the rest of the day unfurled. Given her expression, especially when she looked at me, I knew better than to ask about it now.

Emer was a tiny woman, but she emanated a palpable energy that swept through the room like an angry red wave. Her bow-shaped lips pursed into a moue of irritation as she crossed her arms and lifted her pointy chin in my direction.

"What's she doing here?"

Her tone caused the hairs on the back of my neck to rise, and I stifled a primal urge to defend myself.

"We were speaking about her training," Fergus said, having shifted in his chair to face Emer. "She's not clear about what needs to be done." He looked back and smiled at me. "But I'm sure she'll be grand once she's begun to work with Nuala and Geraldine."

I smiled at Fergus, which served to deepen the furrows of anger on Emer's face.

"Hmph." She blew out a breath and fixed her gaze on me. "I don't see how a woman nearing fifty who's not taken an interest in her heritage up to now can hope to rescue Lorcan." She looked down her nose at me, a feat for one so petite even with me sitting at the table.

"I'm here to learn." My eyes narrowed. "And I'm only forty-five." *Stellar comeback, Aisling.* Everyone's focus shifted to me, and a flush heated my body and crept up my cheeks. Emer's smile of triumph added to the burn of shame filling me. I might not understand what it meant to be a Dreammaster, but I'd learn, if only to show this tiny bitch I could. No. I gave myself a mental shake. I wasn't a child. I'd learn in order to save Lorcan. That was my real goal, and at the thought, a surge of power flowed from my swan pendant to flood my body. The tips of my fingers pulsed with energy. Showing up Emer was an added benefit.

"Aisling came by to see me," Tommy said, standing from his chair. He patted my shoulder, and his touch calmed me. "Can I get you a coffee or cup of tea, Emer?"

She looked at us as if we'd lost our minds. "Tea? This late? I'm fine, Tommy, but thanks." Her tone indicated she was anything but fine. She fixed Fergus with a glare. "We've an engagement, in case you'd forgotten. And as it's ten past five and we're due at Sean and Moira's house at five thirty, I'd suggest we get moving." She huffed. "I don't suppose Sean would take kindly to our being late, unless you want to spoil the surprise party he's worked so hard on."

Fergus checked his watch as she spoke, then looked up, his eyes wide. "Shite, I'm sorry. I lost track of the time." He slid his chair from the table and stood. "If we leg it, we'll be fine. The house isn't too far." Fergus walked away without a glance in my direction, his attention focused squarely on Emer. "Did you drive?"

He stopped in front of her, pulling on his jacket. "Yes," she said as she stood on tiptoes, rested her hand on his chest, and leaned in to kiss him. His back was to me, so I couldn't tell if he kissed her back. He certainly didn't pull away. She rocked back and patted his chest. "But I'm giving that chore over to you." Keys jangled as she dropped them into his hand. "Sean's splurged on champagne, and I plan to indulge, as it's my best friend's forty-fifth. You can keep your head tonight."

"Sounds fair," he said, accepting the keys. He turned and addressed Tommy. "We're good to get started on the bodhran, then?"

"We are indeed." Tommy was still standing. "Come by tomorrow afternoon, and we can start with the frame."

"Just don't be late again," Emer said. "'Tis Friday tomorrow. Our first set is at seven."

"Right. I won't." Fergus paused. "Thanks, Tommy." He glanced at me, then looked away. "Nice to see you again, Aisling."

I nodded and was about to speak, but Emer grabbed him by the hand and dragged him from the room.

"What was she doing here, anyway?" I heard Emer ask Fergus as they opened the inner door to the vestibule. Her voice was challenging. "And what did you mean about seeing her again?"

"I saw her this morning, didn't I? Same as you." There was a pause, and I wondered if they'd left the house, until I heard Emer's voice, low and intimate but still discernible.

"That's better," she purred.

I closed my eyes, trying to ignore the images that danced behind the lids, wishing they would leave, wishing I wasn't such a fool. What in the hell was wrong with me, anyway? I had no business feeling anything about anyone here. The inner doors closed, and a moment later we heard the front door thump shut. I breathed out a long exhale, feeling Tommy's eyes on me. I didn't want to look at him, not before I'd had a chance to compose myself. *And why do you need to compose yourself, missy?* I ignored my internal voice. I wasn't ready to examine why the room seemed dimmer since Fergus's departure.

I smiled up at Tommy, my tone light. "What did Emer mean about their first set tomorrow night at seven?"

Tommy picked up Fergus's cup and took it to the sink. "Fergus and Emer are part of a traditional music group. The band plays at a local pub several nights a month." He came back to the table and began stacking the papers he and Fergus had been looking at. The air in the room had shifted, and I worried I'd said something wrong. I wanted to bolt but didn't want to be impolite.

"Nice. Maybe I'll go listen. If Geraldine allows time off." I forced a laugh, waiting for him to say something about my reaction to Fergus. I'd probably watched the man like some goofy teenager. What had happened to me in the few short hours since my plane had touched Irish soil?

Finally, Tommy spoke, his voice halting. "I'm sorry to say it," he started, "but I have to get moving as well, Aisling." His eyes were full of apologies. "I lost track of the time, and I'm meant to be meeting Geraldine and Mel in an hour for a drink before the art show."

My chest tightened, and I thrust back from the table, catching my chair as it swayed. "I'm so sorry." I cleared my throat, my gaze averted, my cheeks hot. I'd stayed too long. He was ready to be rid of me. I wished I could vanish, like Fergus and Emer had done this morning. "I'll get out of your way."

"There's no rush," Tommy said, but I didn't listen and knocked into the table in my haste to escape.

I shook my head, yanking on my jacket and catching my sweater on the zipper. When I'd finally fumbled free, I zipped the coat closed and picked up my pocketbook. "I'm fine." I blew the hair out of my eyes. "You've been great. Thanks for explaining things. And for this." I touched my pocket where the Druid pen rested.

Tommy watched me silently. What was he thinking? "I have to change," he said finally. "If you'd like to wait, I'll walk you back. I'm going that way." Tommy spoke slowly, and his calm voice settled over me.

I gave a halfhearted attempt at a laugh. "I'll take a walk before I head back, sort through everything in my head."

"Are you sure?" He watched me, his eyes concerned.

I nodded. "Positive." I walked around the table. "I haven't been to the seaside yet."

"Dark falls quickly. You have less than an hour before sunset."

"Thanks. I'll keep that in mind." I headed for the front vestibule. Tommy followed. "A walk will also give me a chance to call my kids." I paused at the vestibule, scrambling for words, when Tommy reached past me to pull open the glass-paned door.

"Things will be better in the morning," he said, his voice gentle.

I looked back and smiled. "They always are." I leaned over and gave him a quick hug. "Thank you, Tommy."

"You're welcome, lass." He followed me out the main door and watched as I headed down the drive. "You're welcome here anytime, Aisling. You've never a need to call in advance or apologize for showing up."

I looked back and waved before turning onto the sidewalk. I needed some space to think about all I'd learned since I'd arrived in Galway. Had it only been nine hours since my bus had pulled into Galway Station? In that time, I'd learned about my biological father, discovered I was going to assist Geraldine in rescuing him in a place called the Dreamscape, met a man who jangled every nerve in my body and made my skin tingle with awareness, and been called to action by Emer's words.

The thought of Emer and her direct glare made me shiver. She disliked me without reason, the thought making me bristle as I continued up the sidewalk. Why did she dislike me so? I couldn't control my mother's decision not to share the truth about my heritage. But her reaction to me seemed like more than just my ignorance as a Dreammaster. Fergus's face flashed to mind. Was it possible she was simply jealous and so she wished me to fail? I sighed. The thought was ridiculous. I was leaving. Soon.

I paused at a stoplight, late-afternoon traffic blurring past as I waited for the signal to change. Emer had done me one favor. She'd cemented my goal. I was going to help save Lorcan. I'd always been an excellent student. My skills were rusty, but I'd brush them off and pay attention to all Granny and Geraldine had to teach me. I had purpose, something lacking in my life for a while now, and at the thought, lightness flowed through my body. I'd become a Dreammaster, embrace my power as best as I could.

The signal changed and I crossed the street, head held high, feet barely seeming to touch the sidewalk, as I headed toward the sea sparkling in the distance.

Chapter Twenty-Three

The sky was darkening by the time I turned into the long driveway to Old Oak Manor, the lights from neighboring homes illuminating my path. I'd spoken to both kids during my walk. They were missing their father and still angry at me for leaving them, although they'd sounded happier than they cared to admit hearing my voice. Thank goodness saving Lorcan didn't entail going back into the dangerous Underworld. Catrina and Conall were only nineteen. They still needed me. Fortunately, I didn't have to choose between my kids and Lorcan. I could assist Geraldine, meet my father, and return home to my kids in one piece. And, in the future, I could introduce them to their grandfather, although the thought of explaining the situation knotted my stomach. As did the thought of my original purpose in coming to Ireland—discovering the power of my dreams. I shuddered. I wouldn't ask tonight. I needed a full night's sleep before I broached that topic.

When Granny's house came into view, I paused a moment to catch my breath and check the time. Six fifteen. Not late. Even a little early.

The old stone of the building blended into the deepening night, and I was thankful someone had turned on a light over the front door. The garden was covered in shadows, and all I could make out in the deepening gloom were fuzzy shapes of trees and bushes and the angles of the bench under the spreading branches of the old oak.

I paused, the bench stirring a memory in the back of my mind, but I couldn't capture the elusive thought. I'd come out tomorrow, take a stroll in the sunlight, and maybe the memory would come. For now, the earthy smell of the turf fire and the curling smoke drifting out of the chimney beckoned to me, and I headed toward the warmth of the house.

I hung my jacket on a hook in the vestibule, returned the borrowed umbrella to the stand, and checked the zipper on my pocketbook that strained to close around the pen box. So far, so good.

At the sitting room door, I paused. Granny sat on the chair across from the fire, eyes closed, a book in her lap and a fuzzy blanket tucked around her legs. Not wanting to wake her, I tiptoed toward the stairs, cringing when an old floorboard groaned under my feet.

"Aisling, is that you, child?"

I peeked into the room, my voice soft. "I'm so sorry. I didn't mean to wake you."

"Nonsense. Come in, child." Granny straightened and put her book on the small table next to her. "Sit down and tell me about the rest of your day. I'm sorry I was asleep when you awoke." Her eyes followed me as I sat on the couch nearest to her chair. "How are you after this morning?" Her eyes clouded.

It was a good question, and I didn't have a good answer. I was clear about saving Lorcan but still reeling at the lie my mother told me. "Confused, I suppose. Still trying to make sense of everything." I settled back on the sofa. "Maeve told me you were napping, so I went for a walk and ended up at Tommy's house. He's a kind man. It helped."

"Good." Granny looked pleased. "Tommy is a balm for any ill."

"I met Fergus on the way. Do you know Fergus?"

"Fergus Hennessy." She grinned. "He's a fine-looking lad, is Fergus. And those eyes." She finished with a silent whistle through pursed lips. "He'd lift my spirits, he would."

I laughed, a deep, honest chuckle of amusement, and some of the tension I'd carried all day fell from my shoulders. "You've summed it up well, and I'm afraid I got lost in those eyes a few times until his lady friend, Emer, arrived and knocked some sense into me with her wilting stare." I put my pocketbook down and rested my hands in my lap. "I'm glad to know Fergus has that effect on other women. I was wondering if I'd lost all sense of decency, seeing as I'm a recently widowed lady."

"Fergus is a lovely man." Granny eyed me. "And you're a lovely woman. No reason you shouldn't feel a pull there and no shame in it." She shook her head as I was about to argue. "You can enjoy the view, child, without climbing the mountain."

Another laugh bubbled up from deep in my belly. "Okay, I'll grant you that." I took a restorative breath. "What I liked about Fergus, almost as much as his eyes, was that he knew Lorcan and could tell me about him."

Granny stared into the crackling fire, watching the flames, considering. The fire popped, and she started, her gaze coming to me. "Lorcan was a lovely, thoughtful man. That's why his disappearance made no sense. You see, Mary had told him about the pregnancy, and he was happy." She paused. "He'd proposed."

"He had?" My belly flopped as I digested this bit of new information. "I wish Mom had told me about him."

"Mary kept too many things to herself." Granny's voice cracked, and she swallowed. "She called me the day she died. We had a lovely chat." Tears glistened in her eyes. "But she never spoke of her illness. I didn't know about the cancer until after." Her hands shook as she wiped the tears slipping down her papery skin.

Maeve bustled into the room as Granny finished speaking. When she saw the tears, she glared at me.

"What have you done, girl?" Maeve asked fiercely.

"I'm fine, Maeve," Granny said, clearing her throat, "and Aisling has done nothing. I'm happy she's here, is all." Maeve huffed, and Granny ignored her. "Are we ready to eat?"

"The food is ready. I wanted to check that this one made it back." She tossed her head at me.

"I apologize, Maeve," I said, hoping my smile would soften her look. "I stopped here to speak with my grandmother and forgot to let you know."

Maeve sniffed. "That's fine, then. 'Tis your granny you should be worried about." She turned and tromped toward the door. "I'll be back in a moment."

"I'll help Maeve, if she'll let me," I said, already rising.

"Thank you." Granny nodded. "Oh, and Aisling, bring the bottle of red wine and the glasses. I left them on the counter by the coffee maker."

The aromas of roast lamb, rosemary, and garlic filled the room as I served our plates. Bright-orange carrots seasoned with thyme and parsley accompanied the lamb, along with a salad of baby greens topped with a zesty oil-and-vinegar dressing.

I poured two glasses of a deep-burgundy cabernet into wide crystal goblets and handed one to Granny.

"*Slàinte.*" Granny clinked her glass to mine.

"*Slàinte,*" I answered, taking a sip. "Mom taught me the word," I said in reply to my grandmother's questioning look. "She spoke about growing up here, about her love of the sea and the deep green of Ireland. I think New Hampshire reminded her of her home."

Granny's chin trembled, but she only nodded and picked up her fork. "Eat, child. While the food is hot."

"This is delicious," I said between mouthfuls, doing my best not to shovel food into my mouth like a woman starved. When my plate was empty and my belly full, I relaxed back into the couch cushions and sighed. "Wow."

Granny chuckled. "Maeve will be happy you enjoyed her meal." She dabbed her mouth with a cloth napkin.

I sat forward and poured the last of the wine into our glasses. "Will you tell me about my mom when she was younger?" I asked, fearful of upsetting my grandmother with talk about her dead daughter.

A rush of emotions crossed Granny's face, joy mixed with grief, but she nodded. "Of course, child. She was a joy, was Mary. And she loved everyone."

The wine brought out Granny's talkative side, and I enjoyed listening to her stories of my mother.

"Mary was kind above all else," Granny said as she finished telling me how my mother saved a young boy she babysat from the bullies in the neighborhood. "Young Steven was always a bit in love with her after she took the broom handle to that nasty Bobby and his sidekick Joe. And I can tell you neither Bobby nor Joe crossed her again. Bobby even asked Mary on a date once."

"What did she say?"

"She turned him down, of course." Granny snorted. "He was still a bully inside, and she knew it. Grew up to be a nasty man. Took to drink. Left his wife." She shook her head. "And now there's me talking too much. That's the reason I don't drink wine too often—and never alone."

I laughed, relaxed and happy. Listening to Granny had been therapeutic for me, and I sensed it had been helpful for her as well, but there was one topic she'd avoided. My heart beat faster as I considered whether to bring up Geraldine's relationship with her sister.

"Mary tried her best," Granny said, as if reading my mind. "Geraldine was never receptive."

"How did you know I wanted to ask?"

"When you're as old as I am, child, you can sense things." She shifted in her seat, folded her hands in her lap, and looked at me. "Mary welcomed her baby sister. Geraldine wanted to be first." Her voice was cool, detached, and I guessed this pained her to discuss. Still, I forged on.

"I don't understand."

Granny took a moment to respond. "Geraldine could not and cannot abide anyone else outshining her, and Mary shone brightly as a child and a young woman." She rubbed her forehead, and I was immediately worried. Had I worn her out, caused her too much pain? "I love Geraldine very much," Granny continued. "She isn't the same young girl she was, and I'd like to think she'd welcome Mary home if her sister was still alive. But she didn't welcome her presence when they were younger."

The fire had dimmed, leaving part of the room hidden in curtains of dark, perfectly mirroring this last part of our conversation. "We don't need to discuss this anymore." I bit my lips. "I shouldn't have asked you."

"You have a right to know." Granny took a moment before continuing. "You should also understand the dream that pushed them apart and sent Mary to New Hampshire."

"We have time," I said. Granny shook her head.

"No. It's easier now, without Geraldine. She becomes agitated speaking about the dream."

"Okay," I said.

"It was October thirty-first, forty-six years ago."

"The eve of Samhain."

"Yes. The time when the boundaries between the human world and the Otherworld are the thinnest. Dreammasters schedule the most difficult dreams on this night, when success is more likely."

I clutched my hands together, waiting.

Granny sighed and rubbed her eyes. I was about to suggest we wait, when she began speaking.

"Mary and Geraldine were together, an unusual circumstance. They'd been whispering between themselves all week, but I'd seen only what I wanted to see. My daughters were getting along. I was cautiously hopeful."

She took a sip of her wine.

"I had a client—what we call a dreamer—that evening. Gerard was left to watch the girls, but they disappeared, and he lost himself in a book." Granny smiled. "Your grandfather and books." She chuckled. "If I lost Gerard, I knew to look in his study at the back of the house. I could count on finding him, nose in a book or pen to paper, for he loved to write as much as he loved to read."

A frisson of energy ran through me. My grandfather and I had that in common. I thought of the pen hidden in my pocketbook.

Granny continued. "Geraldine had just begun her training, and she convinced Mary to practice entering the Dreamscape with her. Mary said she started the dream but that almost immediately she lost consciousness and had no recollection of what had happened. Geraldine must have lost consciousness as well because she couldn't explain the dream either." Granny drew a ragged breath. "I now suspect that the girls somehow opened a portal into the Underworld and sent Lorcan there. Mary's dream the night she died does seem to tie her to Lorcan's disappearance, although I can't explain how she could have opened a portal. The act would not have been intentional."

I shuddered, thinking of Mom's last dream. "The Underworld. It was terrifying."

Granny sighed. "The stories of the land of the monsters paint a grim picture. It's a place separate from the part of the Otherworld where Dreammasters operate. Ancient treaties forbid those connected to the Otherworld to enter the Underworld, which is why no one suspected the girls had gained access. The spell is complicated, involving old magic. Few would know it." She sighed, closing her eyes for a moment. "Old texts might include the incantation to open the boundary, but it's no longer written down and certainly not taught." Granny frowned, her eyes troubled, and I sensed there was something she wasn't saying. "How Lorcan was involved is another mystery." She fidgeted with the cloth napkin still folded over her lap. "The lad wasn't even in Galway that night. There seemed to be no connection between him and the botched dream." She paused. "Had I known what had happened, I would have gone in myself all those years ago." Her voice was soft. "We all assumed he'd been injured or killed."

"Why did Mom leave?"

"The Dreammaster investigation into Mary and Geraldine's actions relating to the unauthorized dream resulted in a suspension of training privileges for both girls. Mary was hardest hit because she was soon to be promoted to Dreammaster. Geraldine was angry. She was unable to train for six months, and all she'd wanted since she'd learned of her heritage was to be a Dreammaster." Granny paused, gathering herself. "Geraldine made Mary's life unbearable." Granny spoke through stiff lips. "Blaming Mary for the suspension and for ruining her life."

"Oh," I said, considering her words. "But didn't Geraldine push Mom into the dream?"

"Yes, but that didn't matter to Geraldine. She had a temper when she was younger." She hesitated. "When Lorcan didn't return, Geraldine's temper spiked. And when she learned of Mary's pregnancy, that broke something in Geraldine. She was erratic." Granny bowed her head, but not before I saw the pinching of her lips and her involuntary flinch.

When she spoke, her voice was choked. "Mary chose to move to New Hampshire before you were born and remain until after your birth."

I frowned, cold fingers of unease dancing along my spine. "Did Geraldine do something to Mom?"

Granny hesitated, choosing her words, speaking with care. "Geraldine's anger was fierce and untamed." Granny sighed. "Mary had every right to be frightened for you and for herself."

Alarm tingled along my spine. "Geraldine wouldn't have harmed us, though."

Granny looked away, again mesmerized by the fire as she twisted her fingers in her lap. When she finally answered, her voice was a whisper I strained to hear. "Of course not."

Chapter Twenty-Four

"Nuala, it's past your bedtime." Maeve bustled into the sitting room, where Granny and I were staring into the smoldering remains of the fire.

The hypnotic crackle and flicker of the red-gold embers sapped what remained of my strength, leaving my body hollow and my limbs shaky. I was happy when Maeve made her pronouncement.

"It's nine. Time to get you tucked up." She came around the couch and held out her hand to Granny.

"I can get up on my own, Maeve," Granny said with a frown. She thumped her cane, her hand gripping the silver swan's head, and rose to her feet. "Aisling, I hope you'll excuse me, but I am rather weary."

I stood as well. "I'll follow you up. It's been a long day."

In front of Granny's room, I bent to hug her good night.

"I am glad you're here, child. And I'm glad we had our talk." Granny patted my back. "I'll see you in the morning."

"Sleep well, Granny."

"You as well, Aisling."

"Nuala." Maeve's voice carried to us through the open door, sharp as a drillmaster and every bit as demanding.

"I think she means business," I said.

"Oh, she does, child." Granny snorted. "Interfering woman. But I'd best do as she says." I waited until Granny had gone into her bedroom before continuing down the hall to my own.

Away from the lulling effect of the fire, my body woke up. My restless limbs forced me to move, and I unpacked as a howling wind battered my windows. The rain had returned, more vicious than before, bringing cooler air with it. I shivered and tugged on a sweatshirt to ward against the cold of the room.

Finished with unpacking, I stood in the middle of the room. Now what?

I browsed through books on a bookshelf in the corner, but my mind whirred like a top. I'd never remember what I read. I'd called the kids. Texted Beverly.

I circled the room again, catching my foot on the strap of my backpack, tripping. After grabbing the bedpost to stop my fall, I picked up the bag and tossed it onto my bed next to my small pocketbook. Then paused.

The pen.

Toeing off my shoes, I crawled to the center of the bed and unzipped the purse. As I withdrew the case, energy from the pen vibrated through the wood into my hand. Once opened, the pen floated from the box into my fingers, as if a piece of my being had returned home.

I rotated the shining cylinder, again admiring the intricate work. I hadn't had time to ask Tommy about the symbology of the tree, but the broad branches seemed to provide cover to the beings beneath, and the long roots were a sturdy base of support and protection. The pen pulsated in my hand, in time with the beating of my swan pendant, like greeting like.

"How do you work?"

It was a pen. It wrote things. I needed paper. I searched in my backpack and pulled out a plain thin spiral-bound notebook. It wasn't fancy, but I'd written my thoughts in notebooks like this since I was a teenager. Mom had offered to buy me fancy journals, but I'd preferred the ease of a notebook I could flip open. I could use the full page, not fight to write into the stiff center of a leather-bound book. In fact, I'd first noticed subtle changes seemingly linked to my dreams after journaling in a notebook similar to this one.

I opened to a blank page, uncapped the pen, and pressed the delicate tip to paper, intending to write my name. But when I scratched the point across the paper, no ink flowed from the nib. I shook the pen to get the ink going and tried again without any luck. I scrutinized the pen, looking for a way to check the ink levels, but I couldn't find any way to twist the cylinder open. With a snort, I slapped the blank page of the journal.

"Magic, huh?" I closed the notebook, replaced the cap on the pen, and was about to put the pen away when it began to vibrate more intensely. What was going on?

Frenetic energy seeped from my body as I held the pen, and a wave of relaxation washed over me. I kept hold of it and waited for inspiration, some direction as to how to use it. Nothing.

I closed my eyes and cradled the pen in both my hands using meditation techniques Beverly taught me. After several deep breaths, as my limbs grew ever heavier, an image flittered into my subconscious. A book. Generic at first, more detailed with every exhalation. A woman with long hair and a flowing gown was tooled into the leather cover. My breath lodged in my chest. My mother's journal. But it had to be my imagination, a product of all I'd seen and heard today, not something real, something I actually had to have in order to use the pen.

Eyes still closed, I took a couple of relaxed breaths, waiting to see if I had any more insights, surprised when the journal in my mind opened. Pages of the book flipped in an invisible wind until they stilled midway. My name was written across the top of the page.

Heart thudding, I opened my eyes and stared at the pen. Tommy hadn't said anything about needing a specific journal. But then, he'd said the Druid pen worked in a specific way depending on who possessed it. I had to figure out my unique way to use the pen.

The pen wasn't pulsating any longer, as if the power had disappeared.

I frowned. Where would I find a leather journal, especially one so specific? I replaced the pen in the case and snapped the lid closed. I stood and walked to the dresser, then yanked open the drawer and shoved it behind my clothes. I didn't need aggravation from a pen, not after the full day I'd had. It was nice of Tommy to give it to me, but this was not a pressing concern.

I hesitated before I shut the drawer, feeling as if I'd let Tommy down. He'd been so excited to give me the pen. Maybe, if I had time, I could find him tomorrow and ask him what I was doing wrong and if, perhaps, the pen needed ink. Maybe even take a walk to town and find a new journal, a special volume I used only with the pen. I sighed and pushed the drawer shut.

I was about to head into the bathroom to prepare for bed, when I paused, breath held, listening. Music was coming from outside my room. Perhaps Granny listened to something as she drifted off.

The tune was familiar, but I couldn't remember where I'd heard it before. My swan thrummed, as if it too knew this melody.

The music called to me, and I followed, heart pounding as I opened my door and peered out. There was no one in the hallway, and I stepped from my room.

The music came from the direction of Geraldine's room. I swallowed. Maybe she'd come home, and I hadn't heard her. I didn't want to bother my aunt if that was the case. Perhaps I should go to bed, leave it alone. But my body didn't listen to my reasoning mind. On shaky legs, I headed down the hall.

At the door to my aunt's room, I pressed my ear against the wood. This wasn't the source. There was only one other possibility.

I turned, my heart thudding against my rib cage, and stared at the end of the hall, at the doorway to the attic.

I gulped, gripping Geraldine's doorframe. My aunt had taken me up those stairs years ago. Today, Granny had told me not to go back.

I shivered, pretty damn sure I didn't want to follow a plaintive song up the dark, old stairs into the unknown. And, yet, my feet moved again, as if being summoned by the strains of the melody. Soon, I was standing in front of the door, heart pounding.

My hand hovered over the knob, my fingers trembling. My logical mind said to turn around, go to bed. My hand didn't listen. At my touch, the handle turned, as if it had been waiting for me to arrive. I pulled my hand away as if I'd been burned and stepped back as the door swung open, breath held as the yawning cavern of the dark attic staircase was slowly revealed.

What should I do? I could turn around, but retreat wouldn't answer why music was floating through the house. Was it real, or was I imagining it? I shuddered at the thought.

The music had a power I couldn't ignore, and before I could retreat, I'd climbed the first step. My hand reached for a switch, as if some part of me had known where to find it, and a dim light flickered on, the yellow glow doing little to dispel the dank gloom. I couldn't see anything but shadows past the top step, but that didn't stop my feet. Thirteen narrow, steep steps later, I stood at the top of the house peering into the attic, my sweaty palms gripping the railing, my feet perched on the tiny landing, poised to turn and fly back down.

The music was louder up here. I blinked into the murkiness until my eyes adjusted to the dim light of the underpowered bulb swinging overhead, searching for the source of the sound. But I saw no radio, no stereo, no music player of any kind. The music came from everywhere and nowhere. I bit my lower lip and swallowed hard.

Small gusts of cool air rattled past old, ill-fitting panes of glass in the uncovered attic windows. Shivering, I moved a little further into the room, rubbing my arms.

Shadowy mounds of junk peppered the floor and hunkered in corners. A musty odor—part old dust, part old damp—tickled my nostrils, and I sneezed. Standing taller, sucking in a breath of frosty air, I took another step into the room and away from escape, bumping into an old trunk as I did so.

"Damn." I bent and rubbed my leg. Why was the stupid thing at the top of the staircase? The music grew louder the further I went, but I still couldn't pinpoint the source. I took a moment to assess my route forward before moving ahead between objects only identifiable as I came near. Trunks. A toy chest. Stands of hanging clothes shrouded in sheets. A movement to my left sent me scurrying into a stack of old papers. Dust flew, and a few papers slid to the ground as I stifled a shriek. "Who's there?" My voice quavered despite my effort to sound commanding. No one answered, and I realized I'd seen myself reflected in the stained, streaky glass of an old wardrobe.

"Get a grip, Aisling," I murmured, continuing. The farther I went, the dimmer the light grew, until I was in near darkness across the room from the staircase. In front of me, dark seeped into the space from the narrow windows, and a furious blast of wind shook the single panes of glass. I wrapped my arms around myself and turned in a tight circle, taking in the murky view from every direction, recognizing the space for what it was—a graveyard of discarded crap.

I sighed. The tension holding my body rigid released, and I sank onto an old trunk. Leaning forward, I rested my elbows on my knees, my head in my hands. There was nothing treacherous about the attic. Yes, it was creepy, but what attic wasn't? Granny hadn't wanted me to come up here because I'd see all her mess.

I blew out a breath. I couldn't explain the music, but I didn't care. It was probably a radio playing downstairs, the sound coming up through old vents. I stood, ready to go to bed, when I heard a creak, followed by the sound of something being dragged across the floor behind me.

My heart started thumping in a heavy rock rhythm, and my body broke out in a cold sweat. Should I dare look? Or should I hightail it down the stairs and slam the attic door behind me? The music swelled, the melody beckoning me to turn, and I slowly pivoted, biting back a scream at what I saw.

A door I hadn't noticed was opening, the light shining from within a tiny glimmer, growing stronger inch by inch as the door continued its arc. The music amplified, as if the door operated like the knob on a radio, turning up the volume. The melody reached a crescendo as the door stopped, standing wide open.

Light from the room flickered, a cheery wave enticing me to enter. I took one step forward and stopped, heart pounding, my swan pendant spreading heat across my chest and through my body. Should I stay, explore? Or run away? The need to know overruled reason, and I took a hesitant step toward the door, thinking of Catrina and Conall, looking forward to the time when I was home and could tell them this crazy story. I took another step, my heart thudding in my chest, a quiet drumbeat of terror, but I kept going. Surely, there was nothing in Granny's house that could kill me.

Chapter Twenty-Five

At the threshold, I paused and peeked inside, on guard for danger, my swan pendant pulsing. What met my eyes wasn't at all what I'd expected, and I released a sigh, unaware I'd been holding my breath.

A welcoming fire and the warmth it emitted lured me inside. Comfort enveloped me as I surveyed the small, cozy sanctuary. Unlike the rest of the attic, this place was clean and smelled of lemon oil and lavender. Tension seeped from my limbs, and my hands flexed and relaxed. The pulse of my swan eased to a gentle thrum. I wondered what I'd been frightened of.

I walked to the fireplace, soaking in the heat, wondering who had started the fire. Candles of varying heights twinkled atop the hearth. A sculpted crystal swan, a foot tall and almost as wide, presided over the room from the center, reflecting the reddish-yellow blaze of the fire. The music was strongest here, and I couldn't explain why or how, but the swan seemed to be the source of the sound.

Magic. Much as I might want to, I couldn't escape the word.

I circled the rest of the space, exploring but not touching, bits of memory surfacing as I went. Aunt Geraldine had brought me here and showed me beautiful stones with sparkling facets, like a king's treasure to my seven-year-old self. They were here, plus many more, gracing the tops of the bookshelves and tables, the myriad colors a rainbow glinting in the firelight.

A tall lamp stood between two mismatched chintz upholstered chairs, emitting a muted golden glow. An antique desk with curving legs and clawed feet pressed against the far wall, the surface stacked with a tower of books that looked as if it might blow over in a strong wind. She'd read to me from a book of fairy tales. A story of love with swans at the end. Where was the book I'd imagined scratched me? I didn't see it in the stack.

Behind the desk, hidden in the gloom, a square table sat beneath a narrow window, the dark beyond the glass causing it to disappear into the wall. I shivered as memory tugged. Geraldine and I sat at this table when she'd brought me here all those years ago.

Back at the fireplace, I examined the bookshelves standing on either side. One shelf was lined with books, mostly fairy tales, myths, and legends, but the book I remembered wasn't here either. The other bookshelf housed rows of journals, all in burgundy save a lone volume of deep-brown leather. The same color as Mom's journal. The same as I'd seen in my vision with the Druid pen.

I looked behind me, just in case, before touching the book. Did I dare pull it out, check the front? I hesitated. I only wanted to see the cover, not read anything inside, but the act of removing the book seemed like a violation of Geraldine's privacy. I pulled my hand away, stopped, reached back, and scooted the brown leather volume out far enough to scan the cover.

"Oh." My breath whooshed out. The cover was the same, portraying the woman with the long hair.

I removed the book and held it close, as if it might answer the questions running through my brain. Was this the book from my meditation, the one I was supposed to use with the pen? I bit my lips. It couldn't be. The Druid pen had nothing to do with Geraldine. It had to do with her father. I wanted to ask, but I couldn't. Tommy told me not to tell anyone he'd given me the pen. I tried to flip through the pages of the journal, but they were stuck together, as if someone had glued them shut. Odd. There was no visible lock. I put the journal back.

It was time to leave this place, although a part of me was reluctant to go. As I headed toward the door, the air grew heavy, pushing against my progress. I was panting at the effort, and at one of the chintz chairs, I stopped and plopped into the seat. Maybe I'd take a short rest before going, and as I thought about it, a fuzzy cashmere throw settled over my legs. I curled my fingers in the soft wool. What could it hurt to sit for a moment? I yawned. It had been a long day.

My head rested back, and I closed my eyes. Maybe a quick nap. I was almost gone, when a howl jolted me to alertness.

"What the hell!" I bolted forward, blood pounding in my head, hands clutching the arms of the chair.

The sound came again, a screech, long and persistent. I whipped around, wide awake, breath held. When the sound came a third time, I released my pent-up breath. Only a branch of a tree against the window.

My moment of relaxation had vanished, and I was about to fold the blanket and leave the room, when I noticed two books resting on the round table next to my elbow. The silver at my throat heated, beating against my skin.

The largest book took up most of the tabletop. A smaller volume sat on top of it. I gasped.

Three regal white swans in a pond of azure blue were embossed on the hard cover of the small book. The same swans that swam across the cover when I was seven. This was the book I'd been looking for.

I picked up the book. It was older than I remembered. The corners of the cover were scuffed as if it had been opened many times. I stared at the cover, breath held in case the swans moved. I'd not noticed the title when I was seven—*Celtic Mythology: Separating Myth from Fact*. Written by Enda Rafferty, PhD. I opened the book to the title page. The year of publication was listed as 1965. There was an inscription on the title page: *To Agnes O'Toole. Many thanks for your help.* My great-granny's name was Agnes. Maybe she was the one who'd helped the author.

Dr. Rafferty was pictured—a smiling man in early middle age with graying hair curling around his ears. A brief biography followed. Enda Rafferty had a PhD in parapsychology, whatever that was.

My heart raced as my fingers held tight to the book, unable to release the volume. I bit my lips, swallowed. It was a book of fairy tales, that was all. There was nothing magic inside, no moving illustrations on the cover. I flipped to the opening blurb.

For centuries, people have explored the rich symbolism of Celtic mythology. But what if the symbolism is more than representative? What if, within the abundant world of fairies and folklore, a kernel of truth, a hidden gem of reality, exists? And what if that reality lives on today, in the magic and mysticism of those who flow from this fantastical lineage? In these pages, you'll discover where truth meets fiction and fantasy usurps reality as we uncover the ancient world of the Celts, a world not so far removed from you and me as one might imagine.

A shiver ran up my spine, my hands tingling where my fingers touched the book, and I dropped it in my lap, rubbing my hands together. What was this book?

At my thoughts, another gust of wind burst past the ancient window glass and circulated through the room, sending sparks up the chimney and blowing the book open. Pages flipped in the breeze, coming to rest at a bookmark midway through the volume. I read the chapter heading. *Caer Ibormeith and Aengus Og: A Dream of Love.*

My breath caught in my throat. Caer Ibormeith. I'd heard her name many times today. But what was her story, and how did it relate to my dreams? I stared at the page, frowning. I could leave it alone, go back to my room, and ask Granny tomorrow. Or, even easier, search the internet, where I was sure to find a telling of the tale. That was the most practical decision.

I tapped the book, reading and rereading the title. I was here now. My heart rate quickened. Maybe a brief scan of the story. Decision made, I picked up the book, glanced around one more time, and settled back into the chair. I'd read Caer's story, then go to bed.

"Caer Ibormeith, a goddess of the Tuatha Dé Danann, is the Celtic goddess of dreams and prophecy and a powerful symbol of love, purity, and fierce determination. She is connected to the swan, also a symbol of purity and love. Determined to choose her mate, Caer pursues her man, the god of youth, love, and poetry, Aengus mac Og, using the power of her dreams to captivate his mind and capture his heart. Caer appears to Aengus in his dreams for a year, wooing him in his sleep with her beauty and the sweet music of her timpan. Caer's grace, intelligence, and loveliness overwhelm him, and each night Aengus reaches for her in his dreams. But the elusive Caer evades his grasp and leaves him as dawn breaks, casting such a spell that Aengus becomes heartsick, his illness preventing him from leaving his bed.

"After a year, the physician Fergne diagnoses Aengus. 'It is love in absence,' he says, and the young god agrees.

""I have seen a young woman, the most beautiful woman in the whole of Ériu,' says Aengus. 'But she only comes to me in my dreams. Before dawn, she vanishes like the morning mist.'

"Aengus's mother, Boann, is summoned, but she cannot discover the whereabouts of the young woman haunting her son. After a year without success, Aengus's father, the Dagda, the great king and father god of the Tuatha Dé Danann, is sent for. The Dagda sends word to his many connections in Ériu, and after another year he receives a report that the woman young Aengus loves has been found.

""She is called Caer Ibormeith,' the Dagda tells his son. 'She is the daughter of a fairy king, Ethal Anbúail, who rules the fairy mound of Sídh Uamuin in the kingdom of

Connachta. You will find her at the Lake of the Dragon's Mouth.'

"With this news, Aengus Og travels to the lake and first spies Caer as a woman standing within a group of three times fifty women, all wearing silver chains. He instantly recognizes her from his dreams. But she is not yet his.

"His father, the Dagda, asks Ethal Anbúail to give Caer to him for Aengus, but the fairy king refuses. He explains his daughter is far stronger than he and it is not for him to offer her to any man, for she will make her choice as to whom she loves. Aengus must win Caer's love for himself. Caer's father also explains that she is a shape-shifting goddess who spends one year as a human and one year as a swan, changing from one to the other on Samhain. Aengus must return in one year to the Lake of the Dragon's Mouth on Samhain and woo her when Caer will be in her swan form. To do so, he must be able to pick her out from her companions, all one hundred and fifty of them in the shape of swans. A year later, upon his return, Aengus recognizes the shining qualities of his love because of the Dreamscape Caer has woven around and between them over the years.

"'I will come to you, Aengus mac Og,' Caer calls to him, 'if you promise I may return to the water.'

"'I promise,' Aengus says. Aengus shifts into the shape of a swan, and together they take flight, circling the lake three times and singing a song so beautiful that all who hear it fall into a deep slumber for three days and nights. They live together from then on, committed to their love for each other.

"Agnes O'Toole, a Dreammaster, explains more about how she, and the other women like her, can help Dreamers change their lives and find their heart's desire by following in the footsteps of her ancient ancestor, Caer."

I dropped my hands in my lap and stared, unblinking, into the fire. I'd heard this story before. Geraldine read it to me up here, in the attic, although she'd left out the part about Dreammasters believing they were related to the Celtic goddess of dreams.

A few weeks ago, I'd have laughed at such a ridiculous notion. But since Mom's death and the magic I'd encountered in only a day in Ireland, I couldn't. Fergus had spoken about my connection with Caer and myth this afternoon, but I'd glossed over it in my fear about saving Lorcan. He'd also said he was descended from Aengus, Caer's lover. Even Tommy claimed he had magical antecedents. And then there was the pen, which floated into my hand as if it belonged there.

I bit my lower lip, my fingers tracing lines down the page of the book. Dreams had plagued me since I was seven years old and had visited this house. Mom had written about my dreams and sending me to Galway to train as a Dreammaster. A shiver ran through me. Two people I'd loved had died because of dreams. I needed to learn more. I bent back to the book.

Agnes: There are still direct descendants of Caer, women called Dreammasters, who, by use of a special process called a Dreamspell, can go into the Dreamscape world to assist those who request their help, called Dreamers.

Enda: There is an old name for Dreammasters, isn't there?

Agnes: Aye, and we still use the name Aislingeach, which means daydreamer. Others know of us by Caer's surname, Ibormeith, which traditional Dreammasters use in their professional capacity.

Professional capacity. My hands trembled, and I almost dropped the volume. Granny had said she had a client on the night Lorcan disappeared. The fact only now registered. Being a Dreammaster was a profession?

Aislingeach. I dropped my head back. Too much like my name, Aisling, to be a coincidence.

Enda: I have heard of the custom of Dreammasters using Ibormeith as a professional name to protect themselves from those who don't believe in Dreamspells.

Agnes: True. Anonymity allows us to work with those who accept our gift and request our assistance while keeping safe all involved in the process. We realize that not everyone is comfortable with the idea of changing lives via dreaming.

Enda: Please explain more about what you do as an Aislingeach or Dreammaster.

Agnes: We dream to open possibilities for our clients. If the circumstances are favorable, the possibilities may become reality. As Dreammasters, we may dream for the well-being of our clients, for health, for peace in relationship, and for love. We may even dream to gently break ties that cause harm in order to restore love and peace. Some Dreamspells are instigated in order to gain wisdom.

Others are prophetic. Still other Dreamspells show past events. The most difficult of Dreamspells are used to shift the reality of the Dreamer who has asked for help. The women in my family have this unique ability to help others in need.

Enda: Tell us, Agnes, about the scope of your power. What issues do you usually tackle?

Agnes: I, and others like me, focus first on issues surrounding love and family, for such things are at the very core of every human heart. I have always felt called to help others find their heart's desire using the dreaming world.

Enda: Isn't it dangerous to change the lives of ordinary people with dreams? How do you ensure that what you do is not harmful or disruptive? Do you believe it is ever proper to refuse to use your gift in aid of another?

Agnes: I'd never turn away one in need, and any dreaming I do is for the good of my client. As you might suspect, a Dreammaster is meant to use her gift ethically. We're taught to carefully choose what we do and whom we help. Dreammasters often dream for love, much like the goddess Caer did. But dreams of love are not all we do.

And while we're taught to refuse to dream if such a dream
would cause harm, I feel it is more harmful to deny help to
the poor souls injured in the name of love. My heart guides
me, Enda, and, truth be told, I choose to help whenever
and however I can.

I lowered the book to my lap, blood roaring in my ears, body cold despite
the fire, while pieces of the story swirled in my head. The faint scent of
expensive perfume floated to me, and I looked up.

Aunt Geraldine stood in the doorway watching me, her expression
hidden in shadows.

"I see you decided to visit my lair," she said. She moved toward me.

I couldn't decipher her tone. Was she pleased? Displeased? Intrigued?
Whatever it was, she'd caught me.

"Shoot." I scrambled with the book and the throw, trying to put one
on the table while pulling the other from around my legs. Apparently,
I couldn't do both at the same time, because the throw tangled in my
legs, and the book plopped in my lap, almost sliding to the floor. "I'm so
sorry, Aunt Geraldine. I didn't mean to—it was the music—and then the
door opened." I was stumbling over words as I grasped the book, ready
to replace it on the round table, when the swans on the cover moved.

I paused, watching as the cover art came to life. I sucked in a breath.
Mom had accused me of making things up. But I'd been right—because
the finely drawn swans were swimming, gliding across the cover of the
book, some fanning their feathers, others dipping their beaks into the
blue water.

"What the hell …?" I'd forgotten my embarrassment at being discovered, too caught up in the strange spectacle before me. "They're moving. Like last time, when they scratched me." I touched a tiny mark on my right hand. "I still have the scar."

I tapped the book as I looked up at my aunt, who now stood next to me. "You said I'd imagined it." I paused, eyeing her. "Can you see that?"

Geraldine smiled and touched the cover. The swans stopped. "It's an old book. It belonged to my grandmother, Agnes."

"Granny's mother." I sucked in a breath. I'd been right.

Geraldine nodded. "Agnes was a very powerful Dreammaster. She taught me much of what I know." She regarded me, one eyebrow lifted. "And you must be special, because the swans don't swim for anyone but me." She paused, head tilted, eyes gleaming. "And you."

"Why me? And why did you lie to me when I was seven? You said I'd scratched my hand on the binding."

"I don't know why the swan pecked you. I'd guess it's the familial connection." She folded her hands in front of her. "I didn't say anything when you were a child because I knew it would upset Mary. She was angry enough just finding you up here."

I bit my lip, thinking back. Mom had screamed at Geraldine. Her face had been so red she'd scared me. "Yeah, I guess it was better you didn't tell her about the swan." I stared at the cover. "So, if I touch it again, will the swans move?"

Geraldine shrugged. "Why don't you see?"

I bit my lip and reached toward the book, pausing before tapping the cover. My eyes widened as the water rippled. "It worked."

I gazed up at Geraldine and she smiled back, until movement caught my attention, and I turned back to the book in time to watch the biggest swan swim at me, its beak aimed at my finger. The razor-edged beak nipped the tip of my right index finger, drawing blood that dripped into the picture, a curl of scarlet blending into the watery blue.

I gasped, watching my blood disappear, barely breathing as my fingertip throbbed.

Chapter Twenty-Six

"**S**hit," I moaned, fire searing through my veins and numbing my arm. I gasped and doubled over. Sweat broke out on my forehead, and my right hand shook uncontrollably. I gritted my teeth, squeezing my eyes closed, fighting the pain. "What's happening?"

"Breathe, Aisling." Geraldine's hand stroked my hair. "Try to relax. The pain will subside faster if you're calm."

"I can't breathe." I straightened, gasped, the tightness in my chest making inhaling next to impossible. I grabbed my hand, hoping to still it but couldn't.

"Relax." Geraldine spoke in a calm voice. She reached over and took my hand, kneading the finger. Heat spread up my neck and into my face. "Take deep breaths, and soon the pain will go away."

"That's not helping," I hollered, trying to pull my hand away. "What did it do to me?" I moaned. Every part of my body ached, stinging from the inside as though a hive of bees had taken up residence inside me and wanted to escape. My swan pendant beat hard against my chest.

"Shhh," Geraldine intoned in a soft voice. "The more you can release the tension, the less it will hurt."

Her calm voice infuriated me. "You know what it is." My raspy voice accused her. "Tell me. What did that damn swan do?" I yanked my hand from her grasp and examined my finger. "It's swollen. And purple." I looked up at Geraldine. "What did you do?" I rubbed my right arm and shoulder, where the pain was the most acute. "I want it to stop. Now."

"The pain will fade." She watched me, her brow furrowed in concern. "I can't make it go away any faster. You touched the book. You started the swans swimming. I didn't cause that to happen."

"You could have warned me." I looked into her eyes.

"I had no reason to expect one to bite you. The swan has only bitten a few times. Once when my granny first showed me the book. Granny laughed at my pain, thought it was amusing." Geraldine shook her head. "Granny Agnes had an unusual sense of humor."

"I'd say." I snapped out the words.

"The swan bit me once again, when I was older." She paused, thinking. "It pecked you when you were seven, which, again, I didn't foresee. And it pecked you this evening." She frowned. "I recall that it's quite painful, although I don't remember pain as intense as what you're experiencing. And you seemed to suffer no such ill effects as a child."

"Only childbirth was worse," I said, but as even as I spoke, the pain was subsiding. I leaned back, resting my hand in my lap. "I don't remember the scratch when I was seven being this painful."

"Don't worry, Aisling," Geraldine said, as if that would make it all better. "The bite of the swan isn't harmful." She leaned over and touched my hand. "It's already better."

"Yes," I said, exhaustion replacing pain. I swiped a lone curl off my sticky forehead. "You're sure this won't hurt me?"

"I've suffered no ill effects. You're young and strong. You'll be fine, Aisling. Trust me."

I raised my finger, examining the now normal pink tip. No more pain. No more swelling. "Remind me to steer clear of your book. That wasn't pleasant."

Geraldine picked up the small volume and tucked it into the bookcase. "It's put away. The danger is gone."

She turned and watched me. I fidgeted under her scrutiny. She'd caught me trespassing. I owed her an apology for that and for accusing her of deliberately harming me.

"About me being up here," I started, clearing my throat.

"I'm glad you're here," Geraldine said, a beaming smile lighting her face. "You heard the music. Caer's music. The song she sang when she and Aengus were united in their love." She paused, her eyes shining. "The music of the Dreamscape."

My eyes widened. I knew where I'd heard the music before. "It's the same music I heard in my dreams when I was younger. I haven't heard it in years." My brows furrowed. "What does it mean?"

"It means you accepted my invitation into my Dreaming Space." She swept her arm around the room. "Where I learned to dream. All Dreammasters have a special place to dream." She pressed her hands together, her voice low and mysterious. "And it means we're ready to begin your Dreammaster training."

"What do you mean? Was this some kind of test?" Heat flooded my body, fueling my sharp words. "I don't like being toyed with, Geraldine."

Geraldine pinched her lips together and raised her chin. "Only Dreammasters, the descendants of the goddess Caer Ibormeith, can hear the music." She spoke in a level tone, but her eyes hardened. "I assumed you would hear the music, but I wanted to see what you would do. If you were too cautious to discover the source, you might not be the woman to save Lorcan."

I digested the information, putting aside for the moment Lorcan and my role in saving him. "You believe you're descended from a Celtic goddess of the Tuatha Dé Danann." I wanted to hear it from her lips. "Is this a common belief in Ireland? Is everyone here descended from one of the gods or goddesses?"

"I know I am descended from Caer, as are you. How can you explain your dreams otherwise?" She watched me through narrowed eyes. "Many Irish are connected to the Tuatha Dé Danann; however, most aren't aware of their antecedents. Those who know have pure bloodlines tracing back to their ancestor or, sometimes, ancestors. They learn about their gifts from their families. These people can and do access their magical abilities and pledge to act in the best interests of those who seek their help."

"Tell me about the other people descended from the gods and goddesses. What can they do?"

Geraldine pursed her lips. She didn't like my questions, but I didn't care. "There are many descendants, all with unique abilities. We don't have time to discuss all of them this evening, but, as an example, Heartseekers concentrate on bringing love into the world. Heartseekers are descended from Aengus, Caer's true love. Heartseekers and Dreammasters share a close connection." She paused. "Others have the power of healing or prophecy. Some use words with magical effect. And there are craftsmen and women who imbue their designs and creations with their particular magic." She checked her watch. "We need to move on."

"Does everyone know about us? Is there some kind of directory to help people find a Dreammaster or someone who can build a magical house?"

Geraldine tapped her fingers on the arm of her chair. "Of course not. Dreammasters and others like us don't advertise what we do. If a person needs our help and voices such a need out loud or within the depth of their heart, they will find us. It's part of the magic that connects all of us to one another."

"I don't understand."

"We live in a magical world, Aisling." Impatience tinged her words. "Not all of it can easily be explained. And not everyone will believe what we are and accept what we can do. They might call us delusional, odd, even dangerous if they learned about us, because many, most even, aren't ready for the truth of our existence. That doesn't negate the help we afford to those who seek us out."

I considered all she'd shared. I didn't doubt my ancestry, not given everything I'd learned. But the fact that she'd lured me up here irritated me. I ignored her impatience. She owed me an explanation. "You tricked me." I stared at her.

"I had to know the truth about you." She folded her arms over her chest. "I set up a small test, and you passed."

"And if I hadn't?"

"I'd have to find another Dreammaster to assist me in saving Lorcan, as I'd originally planned."

I digested this information, fear a fire flickering in my belly. Tommy and Fergus had assured me I didn't have to enter the Underworld as I had in Mom's dream. Still, I wanted to double check. "So, we're going to use a dream to find Lorcan and get him out. We aren't going into the Underworld like my mother did the night she died." She watched without responding. My jaw tensed. "Or have I misunderstood?"

"One of the Dreammaster tenets requires the woman who initiates a dream to finish the dream." She rose and walked to the fire, gazing into the flames, her back to me. "Mother suspects the dream Mary began on Samhain forty-six years ago sent Lorcan into the Underworld." She turned. "If that's the case, Mary left the dream unfinished when she abandoned Lorcan. You're the best person to complete the dream. That is what you will attempt to do, with my help."

"Mom couldn't have known she'd sent Lorcan into the Underworld all those years ago." The words rushed out of me. "And if she had, she'd have said something, tried to rescue him. She loved Lorcan." I took a breath, slowed myself down. "Besides, Granny told me the magic is old and not taught any longer." I spoke sharply, and my eyes drilled into hers. "I still don't understand how any of this happened."

"Neither do I." Geraldine matched my sharp tone. "Whatever happened back then, somehow Mary discovered Lorcan's whereabouts now. Mother suspects her condition may have played into her ability to sense Lorcan." She shrugged. "Maybe she tried to save him on the night she died. We'll never know for certain."

I took a moment before responding, crinkling my brow, as I thought through my question. "I want to help if I can." I paused, watching her. "But aren't you more closely linked to Mom's dream than I am and therefore better positioned than me to save Lorcan? After all, you were there, in the dream. You know how the process works. And you knew him. I'm his daughter, but in reality my connection to Lorcan is pretty tenuous."

Geraldine drew herself to her fullest height. "This was my argument to you on the night I called. I was prepared to do this without you. You wanted to come."

"And I want to be here," I hurried to assure her. "I'll do whatever you ask of me." Thoughts of the dream with Trevor haunted me. "But I'm a newbie. Not trained." I clenched my fists in my lap. Her eyebrows rose, and I rushed on. "Trusting a novice like me must increase the risk to Lorcan."

"You're Mary's daughter, which connects you to her. You're also Lorcan's daughter. You, Aisling, have the strongest connection to Lorcan, even though you haven't met him. This gives you the best chance of connecting with him in the Underworld to dream him home."

I nodded as images of Mom's dream played in my mind: the crashing water, the spiky rocks, the shadowy shapes that growled, the slice of metal that cut into my mother. "But you don't want me to enter the Underworld. You only want me to connect to him using my Dreammaster powers, assuming I'm trainable."

"Correct." She hesitated, as if she wanted to say more, then nodded. "Yes, that is our beginning point."

My mouth went dry, and my body froze. *Beginning point.* What in the hell did that mean?

Geraldine continued, seeming not to notice my consternation. "You're trainable, Aisling. You're a Dreammaster by birth. Your skills are inherent to you, a part of your physiological and mental makeup." She looked me over, tapping her finger on her lips. "I've never known of a Dreammaster who started training in her middle years. But I'm sure you'll do fine." She cocked her head to one side, as if she didn't quite believe her words.

"Okay," I said in a shaky voice. I wished she sounded more confident. But she was right to be wary, although she didn't realize the full extent of my fears concerning my dreams.

"Just follow my directions. I'll teach you all you need to know." She spoke more to herself than to me. "Of course, you'll need permission to enter the Underworld, even in a dream, but I'm working on that." She smiled at me. "We'll be ready. We have to be."

But would we? Now was the time to confess my concerns about Trevor's death, but fear wrapped around my neck and squeezed like strong fingers, locking my words in my throat. I opened my mouth to speak, then covered the action with a yawn. What would I say? What would she say? She and Granny could turn me away. They could report me to the tribunal Granny talked about. The one Geraldine and Mom had faced after their dream on Samhain. I'd never learn to be a Dream-master, but did that matter?

A hollow feeling filled my core, leaving me cold, which made no sense. I hadn't expected to be a Dreammaster. I'd never known such a thing existed. How could I miss something I'd never had? I looked at the door.

Part of me wanted to walk away, head home. I rubbed my sore eyes, longing for sleep. I could go to bed, get some rest, and tomorrow I could confess all to Granny and Geraldine. Let them decide how to proceed.

"It's all so much to take in, Geraldine. I don't even know what Dreammasters do on a normal day." I yawned again, partly for effect. "Maybe we ought to discuss everything in the morning with Granny. I'm exhausted. I need to sleep. In the morning, we can start training me and see how things go. And if I mess up, you can dream as you'd planned."

Geraldine resumed her seat. "I understand your fears, Aisling." She sighed and patted my knee. "As I told you on the phone, I'm prepared to do this on my own, but Mother wanted you." She sniffed. "I said much the same to her as you expressed to me, but she's convinced you're our answer."

I slumped back. I remembered our conversation and the feeling this trip was important for me. I straightened. "Do you think I can do it?"

"Train with me. Allow me to introduce you to the Dreammaster world." She paused. "If you don't feel comfortable after training, I'll understand." Geraldine sighed, rolling her shoulders. "All I care about is finding Lorcan, whatever that takes. I've missed him." She swallowed. "If I was involved in his disappearance, even as an innocent witness to Mary's dream, I must find him. People don't stop mattering even if many years have passed."

I looked at my hands, not sure what to say. She still cared. I could see that. And she had answers I needed. Not only about Lorcan and the Underworld but about the power of dreams. I'd agreed to help. I wouldn't back out before I'd even begun.

I looked up. "Where do we begin?"

Geraldine smiled. "Tell me about your dreams."

Where should I start? "When I was young, the dreams were frightening. Mom taught me ways to keep the worst of the nightmares away. She called my dreams 'slipping around a corner in my subconscious.'

She taught me how to be aware and avoid those dreams." I shrugged. "She taught me a mantra. *I will not slip around the bend, past the place where normal dreams end.* There was a longer verse too. Sort of like a before-bed prayer. For the most part, it worked."

"And when it didn't work?" Geraldine watched me.

"I'd have odd dreams." I sighed. "And sometimes things changed as a result."

Geraldine nodded and folded her fingers together. "You can't run from the truth."

"I don't know the truth." I smacked the arm of the chair. "I know pieces of the truth. It's not the same."

Geraldine nodded, straightening in her chair, the barest hint of a smile on her face. "Fair enough." She picked up the large book still sitting on the table between us. "We'll begin where all Dreammaster training begins—with the Dreammaster pledge."

"What am I pledging to do?" Nerves danced in my belly.

"Dreammasters promise to uphold the duties and responsibilities of our sisterhood. Nothing more." She sighed. "You read the pledge when you were seven." She paused. "Most young women read the pledge at seventeen. I didn't want you to miss out, and I was sure Mary wouldn't allow you to train." She sighed. "But you were too young, and reading the pledge opened you to the nightmares you had for years."

I bit back any response. I'd lost a lot of sleep because of my aunt and caused my mother a lot of worry. But I didn't want to rehash the past, and I wasn't in the mood to absolve my aunt for her actions. "I don't remember a pledge."

"Then it's time for a review." She placed the book in my lap.

The book was old, the leather cover darkened after years of handling, the strap holding the volume closed worn after long use. The image of the goddess Caer was tooled into the leather. I traced her figure, the tip of my finger pulsing in time with the pendant around my neck. The word *Ibormeith* was engraved beneath the woman.

Geraldine spoke, her voice hushed. "Each family has a similar book, which is passed down from mother to daughter. The book contains a list of all the Dreammasters as well as the pledge of our sisterhood. Someday I'll be the keeper of the Ibormeith book. Maybe, in the future, as I don't have a daughter, you'll accept the responsibility from me."

I looked up, my heart racing. Did I want that obligation? "Me? Really?"

Geraldine tilted her head, her eyes considering. "Let's see how training goes, shall we?" She paused. "Open it, Aisling."

I touched the leather strap, reluctant to undo the tie, but a power emanated from the old tome, and I couldn't resist its allure. I untied the strap and peeled back the cover.

The first page was a picture of Caer and Aengus. On the second page, the two had transformed into swans and were flying away from a lake full of swans, as told in the fairy story.

I continued to turn, discovering the list of names Geraldine had mentioned. The lists were divided into family trees, the earliest from several thousand years ago written in ancient Irish. I continued to turn until Geraldine reached out and stopped me.

"Here's our family." I followed where she pointed. "Agnes MacGowan O'Toole." Her finger moved down the page. "Fionnuala Brigid O'Toole Fitzgerald. My mother." I nodded. "Here's your mother." I read her name: Mary Catrina Fitzgerald O'Leary. Next to Mom was her sister, Geraldine Noreen Fitzgerald.

My breath stopped when I read the name below my mother's. "I'm here." I looked up. "How did I get here?"

"You read the pledge."

"Oh." I paused, staring at my name. Aisling Fitzgerald O'Leary Doyle. Tingles ran through my body, and I spread my hand over the page, the power of the book seeping into my skin.

"The pledge is a few pages on."

Nodding, I continued turning until I arrived at a page with an elaborate heading and filled with unfamiliar script. I frowned, looking up at Aunt Geraldine.

"Look," she said in a hushed voice.

When I looked back down, the letters began skating across the page, arranging and rearranging themselves into words I knew. I whooshed out a breath I hadn't realized I was holding when the motion ceased.

"Read it out loud," Geraldine urged. "Say your name where indicated."

I did as she said.

"Dreammaster Pledge

Dear Sister, as you read the pledge below, you formally enter the World of the Aislingeach.

I, (state your name aloud,) agree that by reading this pledge, I promise to uphold the laws of the Dreammaster Sisterhood.

Induction into Apprenticeship and Oath

I, (state your name aloud) acknowledge that I am of the Ibormeith Lineage. I present myself for training, and as I begin this journey, my title shall be Dreamkeeper.

I promise to train and follow the guidance of my teacher, until such time, as determined by my trainer, I am able to fully enter into the world of the Aislingeach. Once my training is complete, I will become a Dreammaster and will be bound by the duties and responsibilities required by the goddess, Caer Ibormeith, who founded our Sisterhood and from whom our Dreaming powers flow.

I agree to accept the lifelong responsibilities inherent in the powers I possess. I acknowledge that said powers must be used with great care. I promise to use my powers only for good and never for evil, to do harm, or for personal gain. I vow to always follow the rules set forth by the Dreammaster Council and to honor any special provisions handed down by the Council with respect to delicate or sensitive dreams. If ever I am accused of breaking Dreammaster rules and in so doing cause harm to a dreamer or anyone associated with the dream, I agree to accept any ruling handed down by the Dreammaster Tribunal regarding punishment, including the loss of my right to dream as a Dreammaster.

We welcome the new Dreamkeeper.

We of the Aislingeach welcome you and recognize that you are now of an age to join into your heritage and take your place as a Dreamkeeper.

Now that you have read the pledge and, by so doing, accepted your duties and responsibilities, your mentor will soon appear to you. Listen to her. Learn from her. All Dreammaster mentors are of exceptional character and will lead you on the true path of your legacy.

Keep Caer in your heart."

I sat back and closed my eyes, memories flooding my brain, my swan pendant throbbing against my chest. I'd seen this book, read these words, with Geraldine's help, right here in this room, thirty-eight years ago, before my mother had slammed the book closed and pulled me away, scolding me for being here with Geraldine.

"This is not something to be fooled with, Aisling." Mother had taken me to our room.

"I'm sorry, Mama." I'd been crying. I'd never seen my mother so angry. "I didn't mean to do anything wrong."

Granny had followed us to our room, angry as well, her eyes beady black, the same beady black I'd carried in my mind ever since.

"You stay with the child," Granny had said. "Hopefully, she didn't do any permanent damage."

"I didn't hurt anything," I'd sobbed.

Granny's face had softened, even as my mother had wrapped me in her arms.

"We know you didn't mean to hurt anything, Aisling," Granny had said, her voice gentle. "I wasn't referring to you, child."

That night, I'd had the first dream.

I closed the book, resting my hands on the cover, the thrum of energy still pulsing through me. It was true. I was part of something I still couldn't fathom. I opened my eyes to find Geraldine staring at me.

"Granny was angry with you all those years ago for showing me this."

Geraldine inclined her head. "Yes. I made a mistake. Mother and Mary had every right to be upset."

"What about my daughter?" I swallowed. "What about Catrina?"

Geraldine nodded. "Catrina is also of our lineage, and should you allow her to read the pledge, she will be a Dreamkeeper." She paused. "Even if Catrina doesn't read the pledge, she will feel the pull of her power, although she won't be able to explain what it is she senses and why her dreams are so vivid."

Could I keep this, her heritage, from my daughter? Could I bear to tell her? Wasn't it best to help to save Lorcan, go home, and resume my life as it was?

I pressed my palms into my eyes. If I trained and Geraldine and I saved Lorcan, I'd have a new father, a grandfather, to introduce to my kids. I'd have no choice but to share this with the twins.

My fingers trembled, and goose bumps pricked my skin as I contemplated meeting the man who had loved my mother and wanted to marry her. I wanted to know the man who would have raised me, had circumstances been different and he hadn't disappeared. I pushed back the fear and doubt that niggled in the back of my mind. Geraldine promised to train me. She wouldn't let me do something I wasn't ready for. I was here. I couldn't leave without trying, not now that I knew the truth about Lorcan.

I looked at my aunt. "Where do we start?"

Geraldine sighed and smiled. "We start with the dream you had on the night of your mother's death."

Chapter Twenty-Seven

Geraldine rose and took the heavy book from me. She walked to the back of the room and placed the book on the large table.

I watched her, wondering what I'd agreed to and if I ought to change my mind. Before I could speak, Geraldine was back.

"We'll only go over the basics tonight." She gave my shoulder a gentle squeeze. "I know you're tired."

I nodded. "I'm wearing out. But I said we'd start tonight, and I meant it." I shivered. "It's cold in here."

"That's easily remedied." Geraldine turned to the fire, which had settled into a steady glow, and lifted her hands to her waist. She took a moment to focus before raising her hands up past her chest. Flames rose, and a wave of warmth coupled with the earthy scent of turf enveloped the room.

"How did you—" I stopped. "Never mind. It's not the strangest thing about tonight."

Geraldine sat back down. "Open yourself up to training, embrace all that you can become, and you'll find magic in almost everything."

Excitement shone in Geraldine's eyes. "Lesson one. Every dream is different. Every dream setting is unique as well." She watched and I nodded.

"I'm following."

"As with regular dreams, Dreammaster dreams begin in our imaginations. Intention sets a Dreammaster's dreams apart. Regular dreams are often random bits of life processed as we sleep. Dreammaster dreams are deliberate and use a specific part of the brain unique to Dreammasters."

"Okay."

"You create the dream setting by blending your intention with the needs of your client. The imaginal setting often derives from the vision of your client. You'll listen, absorb, assimilate, and then execute what the client wishes to achieve."

"Can a client ask for anything?"

Geraldine paused, considering her answer. "Our dreams are limited only by the rules in the pledge. If a Dreammaster is unsure about performing a dream, she will take the matter to the Aislingeach Council. Our elected leader is one of us and we refer to her as Caer, in honor of the goddess. She and the council review and rule on whether a Dreammaster can undertake the dream. Love dreams are the most complicated dreams we can do for a client and must be approved by the council."

"If they approve a dream, can we make people fall in love?" Was that what I'd done with Trevor?

"No. A love dream is the most complex type of dream because two people are involved. One person wants love. The other may not. Dreams cannot force love. A dream is but a suggestion, a shift in reality, to encourage love between the pair. Before granting approval, the tribunal explores all aspects of a case, including if there are any impediments to a union."

She glanced at her watch. "Aisling, I understand you have many questions, and I encourage you to ask them. In fact, why don't you bring up these queries tomorrow? Mother was our leader for many years, and she can give you detailed answers. We need to push on tonight. Once dawn breaks, we must end all dreams."

"Great." I nodded. "I'll talk to Granny." I frowned. "She won't be upset that we started without her, will she?"

"I don't know why she would be. We're only going over the basics." Geraldine checked her watch. "What I propose we do with our remaining time this evening is explore your dream on the night your mother died. With your permission, I'll go into your subconscious with you, and we'll watch the dream through the lens of our subconscious mind, what the Aislingeach call our dreamvision."

"Okay," I whispered, even as my pulse raced at the thought of watching the dream again and seeing Mom attacked.

"Excellent." Geraldine drew a deep breath. "Close your eyes, Aisling, and we'll begin."

I squeezed my eyes closed and clasped my hands in my lap. What was Geraldine going to do? What would I have to do? She said we'd explore the dream the night my mom died, and the thought made my stomach roil. I didn't want to do this.

I lifted my lids and squinted at Geraldine. She sat still and relaxed, her eyes closed.

"Close your eyes, Aisling."

I started at her voice and slammed my eyelids shut. I'd agreed to this. I had to at least try.

"Relax your body, beginning at the top of your head and flowing down to your toes." Geraldine guided me through what was very much like the meditations Beverly led at the end of her yoga classes.

"Remember to take deep breaths." Geraldine's low, singsongy voice acted like a lullaby, freeing my body of tension, hypnotizing me into a heavy stupor.

"You're doing well," Geraldine said. "Continue to let go. The closer we can come to actual sleep, the easier it will be to enter the Dreamscape and access the dream."

Time appeared to stop as I slipped more deeply under my aunt's spell. My body sagged back into the chair. My hands unclenched, allowing my fingers to unfurl. My swan pedant pulsated against my chest, a tiny heartbeat mirroring my internal pulse. The tip of my finger throbbed in a synchronous rhythm. Every breath was a slow-growing ocean wave, filling my body from belly to rib cage to chest with a soft pink energy I could watch behind closed lids. I wanted to stay here, swaddled in the warm glow, safe from harm.

"Come with me, Aisling." Geraldine's voice floated to me through the pink haze of energy. She sounded as close as if she was inside me. Or was I inside of her? "Give me your hand, and we'll enter your mother's last dream."

My body twitched, and my hand was about to move, when I was there, behind my lids, walking through the mist toward Geraldine. Was I in my chair, or had I left? My brain tussled with the question for a moment and abandoned its investigation as Geraldine's hand reached through the pink fog to clasp mine. My palm linked with hers.

"Keep hold of my hand," Geraldine said. "Remember, we are spectators, nothing more, here only to observe and learn."

Geraldine led us to a misty waterway. We floated above the river shaded by overhanging branches, not another creature in sight. This world was as silent as it was absent of other beings—or so I thought until I heard the strains of a melody calling to us through the fog.

"The song." I watched as my breath formed the words in the surrounding air before falling away like sparkling drops of rain into the river below.

"Caer's song to Aengus," Geraldine said. "We'll follow her call."

The music intensified, discordant shrieks of sound ripping through the music, as we approached a small spit of land. Like my most frightening dreams. Only, worse, because I was going willingly.

Geraldine guided us toward the land, and as we approached, we heard a violent storm. Gusts of strong wind etched furrows in the soil and scattered the fog that had surrounded us, but the storm didn't touch us. We continued on, sailing through the turbulence until we hung above a vortex of explosive energy.

I recoiled and would have pulled back, but Geraldine held fast to my hand. "This is it," she whispered, her grip tightening. She looked at me, and her eyes widened. "Don't be afraid. This is a memory, a vision from the past."

I nodded, swallowing hard, eyes averted from the swirling circle of hell.

"Watch."

It was a command, and I turned and peered in, ready to pull back, but the turbulence smoothed to reveal a clear, glass-like screen. As if on cue, my mother appeared on the rocks, Lorcan with her. Wind whipped their hair, and flying debris mixed with dirt and stones assaulted their bodies. I heard my voice calling to my mother within the Dreamvision. I heard her respond, as she had that night in my dream.

"Mom," I called out. I could save her this time. I tugged, but Geraldine wouldn't release me.

"Mary's dead." The mist surrounding us softened Geraldine's blunt words. "She cannot hear you. We can't undo what's been done."

"Lorcan." Mom's anguished voice within the dream was a body blow, knocking the breath from me.

"Lorcan." Geraldine said his name with reverence, and her eyes shone with tears as she watched the scene unfurl. "He is here." She squeezed my hand. "He hasn't changed, you know. He's the same man I loved." She closed her eyes, tears seeping out. "You'll save him, Aisling. I know it."

Images of another dream filled my head as Aunt Geraldine spoke, and I pushed back the pictures burning in my brain. What if Lorcan ended up like Trevor? What if I was dangerous, could harm others in my dreams? I swallowed hard. The words were stuck in my throat, but I knew I had to ask. "Are you sure, Aunt Geraldine? What if I can't save him?" I paused, and she turned to look at me. "What if I hurt him instead?"

Geraldine's eyes widened, and her face paled. "How could you possibly harm him if you do as I tell you?"

"Aunt Geraldine," I started, but before I could consider how I might confess my fears, the wind howled like the primal scream of an injured beast as the storm increased in ferocity. The dream shifted, and even as I pushed back with my mind, images of Trevor filled my subconscious as the screen shifted. One uncarpeted wooden step, the first in what I knew was a long staircase, shimmered before us.

"No." I shouted the word as I screwed my eyes shut.

Chapter Twenty-Eight

My pendant pulsed, warm and protective. I'd make it stop. Like I had when I was a child. I wouldn't let the dream with Trevor get me. I wouldn't let Geraldine see.

I will not slip around the bend, past the place where normal dreams end.

I repeated the words under my breath as I clung to my swan, praying my talismans would save me from exposure.

My arms tingled, and power gathered like a pool of energy in my hands, spreading throughout my body. The energy would keep me safe.

I will not slip around the bend, past the place where normal dreams end.

"Aisling?" Geraldine's voice rose, frightened, questioning.

As my aunt spoke, a force outside of me pushed against my power. I couldn't answer as I struggled to maintain control, all the while pushing away Trevor's face. I was caught up in battle with an unseen enemy, determined to release the contents of my dream to my aunt.

"Aisling, what are you doing?" Geraldine tugged at me, but still I couldn't respond as I dueled with my invisible foe. "Aisling, stop this." I heard the terror in her voice.

"Do you feel it?" I panted. I had to hold on, couldn't risk glancing at my aunt. "The power, pushing back. It's there. It wants to hurt me, and it won't stop." Sweat poured down my back. I closed my eyes and gritted my teeth, hoping to punch up my power, but I was slipping.

"Stop it, Aisling." Geraldine's voice was a command.

"But I can't let you see." My arms trembled as my voice broke. I gasped for breath but held on. If only we could leave this Dreamvision and go back to her Dreaming Space. Then I'd confess everything. But not this way. It was too real, too horrible.

"You must stop this now." The clap of Aunt Geraldine's hands broke the spell. I dropped my arms to my sides.

The force field around me evaporated, and I faced Geraldine. "Please, I didn't mean it." My voice caught on a sob.

"Explain yourself," Geraldine commanded despite her trembling voice.

Before I could say another word, another voice drew our attention to the glassy screen.

"Trevor. How could you do this to me?" My voice. From the dream, the night he died.

Geraldine's eyes widened. The scene changed, the storm broke, and quiet descended, heavy and thick like a curtain covering a theater stage.

On the screen, the rest of the steps of the staircase stacked in descending order. Trevor appeared at the top.

"I'm done with you. I don't love you."

"No," I screamed as I lunged, hands outstretched, and shoved.

Trevor roared, his hands flailing as he tumbled backward down the sharp wooden stairs.

I couldn't watch as he catapulted down. Instead, I fixed my attention on Geraldine, all hope inside me dying as she clutched her hands to her chest, and her eyes widened in horror.

I turned back to the dream at the last moment, in time to watch Trevor land, bloody and unmoving, at the bottom of the staircase. I'd never forget the unnatural twist of his legs, as much as I wished I could.

The scene faded to black. The vortex shrank until, with a pop, it disappeared.

I couldn't breathe. I couldn't turn to look at my aunt. I had no words to explain the debacle we'd just witnessed. I gulped.

"Aisling," Geraldine said in a hushed voice.

I didn't want to, but I looked up.

My aunt's face was a white porcelain mask, her voice a hoarse whisper. "What did you do?"

The trip back to Geraldine's attic space was a blur, and I kept a tight grip on my aunt's hand, afraid she'd leave me behind. I needed to know the truth, but the dream we'd just witnessed was worse than I remembered, and I doubted there could be an explanation other than the one I feared.

When the fabric of the chair pressed into my legs, I opened my eyes to the leaping fire, smelled the earthy scent of peat, felt the wool of the blanket that was still covering my legs, and heard feet pacing the floor.

I watched my aunt circle her small attic space, and I dreaded when she turned around. When she noticed my open eyes, she stopped in front of my chair, one hand resting at her throat, the other folded over her stomach, as if protecting herself. From me.

"Aisling?" Her voice trembled. "Can you explain what we just saw?" Her wide eyes pleaded for assurances I couldn't give.

I gulped, my words dried up and stuck to my tongue. "It's…" I glanced away. "I …" I shook my head. I had no defense.

"You told me your husband fell down a staircase the night he died." Geraldine tapped her chest, taking a shaky breath. "You didn't tell me about your dream."

I heard the accusation in her tone. Anything I'd say now would sound like a justification. But I had to respond. "I dreamed what you saw on the night Trevor left." I was numb except for the pain in my heart. "The next day, he was dead."

We watched each other. I counted my racing heartbeats as I waited for her to say something. She didn't, not at first. She sat next to me, head in her hands, breathing heavily.

I was about to speak, when Geraldine raised her head. "You claimed not to understand dreaming." She looked at me, her eyes narrowed. "You said your mother didn't dream and didn't teach you anything." She paused. "And yet you killed your husband. How did you do it?"

Tears filled my eyes, but I fought against them. My pulse thundered in my ears, and I gulped in air and bowed my head. I wouldn't let her see my distress as the full import of her words slammed into me. Geraldine believed I'd killed Trevor. She'd confirmed my worst fears. I was a murderer. "I didn't mean to do it." My words came out as a hoarse whisper. "I don't know how it happened." She had to believe me. My actions weren't intentional.

"And, yet, he's dead." She swallowed. "I want to believe you, Aisling." Her doubtful eyes met mine. "But I don't know if I can. I don't know if I can trust you to save Lorcan."

I reeled at her words and clutched the arms of the chair. "So it's true. You're telling me I can kill someone in a dream?" I pushed the whispered words through stiff lips as I stared into the fire. I couldn't bear to see my aunt's face as she confirmed my guilt.

She took a moment to answer. "Centuries ago, dark Dreammasters used their powers for evil. Such practices were outlawed, and the methods aren't taught. As I understand, the dreams are complicated. I do not know how you would manage such a dream unless your mother taught you."

I looked back at her and frowned. "Mom didn't finish training before she left Ireland. She wouldn't even tell me about Dreammasters and my inherent powers. How could she have taught me to kill someone via a dream?"

Geraldine sighed. "You said you made things happen with your dreams." She watched me. "Did you want to kill Trevor or think about killing him before you went to sleep?"

Heat flushed my body, remembering the angry words I'd flung at Trevor before he left. I hadn't really wanted him dead, though. I stood. "I was angry. I told him I could murder him." I glanced over at Geraldine's sharp intake of breath. "But I didn't mean it. I didn't want him to die." I hurried on. "Trevor hurt me. He made me angry, but when he left the house, he was fine." I paced the room, gathering my thoughts. I turned toward her. "He was the father of my children. I wouldn't kill him, no matter how mad I was."

Geraldine paused, appearing to ponder my words. "Intention is key," she murmured under her breath. Her eyes focused on me. "You never intended to kill him, you say."

The tightness in my chest lightened, and I sat down on the edge of the chair. "No." I watched her. "You called me, remember? After he left. Did I sound like a woman contemplating murder?"

Geraldine took her time answering. "No." She paused. "No. You were distressed." She tilted her head. "You wanted to get away. To come here. Rather badly."

I closed my eyes, sighing. "I needed a break. I'd decided to come to Ireland, and then he announced his departure. My trip seemed like fate, a way for me to escape, to relax after Mom's death." I sat back. "I didn't know what saving Lorcan entailed, but I didn't care. As long as I wasn't at home. Alone." My lips trembled. "I want to stay and train. If you'll let me." I reached a tentative hand toward my aunt but pulled away at her frosty expression. "I have to be able to control my power. Or make it stop." I gulped. "Please. Help me."

Geraldine watched me, saying nothing. I bit my lip, holding the arms of the chair, praying she didn't send me away.

"We'll begin training tomorrow."

I closed my eyes as the tension drained from my shoulders. "Thank you. I'll work hard, I promise."

"You're on probation. For now."

My heart skipped a beat, but I nodded. "Okay. For how long?"

"For as long as it takes for me to investigate your dream and ensure you aren't a danger to Mother, myself, or Lorcan." Geraldine considered me, her brow furrowed. "For now, we'll keep your dream and the fact that we were here, in the attic, to ourselves."

"Oh." I paused. "Shouldn't we tell Granny?"

"We won't say anything to my mother." Her nostrils flared. "Is that clear?"

"Will you tell anyone else? As you investigate?" My hands trembled.

"There's no time before Samhain. But I'll be watching, Aisling. You'll stop training if I decide I can't trust you, or if your dream places anyone involved at risk."

"Okay," I said, biting my lower lip. "Sure. Whatever you say." Maybe it was best for now. The thought of anyone, especially Granny, learning about the dream made my insides clutch. And she had said not to visit the attic.

"There's no need to upset my mother. Yet."

"Or ever," I said, hopeful that would be the case. "You will help me find out what happened, won't you? You said intention was key. And I didn't intend to kill Trevor."

"We'll see." Geraldine folded her hands in her lap. "Although it seems unlikely, you could have killed your husband."

Hope flared in my heart. "Thank you, Aunt Geraldine."

"Not so fast." She held up her hand. "Keep your intentions pure as you train, Aisling, or I'll be forced to tell Mother, and the disciplinary tribunal, about your dream on the night your husband died."

I shrank back into my seat. "The tribunal?"

Geraldine assessed me. "Nothing you need to worry about yet." She nodded crisply. "Give me some time to investigate. Tomorrow, you'll commence training with Mother and me. You're our best hope of getting to Lorcan in the Underworld. But you have to do what I tell you, no questions. Agreed?"

"Okay." I nodded, a wave of relief spreading through my limbs, although the word *tribunal* echoed in my head.

"If only he'd died a few days later," she said softly. "If it turns out I can't trust you ..." She stopped, staring down at her hands. "Lorcan may well be lost."

Chapter Twenty-Nine

October 27

My heart pounded as I descended the stairs the following morning, my palms sweaty as I gripped the railing. I would be starting Dreammaster training today. What if I screwed up? What if I couldn't do this? Changing reality with my dreams was more responsibility than I was sure I wanted.

I reminded myself that Mom had done this. And she'd been just seventeen to my forty-five.

At the bottom of the staircase, I stopped, gathering myself. All I could do was my best. But then I remembered Fergus's hopeful green eyes. He was counting on me to save his uncle. My stomach clenched in a tight ball of rock. Fergus wasn't the concern here. My primary concern was to understand the scope and potency of my power, and then to learn to control it. Even the thought that I'd killed Trevor by accident was terrifying, and I didn't want Lorcan to end up dead as well.

"Nuala and Geraldine are in the sitting room." Maeve's voice, sharp and piercing, pulled me from my thoughts. "Your granny wanted to be by the fire, so I'm bringing in breakfast." She held a large tray. "You can bring the coffee. 'Tis in the kitchen by the machine." Without waiting for a reply, she turned away toward the sitting room.

The tray was where Maeve had said, and I picked it up and followed her down the hall.

"Aisling," Geraldine said from her seat across the room. "I trust you slept well." The expression in her eyes reminded me to stay quiet about the night before.

"I did, thanks." I settled the small tray on a low table. "How was the art opening?"

"Very nice, thank you." She sipped her tea.

"Good morning, child." Granny beamed at me from her perch in front of another earthy peat fire. "Pour us each a cup of coffee. Maeve refused to make it until you came down."

"'Tisn't good for you." Maeve said, her voice dark. She placed the large tray on the table in front of Granny and bustled from the room.

I watched her leave, wondering if it was just me she didn't like. Fergus had said she was a dragon. She was certainly fierce.

"Here you go," I said to Granny, handing her a cup.

I poured some for myself, added cream, and inhaled the deep smoky aroma before taking an appreciative sip. "Wonderful. This is exactly what I need to get going." I sat. And yawned, belying my words of earlier. Geraldine and I hadn't parted until past two in the morning. Once in bed, I'd tossed a bit before dropping off to sleep as I considered the ramifications of my culpability in the death of my husband and wondered what I'd say to our children.

"I thought you said you were well-rested, child," Granny said. "Training is strenuous work."

I took another sip of coffee as my mind searched for an answer. "I had trouble falling asleep."

She gave me a quizzical look, and I knew my answer was weak. Granny and I had both been dozing in front of the fire before heading upstairs the night before.

"I was up later than I'd intended to be," I added.

"Were you reading?" Granny asked, quirking an eyebrow. "You were dead on your feet when we came up."

"Really, Mother, why the interrogation? Aisling was up when I returned," Geraldine said, her tone exasperated. "I checked in on her, and we chatted." Geraldine smiled at me. "I explained the Dreammaster rules and the basics of how we operate."

Granny narrowed her eyes. "I see. I thought training would begin this morning."

Geraldine placed her teacup on the table beside her. "My overview was general. You're welcome to add anything you'd like, Mother."

Granny hmphed. "No. It's fine." She picked up a scone and buttered it. "Do you have questions, Aisling?"

I bit my lip, looking from Granny to her daughter, understanding now why Geraldine didn't want to mention details about the night before.

I shook my head. "Not now. But I probably will later."

"Excellent." Granny took a bite and swallowed. "Get some breakfast. Emer will be here soon, and we'll get started. She'll be assisting with your training."

"Emer?" My stomach lurched.

"Yes." Granny smiled. "You said you met her yesterday. At Tommy's."

Damn. "Right." I nodded, remembering the tiny woman and the dangerous glint in her eyes when she'd found me at Tommy's, sitting near to Fergus. The prospect of training, already alarming, dimmed a bit more.

"Perhaps Aisling should read the Dreammaster Pledge again." Granny finished her scone and wiped her hands on a napkin. "I doubt she recalls the exact wording after so long."

I glanced at Geraldine, who sighed, looking annoyed.

"She read the pledge last night, Mother."

Granny's eyebrows rose. "I see." She sipped her coffee, watching her daughter from over the rim of the cup. "So, you took the Ibormeith family book from my Dreaming space, Daughter." She paused, eyes beady. "Is there anything else you'd like to share?" She glanced at me. "Either of you?"

I bit my lower lip and looked at my aunt.

"You'd best confess now," Granny said, her tone ominous. "I suspect there's more you're not telling me. I've been a Dreammaster trainer for too long to misread the energetic signs." She pursed her lips as she watched us.

"Fine." Geraldine blew out a breath. "I showed Aisling my attic room. We read the pledge, discussed the basic tenets of our sisterhood, and then we went into Mary's dream."

Granny's face paled. "Why, Daughter? The dream? The attic? I told you not to go up there." She thumped her cane.

Geraldine's shoulders stiffened. "It's a room, Mother. And a good place for Aisling and me to work while she's here."

"We're to work together, the three of us." Granny set her mug on the table with a *thunk*. "Tell me about the dream." She looked at us, her eyes resting on me.

I shrugged. "It was what I saw before. But we weren't in the storm like I was. We only watched. Mom was there. With Lorcan."

"Did you see the attack on Mary?" Granny's voice caught, and she cleared her throat.

"No." Geraldine shook her head, glancing my way. "We exited the dream before the injury to Mary. I didn't think Aisling should witness it again."

I bowed my head. I wasn't about to tell Granny the real reason we exited the dream early.

"Nothing happened that will interfere with training, Mother," Geraldine said.

Granny looked at me, and her expression made me want to crawl under the table. "Was there anything more you wanted to share, Aisling?"

"No," I said, my voice cracking. I looked away, fumbling to pick up my coffee cup, almost choking on the bitter brew as it slid down my throat. I hated to lie.

Granny released a heavy breath. "You should eat, Aisling. You'll need your strength for today."

The doorbell chimed at nine, just as I forced down the last of my scone. Granny's disappointment was a haze shrouding the silent room, making it hard for me to breathe.

"It must be Emer," Geraldine said, putting down the pad of paper she'd been writing on.

"Are you ready, child?" Granny asked, her bony fingers fastened around the top of her cane. She'd spent the past several minutes staring into the fire.

"Yes," I said, my throat thick. "I think so." What I didn't add was how my palms were sweaty at the thought of more dreaming and the possibility that she and Emer might see what Geraldine had seen last night.

"Good morning, Nuala." Emer came into the room carrying a large satchel. Her short, shiny black hair glinted in the dancing light of the fire, resembling the iridescent feathers of the crows when the sun hit them. She even had a pointed chin, rather like a crow's beak, but it didn't detract from her petite prettiness. The thought made my brow furrow.

"Good morning, dear," Granny said, turning and holding out a hand to Emer, who squeezed Granny's fingers and bent to give her a hug.

"Gram sent along a new brand of coffee for you to try." Emer pulled a bag of beans from her satchel. "As Maeve doesn't approve, I'll sneak it into the kitchen later, avoid making her angry." She grinned at Granny, who beamed back at her. My stomach curled, and I looked at Geraldine, who watched the exchange with narrowed eyes.

"Hi, Geraldine," she said. "And Aisling." Emer turned, looked me up and down, and her lips twisted in a way that suggested the very sight of me was distasteful. "Oh, Fergus said to tell you hello." Her eyes shone as she spoke.

I clenched my teeth and plastered a smile on my face, ignoring the flicker of irritation that tightened my chest. "Good morning, Emer, and thanks for being willing to help me."

"It's good practice for me," Emer said as she tossed her bag and coat on the chair next to Granny and took a seat.

"Emer's working on her certification to train young Dreamkeepers to be Dreammasters." Granny spoke with pride, and I clenched my hands in my lap. This day was not starting out too well. "Muirgen, the leader of our sisterhood, is thrilled with her progress. She told me Emer is one of the best apprentices she's had."

Why did Granny's words bother me? Was it Emer's superior grin? Or the fact that I'd disappointed my grandmother, and I knew it? "That's wonderful."

"I'm enjoying the process," Emer said. "Being a trainer has always been my ambition. But, then, I've always embraced my heritage and wanted nothing more than to use my gift from Caer to help others."

I heard the snub, but still I smiled. "What a lofty goal." I'd had about enough of Emer's perfection, and the way Granny beamed at her. All of a sudden, I was glad I hadn't told Granny about the Trevor dream. My chest tightened as images of his fall flooded my mind. Trevor hadn't deserved to die. I hadn't wanted him to die. At least, I didn't think I had. I should have opened my mouth, spit out the words. My stomach churned at the thought of Granny's expression if I had.

"Here's your tea, Miss Emer." Maeve bustled into the room with a tray containing a teapot and a cup.

Miss Emer?

I almost snorted and glanced over in time to see Geraldine cover her mouth to hide a grin.

"Right," Granny thumped her cane, shifting my attention to her. "We should get started."

"I agree," Geraldine said. "I thought we could begin with connecting to the Otherworld this morning, beginning with a journey into the realm. Emer and I will accompany Aisling. I'll need to go into the office later, and I'd like to be with her on this first trip."

"Grand," Emer said, glancing at her phone. "I can't stay all day either. I have to be out of here by two. The band's playing at Milligan's pub tonight, and we've a practice at four. I'll need to pop home to change and grab my music."

"Perfect," Granny said. "I'll connect with you and join in the blessing, but I won't accompany you into the Mist. Three of you entering is enough. And I know Ailing will be in good hands." She reached over and gave my hand a squeeze. "You won't see me once we've begun, child, but I'll be watching. I'm sure you'll make excellent progress." She smiled at me. "Maybe you can even enter the Dreamscape before training is finished for the day. I'm certain you'll be an apt pupil."

I smiled, hardly daring to breathe, hoping Granny was right.

Geraldine focused on me. "We're going to start with entering the Mist."

"What's the Mist?" I asked, my voice breathy.

Geraldine explained. "The Mist is the place where all dreams begin and where normal dreams occur—the surreal place between reality as you know it and the land of the subconscious you experience when you sleep. Most people don't remember their dreams, but all dreams exist in the Mist. Dreammasters can go deeper. We have an extra level of subconscious that allows us to go past the Mist and into a place we call the Dreamscape. But in order to enter the Dreamscape, we must begin in the Mist."

"What do I do?" My belly fluttered.

"Before we can head into the Mist, we'll ask Caer to bless all we are about to do," Geraldine said. "Listen closely. It's important you remember the process. You won't be able to refer to a manual when you're dreaming for a client."

"Okay." My swan pendant started to heat, the vibrations helping to relax me.

"To begin, close your eyes."

I looked over at Granny, who winked at me before closing her eyes. I followed her lead.

Geraldine spoke, and I repeated the words in my head.

"As we enter into the Mist
And venture into our dreaming realm,
Please bless this dream, dear mother Caer
May we do only good and cause harm to none."

My swan pendant palpitated against my chest like a second heartbeat, and tingles spread through my body.

"I will now set a sphere of protection to safeguard our practice and shield us from any outside influences or malign entities intent upon doing harm. You might feel the energy as it surrounds you."

Geraldine hummed softly, the low melody reminiscent of the music from the night before. I saw Geraldine, Granny, Emer, and myself behind my closed lids, arranged as we'd been in our chairs. As I watched, a midnight-blue field of energy flowed from Geraldine's palms and cocooned us.

Deep purple flared from Emer and mingled with ruby-red sparks from Granny to mix with Geraldine's energy. I watched transfixed until I realized I was emitting flickers of emerald green.

"Well done, Aisling." Geraldine's voice flowed over me. "You already have a powerful energy field." She paused. "Now, we'll center our energy and use our breath to enter the Mist. Begin by focusing on bringing your breath into your belly. You must start by relaxing, making your exhales longer than your inhales."

I brought my attention to the center of my body, feeling the emerald power coiling in my belly as my breathing slowed.

"Imagine you're heading to sleep and allow your body to release deeply into the experience." Geraldine's voice was soothing, and I focused solely on her words.

"Very good. Now bring that power up into the center of your heart, allow it to circle there until you feel ready, and then send it into the center of your head."

As I followed her instructions, I soon became aware of something nudging the edge of my mind. I wanted to grab at it before it slipped away, afraid of missing whatever was waiting for me. But the more I tried, the further away it seemed.

"Continue to relax, Aisling, as we take the three breaths that will deliver us into the Mist." Her voice was low and rhythmic. "Breath one, surround and connect us." As Geraldine spoke, a golden band of light drew our energies together, connecting the four of us.

"Breath two, guide and protect us." A field of pink light shrouded us, creating a shimmering veil, and I felt as if my spirit lifted from my body.

"Breath three, gently release us into the world of dreams."

As Geraldine uttered the final words, the elusive something my mind had been chasing became clear, and I found myself standing by a pool in a forest. Glittering mist swirled around me, so thick I didn't see Geraldine and Emer.

"Geraldine." I called into the mist. "Emer." Neither answered.

I should have been worried. But I wasn't. I was caught up in the beauty, absorbed into the peaceful strangeness of this place. My swan pendant continued its familiar thrum, and the emerald energy I'd witnessed before circled me protectively.

Brightly colored creatures, tiny beings with transparent wings, zipped through the sparkling air, chattering among themselves as they twisted around me, circling through the tree branches, zooming into the never-ending cerulean sky above.

I wished I could fly with them, and as I wished, my feet lifted from the ground. I spread my arms, allowing the air to carry me over the world below.

The landscape was a gardener's vision: the leaves on the trees were profuse, the shrubs and bushes were deep green and abundant, and the plentiful flowers were vibrant, painted in fuchsia, red, and yellow.

One of the wee creatures buzzed closer, circling my head, and I recognized she was a tiny fairy with flaming hair and sparkling eyes like I'd seen in old books my mother had read me. She smiled, then flew off, beckoning for me to follow.

I did, but she was faster and disappeared. Alone, I floated above the river, twisting from my back to my front, laughing when a small red-feathered bird settled on my belly.

I stretched and soared upward, as light as a breeze, turning somersaults like I was a child again. I hadn't played in too long, and I didn't want the fun to end.

"Very good, Aisling." Emer joined me. "This is the Mist, where we all have dreams."

A part of my mind registered Emer and her words and the fact that she'd disrupted my fun. Pinpricks of irritation flickered throughout my body.

"This is a dream, then? Not real." I realized as the words formed that they weren't coming from my mouth but seemed to flow from my mind directly into Emer's.

"It's a dream," she said. "And yet not a dream because we've entered with intention." She giggled, surprising me as she looped around me.

"Sort of like lucid dreaming?" I asked.

"Right. The extra layer in a Dreammaster's brain allows us to dream in a different way. If this were a normal dream, whatever was on your mind before sleep would play out in your subconscious. And you might or might not remember it in the morning. After our training, you'll remember everything. Just as you will after you dream for a client."

I couldn't imagine having clients. Right now, arriving in the Mist was enough.

"No one else sees my dreams in the Mist, right?"

"No. Your dreams are yours alone. I'm only with you now because we came in with the intention of working together. Geraldine is waiting for us."

As she spoke, a formation of fairies swooped around us like an undulating river of color.

"So, can you see the fairies?" I said, shooting her a sidelong glance.

She smiled. "Yes. The fairies aren't part of your dream or my dream. They're here to greet us."

"I've never seen fairies in my dreams."

"Now that they know you, you'll see them again. The fairies live in the Otherworld, which is just beyond the moonbeams." She pointed, and I followed her finger. On the horizon was a half-circle of opalescent orange radiance shooting beams of light toward us.

"Oh." The word escaped like a slow sigh from my lips. "It's beautiful."

"Yes. But it's more than you can see or even imagine. The Otherworld is beyond the borders of your thinking, human mind." She zipped ahead, mingling with the tiny creatures. I followed easily.

"We can't go there, then?" I asked.

"You're kin to the fairy world, Aisling. You're connected to the fairies through our ancestor, Caer. The goddess is part of the supernatural tribe of beings known as the Tuatha Dé Danann—or the Tuatha Dé. As such, she is part of the Otherworld, and so are we. When we enter into the Dreamscape, we're in the Otherworld."

"Will the fairies be there too?" Now we were soaring with the fairies, following the beat of their intoxicating song, dipping and rising as free as the crows glided from rooftop to treetop to ground and back in Granny's garden.

"The Dreamscape is reserved for the descendants of Caer." She turned to watch me for a moment, smiling. "It's a beautiful place. A wonderful, magical landscape where we can dream with the dreamers who request our help." She spiraled upward, beckoning to me to follow.

"As I said, your dreams are yours alone. Only if you expressly wish to share a dream could another person witness it. Which is usually only in cases of disciplinary matters brought before the Aislingeach Tribunal."

The Mist was cool suddenly, the haze heavier. The joyful sound of the fairies dimmed as I considered what Emer had said. I hadn't wanted to share my dream of Trevor, yet Geraldine had seen it. Had some part of me wanted to show her? But I'd fought so hard to keep the dream from her. Or had allowing Geraldine to witness the dream when Mom died also conferred permission to my aunt to view the dream of Trevor's death? That was the only reason that made sense, if I believed Emer.

"Aisling?" Emer's voice called to me, and I hurried to catch up to where she waited. The fairies had gone on ahead; the end of the swarm was barely visible. "Come on."

I was overthinking things. I'd ask Geraldine later. Or not.

"Coming," I called, and my body took off.

I reached Emer's side and paused, hanging in midair. "Am I moving, or is my mind making it happen?"

She laughed. "It's amazing, isn't it? Our minds are very powerful, more powerful than we realize. As a Dreammaster, you'll use your mind in ways you've never imagined."

She touched my arm. "We're almost there. Come on."

"Where are we going?" I called after her.

"Because you're doing so well, we're heading on into the Dreamscape."

"Wait a minute." I wasn't ready to go further. The Mist was wonderful, but the next step required something deeper, something I was scared I couldn't achieve.

"You'll be grand, Aisling. Trust in yourself."

Emer landed next to Geraldine, who waited on a small beach. I touched down next to them.

"You've done well, Aisling." Geraldine smiled, her face alight. "How do you like the Mist?"

"It's amazing." I looked around the barren strip of land where we stood. "What's this place?"

"This is the entrance to the Dreamscape." Geraldine opened her arms as if to embrace all the scene before us. "Only Dreammasters can leave the Mist and enter this part of the Otherworld. The dreaming realm. From this place, a deeper form of dreaming is possible."

No tree, shrub, flower, or blade of grass decorated the landscape. My shoulders slumped as I took in the desolate view. "But there's nothing here."

"Not yet." Her eyes sparkled. "But there will be."

CHAPTER THIRTY

My heart thumped in my chest. "What does that mean?"

"One step at a time, Aisling." Geraldine said. "First, I want you to practice the Aislingeach invocation I recited earlier. This will make the dream yours and allow you to set the Dreamscape."

"I still don't understand," I said, looking from one to the other.

"Trust us," Emer said, her eyes glowing. "It's amazing."

"Repeat after me," Geraldine said, and she began.

"As we enter into the Mist
And venture into our dreaming realm,
Please bless this dream, dear mother Caer
May we do only good and cause harm to none."

I repeated the words, surprised at the power surging throughout my body.

"There's one more piece to the process," Emer said. "Raise your hands, palms toward the Dreamscape." Emer demonstrated, and I did as she asked. "If you were going to dream for yourself, what would that dream look like?"

I bit my lips. "I don't know."

Geraldine took over. "What represents a safe, welcoming place for you to find the answers or changes needed in your life? And remember, today we are learning and practicing, so this place, this dream scene, is yours. When you work with clients, their needs set the scene."

I closed my eyes and considered her queries. Nowhere felt safe to me right now. Maybe in my garden, surrounded by my herbs and flowers. But no. Home wasn't comforting, not after Trevor's death.

The tip of my right index finger throbbed where the swan had pecked it, and I pressed it with my thumb. Why did it hurt?

"Excellent, you've chosen well." Geraldine's voice was approving.

"What?" I hadn't decided anything. My eyes snapped open, and I gasped. Granny's garden spread before us. Granny's garden was peaceful, but I hadn't considered it.

I gulped. "I didn't do that." The pain in my finger intensified. I increased the pressure from my thumb, trying to ignore the burning sensation.

"You did." Excitement brimmed from Emer's wide eyes. "And quickly too." She touched my arm. "Shall we go inside?"

"No." I shook my head, taking a step back. "This is wrong. I considered my garden at home, not Granny's."

Emer looked from me to Geraldine.

"Aisling?" My aunt watched me with narrowed eyes, and her voice had a note of warning in it, as if I'd said something wrong.

I bit my lip, unsure of what to say. But what happened didn't make sense. "If I was supposed to imagine this before it appeared, I didn't."

Geraldine's lips twisted as she considered me. "You spent time in Mother's garden yesterday after an emotional morning."

Emer frowned.

I didn't want to explain, but it wasn't fair to Emer. "I learned about Lorcan."

"Ah." She nodded.

Geraldine continued. "You also sat on Mother's bench, an object soaked in her energy and forged from the magic of my father's skill as a woodworker."

This tallied with what Tommy had told me, but it didn't explain the scene before us. "What does that have to do with this?" I swept my arm in front of me.

"The bench is a haven, a place of security, as Father designed it to be. I believe you absorbed the peace of the place, and it is now re-created in your Dreamscape."

I was about to object again, but pain shot along my arm, causing me to sway. As I opened my mouth to ask Geraldine what was happening, the pain intensified, and I doubled over.

"Aisling, are you okay?" Emer grabbed my arm. "What's wrong?"

"Sorry," I said, taking deep breaths. My pendant burned as hot as my finger stung, but the energy was different, almost like a warning. "I was dizzy." I slowly stood, the pain in my finger lessening. "I'm better."

Geraldine watched me but asked nothing. I'd speak to her later.

"Aisling?" Emer was watching me, frowning.

"I'm fine." I smiled through the residual pain, nodding until Emer's concern faded.

"Coming into the Dreamscape for the first time is an adjustment," Geraldine said. She patted my back, her smile encouraging. "You've taken to dreaming like you've been at it for years. Be glad it's been easy and don't fret."

Did Geraldine's words have a double meaning? Did she still have doubts, even suspect I knew more about dreaming than I'd admitted? I choked back my questions and fears, knowing I'd have to wait until later for answers.

I touched my stomach to quell the internal flutters, noting the pain in my finger had subsided. Clearing my throat, I shrugged back my shoulders. "I'm ready. Let's go."

I followed Emer and Geraldine from the beach into the garden at Old Oak Manor. The scene was beautiful, filled with flowers and trees and even buzzing, circling insects. I sniffed and scrunched my nose. I didn't smell anything.

Emer and Geraldine led me past the bench under the oak tree and into the middle of the garden.

"Brilliant," Emer said when I'd joined her. She turned in a circle, her arms outspread. "You've captured every detail of Nuala's garden."

"I don't understand how I created any of this."

"Your mind created it." Emer's voice insisted I believe.

"Right." I rubbed my forehead. Her eyes narrowed as she watched me. "I guess I'm nervous."

Emer chuckled. "Of course you are. You're just not used to doing this. But you're brilliant. This garden is grand." She patted my arm, smiling. "After a few more practice runs, it'll feel natural."

"Relax, Aisling," Geraldine said. "Your progress is remarkable."

"But nerves are normal," Emer added. She began to walk, and I followed. "Right now, we're here in your Dreamscape via our minds. The process is similar to a dream but with elements of a deep meditation. You can work for clients from this place, but your work becomes easier, seamless, when you enter into your Dreamscape in your full body. When you're ready, and you're here fully in your body, it changes how you interact with the scene and your client. Your connection with your client will be deeper. And you'll be able to feel the essence of everything you've created." She swept her hands around the garden.

"I feel the grass." I took a half step, watching the grass sink beneath my foot. "It's springy."

"Can you really feel it, though?" Her eyebrows rose. "You believe you feel it, and so you do. What we can achieve as Dreammasters is incredible, even without entering bodily into the Dreamscape, but although you feel the touch of the grass, it's a sensory detail created and living in your imagination. When you enter bodily, it's a novel experience altogether." Her tone grew serious. "You entered the Underworld in your corporeal body. Did it feel as this feels?"

I took a moment to think back to the dream with my mother. "No." I shuddered at the memory. "That was frightening. The stones were rough. I was wet when I awoke, and there was dirt on my feet."

"Exactly." Geraldine took the lead, and we strolled after her. "Can you sense the difference now?"

"I think so." I bent to touch the grass, which looked soft and damp like it always did in Granny's garden. My fingers seemed to touch the blades, and I felt a tickle on the tips, but there was no wetness when I pulled away. "It's different." I rose. "I don't smell anything either."

"Yes, well done," Geraldine said. "Being here in our dreamvision is more like a regular dream in the Mist, although we can still work for our dreaming clients. But it's better to dream in your full body when you work as a Dreammaster."

"We could work on that tomorrow," Emer said, her eyes shining.

My insides churned. What if the Trevor dream appeared again? "I don't want to go too fast." The words spluttered from my lips.

Geraldine and Emer turned in unison to watch me.

I wrapped my arms around my middle. "It's just a lot to take in."

Geraldine nodded, considering. "It may be too soon." She pursed her lips. "I can't work with Aisling all day tomorrow. I have vital business meetings I must attend at Milligan's in the afternoon. Mel needs me in the office."

Emer scowled. "We'll run out of time." She fisted her hands on her hips. "I can guide Aisling. Check with Muirgen if you're unsure. I'm certain she'll vouch for me."

"I should be here," Geraldine said, her voice hardening.

"That's silly, Geraldine. I'm qualified."

My eyes darted from one woman to the other as their debate continued. All I heard was blood rushing through my veins. I wasn't ready. I couldn't do this. They shouldn't trust me to save Lorcan.

I looked around, astounded, at the garden spread before me. The Dreamscape was magical, but I didn't think I was part of that magic. I hadn't created this scene. But if I hadn't, who had?

As my thoughts whirled, my eyes focused on my aunt. Had Geraldine helped me out in some way? Pain pounded in my fingertip at my thoughts, and I gasped, doubling over and grabbing my right hand in my left. This pain was another thing I didn't understand.

"Are you okay, Aisling?" Emer's eyes widened, and she bent toward me, rubbing my back. "What's happened?"

I bit back another gasp and stood, pressing my thumb into the tip of my index finger. "A swan pecked my finger yesterday, and—" Before I could continue, Geraldine hurriedly broke in.

"She reached toward a swan on the riverbank yesterday as she walked to the house." She gave me a warning look as she inspected my pulsing fingertip. "But it will heal." She patted my hand. "If the wound isn't better tomorrow, we'll call Dr. Higgins."

I was confused. Why couldn't I tell Emer what had really occurred? She would understand about the book. She was a Dreammaster too. But Geraldine's slight shake of her head made me keep my mouth closed.

Emer watched us, her eyes disappearing behind her frown. I hesitated for a moment longer before acquiescing to Geraldine. For now.

"It was a silly thing to do. They're just such magnificent birds." I tugged my hand free. "Maybe I should see the doctor." I didn't add that I wanted another opinion. Geraldine might not know what her grandmother had done to the book. Maybe the swan was dangerous. "The pain comes and goes."

"Another reason to wait until I can be with you when you enter fully into the Dreamscape." Geraldine looked down her nose at Emer, her eyes challenging the younger woman to argue.

Emer looked as if she was about to protest, when the garden began to vibrate, tossing the three of us to the ground.

"What's happening?" I said, pushing to my knees and swaying as a wave of dizziness swept over me.

"I don't know." Emer's eyes were wide, her pale face now pasty. "This has never happened before."

Her words stopped my breath. What was going on? Had I caused this?

"Where's Geraldine?" Emer's voice broke through my thoughts.

I searched beside me where Geraldine had been standing, but my aunt wasn't there. She'd fallen with us. So where was she now?

"Geraldine," I called, my voice lost in the rumbling. "I don't see her. We need to get up." I knew the shaking would knock me back to my knees, and I crawled toward the bench for support. "Come on, Emer."

At the bench, I pulled myself upright and extended a hand to Emer, who'd followed. Hanging on to the back of the bench, we searched for my aunt.

"She could be injured," I said. "We need to get her and get out of here."

"I agree," Emer panted. "But where is she?"

Before we could move, the trembling Dreamscape pulled us into a dream. Emer gripped my hand as the sitting room in Granny's house materialized, replacing the garden. The bench disappeared, and we clutched at each other to stay upright, taking in the scene before us. Clearly, neither of us had conjured this.

Granny sat slumped in her chair, her arms dangling, her face slack.

"Granny," I screamed, fear a band of ice around my chest. "Can you see that?" I yelled at Emer, my body ice cold. "What's happening?"

Sweat beaded on Emer's brow as her chest rose and fell with each rapid breath. "Something infiltrated our dream. But I don't know how." Her voice shook. "Geraldine set protections. I don't understand." Her eyes darted to me. "We have to get back to Nuala. Follow me."

But before we could move, a blanket of darkness spread over Granny. "We don't have time to get back," I hollered. "We have to stop that, whatever it is."

I was hollering at her, hoping to get her to move. "Emer." But her eyes were pressed closed, and when I yelled her name again, she didn't respond. Or couldn't. I'd seen this before, but not in a dream. At my house, on the morning after Trevor died. Beverly had been rooted, unable to see me or respond. Until I cleared away the shadows in front of my house. Now it had happened to Emer. I was on my own.

I had to help Granny. But, first, I had to calm down. I took a deep breath, tuning in to the pulsing of my pendant and allowing the emerald energy I'd conjured earlier to flow from my belly up through my heart and into my hands. At the touch of my power, pain stabbed my index finger. I exhaled with force, determined to ignore the pain.

Raising my hands, I sent a stream of glowing green toward the dark wall ensnaring Granny. Rather than dissipate, the fog deepened to inky black and swept from Granny toward me, knocking my hands to my sides.

I struggled to remain standing as the energy buffeted Emer and me. Emer swayed and fell, her eyes rolling back in her head, and I bit back a scream. I couldn't help her and save Granny. One step at a time.

I was fighting a foe I didn't understand. The pain in my finger intensified. Despite the pain, I raised my shaking hands again, biting back a scream when my entire arm seared as if on fire. The opposing energy was powerful, nearly tumbling me to the ground. I held firm, searching for Granny in the gloom.

Something growled deep within the blackness. I yelled, cursing the swirling black, and pushed with my mind until rays of deep green surged from my hands, thrusting against the merciless gloom. Even when nothing seemed to change, I kept going, watching as the green vanished into the dark, until a crack appeared.

"Yes," I hollered, as the bones in my arms rattled. "Go away." I held on even when my finger swelled up, thundercloud purple, threatening to burst. I wanted to close my eyes, sink to the ground, cradle my right hand. I wanted the pain to stop. But I wanted to save Granny more.

When I was ready to collapse, certain I was losing, the reach of my green light widened. I held on, watching as my emerald force encompassed Granny, colliding with the black haze around her. A flare of light exploded, and my breath caught in my throat. Had I killed my grandmother in some kind of mind-induced explosion?

When the spark settled, I could see that the blackness had dissipated, the garden of my dream vision was back, and Granny was stirring.

Emer shifted next to me, pulling herself to her knees as the Dreamscape returned to Granny's garden. I reached out to help her up.

"Nuala?" she said, her breath ragged.

"I think she's okay." I was panting, struggling to catch my breath. "I used my energy. She moved. We need to get back." My words were choppy.

"Geraldine?" Emer gasped. "We have to find her."

"I'm here." Geraldine's raspy voice drifted to us, and I looked toward the far wall of the garden, spying my aunt curled next to a rosebush. "Aisling." She reached out a trembling hand.

"Hold on, Geraldine." I scrambled to her, offering her a hand and hauling her to her feet. "What happened?"

"Don't know," she said, her face blotchy, her breath catching in her throat. "I must have lost consciousness." She blinked rapidly, her fingers tapping against her chest. "It was like the dream. All those years ago. The dream with your mother."

I frowned. "We weren't in the Underworld, though."

She shook her head. "I don't understand."

"It doesn't matter," Emer said. "Let's get out of here."

Geraldine and I followed Emer as she led the way from the Dreamscape, closing the portal into the realm with another verse.

"As we leave the Dreamscape,
Having completed our dream
We thank the goddess Caer
And the realm of the Otherworld.
May all we achieve as Dreammasters
Fulfill and subscribe to the tenets of the Aislingeach Sisterhood."

I repeated the words to myself. Back in the Mist, we rushed to the river and followed it. My rasping breath was like sandpaper against my throat as I imagined Granny injured—or worse. Finally, we were back at the glade surrounding the pool of water where we'd started.

"Close your eyes and take slow breaths like you did as we began," Emer said. Her voice shook. "See yourself back where you began, your body in the chair in the sitting room at Old Oak Manor." She paused, and I did as she'd instructed.

"We'll take three breaths as we leave. Repeat what I say, and once you feel your body solid and present in the room, open your eyes. I'll meet you both there."

"Breath one, surround and connect us." As I repeated the words, golden cords of power extended to touch Emer, Geraldine, and me, connecting us to the human realm and our starting point.

"Breath two, return and protect us." With my second breath, the force field of shimmering pink light enveloped us once again and lifted us from the Mist realm.

"Breath three, gently release us into the world of human beings." As I uttered the final words, my body released onto the soft sofa, where I'd started this adventure, and I opened my eyes.

"Granny." I stood, wobbling as my body reoriented back to the human world. My finger still ached, and I glanced at the tip. The purple puffiness was reversing, slowly returning to normal.

"Aisling." Granny mumbled, her voice slurred. "All wrong. Take care." She touched my arm with icy fingers. "Your power." She sighed, as if the words were too much. "Saved me." She rested her head against the back of her chair.

Geraldine hurried to her mother's side. Emer hung over the back of a chair, her face chalky, her eyes fever bright.

Geraldine searched her mother's face. "Mother, can you speak to me?"

"Why?" Granny gasped, clutching Geraldine's hand, her eyes wide in her pale face. "Why, Daughter?" A tear slipped down Granny's cheek.

Geraldine looked up, her face flushed and her voice frantic. "We need Dr. Higgins."

"I'm on it," Emer said, grabbing her phone from the table where she'd left it.

"Aisling," Geraldine said, "get Maeve. Tell her Mother's ill."

I nodded and ran to the kitchen, flinging myself through the door as I called out.

"Maeve, we need you. Granny isn't well." I clung to the doorframe, afraid my knees might buckle. Maeve's eyes widened, her face paled, and she rushed past me without a word. I bent my head, struggling to catch my breath.

"Aisling," Tommy said next to me, and my head snapped up. I hadn't seen him in the room. "What happened?" His voice was gentle.

"We were training. In the Dreamscape." I paused for breath. "A black cloud encircled Granny. Geraldine lost consciousness. Emer couldn't move." I choked on my shaky breath. "I had to fight it off." My eyes filled with tears, and the horror of what happened flooded my system. "I have a power. It's emerald green, and it broke through." I blinked up at him. "I don't understand it all." I pushed from the door. "I need to see if Granny's better. She was dizzy."

"I'll come with you." Tommy followed me to the sitting room. "How is she, Maeve?" His calm voice flowed over the room.

Maeve was patting Granny's cheeks, and Emer was on the phone. Granny's housekeeper looked over at us.

"She's awake but very weak." Maeve pierced me with a stare. "She says you saved her."

I nodded, biting my lips. "I guess so. But I don't really know how."

"Doesn't matter how. As long as Nuala's well." It wasn't a thanks, but she didn't look angry at me either. I released the breath I'd been holding.

Emer disconnected from her phone. "Dr. Higgins is on his way."

Chapter Thirty-One

"I should be with Granny." Seated in Tommy's kitchen, I fidgeted with the handle of my coffee cup. I knew I was whining. At least a bit. I'd allowed him to drag me to his house after Dr. Higgins had given Granny the all-clear. Geraldine had assured me Dr. Higgins knew all about Dreammasters and was well able to care for Granny. She'd encouraged me to go with Tommy. But leaving felt wrong, as if I'd deserted my grandmother.

Tommy turned from where he was standing at the sink and faced me, crossing his arms over his chest, his eyes zeroing in on mine and holding them. "Nuala needs rest. Maeve will keep watch and call if something changes. There's nothing you could do at Old Oak Manor besides get in Maeve's way." He smiled. "We both know that wouldn't help anything."

I sighed, the force of my exhale lifting the hair off my forehead. "I have questions, and I need answers." Pushing back from the table, I stood and paced the room. "What happened in the Dreamscape? What if it happens again?" *What if it was my fault?* I couldn't voice the last question, however—not until Geraldine had time to speak to me. When I'd tried to talk to her about it, she'd brushed me off and hustled to work for an afternoon meeting. I had no idea when she'd return. I stopped across the island from Tommy. "I appreciate you taking care of me, but you can't answer my questions, and even if you could, Geraldine wouldn't want you to."

A frown crossed Tommy's face at the mention of Geraldine's name. It was gone as quickly as it appeared. He leaned against the counter and watched me a moment longer. I sensed he was weighing his words. I hoped he'd offer insight or clarity regarding my grandmother, despite Geraldine's admonition to speak only to her. But he offered nothing but banalities.

"Why don't we go out back? I can show you my woodshop. We could sit in the garden while the sun's shining, enjoy a beer or a glass of wine, and let nature soothe your nerves."

I wanted to slam my hand on the wooden surface of the island. "I don't want to escape into an afternoon of drinking." Part of me wanted to scream. Why was Tommy so calm? Didn't he understand that something had been gunning for Granny in the Dreamscape?

His eyes narrowed, and his voice deepened. "I understand the danger your grandmother faced."

My body froze, limbs rigid. "How did you know what I was thinking?"

Tommy bent his head a moment before looking back at me, his expression inscrutable. "'Tis one of my gifts. I can intuit the emotions and thoughts of others. Rather like the way you have an energy that supports you and helped you to save your granny." Tommy paused, as if waiting for me to question his power. I nodded, needing no further clarification. Beverly believed in the empathic ability to read another's emotions. Tommy smiled and continued. "I also have a deep connection to the earth. I know you like gardening, and my small patch of soil is rather special for many reasons." His eyes sparkled, and his tone hinted at mystery. I followed him despite myself.

Tommy led the way through a double sliding door and into a glassed-in conservatory. "I had this added to the house a few years ago. Even when it rains, I can always feel as if I'm outside."

A rattan couch and two matching chairs circled a glass-topped table. The couches were upholstered in a calming ivory with silk throw pillows for added support and comfort. A matching rattan ottoman sat in front of the chair nearest a circular wood stove, and I imagined Tommy sitting here on a rainy afternoon or evening, his legs propped up, fire crackling, book in hand.

"It's beautiful." My shoulders relaxed despite myself as the fire in my belly calmed. I took a breath and walked to a window, gazing out into his rear garden. The afternoon light was fading, wrapping the outside world in gentle purple hues. "And that's your woodshop." I nodded at the white-painted building with large windows at the end of the driveway.

"Aye, it is. Your grandfather and I converted it from a garage to a shop years ago." He paused. "I've filled it since then with all the tools of my trade." He headed for the door onto a slate patio. "I'll show you the inside." Tommy left the conservatory, and I followed.

The late-afternoon sun wasn't as warm as it had been when I followed him up the street, and I wished I'd brought my jacket out with me. A round table and four chairs sat to the side of the patio, next to a covered grill. Round planters sat at the four corners of the slate, most of the spring flowers now dormant, although a few hardy blooms remained. Several raised beds filled a majority of the backyard, the faint scent of mint, coriander, and dill mixing with the smell of the sea.

"What do you have in the beds besides the herbs?"

"Ah, well, I've got winter squash coming into its own, as well as parsnips and beets." He talked as he walked. "The herbs are near to done for the season, but I still get a few clippings for cooking. I've potted my favorites to use over the winter. You'll see them in the woodshop, along with hot peppers."

I cocked my head, and he chuckled. "I make a potent arthritis cream, and I need a supply of fresh, organic chili peppers."

"You'll have to teach me your recipe. I love compounding ointments with herbs."

"I'd be pleased to, lass."

Tommy stopped at a double-paned glass door and withdrew a shiny golden key from his pocket. He ushered me inside and followed. Sawdust hit my nose as soon as I stepped in, and I fought the urge to sneeze. He was correct. Tools filled the space. As did a row of herbs and the aforementioned hot peppers, their shiny red skin a pop of color among the green of the herbs lining a bench beneath a wide window.

"You'll have to tell me what's here," I said. "I know almost nothing about woodworking."

Tommy cleared his throat. "My first purchase was the bandsaw, just there." He led me to a tall, narrow stand with a long, sharp blade extended from the top down to a metal plate. "After that, I added this table saw"—he moved on— "and these planes for smoothing the wood. Nuala and Gerard gave me this set of chisels." He picked up a sharp instrument from a workbench. "And Gerard helped me install the shelves in the back there, where I keep various types of wood. I can't pass up an exotic sample when I come across one." He walked to the shelves lining the back wall of the workshop, running his hand along a pale wood. "This is ash. 'Tis what Fergus and I used today to form the rim for his bodhran."

Fluttery sensations circled in my belly at the mention of Fergus. I pretended they weren't there.

Tommy picked up a mold with a section of ash formed and clamped around it. "We made good progress. Once this sets, we'll glue two dowels in the shape of a cross in the back so Fergus can easily hold the drum. After, we'll stretch the goat skin over the top."

Being out here with Tommy was soothing, although I couldn't explain why, as was the smell of the sawdust and the way the sun picked up the dust motes that floated in the air. "I hope you're done before I leave. I'd love to see it finished and hear Fergus play."

"You may well be able to," he said. "I want to check how this is drying. Give me a minute, and we can sit outside."

I nodded, and as he scrutinized his handiwork, I meandered between the saws and other equipment. Shelves along another wall held projects Tommy had completed, and I walked closer to see what he'd done. A row of intricately carved ornaments, some small enough to wear as a necklace, caught my eye, and I leaned in, intrigued by the spiral designs and the way the oiled wood glowed, as if alive from within. I gently touched one, feeling the heartbeat of the wood pulse into my fingertip and send a thrum of heat up my arm. My swan pendant throbbed in time. I pulled away slowly, my breath caught in my chest. A rustle behind me made me jump and turn. Tommy stood there, watching me, a mysterious, shadowy look in his eyes.

"These are beautiful," I said with a hard swallow, hoping I hadn't offended him by touching.

"Aye," he said in a soft voice. "Celtic knots are beautiful. They have no beginning or end but loop back to where they started. Because of the never-ending nature of Celtic symbols, they're said to represent eternity."

"What's this one?" I pointed at the one I'd touched, an intricate knot with four equal sides. "It's almost like a four-leaf clover but more detailed."

"This is the Dara knot. Dara comes from the word *doire*, which means 'oak tree.' The oak is strong and long-lived and has deep roots. Because of this, the Dara knot is a symbol of strength, including inner strength. Keeping the symbol close can help to focus and enhance our own innate tendencies." He paused, watching me. "You're more than welcome to take it, lass."

I glanced at Tommy, and when he nodded, I picked up the carving and traced the intertwined lines as warmth flooded into my fingers. "It's warm, like it's been sitting in the sun all day." I looked up to find him watching, his expression alert. I wasn't sure if I should continue. "I'm imagining it, I know." I looked back at the carved wood. "It's beautiful, Tommy." I paused. "Thank you."

"You're welcome, lass." He handed me a length of black leather. "You can wear it around your neck if you'd like. Or keep it close by to soak up the energy of the knot." Tommy took a breath. "Don't discount what your senses tell you, Aisling. Even if what you feel seems unusual." He took my arm. "Remember what we discussed yesterday. There is magic. You only have to believe."

"Magic," I whispered. It explained what I'd felt. "You make magical things, then?" I looked from him to the Celtic knot resting in my hand.

Tommy grinned. "Woodworking is a magic unto itself." He reached past me to pick up a short, dark wooden stick with a rounded end. It was varnished to a high gloss. "Shillelaghs are one of my favorite pieces to create. Blackthorn wood. Sturdy and strong. They make excellent weapons. Longer ones are good for use as walking sticks." He ran a hand down the stick, and the wood seemed to glow as he touched it. "Beauty and power combined, with a little of my own personal magic sprinkled in. For good measure."

"I saw a brass tub of them in your vestibule." I gulped, wondering if I dared touch the wood. I kept my hands at my sides, the wooden Dara knot still warm in my clutched palm.

"I always keep them nearby." He winked and replaced the shillelagh. "Come into the garden with me. I have warm blankets for our legs now that the sunlight is dimming. I'd like a glass of our famous Irish beer, and I'll bet you've not tried it yet."

"I'm not really a beer drinker," I said, following him.

"An Irish lass who doesn't like beer." He teased me and I shrugged. "No matter at all. I've got wine and whiskey as well."

"Maybe," I said, feeling my resistance ebb away. It was late afternoon, closer to evening. Training was over for the day. And Maeve would call if Granny was in danger. "Maybe just a glass."

Tommy chuckled. He grabbed two cushions from a storage closet by the door, handed me two blankets, and gestured for me to precede him out. Tommy turned off the lights and locked the door. "'Tis time to relax after the stress of the day, and I'd appreciate the company."

CHAPTER THIRTY-TWO

Tommy

"**S**ettle into a seat, lass, and cover up with the blanket. I'll fetch a sweater you can slip on to keep your arms toasty." He handed her a cushion and a blanket.

Aisling dropped the deep-green cushion on the seat of an armchair and plopped down, pulling the blanket up to her shoulders and tucking it in behind her. She shivered. "Thanks. A sweater sounds lovely."

He placed the second cushion in the chair across from her. "White or red?"

She frowned, then smiled as she answered. "White sounds nice, thank you." She scrunched under the blanket, her forehead wrinkled. "It's not like I'll get answers from Geraldine tonight."

Her eyes clouded, and Tommy wondered what it was she wasn't telling him about her time in the Dreamscape. He understood her fear surrounding Nuala, but he knew there was something else, something deeper she wasn't saying. He'd give her time. Maybe she'd confide in him.

"Grand. I'll be half-a-minute." Tommy headed to the laundry room adjoining the kitchen first, opened a floor-to-ceiling cabinet, and pulled out two woolen sweaters. In the kitchen, he grabbed a bottle of chilled chardonnay, two cans of Guinness, and two glasses, then returned to the patio.

"Here you are, lass." He handed her an off-white wool sweater.

"This is beautiful." Aisling traced the woven triangles of wool before pulling the sweater over her head. "I need to find a sweater before I go home."

Tommy wondered how long she'd protest the fact of her belonging in Ireland. He knew she had a job and a family in America, but she was a Dreammaster, a part of the fabric of Ireland. She could easily come to Ireland and bring her lass and lad with her. But 'twas not for him to tell the woman what to do or influence her life decisions. Instead, he picked up the corkscrew.

"'Tis a honeycomb stitch, a very traditional weave." He poured the wine, the golden liquid filling the glass halfway. "You can find a nice selection in downtown Galway." He handed her the glass and began to pour his Guinness, taking time as the foamy layers cascaded to a still deep black. "'Tis is a pity we won't have the time to head to the Aran Islands, where the island women hand-knitted the sweaters for over a hundred years. But perhaps we'll go on your next visit."

Aisling sipped her wine and snuggled back in the chair. "Sounds lovely, but I don't know when that might be. I've got to figure my next steps, probably sell my house. And the kids won't want me to leave again too soon." She shook her head with a smile. "Someday."

"Why not come back for the winter solstice, the twenty-first of December?" He warmed to his idea. "'Tis one of my favorite times of the year. There'll be bonfires and music and dancing. And Christmas soon after. 'T'would be a grand time for your young ones to get to know their Irish family." He sipped his beer and smacked his lips. "Brilliant." He sighed. "I do love Guinness."

Aisling looked doubtful. "It looks strong. Not my taste."

"Yer grandfather'd be right disappointed to hear you say so, lass. 'Twas Gerard himself introduced me to the black stuff, as they call it in Ireland." He grinned. "I'll get you to try it yet. And once you do, you'll be hooked." He winked and sipped again. "My father didn't believe a brew from the human realm could be as good as I claimed." He raised his eyebrows, a twinkle in his eyes. "So, I snuck one to him. He loved it. Said it was as good or better than the mead and ale from my home realm."

Tommy winked at Aisling as the warm glow of the beer spread through his system.

Aisling frowned, her gaze quizzical. "What do you mean, *human realm*? Where are you from, Tommy? I had the impression your father lived in Ireland."

Tommy tilted his head. "He does, and yet he doesn't."

She sipped her wine as she regarded him with quizzical eyes. "I hesitate to ask exactly what that means, especially considering all I've discovered since I arrived." She shook her head. "Was it only yesterday?" She paused. "You'll be filling another glass for me—of that, I'm sure—as we delve into your story. So go ahead, tell me about your father and where you're from."

Tommy laughed outright. Aisling was an unexpected joy, and she made him feel rather like how he imagined parents might feel when their offspring grew up to be enjoyable adult company.

"I suppose my origins aren't any stranger than yours. And I appreciate your willingness to listen." He paused, gathering his thoughts. "You were in the Dreamscape today." She nodded. "I'm sure Geraldine or Emer told you that the Dreamscape is part of what we call the Otherworld."

"Emer did, yes." Aisling clicked a nail against her glass. "She said I was part of the Otherworld because I'm descended from Caer." She blew out a breath. "It's hard to believe, but after today it's harder to deny."

"I'm happy you're open to your history. And you should also know Caer does exist even now, although she retreated with the other gods and goddesses and the fairy folk into their own world after being defeated by an invading people, the Milesians."

"I've read of the conflict between the Milesians and the Tuatha Dé Danann. I guess you're telling me that story wasn't a myth either."

"No, lass, it wasn't. The Tuatha Dé Danann retreated underground, to the Sídhe, or fairy hills of the Otherworld. You'll see the fairy hills dotting the countryside of Ireland. All the gods and goddesses, and all the fair folk, live in the Otherworld, which is divided into realms or underground cities scattered all about Ireland." He took a deep swig of his beer, draining the glass. "The gods, goddesses, and fairy folk still live in the Sídhe and are called Daoine Sídhe or People of the Sídhe."

Aisling finished her wine and held out her glass. "If you're about to tell me you're from a Sídhe, you need to refill my glass." He did as she requested, and Aisling settled back into her chair.

"You've guessed correctly, lass. My father is the king of the Daoine Sídhe in western Ireland. He's called Finvarra, and my mother is Queen Una." He took a swig of his beer. "I'm the eldest of seventeen children, all males. We're a boisterous family, to be sure."

Aisling shook her head, a quizzical smile on her face. "Three days ago, I'm not sure I'd have believed you." She closed her eyes and took a deep breath. "But, after today, I can't even begin to find an argument to counter what you've told me." She paused. "So how and why did you end up here?"

Tommy took a moment to consider his answer. "My father sent me to this realm on a mission, one I've yet to accomplish." Should he tell her more? Not yet. Soon, he'd explain the exact nature of his mission and how it concerned her. Tonight, he'd show her a bit more of the magic of the Otherworld. He reached into his bag and pulled out another can of Guinness. "I'll be here until I've finished the job Father set for me. He'll expect me home after." His shoulders stiffened. He'd not be returning. Of that, he was certain. Eilish was here, in Ireland. And once the Fomorian was found, she'd come back to him, as she'd promised long ago. They could be together.

"Tommy?" Aisling was watching him, her eyes concerned. "Don't you want to go home?" Aisling twirled the base of her glass in her fingers. "What about your family? I'm sure they miss you."

He rubbed a hand through his hair, the familiar heaviness spreading through his body at the thought of the leaving his life in Galway. But it wasn't as if Father could force him back. "I go home to visit from time to time. And suppose I should want to go back permanently. There are advantages. For one, I'd age more slowly. Time doesn't pass in the Sídhe like it does here. My family's barely changed since I left, while I've added forty-six years of wrinkles." He snorted. "I age slower than humans, and I've kept my stamina and health, but I look older than my parents." Aisling smiled. "Additionally, in my father's kingdom, life is easier, without some dangers one faces in the human world." He tapped his hands on the table. "But I've become accustomed to this place, to my house, to my friends. I find I'm not in any rush to leave, and I can't leave until I finish my task, so 'tis a moot point. Besides, I have companionship from home frequently." He grinned and pointed into the garden. "You see the tree in the corner?"

Aisling turned to look at the large tree, the autumn leaves still clinging to many of its abundant branches while those that had fallen created a spreading red blanket on the ground. "Yes. It's beautiful." She stared at the tree longer, and her voice was hushed when she spoke again. "Glowing, even."

"Aye, that it is." Tommy matched her tone, his being vibrating in time with the light filling and spilling from within the tree. That she could see the light told him more about Aisling than any report from Emer about training ever could. "It's a hawthorn tree, also called a fairy tree." He bent lower, pointing. "If you look closely, you'll see small dwellings under the tree."

Aisling squinted, leaning over the arm of her chair. "Yes, I see something," she said with a rushed exhalation. She sat back, her eyes wide, and looked at him. "What's there, Tommy?"

He touched her hand. "Follow me and see." Tommy stood. Aisling waited a beat, then did as well.

They walked side by side to the tree overhanging the back corner of his garden, stopping where the farthest branches came close to the ground. Molten light seeped from under the branches, emitting a gentle warmth that flowed into his pores. The feeling of home. The thing he missed the most. He glanced at Aisling standing motionless yet relaxed next to him. Her cheeks had taken on a pink flush, and he knew she felt the warmth as well.

"Peek under, lass," he whispered.

Aisling squatted, resting her elbows on her knees, and watched, her breathing shallow. A minute later, she spoke softly. "I see houses and little doors in the tree's trunk. There are paths between each of the dwellings." She paused a moment. "It's like a tiny town."

"Yes," he whispered, kneeling on one knee next to her. "Do you see anything else?" He paused. "Don't doubt your eyes, Aisling. Believe what they show you."

She focused, silent for several minutes, and then started and almost fell backward. "Tommy." She reached over and grabbed his arm to steady herself. "Something's moving." She dropped to her knees, creeping closer to the base of the trunk. "No way," she said, transfixed. Aisling sat back on her heels and looked up at him, her mouth agape, too overcome to speak. Finally, she found her words. "It looks like the small creatures I saw in the mist. They flew with me." Her eyes shone at the memory. "Do they live here?"

Tommy nodded, meeting her smile with his own. "They'd be what you'd call pixies, and some of them do live here. Although many visit and go back." He rested his elbows on his raised knee. "I awoke a few mornings after I moved into the house and discovered the village. The hawthorn was one reason I bought this house, being from the fairy realm myself, but I hadn't expected some of my fairy friends to join me and offer their help and support." He placed a hand on her back. "They only allow a select few to see them, you know."

Aisling watched, as wide-eyed as a small child on Christmas, as the fair folk went about the business of life under the hawthorn. One or two flew close to her, their wings tickling her cheek, and she giggled, touching her fingers to her skin.

"Wow." She rose and turned to him. "I'm honored to have been chosen." She quirked her head. "Are you that small in the Otherworld? And I apologize if that's insensitive. I just wondered ..."

He smiled. "Come on back to the table." He put an arm around her shoulders, and they walked across the yard. Once they settled in their chairs, he poured his beer and her wine before speaking again. "Like here, we're all very different in the Otherworld. My appearance, even when I'm in my home realm, is very similar to how I look now. I'm more closely related to the Tuatha Dé Danann. We're larger. Stronger, if you're only counting muscle mass. Many of the fairy folk are as large as me, including the pixies. Most pixies can assume different sizes and do so depending on the situation. In a fight, they're a skillful bunch and difficult to stop once goaded." He took a sip of his Guinness. "Those of us from the Sídhe work together. We've learned to make up for one another's weaknesses. For instance, my kind isn't bothered by iron or salt. But the presence of either near the fair folk can cause them illness, even death."

Aisling took a moment to digest this information. "This is unbelievable." She reached over and covered his hand with hers. "Thank you for showing me, for teaching me."

Tommy squeezed her hand, pleased at her response. "'Tis few I'd show, especially not so early in a new friendship. But your connection to my world is undeniable, as is my link to your Dreammaster roots."

"It's all so much to take in." Her face clouded. "It's also an enormous responsibility. Learning, training, understanding how it works." She rubbed her forehead. "I worry I'll never quite get it, never fit in." She bit her lips. "That I'll cause more harm than good in the end."

This was the unspoken worry he'd sensed from her earlier. "But why would you say that Aisling? Why would you believe you'd cause harm? You saved your grandmother."

She lowered her face into her hands, doubt wafting from her like a deadly vapor. He reached over to touch her shoulder.

"Geraldine and Emer were nothing but complimentary about your success today."

Aisling raised her head, her eyes frightened. "No one can explain what happened, though. You don't know. Neither Geraldine nor Emer understand." She took a shuddering breath. "I'm the novel variable. What if..." She paused. "What if whatever attacked Granny got to her because of me?" She bit her lower lip. "Or what if I did it without meaning to? What if my power is somehow dangerous?"

Tommy sat back, unable to answer as he watched Aisling. Where were these doubts of hers coming from? "Do you remember doing anything to harm your grandmother during your training?"

"No," Aisling said in a whisper.

"Did you go into the Dreamscape intending to do harm?"

"Of course, I didn't." Aisling's eyes sparked. "I went in with Geraldine and Emer. I didn't know what I was doing. They guided. I followed." Her brow furrowed. "But I can't explain the scene of my Dreamscape."

She looked at him. "Granny's garden appeared before I'd decided on the setting."

A chill ran up Tommy's spine despite the wool sweater and the blanket over his knees. What Aisling was describing made no sense. Nuala and even Geraldine had told him that an integral part of creating the perfect Dreamscape included a picture of the scene within the mind of a Dreammaster. How had Aisling created a scene she hadn't even imagined beforehand?

* * *

Aisling

"Tommy?" The early evening breeze carried Fergus's raised voice to us from the front of the house.

"Damn," Tommy said under his breath, scowling as Fergus began pounding on the door.

"Aren't you going to answer him?" I asked, surprised at Tommy's reaction. "He sounds like he needs something."

"Yes." He glanced toward the front of the house and then back at me. "We have to discuss this more." His tone was urgent.

"Why?" My anxiety heightened, setting my pulse racing.

Tommy's brows drew together. "What you've described doesn't tally with what I know of the Dreamscape."

"Tommy." Fergus sounded panicked. "It's my guitar. I need your help."

"Have you worked with the pen yet?" Tommy gripped my hand, holding my gaze in his.

I shook my head. "I tried, but I couldn't figure it out. Is there anything special I need before it will work?" The journal I'd seen in my meditation flitted through my mind. "Like a specific book or journal?"

"Maybe. I can't say for certain. The pen will work differently for you than it does for me." He leaned in closer, concern clouding his eyes. "Work with it tonight. Figure out how to protect yourself."

"I need protection?" My chest tightened. "How do I do that? And what if the pen still doesn't work for me tonight?" I had to find a journal. I had no idea where to look.

"It has to work. Ask the pen." He swallowed. "And figure out how to communicate with me." He squeezed my fingers. "Promise me you will."

"But I don't think I can," I said. "I saw a book—"

"You have to do this, Aisling," he said, his voice tense. I wriggled my fingers. His grip hurt. "I'm sorry," Tommy said under his breath, releasing me as Fergus rounded the corner of the house.

"Tommy." Fergus had a guitar in his hands. He paused, his eyes lingering on me, a slow smile spreading over his face. "Aisling. 'Tis an unexpected pleasure to see your lovely face."

"Hi Fergus," I said, my insides melting. I was surprised I didn't bumble my words.

"Excuse us, Aisling." Fergus gave me another soul-shaking smile before turning to Tommy. "Didn't you hear me?" He started toward us. "I'm in a real bind." He extended the guitar toward Tommy as he reached the table. "I knocked this to the floor, and the neck broke."

"Let me see." Tommy took the instrument in his hands and examined the damage. "I can't fix it before your gig tonight. But you can borrow my old one." Tommy rose.

"Grand. You read my mind." Fergus let out an audible sigh of relief.

"Follow me." Tommy started toward the garage. "Wait there, Aisling. I won't be a minute."

"I ought to head back," I said, but Tommy and Fergus had disappeared into the workshop, oblivious to me. I sighed and sipped my wine, wondering why Tommy was particularly worried about my dream scene when Geraldine hadn't been.

"This isn't as grand as yours," Tommy said a moment later. The shop door closed with a *thud*, and the men headed my way.

"Brilliant," Fergus said. "Emer's angry. I've missed practice, and she's sure I'll bollox up the gig tonight." I heard his grunt of irritation. "As if we haven't played most of these numbers more times than I can even count."

"You'll be fine, lad."

Fergus stopped behind my chair, electrifying the surrounding air. He touched my shoulder, sending a current of awareness flowing down my arm to pool low in my belly. Bending, he kissed my cheek, his deep voice murmuring in my ear. "If I'd known you'd be here, I'd have broken my guitar earlier."

My heart thundered in my chest, and heat built in my belly. He smelled clean. Pure and crisp like a mossy wood after a rain. Something in his eyes made me want to reach up and touch his red-gold curls, rake my fingers through and make my own mess.

Tommy cleared his throat, breaking the spell. Fergus rose, and I looked away, studying my hands. What had come over me? I had no business feeling anything for a man I barely knew. And, anyway, wasn't he dating Emer?

"You're on in an hour, lad."

"Shite, is it that late?" He tucked the guitar under his arm. "You'll both be there tonight, won't you? It'll be great craic."

"I'd planned to come if Aisling will join me." I looked up at Tommy and he winked, making me smile.

I had to figure out the pen. But, despite my better judgment, I wanted to hear Fergus play. "Before I agree, I have one question. What is great crack?" I raised my brows, looking between the two men. "It sounds a little iffy to me."

Tommy chuckled. "Craic means fun."

I laughed. I had lots to learn about Irish vernacular. "How can I refuse an invitation to great fun? I'd love to come along." I glanced at Fergus, who grinned. "But I'd like to check on Granny first."

"Grand. Don't be late." He checked his watch, let out a whoop, and jogged down the drive.

CHAPTER THIRTY-THREE

Night had fallen by the time Tommy and I looked in on Granny on our way to town. After Maeve's assurance that my grandmother was resting peacefully, Tommy took me to a large pub on a busy corner near the downtown pedestrian area. I was shivering by the time we arrived, my hands stuck deep into my pockets, the damp night air seeping into my bones even though I still wore the sweater Tommy had loaned me. The cold air didn't seem to bother him at all, and I wondered if he had a magical way to heat himself. What, exactly, were his powers as the son of a fairy king? I'd experienced the calming nature of his presence, but there had to be more he could do. While the busy sidewalks of Friday night Galway weren't the place to discuss it, I did ask him about the journal I'd seen in my meditation. "My mom had a journal like it, but I couldn't find it after her death."

"It sounds like something Geraldine had when we were first married," he mused. Did his skin glow in the light of the streetlamps? I was being fanciful. "I thought it had something to do with being a Dreammaster, but you can't ask her. You can't mention the pen." He was insistent on that point.

I didn't tell him I'd seen the journal in Geraldine's dreaming space. She didn't want me to discuss our time in the attic with anyone. And Tommy didn't want me to discuss the Druid pen with her. Frustration built inside me until I felt as if I was going to burst. "What if I can't find the right thing to use? Can you conjure something for me?" I leaned closer to him and asked the last question softly.

Tommy chuckled and wrapped an arm around my shoulders. "You're freezing." As he spoke, the cold fled my limbs and heat filled me. "I can't conjure things, Aisling, but I might be able to obtain a notebook from a friend here in Galway, a woman with considerable power." He squeezed me. "Or we could ask Nuala. But only as a last resort."

"Okay." I nodded. He released me, and I shivered in advance, ready to be cold again, but the heat from his touch remained.

"Here we are," Tommy announced, leading me past a building two stories high and fronted by long, low windows, behind which a sizable crowd had already gathered. The merriment from inside spilled out to the sidewalk, raucous voices and laughter blending with lively music.

"Milligan's Pub," I said. "Like the store downtown?"

"Yes." Tommy nodded, and a smile creased his face. "Mel Milligan has made a name for himself throughout Ireland. Milligan's is one of the largest business conglomerates in the country. He's come a long way from the young man I befriended so many years ago."

I heard the pride in Tommy's voice and wondered at my reaction to Mel. I trusted Tommy. So why did his friend bother me so much? And why did my contact with Mel and his son burn them? The only other person I'd burned was the monster-man from the bus. Why those three and no one else? I didn't understand my power, and I needed to. But who could I ask? Tommy, Mel's closest friend. Or Geraldine, Mel's employee.

Neither choice was a good one. Unless I asked Granny. I'd do that. As soon as she'd recovered.

"So it seems," I said. "He must be a talented businessman to have had such success. How did Geraldine come to work for him?"

"She started working for Henry Osheen in Dublin after Mel had moved to Galway. Mel already worked for Henry and had for years. He was, still is, married to Henry's daughter, Neassa. Henry sold part of the business to Mel years ago, but Mel and Neassa didn't take control of the operation and change the name until after Henry Osheen's death."

"Mel changed the name?" I frowned. "Didn't that upset Mel's wife and the rest of Mr. Osheen's family?"

"Nah. The place is still a family affair, and Mel is a trusted and respected member of the community with a reputation for taking good care of his employees. In fact, he brought Geraldine back to Galway from Dublin when she asked to move about a decade ago. She wanted to be closer to her mother."

"That's nice," I said, wondering why he hit me so wrong. "His son's an odd one, though."

Tommy's brows rose, and he held my gaze in his, his eyes bright with intensity. "Why do you say that?"

His tone alerted me I'd gone too far, and I shook my head, wishing I could withdraw my words. "I'm sorry, Tommy. It's just Torin was an ass when I met him the day I arrived in Galway. He came on to me. And he's married." My skin crawled as I remembered his touch. I pinched my lips closed. I'd said enough for tonight.

Tommy must have sensed there was more I wasn't saying, because he moved us out of the way of an arriving party, his eyes boring into mine. "Torin's attitude toward women is reprehensible. I'm sorry he was disrespectful, Aisling. But there's more you aren't telling me."

"It's nothing," I said.

He didn't look away. "Out with it."

I paused, considering my words, settling for a half-truth. "Torin's creepy. His touch made my skin crawl. I don't like men like him." I bit my lip at Tommy's expression, afraid I might have offended him. "This is why I didn't want to say anything. I've upset you."

"No." He shook his head. "Maybe. But not because of anything you did." He paused. "Are you sure there isn't more?"

I wanted to say that Mel was just as creepy as his son, but I didn't. "No. That's it. I hope I didn't offend you."

Tommy watched me a moment longer, his eyes narrowed and his expression stern.

I sighed, looking away. "I shouldn't have told you." I looked back. "Ignore me, Tommy. I was tired. I'm sure I overreacted."

"You did nothing wrong, lass." Tommy patted my arm, but emotion flickered in his eyes. Was it anger? Concern? Maybe a mixture of both. "I'm glad you told me."

"Don't tell Geraldine. She works for Mel. And she works with Torin. I don't want to upset her."

"No, lass. I won't." He stared at me for a moment, as if considering asking me more. Finally, he took my arm. "Let's go inside. It's cold."

Tension seeped from my limbs at his words. I didn't think I could obfuscate anymore tonight. If he'd grilled me longer, the truth might have slipped out. Tommy opened the door, and a wave of heated air enveloped me, luring me in.

The aroma of food blended with the sweet, fermented odor of beer assaulted me. The place was a frenzy of smiling people, and I pushed past the crowd at the entrance, noting the boisterous line of drinkers at the curved wooden bar. A group shoved past us, jostling me farther into the room, and I glanced back to make sure Tommy was still with me.

He smiled and pointed toward the next room. "The staircase is at the back." His shout was muffled by the noise of the crowd. "Go on through, and I'll follow. Live music is upstairs."

I nodded and began shoving my way through.

"Where you off to, darling?" A man grabbed my elbow, stopping me. "Why don't you let us buy you a pint?" He slurred, his unfocused blue eyes squinting at me, his wide mouth curved in a drunken smile. "We're celebrating."

"No thanks." I smiled, shook my head, and plowed on.

The crowd thinned, and Tommy stepped beside me. "Poor lad. You broke his heart." He grinned and sidestepped around customers. "Follow me."

The stairway was calmer until we reached the second floor, where even more people gathered.

"Over here," Tommy yelled, pulling on my arm and nodding for me to follow him. He headed into a swath of people, disappearing like a dinghy sucked into a hurricane.

"Will you never learn, woman?" A familiar voice teased me as a firm hand gripped my elbow. "You have to move quickly in Ireland." I turned to gaze into Fergus's sparkling green eyes. He touched my cheek, the light brush of his fingers heating my skin. "I'm glad you came."

"Me too," I said, my tongue suddenly too large for my mouth. Why did I act like a schoolgirl every time I saw this man? "I've lost Tommy."

"We'll find him, shall we?" Fergus gave a gentle tug, and I followed. He knew everyone, nodding and calling to people as we passed. Several of them looked me over, their glances curious.

"We've a table over here near the front." Fergus leaned in, his breath a whisper on my skin. The crowd thinned as a grouping of tables came into view. "Always save a seat for Tommy and any of his friends." He stopped at a table close to the raised stage. "But I hope you're also here as my friend. I heard how you saved your granny. You'll make a grand Dreammaster." He ran his hand up my arm to the back of my neck, his fingers pressing into the soft skin, and I trembled. No one had touched me this way in a very long time.

Then, to my shock, Fergus pulled me closer and grazed my lips with his. I tasted the sea-salt fresh air of Galway mingled with the faint tang of beer before he pulled away. "I hope you enjoy the show. I've a tune especially for you." He held me a moment longer, and I wondered if he could feel my pulse racing or read the confusion I was certain must be in my eyes.

He'd left Tommy's yesterday with an offhand good-bye to go on a date with Emer. I'd assumed they were together and that he was frustrated with me about doubting whether I could save Lorcan. But then, barely an hour ago, he'd wrapped me in his spell on Tommy's patio. And now he'd kissed me in public, as if we were an item. Whatever Emer had said about my training today, Fergus must believe I was prepared to save his uncle. Did he like me? Did he like her? Was he drunk?

"Fergus, lad." Tommy spoke from over my shoulder, his voice barely discernible above the din. "Why aren't you on stage?"

"Just making sure Aisling found the table." His fingers lightly brushed mine, and he was gone.

I slid into a chair next to Tommy, and none too soon for my shaking legs. I touched my lips, which still tingled from his kiss. The man had an effect on me, that much was certain, and I wasn't sure I liked it. I wasn't looking for romance so soon after losing my husband—or killing him, as the case might be. As attracted as I was to Fergus, being in a relationship with any man didn't seem like an option until I knew the exact danger my dreams posed.

A snippet of a melody flowed through the room, pulling my eyes to the stage, where Fergus had settled onto a stool, picked up a fiddle, and begun tuning the instrument. An open guitar case was stowed at his feet.

Another man climbed onto the stage and pulled a stool next to Fergus, nodding a greeting. Strains of concertina music intertwined with Fergus's fiddle, starting and stopping as they made adjustments.

"I'm heading up for a pint, lass," Tommy said. "Would you like a glass of wine?"

I hesitated. "What about food?"

"I thought I'd put in an order while I was up there. They do a tasty lamb stew served with soda bread."

"Perfect," I said, my stomach rumbling.

"Wine?"

"Sure. A glass of white."

A few minutes later, Tommy returned with the drinks. Shortly after, a harried server plopped two steaming bowls of stew in front of us. I scooped fragrant chunks of tender lamb into my mouth and moaned. Perfection.

The rest of the band assembled and began warming up as we ate.

By the time the waitress took our empty bowls and brought Tommy another beer, Emer had joined her bandmates, her flute in hand. When she saw me, her eyebrows rose. I watched as she marched to Fergus and spoke, wildly gesturing with her free hand.

"Our Emer's fixated on Fergus." Tommy leaned near, his face red from the heat or the beer or both. "Fergus won't ever give the lass what she craves, but there's no telling a heart how to beat, now, is there?" He watched me a moment longer, then raised his glass to his lips.

I frowned. Was he warning me about Fergus? About Emer? Or were his words a subtle warning to me to abandon my foolish attraction to his friend?

I sighed. I'd be gone in less than a week, so what did it matter? I relaxed back in my seat, full, warm, and pleasantly drowsy. Until I remembered I had to go back to Old Oak Manor and figure out how to set protections with the Druid pen. I sat upright, my muscles twitching with the need to move. I should go now. Figuring out the pen could take all night. And there was no guarantee I'd find an answer.

A hush fell over the crowd at the introductory strains of a melody, and all eyes fixed on the stage. Any thought of leaving disappeared when the band broke into a toe-tapping jig. My fingers played the beat on the tabletop as I listened, transfixed by the perfectly choreographed musicians. The first tune flowed into the second, and my flagging energy revived. When the first set ended, I decided to stay a while longer.

"But I have to go after this round," I told Tommy. The pen wouldn't figure out itself.

He nodded. "I'll go with you, lass. Make sure you get home safe."

"No, you stay," I said. His cheeks were rosy, his eyes sparkling, and I wondered if it was due to the handsome woman, Doreen, who'd joined us.

"We'll see," he said as the second set commenced.

Again, the music captivated me, and I found my eyes irresistibly drawn to Fergus, who had gone from fiddle to guitar and back to fiddle. I watched his fingers fly over the strings, absorbed in his every movement, keeping time with the music. When he looked up and his eyes met mine, I couldn't look away as he wove a lyrical spell that wrapped around my thrumming heart. I pressed a hand against my chest, afraid it might burst.

As the music ended, Fergus stood, fiddle in hand, and approached the central microphone. A blond woman who'd been playing the bodhran moved from her stool to a keyboard on the side of the stage. She looked at Fergus, who nodded. The rest of the band remained still as she played the opening of a ballad I recognized, although I couldn't remember the name.

Fergus began to sing, his voice clear and deep. His bandmates joined in, adding depth and harmony with banjo, guitar, flute, and concertina. But the voice of the man was the instrument I focused on.

The words Fergus sang were in Irish, but I felt each of them like a beat of my heart, especially when his eyes found mine once again. He broke from singing and joined in with his fiddle, still watching me. Was this the tune he'd promised to play for me? My body trembled at the thought and at the intensity of his gaze.

When the ballad ended, the room erupted in applause. The players bowed, and the blond woman announced a break before the third set. Fergus was still watching me. I wanted to go to him and tell him his playing was lovely, his voice amazing. I wanted to reach out and touch his face, look deeply into his eyes, see if what I was feeling would be reflected back to me.

Fergus made a move to step down from the stage, when Emer stopped him. She shot me a glance, and I had no trouble interpreting the territorial look in her eyes. Emer took hold of Fergus's arm and leaned in, whispering fiercely in his ear. He nodded and turned, following her to the back of the stage.

My cheeks burned as I watched him walk away. I closed my eyes and conjured Trevor's face, burning his image into my brain. He was dead. Was it my fault? I swallowed with difficulty as I considered that question. I could change things with dreams. I probably killed my husband. Discovering the truth was why I was here. I should thank Emer for ruining the moment of insanity between Fergus and me. He was a flirt, and I was weak. I was also a possible murderer. I had to remember that fact. I rose, tapping Tommy, who was engrossed in conversation with Doreen. It was time to go back to Old Oak Manor.

"Aisling, lass." Tommy grinned, and I couldn't help but smile back. "Where you off to, then?" His accent was thicker after several pints of Guinness.

"I'm heading back to Granny's."

"Aye, I'll come with you." He made to get up, stumbling a little, and I stopped him with a hand on his shoulder.

"You stay." I smiled at Doreen. "It's been wonderful, but I'm worn out." I checked my watch. "It's early still, just past nine. I'll walk back. I remember the way."

"No, I'll come." Tommy started to rise and stumbled.

"You sit, Tommy dear," Doreen said. "I'll get my Paddy to give Aisling a lift." She shifted her gaze to me. "My son drives a cab, but he took tonight off. He can have you home and be back before the next set starts."

"You don't need to do that."

"Then I'll be coming along." Tommy stood and wobbled.

I exchanged an amused look with Doreen and gave in. "Fine. If Paddy will take me back, I'd appreciate the lift."

Doreen sent a text, and a few minutes later, a tall, skinny man with thinning hair, wide-set eyes, and a gentle smile arrived at the table. Doreen made the introductions, and I bent, gave Tommy a quick kiss on the cheek, and followed Paddy.

Outside the bar, Paddy told me to wait while he fetched the car, and I breathed in the clear air, the cold of it frosting the inside of my nostrils. I rubbed the tip of my rapidly cooling nose, wishing I'd insisted on going with him. Moving wouldn't be as chilly.

"Aisling." I turned at the sound of Fergus's voice. "Are you leaving?" He walked toward me, his hands stuffed in the pockets of his jacket, his eyes a darker green in the night shadows.

My stomach flip-flopped. Trying to figure out my feelings for Fergus wasn't a good idea tonight. Or ever, given my situation. I stifled a yawn, thoughts of bed flitting in my mind. But I couldn't indulge in sleep. Not yet. I still needed to figure out how to work the pen. Then there was training tomorrow. I sighed.

"Yes, I am," I said, and his face fell, causing my breath to catch in my throat. "I'm exhausted after training. And I want to check on Granny."

Fergus reached out, softly touched my cheek with his fingers. "Aisling." His voice was barely above a whisper. "You disarm me." He cupped my cheek in his hand.

I couldn't move. All of me was wrapped up in him, resting in the palm of his hand, waiting to see what might happen next.

Rather than speak, he drew closer to me, pulling my face toward his until my eyes closed and our lips met. His touch was feather-light yet whirlwind strong, and I quaked to my very core, as if the reverberations of his simple kiss could split me in two. He pulled back slowly, and I opened my eyes, locking my gaze with his. And saw Trevor's face, as if his ghost had shrouded Fergus's features.

I pushed away from Fergus. "This isn't right," I said, backing away until he was forced to drop his hand. "My husband just died."

I heard his sharp intake of breath. "That doesn't change how I feel."

"You just met me. You don't know me."

"I know you're strong and beautiful." He took a step toward me, but I put out a hand to stop him. "I know you'll save Lorcan."

The breath rushed out of my lungs. This was what he cared about. "What if I don't?"

His eyes clouded. "But you will."

"I've barely begun to train, Fergus." What had I been thinking, allowing my middle-aged hormones to make a fool of me? "I want to help save Lorcan. I don't know how to do it yet. There's so much more for me to learn." *And no one's assured me I won't kill the man if I tried.*

"But you've done so well after just one day." He reached for me. I sidestepped him.

"What about Emer?"

At that, his eyes widened, and he looked abashed. "Emer's a close friend."

My body filled with heat, and the need to defend Emer bubbled up. "Anyone can see she feels much more than friendship for you, Fergus."

He shoved his hands in his pockets and looked away. "I didn't mean to upset you," he said in a soft, sad voice. "I thought you felt what I did."

I sighed. "I don't know what I feel right now. You're attractive. You're talented. And I do feel drawn to you." His eyes lit up, and I hurried on. "But that's attraction, Fergus. Nothing more. And I just can't handle it right now." I glanced away. "Not until I understand."

"Understand what?"

"Aisling." Paddy called to me from the curb and honked his horn. His timing couldn't have been better. "That's Paddy. He's taking me home." I reached over to touch Fergus's hand, and his fingers linked with mine. I allowed the heat from his grip to fill me for a moment. "Thank you for the song. Your music, your voice—" I stopped, not sure what to say, how to express what the music meant to me. "It's beautiful."

"Fergus, we're up in five." Emer's voice, shrill and demanding, shattered the mood for good. She stood in the doorway of the pub, watching us, her eyes slits of glowering anger, her lips fixed in a flat line of distaste.

"Good night, then," Fergus whispered, his eyes shadowed as he pulled his hand from mine.

"Good night." I watched as he turned and walked to Emer. She took hold of his arm, leading them both back inside. My shoulders drooped as I turned away.

I crept into the silent house as the grandfather clock struck the quarter hour, happy for the key Granny had given me and the lamp Maeve had left on in the front hall. Dim light from the banked fire cloaked the sitting room in a golden haze, but Granny wasn't in her chair. She'd be in her bed, and I wanted to check on her, but I figured Maeve or Geraldine would have called Tommy if Granny was worse. I'd wait until morning.

In my bedroom, I switched on the bedside lamp and dropped onto the bed to pull off my boots. I pulled out the carved Celtic knot Tommy had given me, strung it on the length of leather, and tied it around my neck so that it hung under my swan, tucked beneath my sweater. The wood warmed my skin, and I hoped it worked as Tommy said and focused my power.

Yawning, I considered a shower to wake myself up. I'd promised Tommy I'd figure out the pen. The thought exhausted me. I plopped back into the center of the bed and spread out my arms. My fingers grazed something resting on the duvet, and I sprang upright and swiveled around, my heart pounding.

A wrapped package I hadn't seen sat there, and the breath I'd been holding rushed out. Nothing nefarious. I reached out and took hold of the package, then pulled it to me. A card was taped to the paper. I opened it.

Dear Aisling,

Enclosed you'll find your Dreammaster journal. Upon the beginning of Dreammaster training, every woman in our lineage receives this gift from the goddess Caer. The journal arrived late today. I asked Maeve to place it in your room so you'd see it when you returned.

You can use the book for anything you'd like to keep note of. Many women use the journal to keep track of training and for any thoughts and realizations that arise during the process. The journal has magical properties. Your touch, coupled with your intention to secure the journal, will lock it. It unlocks in the same way. No one else can lock or unlock the journal, and no one else can see your entries unless you allow it. Work with the journal, and it will show you how to proceed.

Mary loved her journal. Perhaps you found it among her things. If you did, keep it as a remembrance of your mother. I still have mine.

You excelled in your training today, Aisling. You saved me. I am very grateful to you and the strength of your power. You should be very proud of yourself.

With love,

Granny Nuala

My fingers tingled, and my swan pendant began its familiar pulse, its heat blending with the heat from the Dara Knot as I gazed at the rectangular package. Granny had said *journal,* and that it was a gift from the goddess. Was that literal? Tommy said Caer still lived in the Otherworld. Had she somehow sent the journal to me? Could this be the book I sought?

I held my breath and tore the paper where a shiny line of tape held it fast. I removed the paper, taking my time, my heart beating faster as the brown leather cover slowly emerged until the paper was off, discarded on the floor. I released my breath on a sigh. This was the book I'd seen in my meditation. It was the same as the journal my mom had used to write about my dreams and the same as the book I'd found in Geraldine's bookcase. I traced the engraving of the woman and the swans tooled into the buttery leather cover. Caer, in her flowing gown, her long hair falling past her shoulders. Two swans at her feet, heads touching, their necks bowed to create the shape of a heart.

Excitement beat within me, and I sprang from my bed and dug through my drawer. My fingers grazed the wooden case, and I clutched it and pulled it out. Back on my bed, I opened the box. The pen floated from the crushed velvet lining and nestled into the fingers of my right hand.

Giddy, I uncapped the pen and picked up the journal in my left hand, holding the two objects in front of me. Each one pulsed in time with my swan, emitting a warmth that circled me, as though I were a babe being held safely in her mother's arms. Maybe this was protection enough. I certainly felt secure at this moment.

I frowned. It couldn't be this easy. Tommy had told me to work with the pen and discover how I could best use it. Pens were for writing. So I'd write.

I touched the cover of the journal. "Unlock please," I whispered. The cover opened to my name inscribed in elegant cursive on the first page. I hated to spoil the empty beauty of the heavy ecru paper, but I had a mission to complete. And then, I needed to sleep.

I touched pen to page, and the words flowed.

I started training today. The mist was incredible. The Dreamscape was beyond what I'd imagined. But I don't believe I set my own scene. I can't explain what happened.

I continued writing, describing in detail the attack on Granny and how my emerald energy pushed away the fog.

Now, I need to understand how to use the Druid pen for my protection. Could you send me a message to guide me?

I waited, pen poised over paper, reminded of the automatic writing workshop taught by a spiritual guide at Beverly's yoga studio. I'd had little success, and Bev and I had laughed at the nonsensical series of words splayed across our pages. Now, I forced my hand to relax, closed my eyes, and focused on breathing deeply.

My eyes popped open when my hand began to glide across the page. I gaped at the words that appeared.

Write a verse but be precise.
Your intention is key,
Your words, the device.
If you do not write with care
The outcome may skew,
Leaving you in despair.

> *What you ask for matters not,*
> *Guidance, protection, notification, and more,*
> *But leave nothing to chance as your words you plot.*

I waited several minutes after the pen stopped in case it had more to say. No one would believe I'd done this. Even I found it improbable. But the verse was the proof.

Now, what about a verse for protection? And I needed one to send to Tommy. I checked my watch. It was after eleven. Way past time for me to be asleep.

The protection verse would be easy because I wasn't in any danger. I was going to sleep. Not into the Dreamscape.

I had it. Short, sweet, simple. And, hopefully, effective.

> *Keep me safe as I rest tonight,*
> *Protect the house and all inside.*

Not great, but my eyes were drooping. I'd play with it more tomorrow. Tommy next. I jotted down the lines as they came.

> *Tommy, I hope this verse gets to you,*
> *I'm home and safe and sleepy too.*
> *Good night, sleep well, and thanks for the talk,*
> *I'll come by soon on my next walk.*

I wasn't a poet. That was clear. But I'd done what Tommy asked.

I closed the journal, touched the cover, and asked it to lock. I wondered where Mom had hidden her journal. She must not have wanted me to find it. And I couldn't have opened it or read anything inside even if I had.

I yawned, hid the journal and the pen behind my clothes in the drawer, changed into pajamas, and snuggled into bed.

As I drifted off to sleep, I worried I didn't know enough to set proper protections. I dismissed my concerns. Everything was fine.

Chapter Thirty-Four

October 28, Old Oak Manor

"Excellent, Aisling," Geraldine said, tapping the clipboard in her lap. I'd led us into the Dreamscape three times and practiced blocking energies intent on sabotaging my dreams, which mainly consisted of directing the green force to surround and sweep them away. "You've mastered all we've taught you. You're well on your way to earning the title of Dreammaster." She paused, peering over the rim of her stylish reading glasses. "Now that you have the basics mastered, I want to teach you how to connect with your dreaming client."

I wanted to be as pleased as my aunt sounded, but doubt prickled my skin and flooded my mind. October 31 was only days away. Everything was so new. And I didn't agree with Geraldine's assertion that I'd mastered everything. If I had, why did Granny's garden continue to appear as my dream scene in the Dreamscape before I'd even had a chance to come up with my own setting? I'd tried to ask this morning, before we got started, but Geraldine had barreled over my morning questions with a flip of her hand and a promise to address any concerns later. But later when? I rubbed the tense spot between my eyebrows. Now, there was something else to master. I was never going to remember everything when I had to do this on my own.

"Really? I'm still not convinced I'll be ready to go it alone and dream Lorcan out of the Underworld. And there's the issue with my dream scene." And the possibility that my dreams were dangerous, and I'd killed my husband. Geraldine said she'd investigate my dream on the night Trevor died. But she hadn't mentioned it since the night she discovered me in her attic space. She'd said it was unlikely I'd killed my husband. But I wanted certainty. I couldn't risk hurting anyone else. Again, I wondered when she'd have time to speak with me and answer my questions.

I sank into a chair and glanced at my watch. It was nearing one; we'd been working nonstop since nine, and we'd missed lunch. My body was wearing out. "And why do I need to learn to connect with a client when my dream is to save Lorcan?"

"Our pledge requires that we never dream for personal gain," Granny said. "For that reason, Dreammasters dream only for clients, called dreamers. Geraldine will act as your client."

"Dreammasters aren't allowed to use their power for themselves?" I thought back to my dreams that had changed things. Was this something else I had to confess to?

"No, we're not," Emer said. "But it does happen unintentionally as our powers begin to manifest. The Aislingeach Council allows latitude to the trainer to decide if those early dreams ought to be punished. Few Dreamkeepers face discipline."

I sighed. That was good enough for me for now.

"Dreammasters are allowed to request a dream from another Dreammaster," Granny said. "Having a third party conduct the dream keeps the process free of manipulation and coercion. Dreammasters have human qualities, after all, and we all face temptations."

"Makes sense," I said, all the while wondering how I was going to keep another thing in my stuffed brain. My headache was rapidly intensifying. "But it still doesn't explain my dream scene."

"Your scene is fine," Geraldine snapped, a note of irritation creeping into her voice. "You'll be ready. Learning to connect with your client will alleviate some of your concerns. You will set the intention for the dream. The process grounds you in your body. This is necessary as you'll be traveling from this mundane human realm into the ethereal otherworld realm. And if you run into issues, I'll be there to assist."

"That's a relief." I sighed and took a deep breath. "Although, I still wonder if I'm the right person to lead this dream."

"Stop fretting." Geraldine spoke sharply even as she smiled at me. "Things are well under control. All you need to worry about is your training."

"Which is going very well," Granny said, but her brow was creased. "What did you mean about your dream scene?"

"It shows up so fast," I said, "before I have a chance ..." Pain shot from my finger up my arm, stealing the rest of my words. This had happened the day before when I'd questioned the scene that appeared in my Dreamscape. The pain had stopped me. Was this a warning not to speak? Or a way to keep me silent? My eyes slid to my aunt. Here was another question she needed to answer.

"Her scene is your garden," Geraldine said, her words clipped. "Which makes sense. She found respite there on her first day."

Granny's brows arched as her eyes narrowed. She looked from her daughter to me. "Before you have a chance to what, Aisling?" she asked, ignoring Geraldine.

"To imagine it," I croaked, pressing the tip of my finger with my thumb. Geraldine shook her head, looking like she might explode.

"It was rather odd how fast Aisling created the scene," Emer said in a cunning voice. "Like she'd done it hundreds of times before." She tilted her head. "Are you sure your mother didn't teach you how to Dream?"

"Of course I'm sure," I said, barely controlling the anger roiling through me. She'd shot me poisonous glances all morning and made a few snide comments about the timbre of my voice when I asked to enter the Dreamscape. Geraldine had noticed Emer's attitude toward me. I saw her interested glances. But my aunt had kept any questions or comments to herself and focused on training. Which was best. Because I knew Emer had seen Fergus holding my hand the night before, and I had a feeling she'd seen us kiss, and that was something I didn't want to discuss.

Emer flopped in a chair, swiping her silky fringe out of her eyes. "Hmm. Well, you've caught on quickly for a novice."

Geraldine sighed. "Aisling's training is going well. She's a natural. Mother, you've said Mary never used her Dreammaster abilities, correct?"

"She did not," Granny said. She was watching Geraldine, a curious glint in her eyes.

"I've never done any of this before." I swiped away the lone curl that liked to hang in the middle of my forehead. "I'm sorry I said anything."

"Perhaps I should accompany Aisling into the Dreamscape next time," Granny said in a too casual tone. "I have been at this longer than anyone else here. I'd like to see what's happening with her dream scene."

"That's hardly necessary, Mother." Geraldine slapped her clipboard. "Especially not as your leg still hurts you. Unless you doubt my abilities." Granny sat back, saying nothing, but her eyes never left Geraldine's face. Geraldine huffed and looked away. "Let's discuss connecting with your client, Aisling. The process is quite simple."

My stomach growled, but if anyone else heard, they said nothing. "Simple is good," I said, forcing a smile to my lips.

"You and your client will meet somewhere private. The best situation is to have them join you in your dreaming space."

"I don't have one."

"For this dream, we will use my space in the attic." She paused, eyebrows raised. Granny shifted, and I wondered if she'd object. But Granny said nothing, and I kept quiet. "You will review the facts of the dream you're about to do. Once the client, or dreamer, has affirmed the facts of the dream, you will ask her to close her eyes and join you in the Dreamscape using the words you learned yesterday."

"Does the client go into the Dreamscape with me?"

"The client enters the Dreamscape within their subconscious mind. Because of the special Dreammaster connection you forge with your client, the dream will seem real to them."

"It's not safe to take your client fully into the Dreamscape," Emer said. "You've read the stories about humans being captured by fair folk and taken into the Otherworld?"

I nodded. "As I recall, the humans don't fare too well."

"The stories are mixed," Emer said. "Musicians are often taken by the fae, or fair folk, for a night of revelry and returned unharmed. Other humans stay or are kept for too long and when they do make it back to the human realm find many years have passed and their loved ones are dead." She sighed with a shrug. "The fae are a capricious lot. One moment they might like a human. The next, the human may say or do something considered offensive. The fair folk are no more prone to kindness than human beings. They can be beneficent. They can be cruel. We are part of the fabric of the Otherworld and the fae. We can enter our realm without danger. Our clients cannot and therefore aren't allowed to enter the Dreamscape."

"Emer is correct," Geraldine said. "Whether the dream is a simple one or more consequential—for instance, a dream for love—your client will always engage via her subconscious mind. You may choose to use your dreamvision for simpler dreams. You must enter fully into the Dreamscape for more complex dreams. And you may choose to enter the Dreamscape in your full body for every dream you do."

"Because the dreamer is going to experience the dream as if she's there, the dream scene is vitally important," said Emer. "Your client will give you the details of the scene within which they wish to dream. You must create the scene they require so that they are relaxed during the process."

"Do they know where they are? Are they aware of the Mist and the Dreamscape?"

"No. The client knows only what they've told you about the specific dream they wish you to perform and the instructions you give them as you prepare them for the dream. The client, or dreamer, enters the Dreamscape within her mind when accompanied by you and for their specific dream. Even though they aren't fully in the Dreamscape, your power creates the magic necessary for success. It is vital that you don't lose your link to your client, or the process becomes dangerous for both of you."

Emer continued. "If a client breaks away from the dream, their mind can be accosted by entities within the Otherworld. The Otherworld isn't a benign place. There are good and bad beings residing there, and many don't like humans. Trying to reestablish your connection with a client if such a break occurs puts you in danger as well."

"Take great care of your clients," Granny said. "'Tis part of the Dreammaster pledge to act only for good, and this includes ensuring the safety of the person for whom you're dreaming. Therefore, if there are any questions concerning the dream, it is vital to consult with the Aislingeach council ahead of time. Nothing must be left to chance."

My mouth went dry as I listened. Bad beings in the Otherworld. Keeping connected to my client. So many ways I could screw up this dream. I was realizing that nothing about this process was going to be easy. I clenched my fingers into balls in my lap. What had I agreed to?

"Aisling?" Geraldine's sharp voice broke into my thoughts.

"Yes." I forced a smile and looked at my aunt. "I heard it all. What next?"

"Next, we practice," Geraldine said. "Emer will act as your client for today. Let's see how you do making the connection."

On my first two attempts I failed. Emer put up barriers to our connection, and I knew she was enjoying herself. Her snarky smile gave her away. On the third attempt, I tried a different approach, using my energy to envelope her, subduing her energetic attempts to thwart my efforts. And I succeeded.

"Well done," Granny said, her face beaming when I brought Emer and myself back from a short jaunt to the Dreamscape. "Using your energy to calm Emer and bring her deeply into the meditation was exactly the right choice."

"I didn't think you were going to catch on," Emer said, her smile grudging. "But when you pulled in your energy, you relaxed me past the point of resistance. Well done."

"Yes," Geraldine added. She jotted notes on the paper on her clipboard. "I believe that's enough for today. We'll proceed bodily into the Dreamscape in the morning." She looked over at me. "You're ready. And, by then, we'll have word from King Finvarra and the Aislingeach Council about the status of the dream."

"The Fomorian king will never admit a human into his realm, even via a dream," Emer said. "The Aislingeach council will probably label the dream dangerous and recommend we don't try as a result." She sniffed. "Fergus thinks it's silly to even ask the Fomorian king. And to worry about gaining permission to use a dream in the Underworld. All we're doing is alerting the Fomorians to our intention."

"It's a matter of courtesy," Geraldine said. "Our dream will break the treaties."

"The Fomorians broke the rules first forty-six years ago when one of them came into Ireland," Emer said. "He was likely the reason Lorcan got pulled into the Underworld. We don't owe the Fomorians a thing."

My ears perked up. "A Fomorian came into Ireland? Despite the rules in place?"

"Yes." Geraldine pursed her lips. "It may or may not be related to Lorcan's disappearance."

"Wait." I cocked my head, watching her. "How could the two events be connected?"

"King Finvarra, Tommy's father, noticed a disturbance in the Otherworld on the eve of Samhain forty-six years ago," Geraldine said, barely concealing her irritation. "The same night Lorcan disappeared. But there is no clear-cut evidence the two events are related."

"But it is a pretty big coincidence," I murmured.

Geraldine scowled. "No one, Fomorian or otherwise, passed Mary and me that night. Neither did Lorcan."

"You claim you were unconscious," Granny said, her eyes beady. "You wouldn't necessarily have seen anyone."

"Really, Mother. I think I'd have noticed a monster." Geraldine's face was suffused with red. "This talk is a distraction serving no purpose except to alarm Aisling."

I bit my lips, watching their interaction, not so much alarmed as curious. Why had no one mentioned this before? It seemed like it did relate to all we were doing. Especially considering how my mother died at the hands of a monster.

"Hmm," Granny said, before turning her attention to me. "The arrival of the Fomorian is under investigation. He has eluded capture. As you know, what happened to Lorcan has been a mystery until now. Despite the fact that a Fomorian broke the treaties years ago, the Dreammaster pledge requires us to follow the decisions of the Dreammaster Council. The council requires us to inform the Fomorian king of our intentions. We will do so, hoping that our actions will smooth the way for the dream.

"If we don't," Geraldine said, "and our incursion is discovered, the Fomorians might retaliate."

"Since when did you care about the rules?" Emer asked Geraldine, her nostrils flaring. "It's a stupid plan to alert the enemy. Fergus says—"

"I don't care what Fergus says—" Geraldine stated.

Granny interrupted. "The council hopes that by contacting the Fomorians, they will decide to return Lorcan." She held up her hand when Emer opened her mouth. "I tend to agree that it's folly to alert the Fomorians to our intentions. But I'm no longer in charge of the Sisterhood. Muirgen, as our leader, makes these decisions along with the council. What this means is Aisling will need to be well prepared and ready to find, connect with, and save Lorcan." She turned to me. "The faster you are in and out of the Underworld, the less likely the Fomorians can sabotage your dreaming efforts. The last thing I want is for anyone to get hurt."

"We risk Lorcan being hurt," Emer said. "The Fomorians will be watching him once they know our plans. They could invade the dream and hurt him or Aisling."

Her words sent a chill through my body. "I can understand how they might hurt Lorcan. He's there, in his body. But I'm only going to the Underworld via my subconscious mind. How can they get to me? Is there some way the Fomorians can infiltrate Dreammaster dreams?"

"Fomorians are powerful," Granny said. "They have special magic that could interrupt your dream and potentially cause you harm."

"So, would I lose my mind?" I swallowed hard, wishing I could clear the lump in my throat.

"I'll be there to assist you," Geraldine said. "You'll be fine."

I looked from Granny to Emer to Geraldine. "That's not reassuring."

"You will be prepared, Aisling," Granny said. "And we'll set extra protections." She pulled in a ragged breath that did nothing to soothe me. "It's a better solution than having you go into the Underworld fully in your body. Then we risk you being trapped or killed."

My body froze, and my heart stopped. Only for a moment, but it was long enough. "I do have kids to go home to, you know?" My whispered words were pathetic, and I regretted saying them as soon as they passed my lips. I'd perform the dream to the best of my ability. There was no turning back. But I didn't think it was unreasonable to not want to die or go mad. For my sake as well as the sake of my kids.

"Fine." Emer slapped the arm of her chair. "Stop, then. I always knew you would."

Her words and the spark of anger in her eyes burned through my chill, and I leaned forward, holding her gaze. "I never said I was going to stop. I want to save Lorcan. But it seems like the odds are stacked against us, and I do have two kids who need me."

Emer watched me, saying nothing.

"Lorcan must be saved. I want him out of there. I want to know the man who gave me life." I lowered my voice to a growl. "But if you think you can do better, with your *strong* connection to my father, be my guest."

Emer clamped her lips together. I sat back with a nod and looked at Geraldine. "Given that this entire operation is a bit of a mess, I suggest we continue training. I need to know as much as I can before I attempt to save Lorcan." I ignored my rumbling stomach and looming headache. "What's next?"

Emer glared at me a moment longer, as if deciding how to react to my words. Finally, she spoke. "Why not take her fully into the Dreamscape now? We have an hour. All we need to do is introduce the process."

My heart raced at her suggestion. I wasn't ready. But was I ever going to be? "Yes. Let's do that."

"We need more time," Geraldine said, closing the pad where she jotted notes as if the matter was decided.

Geraldine was stalling. I wondered why. Did she worry about me? Maybe she suspected I was more dangerous that she'd led me to believe.

"Muirgen says to allot one hour," Emer persisted. "Dreammasters aren't supposed to take forever on a dream, Geraldine."

Geraldine bristled at her tone. "Tomorrow will be fine, Emer. I'm directing this operation, not you."

"I think Emer's correct, Daughter." Granny thumped her cane. "I'll accompany them. Emer can lead the way. The more practice Aisling has, the easier the dream is on Samhain. I have no plans of losing my granddaughter or Lorcan. We don't have time to dilly-dally."

"I don't have the time today," Geraldine said, glancing at a tasteful jeweled watch circling her wrist. "There's a vital meeting at work that begins at two. I must leave."

"Nuala and I can do this," Emer said. She looked at me. "What do you think, Aisling?"

"I'm ready." My voice croaked on the last word, hinting at the fear laced with my determination. Geraldine's insistence that we wait fueled my doubt, and I hoped I wasn't making a terrible mistake.

"You're afraid," Emer said matter-of-factly. "And I understand. But what you need to remember is that your powers allow you to enter the Mist and access the Dreamscape in full-body form, not just in your mind. You're a Dreammaster." She stood and stretched. "You'll have to do this to save Lorcan. And you'll have to bring him out of the Underworld into the Dreamscape in his full body form. Practice will make it easier."

"How do I connect with Lorcan via my mind and manage to bring his full body out of the Underworld?" My mind was still working to wrap around the concept.

"The same way your mother connected to you," Granny said. "All that we do as Dreammasters is based on intention and energy. Let's practice going fully into the Dreamscape today. Tomorrow, we will teach you how to connect and bring Lorcan into the Dreamscape."

I nodded. "Fine."

Geraldine snapped closed her briefcase and rose. "I suppose the three of you aren't going to listen to me," she said, her lips compressed into an angry line. "I want it noted that I don't believe this is a good idea. Unfortunately, I must leave." She turned to me, her dark and disapproving look matching her tone. "Good luck, Aisling."

I watched her leave, fear and guilt sitting heavy in my chest. I didn't want to oppose my aunt. But I wanted to be ready. I clutched my pendant, which throbbed as if my determination had somehow found its way into the silver. The carved Dara knot was warm beneath my sweater, but the spreading confidence I'd felt had vanished. I rose and walked the perimeter of the room, my limbs twitchy with the need to move.

"It makes sense to move forward," Granny said, "rather than going over skills you've mastered. And I'd like to watch as you create your dream scene."

"I think that's an excellent idea. I'd like your thoughts." I paused at the windows, staring into the garden. My heart pounded as I contemplated the next steps. What would it be like to be in the Dreamscape in my full body? What if I couldn't do it?

"This is what you're meant to do," Emer said, her voice softer, kinder than I'd heard it. "Your natural instincts will take over. And we'll be there to guide you."

"Trust us." Granny watched me with her beady eyes. "Trust yourself, Aisling."

I turned to find them watching me. I kept my eyes on Granny's. "I do trust you." What I didn't add was how much I doubted myself. I shuddered as I thought back to yesterday and the sight of Granny slumped in her chair, the throbbing of my finger as I struggled to save her. Had I caused that? She could have died. Things could be worse if I took this final step and entered fully into the Dreamscape. I could harm Granny and Emer. I should voice my concerns. Be open and honest. Only by learning the truth could I fully trust myself.

"I really don't understand what's holding you back," Emer said in a challenging voice. She stood with her hands on her hips, her eyes hard blue points.

My mouth opened, ready to confess to murder, but the fear and the throbbing in my finger kept me quiet. That and the fact that Geraldine had warned me not to say anything.

"Grand. Two days wasted." Emer shook back her short black hair, slipped her purse strap over her shoulder, and turned to leave, dismissing me and my doubts, treating me as if I didn't matter, like Trevor had. Like my mother had when she hid the truth from me. Heat, like a molten fire in my belly, spread throughout my body. My fingers fisted.

"Wait one minute. I didn't say I wanted to stop working." My voice was hard, demanding a response. I was sick of people walking away from me. Emer turned around.

"I just found out about this stuff. You've known who you are for a lifetime, but I've had a different life. I'm a mom, something you're not." Emer blinked, the color draining from her face before she looked away. "I was a wife as well. Something you're also not." Her gasp was satisfying, fueling the sizzling anger throbbing through my veins. "My life has been as meaningful as the life of a Dreammaster and just as worthwhile as doing a dream for someone for love." I snorted at the word. "And, as for love, let me tell you, it isn't all it's cracked up to be."

I looked up at the ceiling, lost in my rant. "Husbands can cheat and leave, and kids grow up and they leave too. But it was my life, and I understood it. I miss it. This is new, daunting. Scary." My voice hitched, and I took a steadying breath.

"Aisling," Granny's voice was soft. "We understand, child. This is all very new. And Dreammasters must act with care. But I believe you can do this."

"How do you know?" I turned to face my grandmother. "What if I do this in a few days and hurt Lorcan?" My voice cracked as if penetrating thin ice. "What if I accidentally kill him or someone else? You can't tell me that dreams are always safe. You said that entering a dream with the wrong intention could cause harm." My heart pounded, and I stared into my grandmother's eyes, willing her to reassure me that all my fears were unfounded, even when she didn't understand the truth of Trevor's death and where my terror stemmed from.

Granny leaned forward, watching me, a deep furrow between her brows. "What are you afraid of, Aisling?"

"I'm afraid of ..." I wanted to blurt it all out, was about to tell Granny the truth about my involvement in Trevor's death and my fear that I'd hurt her the day before, but before I could say more, pain shot through my right index finger and bolted up my arm.

"Ahh." I bent forward, grabbing hold of the chair I'd been sitting in, breathing as if I'd been in an uphill race. I rubbed my hand up and down my arm and pressed my thumb against my finger. I stumbled around the chair and plopped into the seat.

"What's wrong?" Emer's narrowed eyes watched me.

"Aisling?" Granny said, her voice sharp with concern.

I took a shuddering breath, fighting the pain. "This hurts." I held up my finger, which pulsed red hot and swollen like a miniature balloon.

"Is this the finger the swan pecked?" Emer walked to me and took my hand in hers. I gasped when she touched the tip of my finger. "It's hot."

The pain was worse than the initial peck. I was done lying. "It was a book." As I said the words, my vision blurred, and I almost fell.

"A book? That's not what Geraldine said yesterday." Emer pushed me into a chair. "I'm going to call Dr. Higgins. This sounds like more than a paper cut."

"It wasn't a paper cut. I got pecked." Intense pain stole my voice and made my breath ragged.

"What book, Aisling?" Panic filled Granny's voice, and she thumped her cane. "Where did this ..." Granny's voice faded, and I wasn't sure if my hearing had failed or she'd lost the ability to speak.

"Granny," I croaked when she didn't finish her question. "Is she okay?" I tugged at Emer's hand.

"Pecked by a book?" Emer asked, disregarding my concern. "Can you explain how you managed that, then?" she asked, searching my face.

"Not by the book." I gasped. "The picture," I said before my head lolled back and the dream sucked me in.

I was there, in the thick of a dreamvision with none of the preliminaries Granny or Emer had taught me. I'd had no time to set my intentions, to protect myself from destructive energy, or to imagine my Dreamscape scene, but, as before, my Dreamscape was there waiting for me. Today it looked exactly like the sitting room where I'd spent the afternoon training with Geraldine, Granny, and Emer. The fire was burning in the hearth. Emer was kneeling at my feet, holding my hand, staring at my throbbing finger. And Granny was asleep in her chair.

Granny was asleep. No. She was more than asleep. She was unconscious. A murky energy surrounded her, the same dirty circle of smudge that I'd seen enfold her yesterday, little fingers of it pressing into her head and circling her neck, as if it intended to strangle her. That wasn't right.

I fought with myself to break free of the dream, but I couldn't. I was immobilized within the Dreamscape, only able to watch as Granny seemed to sink further into herself until she shuddered, took a rattling breath, and then seemed to stop breathing altogether.

"Granny," I screamed in my head. Granny didn't answer. Had I started this dream? Was I hurting Granny? I didn't remember doing anything, but I knew I had to do something now.

Energy thrummed in my belly, and heat spread from my chest into my swan pendant, which beat hotly against my skin. I summoned my power, bringing it up from my belly, a warm river of emerald energy pumping into my heart and throughout my limbs. From my heart, I drew the energy up into the space behind my eyes and surrounded Granny with it, covering her and sweeping the dark energy away, sending it into the cleansing aura of the Dreamscape, watching as it separated into droplets and disappeared into the mist.

"Come on, Aisling. Take a deep breath. Come back. You're doing great." Emer coaxed me back from the Dreamscape.

I breathed deeply, focusing on slowing the energy whirling in my system, and opened my eyes. Dr. Higgins was standing over Granny, speaking in a low voice. Granny's answer was mumbled, but she was alive.

"How is she?" I sat up too fast and dropped my head in my hands.

"She's fine." Emer knelt before me. "You brought her back. Like yesterday."

"The green energy," I said. "It flowed around her and covered the dark energy." I didn't like her look, her narrowed eyes and pursed lips. Blood pounded in my ears. Emer suspected me of something. The problem was, so did I. "It was like yesterday's dream. I saw the dark energy siphon from her, like some sort of infection being drained." I looked up at Dr. Higgins, who'd walked to where Emer knelt.

"That makes sense," he said. He turned when Maeve bustled into the room to fuss over Granny. When he turned back, his eyes were clouded, and his voice was quiet and serious. "I did some reading yesterday. Because I've never encountered anything quite like this." He cleared his throat. "From what I found, I suspect that something or someone has been trying to steal Nuala's powers." Tommy had explained that Dr. Higgins was also a descendant of one of the Tuatha Dé Danann gods, a healer called Dian Cécht. He understood our powers and our mission to save Lorcan.

"What?" Emer shot to standing. "My gram told me that's not happened in centuries."

"Yes." Dr. Higgins pinched the bridge of his nose. "The Aislingeach Council outlawed the practice over four hundred years ago after several Dreammasters lost their lives and their minds. Horrible practice." He shook his head. "Nuala may be confused for a day or so. Especially as this is the second day it's happened." He looked from me to Emer. "I'd take a break from training for a day if you can. She needs her rest. And I need time to figure out who's behind this devilish action. Whoever it is, the council must bring her to justice." He stared at me, and for a moment I was worried he was accusing me. Could he read the doubts in my mind about my trustworthiness?

"We'll do what we have to for Granny," I said.

"But we can't stop." Emer scrunched her hands in her hair. "We don't have much more time."

"Nuala can't help you for at least a day," Dr. Higgins said. He checked his watch. "It's two thirty. Maybe it's a good time to break until tomorrow." Emer opened her mouth, and he held up his hand. "I understand your mission for Samhain, but this mission may place Nuala in danger. If that's the case, I'll have to insist she not take part in any more training." He looked back at me. "What were your observations, Aisling? Emer told me you dived into the Dreamscape as if you'd been doing so since you were seventeen."

The doctor's eyes narrowed as he watched me, and I wanted to run out of the room and hide. Or confess. At that thought, pain shot through my fingertip and seared up my arm. I crossed my arms to hide the resulting tremor and banished any thought of confession, and the pain subsided.

"A force pulled me in," I said. "I saw Granny droop. I knew she wasn't well. But I didn't try to get into the Dreamscape, and I don't know how I got there."

"Your finger hurt," Emer said. "And then you were gone."

"Show me the finger." Dr. Higgins held out his hand.

He took my hand, prodding my now normal finger gently and with clinical detachment.

"It's fine now," I said. "Not swollen. No pain at all. I don't know what set it off before." But I did know. Or I thought I did. Whenever I started talking about the book and the swan, pain seared from the tip of my finger up my arm. I almost spoke up, but Geraldine was keeping my dream the night Trevor died to herself for now. Before I spoke of the peck to the doctor, I'd speak to my aunt.

He examined the wound. "There's a small mark here, but it looks clear of infection." He released his grip, tilting his head, considering the options. "Maybe you hit it on something?"

"Maybe." I nodded. The look in his eyes, as if he knew I was lying, made me reluctant to tell him about Geraldine's book and the swan. Plus, I didn't want to make Geraldine angry when she'd asked me not to say anything.

"First, Geraldine said a swan by the river pecked you." Emer's eyes narrowed. "Today, you said something about a book." She had to butt in, and I mentally kicked myself for saying anything.

"A book?" Dr. Higgins quirked his eyebrows.

I shook my head. "I don't know what I was saying. It must have been the dream pulling me in." I pulled my hand away from his.

"Hmm." He considered me for a moment longer. "If you have any more pain, come see me."

"Aisling." Granny's soft voice floated to us.

"Granny." I scrambled to my feet and hurried to her side. "How are you feeling?"

"A little tired, child, but I'll recover." She reached for my hand, her worried eyes searching mine. "You must be careful." She paused, gathering breath, her grip strong.

"Don't speak," I said, squeezing her hand. "We can talk later."

Maeve growled, and I sensed a protest.

"Or tomorrow."

"No," she shook her head. "Now. While we can."

"But we'll have tomorrow."

"Maybe."

I frowned, about to question her more, when she coughed and motioned for her glass of water. I handed it to her. She drank, handed the glass back to me, and grasped my wrist in her cold fingers. Leaning closer, she spoke urgently. "Your energy is wrong. Too much fear and doubt." She swallowed, and her eyes closed.

"Granny," I whispered. "Please." She had to be okay.

"There's danger and darkness in your dreams. A force, preying on you—on your energy. Fight it, child." She dropped back and sighed. "Geraldine," she whispered. "Mother."

"My mother, Granny? Are you speaking about Geraldine and my mother?" She looked at me, her eyes drooping. "What do you mean?"

"She should be in bed," Maeve said, pushing past me to Granny's side.

"No," Granny murmured. "Must explain to Aisling." Even as she spoke, her eyelids lowered, and her chin sank toward her chest.

"To bed with ye," Maeve said, gently removing the blanket covering Granny's legs.

"I'll help you," Dr. Higgins said.

"Aisling, take care," Granny said, her voice drifting from soft to softer as the doctor and Maeve escorted her from the room. "Not what it seems."

"Granny," I said, starting to follow, stopped in my tracks by a sharp look from Maeve.

"Leave her be. You can speak with her tomorrow," she said, and her tone precluded argument.

"I'll see you tomorrow, Granny." But I didn't think she heard me.

"I guess I'd best leave," Emer said. "We'll start early tomorrow." With a nod, she followed them from the room.

I dropped into a chair, my head in my hands, elbows resting on my knees. I massaged my temples, my skin hot. Too much had happened since I'd arrived; most of it I couldn't begin to explain.

What I hadn't told Dr. Higgins was that my finger had started to throb this morning after I was about to confess my dream of killing Trevor, almost as if my body were warning me not to say anything. And my finger throbbed before I was pulled into dreams I hadn't started. Or did it throb when I was about to cause harm? I didn't know anymore. I rubbed my tired eyes. Why did my finger hurt at all, and would I ever find a way to make it stop? And what did Granny mean about the danger and darkness preying on my energy?

I blew out a breath, kneading my neck, but doubts still circled in my mind and refused to allow me to relax. Granny could clarify my questions, but Maeve would never let me near her. I wished Geraldine was here—I could broach my concerns with her.

Chapter Thirty-Five

"How could she do such a thing?" Maeve's shocked voice carried up the stairs. I paused halfway down, not wanting to interrupt. Was Geraldine home? Or had the doctor stopped by to check on Granny? Or maybe Maeve was on the phone. When I heard nothing more, I continued my descent.

"She's not shown her face since dinner." Maeve was speaking again, and my ears perked up. Was she discussing me? "She said something about a headache." She *was* discussing me. Nerves danced along my spine. Who was she talking to and why? "Go on with you," she bleated. Another pause followed this. "Jesus, Mary, and Joseph, what's the world coming to?"

Her exclamation made me jump, and I caught the knobbed end of the banister before I lost my footing. Someone was saying unpleasant things about me. I took a step toward the kitchen, sure Maeve was speaking on the ancient landline hanging by the door. My heart thumped as I drew closer, hoping I'd hear more and discover what horrible thing I supposedly had done. Was it Geraldine? Had Granny called her daughter to share her suspicions?

I stopped outside the kitchen door, breath held, hands clasped at my heart. Silence greeted me from within the room. Had she hung up the phone? I was being an idiot. I should move, stop listening in on a private conversation. But I couldn't get my feet started.

Maeve cleared her throat, and I thought my racing heart would give out. "Don't you worry, Geraldine. I won't let her near your mother." A pause. "I'm on top of things, I am. I'll see you when I see you." A clatter followed as she replaced the landline on the base.

Shit. I was about to be discovered. I had to hide. Or obfuscate. Breath held, I tiptoed back to the base of the staircase, took two steps up, and made as much noise as possible coming back down. Maeve's head popped out of the kitchen, followed by her petite, round frame.

"Hi, Maeve," I said, noting her scowl and answering with a smile. "I came down for a cup of tea." I dangled a tea bag of my favorite calming brew from my fingers.

"Suit yourself." Maeve's body blocked the kitchen door.

"Do you mind?" I gestured to the kitchen, and she moved, albeit with a frown. "Thanks."

Maeve followed me into the room, and I felt her eyes on me as I filled the electric kettle and switched it on.

"Do you know if Geraldine's coming here tonight or going back to her place?" I asked, curious to hear how she'd respond. It was nearing nine in the evening, and I'd heard nothing from Geraldine, although, given her call, she'd heard about the dream this afternoon and that Dr. Higgins believed some entity was trying to steal Granny's powers.

I froze, mug in hand, as I replayed Maeve's side of the conversation in my head. Geraldine thought I was dangerous. Granny's earlier comments about the danger and darkness of my dreams indicated she was worried about the same thing. But they couldn't suspect me of trying to steal Granny's powers. I hadn't known such a thing was possible until Dr. Higgins spoke of it this afternoon. I wanted to scream, to barrage my aunt with my questions, to release all the doubt and frustration bottled inside me. But it seemed Geraldine had made up her mind about me.

"I don't keep track of Geraldine." Maeve snapped.

"Of course." I dropped the tea bag into the mug.

Maeve snorted and bustled around the kitchen. She was a good bustler and a very efficient housekeeper. But tonight I sensed she was moving to move, trying to look busy so she could keep an eye on me. With a shaking hand, I poured hot water into the mug. I didn't know what to ask her to get more information.

"Geraldine's a busy woman," Maeve said brusquely. "Has meetings, important things to do. She can't babysit you all day long, now, can she?" She slapped a towel on the counter by the sink. "And neither can I. I need to check on your Granny."

"Can I come with you? I'd like to see her."

Maeve rounded on me with the ferocity of a rabid dog. "You stay out of your granny's room." She stepped toward me, wagging a finger in my face. "You stay away from Nuala, do you hear? She doesn't need you pestering her. Not after what you did to her." She bit back a sob.

"I'd never hurt Granny," I said, pressing my hand to my heart. Maeve's expression said it all. She didn't believe me. I closed my eyes, hoping to calm my nerves and push away the thrumming behind my eyes that had taunted me since lunch.

"That's just what you'd say. Geraldine warned me." She stopped, crossed her arms across her ample midsection, and looked away.

"Fine." I took a deep breath. "I won't see Granny. But I had a few questions for Geraldine." I'd spent a solitary late afternoon and evening waiting for my aunt, working with the Druid pen and wondering if I shouldn't be doing something useful to prepare for Samhain. Which was pretty hard to do when Geraldine was the one with the information I needed to get into the Underworld.

"And you'll ask them tomorrow." She narrowed her eyes, her body positioned by the door. "You have a room and a chair. Surely you know how to read a book." Maeve snorted. "As soon as I check on Nuala, I'll be closing up the house for the night. You needn't bother coming back downstairs."

"Okay." I swallowed, wishing there was some way I could reassure her, convince her I hadn't tried to hurt my grandmother. But I knew she'd dismiss my words. My heart sat heavy in my chest as I made my way across the kitchen, mug in hand. "An early night is a good idea."

Maeve followed me from the room and up the stairs. I looked back toward Granny's room when I reached my door. Maeve was watching me. I looked away and stepped into my room.

I was hollowed out, hurt that Geraldine considered me a threat to her mother. But maybe she was right. Could I guarantee Granny was safe from my dreams? After all, I'd been present on both occasions when Granny had been sucked into dangerous dreaming scenarios.

As I sipped my tea, I prepared for bed. Snuggled in warm pajamas, I climbed beneath the covers, leaning back against the pillows, my head pounding with worry and concern. I didn't want to be dangerous, but Trevor's death was a strong indicator my dreams posed a threat. My chest felt weighted, making breathing a struggle. I couldn't go back in time and save Trevor, but at least there was something I could do to keep Granny safe tonight. I pulled out my journal and pen.

First, I reviewed my notes for my aunt and scribbled down a couple of new thoughts.

1. Concerned about the dreams and danger to Granny. Do you have any thoughts?

2. Still uncertain I can be trusted. Need answers about the dream on the night Trevor died.

3. Pain continues in my finger, but I don't understand why.

4. My dream scenes continue to appear without my intention.

5. Granny says my energy is wrong.

I bit my lip, tapping the pen on the last comment, considering what Granny had said to me. Too much fear and doubt. I could only consult Geraldine, per her instructions. My stomach tightened. Geraldine and I had to speak tomorrow, or it was time for me to take my questions to Granny, even if it meant confessing my fears about Trevor's death.

I yawned. Tonight I'd rest after I cast my ring of protection. I wrote my verse in the journal with the Druid pen.

> *Tonight, I set a circle wide,*
> *to protect myself and all inside,*
> *from any threat I may pose,*
> *from my dreams when in repose.*
> *Include Granny within the ring.*
> *Protect her from danger coming from me.*
> *I set my intention for only the best,*
> *and cast my circle before I rest.*

Putting the journal aside, I closed my eyes and relaxed, allowing my breaths to be slow and deep. The green energy radiated from my core, into my heart and head and beyond, flooding every corner of the room. I finished with a visualization of Granny, watching the protective energy cradle her.

Opening my eyes, I looked around. The room looked cleaner, safer. Or, at least, I felt better.

I snapped off the table lamp and snuggled down under the covers, listening to the heavy rain lashing the old stone of the manor, relaxing into the soporific spell of the pounding water.

* * *

"You should be afraid and filled with doubt." A soft female voice of indeterminate age taunted me, a presence deep within my subconscious. I didn't recognize the speaker, but I struggled, pushing against the phantom in my mind, willing the words to stop. They didn't. "Everyone leaves you. You're all on your own. With such burdensome responsibilities." The voice rose, louder and louder, until it shouted. "Alone. So alone and afraid."

"No," I whispered, writhing in bed. Was this real or a dream? "Safe. All safe."

"There's no safety, Aisling." The voice taunted me. "Only duty and responsibility. You can't handle it. You're afraid."

"No." My voice was guttural, a strangled cry struggling out of my body. "No." I thrashed from one side to the next, finally curling into a ball, falling back into a tormented sleep.

Wind and rain woke me next, buffeting my body. I stood at the edge of a cliff, watching the ocean roil below me, fog rising from the waves like steam whistling out around the lid of a boiling pot of water.

"Aisling." A voice rose in the fog to reach me. It was my mother. "Aisling, go back. You're not safe."

I looked into the face of my mother far below me. I was back in the Underworld. Fear pumped through my veins in an icy stream as the pendant around my neck pulsed and the tip of my finger throbbed. Why was I here? Had my mother pulled me in?

"I'm working, Mom. To save Lorcan."

"Go back, Aisling," Mom yelled, her voice broken by the blustering storm. "Quickly. All is not as it seems."

And then Granny was standing next to my mom. She reached out but was too far away to touch me. "Trust yourself, child. And go back now." Granny's form wavered, and I screamed as she faded in and out of view.

"She's not strong enough to be here," Mom yelled. "Leave and take her with you. It's not her time or her place to die."

The fear welled up, choking me, making me pant for breath. Granny couldn't die. I forced back the fear, pushed against the pain in my finger, and took a cleansing breath, focusing on Granny. I knew in my heart that I was the only one who could save her. "She won't die."

My emerald energy was there as I said the words. I sent it up and out from the place between my eyebrows, surrounding Granny with the beam of light. I pulled Granny's form closer to me and shot us both up and out of the Underworld, through the Dreamscape, and back to Old Oak Manor.

A coughing fit awakened me, and I became aware of lying in my bed, my nightgown damp from my journey. I pushed up, confused about the dream, baffled how I'd managed to get into the Dreamscape bodily, let alone the Underworld. I'd taken precautions, set the ring of safety before I slept. What had happened?

I took deep breaths, allowing the pounding of my heart to calm before I swung my legs to the floor. I had to check on Granny. My head spun, and I gripped the mattress until the sensation passed. If I was unsteady, I could only imagine how the journey had weakened her.

Before I could move, a powerful beam of lightning shot into my room. Balls of electricity bounced off the walls as if a violent tennis match was being played by invisible opponents, striking at me until I dived under the blankets, hoping that Irish wool and deep-down duvets would repel an electric current. It was as if the Underworld had followed me back to Galway, and I lay still, holding my breath, waiting for the next strike, hoping the violence was directed solely at me and not Granny. As the tempest calmed, sleep sucked me in, and I fell under its spell and into another dream more dreadful than the last.

I was standing at Granny's bedside, staring down into her face, the carpet pressing into my feet, shivering. I reached out and touched Granny, her skin warm beneath my fingers. I was here, in her room, in a dream. Frowning, I bit my lips. This made no sense. I took a step back. I had to leave. My finger throbbed.

Movement from above Granny pulled my attention. Five undulating fingers floated from a milky palm, like anemone waving in a murky sea, reaching for Granny, who lay unmoving in her bed. A voice murmured, the whisper barely intelligible, although I caught a few words: *empty, cold, death.* My heart raced. I wanted to go to her, but I was frozen in place and only able to watch as the fingers unfurled, stretching toward Granny.

"Mary shirked her duties as a Dreammaster." It was the same voice I'd heard before. "She was untrustworthy. Trevor left, shirked his responsibilities. He failed in his duty of trust." The voice became Granny's voice and grew louder. "If you cannot be responsible, no one can trust you, and you fail." The fingers drew closer, approaching Granny's temple. "Responsibility and trust and failure, Aisling. Are you the same as them? Or are you afraid? Are you so scared that you cannot act, cannot take responsibility, cannot prove you're trustworthy?"

Red waves of anger swelled in my chest at the words, pushing out terror. I was responsible. I was trustworthy. Why had no one ever seen that? Not even my grandmother. I watched, mentally encouraging the fingers as they continued their relentless journey toward Granny.

"What will you do, Aisling?" Granny's voice taunted me, pushing the anger into a fever. "How can you earn trust and prove your worth when no one has trusted you before? Not Mary. Not Trevor. Not even I trust you." Granny's head rose from her pillow, and she stared into my eyes.

"I can never trust you. Look at what you're doing to me now." The fingers fastened to Granny, pulling at the side of her head, stretching it into a cartoon shape. Moments later, they withdrew, each digit extracting a strand of ruby-red light from Granny. Granny's face deflated like a popped balloon as the last of the strands exited her body, and she dropped, motionless, onto her pillow.

The anger that had filled me whooshed away as Granny shrank, replaced by a cold, prickly dread. "No!" I screamed.

But the fingers continued their work, ignoring me. They carried the strands of red to a matching hand with a matching set of five fingers holding a sparkling orb of crystal deep within the palm. Poised above the orb, each finger released its strand into the orb until they blended together. Then the fingers stoppered the orb, sealing the coiled red inside.

"Stop. What have you done? Don't do this to Granny." But my voice reverberated inside my skull, and the hands took no notice.

"She will die if all is not restored by daybreak on Samhain." The hands with the orb cradled within the joined palms disappeared.

I wanted to call out, to wake up, to alert someone, anyone, that Granny was in danger. But the paralysis held on even as my index finger pulsed with pain. I focused on each part of my body, straining to move, but every limb was heavy, as if stuck in thick, squelchy mud. All the while, my mind whirred. Was Granny dead, just like Trevor? And was I responsible?

CHAPTER THIRTY-SIX

October 29, Old Oak Manor

"Wake up." Screaming accompanied by pounding on my door woke me. I sat up too quickly, my head spinning. The world was still dark beyond the sheer curtains, and rain pounded in a harsh staccato rhythm on the panes of glass. Feet stomped down the hall, and the pounding resumed, along with a holler to Geraldine.

"Maeve," I mumbled, shaking my head and rubbing my eyes as I struggled to orient myself. Something wriggled at the back of my brain, waiting for me to remember. What was it?

"Wake up, Aisling." My door opened. Aunt Geraldine stepped inside and snapped on the table lamp by the bed. "My mother is ill. I may need your help."

"Granny." My head spun as the dream tumbled back into focus. My body trembled at the images, and I was happy to be sitting.

"Aisling, are you unwell?" Geraldine stepped nearer. "You're very pale." She leaned over and touched my forehead with the back of her fingers. I flinched, remembering the fingers from the dream last night. Geraldine noticed and pulled away. "Your clothes are dirty. Were you outside in the rain?"

I glanced down at my pajamas. Stains streaked down the front of my shirt, lines where water had soaked me and dried the fabric a different color. "No, I was asleep." I looked back up at Geraldine and shrugged. "I don't know." How could I tell her what had happened last night? Especially if I harmed my grandmother.

Geraldine's eyes narrowed, considering. "I think it's best that you wait here, Aisling." She spoke as if I was a child in trouble.

"I want to see Granny." I scrambled from the bed, noticing a gritty feeling on my sheets and between my toes. Sand. From the Underworld. It had happened. And Granny had been there and was weakened because of it.

"Come along, the pair of ye." Maeve burst into the room, her eyes wild, her curls woolly from sleep. "Nuala's not getting any better the longer we wait."

"No." Geraldine's voice was sharp, and Maeve jumped, believing Geraldine was speaking to her.

"Don't take that tone with me, girlie."

"I wasn't speaking to you, Maeve." Geraldine looked at the housekeeper. "I was speaking to my niece. She's not feeling well this morning, and I believe she ought to stay here while we investigate."

"I'm fine," I argued, fighting against a wave of nausea. I had to see my grandmother. To ensure she was okay.

"You're not," Geraldine snapped back, her eyes sparking a warning not to argue. "You're about to fall over as we speak. Stay here and wait for me."

She turned, as precisely as a soldier, and strode past Maeve, who looked from me to the retreating form of my aunt before following Geraldine. She glanced back at me once, a question in her eyes, but I had no answers. My knees threatened to buckle, and I sat back on my bed, reaching over to wipe the sand from between my toes until, feeling lightheaded, I was forced to sit up.

What could I do now? What was Geraldine thinking? And was it possible I'd done something awful, some irreparable harm to my granny? "No, I couldn't have." I sank against the pillows at the top of the bed, burying my face into one. I thought back to what I could remember of the dreams I'd had the night before. So much for setting protection around my space. I'd screwed that up as well as everything else. I'd hurt Granny. Just like I'd hurt Trevor. I was a menace.

I wallowed in my wretchedness for a few minutes, each breath a struggle as the dreams from last night replayed in my brain, but something didn't mesh.

A new thought came to me, and I sat up. In every dream I'd had in which someone had been harmed, a force had pulled me in. It had happened when Mom died, when Trevor died, and when I'd watched the fog surround Granny. Last night was the same. I hadn't intended for any of the dreams to happen. In fact, I'd intentionally tried to protect against dangerous dreams coming from me last night.

I rubbed my eyes. Maybe I was grasping at something, anything, to prove I wasn't dangerous.

"Aisling, what happened last night?" I hadn't heard my aunt return, and when I looked up she was watching me, her lips a straight line, her eyes filled with anger. "My mother is very ill. Dr. Higgins is on his way. And I believe you know something about this."

"I don't know." I sighed out a sob. "I set the protections like Granny said. But I was back in dreams. All night."

"What did you do to my mother?" The way she said "my mother" seemed to negate any claim I had on Granny as my grandmother, leaving me excluded. I shivered.

"Fingers took something from her. Put whatever it was in an orb. I watched but I couldn't stop them. And then she sank like she'd been drained." Her sharp intake of breath brought me to my feet, and I grasped the bedrail to keep from falling. "I swear, I don't know what happened." But Geraldine wasn't paying attention to my words any longer.

She pointed a shaking finger at me, her face pale. "You took her powers."

"No. I swear. I didn't." I lurched around the bed toward her. "Please, believe me." I clutched at her hand, but she pulled away as if I'd burned her. "Please, Aunt Geraldine. Help me." I was crying, and she watched, unmoved.

"I can no longer help you, Aisling. You've broken trust, just as Mary broke trust with me all those years ago and lost the man I loved. How can I believe you will save Lorcan and not kill him? How can I help a woman who is so bent on destruction that she'd try to kill her elderly granny? My mother only wanted the best for you." Geraldine's eyes filled with tears. "And you betrayed her." She seemed to rise taller before my shrinking form. "How dare you?"

I sank to the floor, sobbing, aware only of my rasping breath and Geraldine's footfalls walking away.

❦

After waiting half an hour with no word from my aunt, I decided to check on things myself. The knob of my bedroom door didn't turn when I tried it. I stared at the knob as if the polished brass could speak to me. It had never been stuck before. My brows narrowed. Or was it locked?

Surely Geraldine wouldn't lock me in. I tried again, the knob rattling as I twisted left and right. Nothing.

"You need to stay where you are for now, Aisling." Geraldine's voice floated through the door.

"Why?" My voice was sharp. "What have I done?"

"I think you know." She released a weary sigh. "Although, I have no idea how you figured out how to do such a complicated spell." Her voice tensed. "I hear you tried the same thing after I left yesterday."

"I did no such thing. The dream pulled me in, and I saved Granny. Ask Dr. Higgins."

"Who do you think told me about yesterday's attempt?"

My shoulders sagged. Dr. Higgins had watched me yesterday as if he wasn't sure if I could be trusted. He must have thought I'd tried to hurt Granny, and if he was against me, proving my innocence was going to be tough.

"Come on, Geraldine," I pleaded. "You can't really think I'd know how to do such a thing." I laid my head against the door. "How could you even think this of me?"

"How could I think this?" She laughed, not a cheery sound. "I don't believe my suspicions are as farfetched as I wish they were." Her voice lowered to a hiss. "After all, you're the woman who murdered her husband. How did you learn to do that? Why is it such a stretch to think you could steal Mother's powers?"

"You weren't convinced I hurt him." I slammed a hand against the door. "You said you'd help me find out the truth. You also said intention was key. Why would I intend to hurt Trevor or Granny?"

"You're full of excuses, Aisling, but we both know this isn't my fault. Right now, I have no time to listen. I have to figure out how to save Mother and poor Lorcan without your help."

My veins filled with ice. "I didn't do this. Let me help." I pounded on the door. "Geraldine, listen to me. He's my father. He was in love with my mother. I want to save him. And I need to find out what happened to Granny."

I pounded again, but when there was no answer, I stumbled back, trapped and presumed guilty.

I shook my head, leaning against the bed as my mind raced. She didn't understand about Granny either. She hadn't seen the dream. I shook the bedpost, causing the entire bed to shimmy. Something had pulled me in, and I hadn't gone in willingly.

"It wasn't me," I hollered, not expecting an answer and not receiving one. But it didn't matter. I pushed away from the bed, purpose fueling my movements. I'd show everyone I was trustworthy, contrary to what the voice in the dream had said. I'd save Lorcan and Granny, and I'd prove my innocence. The dream last night wasn't my fault. I was sure of that. But, first, I had to get out of here.

I hurried into the bathroom, where I'd left my jeans to dry after yesterday's rain, but a glance in the mirror stopped me. Leaning in, I touched my face where sand had dried, bits of it flaking into the sink. My hair was flattened from sleep and crusty with seawater.

A shower was mandatory before anyone would take me seriously.

After my shower, I pulled on jeans and layered a long-sleeved T-shirt under a soft wool sweater. Opening the curtains, I noted that while the sun was up the sky was filled with heavy gray clouds and rain was still falling. I'd need both a jacket and an umbrella. I stared outside a moment, watching as the wind whipped the garden into a frenzy, until a spiky branch from the old oak tree screeched down the window, causing me to jump. Time to go.

I paused. But where was I going? The thought of flying home crossed my mind, but I banished the notion as I gazed around my mother's girlhood bedroom. Mom wouldn't want me to abandon Granny and Lorcan. A surge of power flooded my system, heating my hands as my pendant pulsed against my chest. No more running. I'd make this right and clear myself in the process.

I could go to Tommy. But Geraldine would think of looking there first. I didn't know anyone else in Galway. But if I didn't go there and explain everything to Tommy, including the dream the night Trevor died, Geraldine could sway him to her side. An idea sprang to mind. I could use my journal and the Druid pen. Warn Tommy I was on the way. It was early. He'd see the note and write back. It was the best option I had.

I rifled through my backpack for the items. Opening the journal, I paused. How could I phrase this without making myself sound guilty?

> *To Tommy:*
> *It's Aisling ...*
> *I need your help,*
> *And a place to hide.*
> *So I can explain,*
> *And make things right.*
> *Everything's wrong.*
> *Bad dreams last night,*
> *Granny's powers ...*

Muffled voices in the hallway and the mention of my name made me pause.

Geraldine spoke, "I must search her room."

"But why would she harm her grandmother?" Dr. Higgins's voice.

I froze, the verse forgotten. Like hell I was going to allow my aunt to rifle through my stuff.

"She's been trying to hurt my mother all week." Geraldine sniffed. "This morning, Aisling said she put the powers in an orb. She must have hidden them in her Dreamscape or brought them back here. Until I return them to Mother, there's a risk of Mother dying. She's lost to us if the orb is broken."

"Dear God have mercy," Maeve wailed.

"She knows far more than she's admitting." Geraldine sounded so sure, so authoritative.

My jaw tensed. I had not said I put the powers in an orb. I'd said the *fingers* I saw put something in an orb. Full-body heat swept through me. Geraldine was offering her interpretation of my dream without allowing me a defense. But there was no reason for Dr. Higgins to believe me over a woman, a Dreammaster, he'd known for years.

I closed and locked the journal and stuffed it in my backpack before pulling on my boots. I tiptoed to my door and pressed my ear against the wood, but I didn't hear Geraldine. Had she, Maeve, and the doctor left? This could be my chance. I quietly turned the knob twice, but to no avail. Damn. Still locked.

"Geraldine has every right to be suspicious of the girl." Maeve's voice trembled, shocking me into stillness. "I hate to speak bad of family, but Aisling's not good for Nuala, she isn't." Maeve was devoted to Granny, and I couldn't fault her instincts, considering my own previous doubts about whether I was a danger. But I wasn't a danger. Not to Granny. I was sure of it. I loved Granny.

"Calm yourself, Maeve." Geraldine's voice was soft. "Aisling will face the consequences of what she's done. I've notified the Aislingeach Tribunal."

I bit my lips together to keep from shouting at my aunt. She'd convicted me before I'd had a chance to explain my side. No doubt she'd sway the tribunal, destroying any chance of a fair hearing.

"What do you mean, she isn't good for Nuala?" Dr. Higgins said.

I glanced behind me, wondering if I could climb down the drainpipe on the wall outside my room and make for Tommy's house. As long as the drainpipe held. I fisted my hands. And I didn't look down. A wave of dizziness hit at the thought. I hated heights. So how was I going to get out of here? And then I remembered the other door out of my room. The one no one thought about any longer.

"Nuala's always weak after being with her," Maeve said.

"Nuala's excited to have Mary's daughter with her after so long," Dr. Higgins said, his voice calm.

"It's more than that, I'm sure," Maeve sniffed. "What about the night-clothes?"

"What about them?" Dr. Higgins sounded mildly interested, as if he was indulging an overwrought toddler.

"Both Nuala and Aisling had stains on their pajamas this morning," Geraldine said, "as if they'd been outside in the rain."

"But it was in a dream, wasn't it, Miss Geraldine?" Maeve said. "You said they were both in the Dreamscape last night."

"I come back to my earlier query. Is Aisling capable of doing that on her own?" Dr. Higgins asked, again the voice of reason and calm. "She's only been at this three days."

"Her training's gone very well," Geraldine said. "I'm sure she could enter the Dreamscape alone."

Heat flowed through me, and I wanted to pound on the wall and challenge my aunt. I'd never entered the Dreamscape alone. And I'd never gone in bodily during training. I hadn't had a chance to learn that step the day before. Saving Granny had preempted my lesson. The only time I'd only entered a dream in my full body was when my mom connected to me and pulled me into the Underworld. So, what had happened last night? Because for the second time I'd gone fully into a dream. I'd been wet, dirty. I bit the inside of my cheek and closed my eyes, my mind reeling. My swan pendant throbbed against my chest, and I nodded to myself. There was only one way any of this made sense. The only reasonable way to explain what happened last night was that someone pulled me into the dream with them. Someone who wanted to implicate me in the theft of my grandmother's powers. My eyes popped open. I needed proof.

"Why would she?" Dr. Higgins asked. "Is there something more you're not telling me? A reason you suspect Aisling is dangerous?"

I'd heard enough without waiting for Geraldine's answer. She'd tell the doctor about Trevor. I'd never escape once that happened. Time to go.

I stepped from my door, stuffed my phone into my backpack next to the pen and journal, and added my passport, wallet, and the notebook I'd brought from home. I grabbed my waterproof jacket and a travel umbrella and, as an afterthought, shoved a change of clothes in as well. Then I tiptoed across the space and into the bathroom, heading for the unused adjoining door between my bathroom and Granny's. Unless someone had locked it from the other side, it ought to still work. I crossed my fingers.

It took some jiggling, and I paused every few seconds to listen for sounds of Geraldine coming for me, reinforcements in tow. Finally, the handle turned, and I pulled, but the door resisted, years of swollen wood and settling joists hindering my progress.

"You're going to open." I tugged harder, the rubbing wood squealing in protest. "Damn." I stopped, holding my breath as I listened for any reaction to the noise. Nothing. I was thinking I'd have to try again, and I wished I had oil to smooth the process, when I thought of the pen. Of course.

I fumbled through my backpack, fishing out the pen and leather journal. I touched the journal, and it flipped open, as if it could read my mind and knew what I wanted. I stared at the blank page before me and considered my words. Words mattered. Intention was key, which seemed to be a recurring theme with all magic. I frowned. Which was why the failing of the protective spell last night made no sense. Unless I'd been too specific. I'd set protections against *my* dreams. But if something else had pulled Granny and me into dreams, my protections wouldn't have worked. The old clock downstairs chimed the half hour, pulling me back. I started writing.

> *Stuck like glue, the door between*
> *Must be released for escape unseen.*
> *Answers I must seek and find*
> *To prove I'm not a dangerous kind.*
> *Please do help me to get free*
> *And find the answers that I seek.*

Old hinges whined a bit when I tugged again, but the wood released its hold, and the door swung open. I held my breath as I peered inside Granny's bathroom. Empty. I breathed out a sigh, shoved the locked journal and pen back in my bag, closed the door, and crossed the yellow-tiled floor to the other side of the room, peering into the bedroom.

The large bed dominated the room and engulfed Granny's slight frame. Draperies shrouded the windows. Shadows ringed the periphery of the room. Aside from Granny and me, the room appeared to be empty. Creeping to her side, I picked up her hand lined in prominent blue veins, the faint pulse reassuring.

"I'm so sorry, Granny. I would never hurt you." A spark shot between Granny's palm and mine, a message from her to me. Having her powers taken was like cutting off the fingers of an artist. I wouldn't have done something so awful. I couldn't have.

"It's intention," I whispered, not expecting a response. "And I don't intend to cause harm. I don't. I can't do complicated dreams. I can't go into the Dreamscape alone. Someone else did this. And I'm going to find out what happened. And then I'm going to save you and Lorcan and prove myself to Geraldine. I promise."

Granny sighed, and her fingers moved in mine. I squeezed gently and set her hand down. "I love you, Granny, and I don't want to lose you. But I have to leave here to find answers. I promise I'll be back."

I slipped from her bedside toward the doorway.

A deep voice stopped me. "You don't have much time."

I bit back a scream and spun around, my hand to my chest as Dr. Higgins stepped from the shadows into the light.

"You need to leave, Aisling, if you intend to do as you claimed." He came closer to me. "I don't think you harmed your grandmother, so I'm going to let you go." He took my hand and raised my injured finger to look at it. "How did this happen? No one explained."

"I cut it on a book."

"Not a paper cut." It was a statement. He was watching me.

"No." I shook my head. "Look, it sounds preposterous." I shrugged. "But, then, given everything else, maybe it doesn't." He smiled. "An illustrated swan on the cover of a book came to life and pecked me."

His eyes narrowed. "Where did you find this book?"

"Geraldine's dreaming room in the attic."

"When did this happen?"

"My first night here. Music led me up there." I closed my eyes and sighed. "It was wrong to go, but then Geraldine found me and said I heard the music because I was Caer's descendant. She said the swan bite wasn't harmful." I gasped, unable to continue, as the familiar pain coursed through my finger and arm. The doctor raised his eyebrows and I shrugged. "It hurts when I talk about it."

"Hmm." He examined my finger again. "I'm not sure," he murmured. "But I wonder."

"Wonder about what?"

He released my hand and focused again on me. "I need to think. Do some research. But you should tell Tommy what you've told me. And continue to train. Tommy can direct you to Dreammasters willing to help you. Not everyone will doubt you, not if you explain to them what you've explained to me." He looked into my eyes, as if he could see my thoughts. "You're very like your mother. She would have made an excellent Dreammaster, had she stayed and trained." He sighed. "Don't give up. Samhain is only a few days away."

"I'll go to Tommy."

"Excellent."

"I don't want to get him into trouble."

"Tommy knows how to take care of himself. And he can protect you."

"Tommy and training." I nodded. "I can do that. And you won't say anything?"

"No, but hurry. Go now, and you'll have no trouble leaving unseen."

Chapter Thirty-Seven

He'd left before sunrise, following a predawn summons from his father. The missive had appeared on his bedside table with a pop and a wink of magical light, waking Tommy from a deep sleep. He'd fumbled for the thick paper and paused, noting the official seal of the king. Father only sealed vital messages and only the intended recipient could break the wax lock. Tommy had frowned, not able to recall the last time King Finvarra had sent him a message like this. It had happened once, perhaps twice, during his time in Galway. Usually, the fair folk relayed messages from the king via the hawthorn tree in back.

Tommy shifted to sitting and broke the seal, which snapped and sparkled as the wax melted away, disappearing into the air. As he read the words, the hair on the back of his neck raised.

Trouble in the north. Activity on the island. Meet me at the castle to discuss. Hawthorn not safe. Hurry. Father.

He'd hated to wake his friend, but Tommy didn't own a car, and given the remote location of his destination, a cab wouldn't work. He'd never get one back to his house. As Fergus lived closest to him of all his friends, Tommy found himself knocking on the lad's door at half five in the morning.

"Jaysus, stop your hammering." Fergus pulled open his door and peered at Tommy through half-open eyes. "Tommy." He rubbed a hand over his bare chest. "What in the feck are you doing here?"

"I need your car," Tommy said, tamping down impatience. "I've had a cryptic note from my father to meet him at his castle."

"And the tree wouldn't work?" Fergus yawned. "You had to wake me."

"He said the Hawthorn wasn't safe." Tommy gripped the doorframe. His father was seldom in touch, and almost never had he sent a warning so dire. Tommy sensed the impending danger, feeling it as a building pressure in his chest. He knew he had to act.

Fergus watched him for a moment, and Tommy wasn't certain if his words had penetrated. "You'll let me know what you find out. We need a break, and that's a fact. The damn Fomorian has had his way for too long."

"We do. And he has." Tommy glanced at his watch. "He said to hurry, lad."

"Sure." Fergus nodded. "Sure and you can take the thing," Fergus said, waving Tommy inside. "As long as I can find the fecking keys. A minute," he mumbled, heading to the back of the small cottage he lived in at the edge of his parents' Galway city property.

Tommy stepped inside, leaving the door cracked, ready to get on his way as soon as Fergus returned. He heard talking, didn't really want to listen. He didn't need to know if Fergus had overnight company.

Fergus emerged from his bedroom, still mumbling under his breath. "Don't know how the fecking things ended up under the bed."

Tommy wasn't surprised. Fergus was no housekeeper. Not that it mattered.

"Thanks a million, lad," Tommy said, accepting the keys. "I'll fill it with petrol for you. I should be back by early evening." He knew how his father liked to talk. And if he was going to the Otherworld, he'd want time to chat with his mother. He missed Queen Una. She was the calm, centered stability of his family. He planned to spend the day. Unless his father's news meant he had to return more quickly. "Or earlier."

Tommy stepped outside, turned to wave, and was greeted by the door closing in his face. He shook his head and rounded the cottage to the small drive where Fergus parked his subcompact metallic-green Volkswagen.

The drive was only thirty-five kilometers, made even quicker by the lack of traffic on the roadways and roundabouts so early in the morning. Still, Tommy was sweating by the time he pulled off the road outside of Tuam. He parked in the center of a copse and added to the seclusion with a series of spells he cast to keep the car and his presence hidden. Then, he turned to follow the track to the Sídh of Cnoc Meadha or Knockma Hill, as at the locals called it, which hid the entrance to his father's kingdom.

The climb was rocky and steep, but Tommy made the hike with ease. He claimed his age as sixty-six to his Irish friends, but his actual age wasn't easily translated into human years. Suffice it to say, he was far older; however, his bloodline allowed him to age more slowly, even while living in Ireland, and he retained his youthful vigor despite the lines and wrinkles of the human aging process.

At the rocky top of the hill, Tommy paused, looking around him. The world was still shrouded in darkness, obscuring the spectacular view of County Galway he knew spread beneath where he stood. Sunrise wasn't for almost an hour. Still, the peace of the spot soothed him, and he took a deep breath and closed his eyes. The energy of his homeland called to him, flowing from his feet into the rest of his body. The warm wind of the Otherworld circled him, carrying with it the fragrance of his land—a mixture of rose and honeysuckle blended with salty ocean breezes and sprinkled with magic.

He opened his mouth, about to speak the words that would open the realm to him and allow him to enter, when he sensed a presence settling next to him.

"You woke me, my son." King Finvarra's baritone voice spilled into the dark of early morning, rumbling over the land like a gentle roll of thunder. He snapped his fingers, and a pool of light shone down upon them. "What brings you to your home so early? Is there a problem?"

The sense of urgency twisted into a squeezing hand of dread tugging at Tommy's gut. "I received your missive. This morning. At my bedside." He turned to stare into the deep brown of his father's large expressive eyes.

"I sent no note to you, my son." The confusion on his father's face told Tommy he spoke the truth.

"So there's no emergency in the northern counties. No large influx of Fomorians onto Tory Island?"

"We do have reports of some activity, yes." The king nodded, his golden hair glimmering in the pool of light. "Nothing to cause us great concern; however, it's most vexing. As soon as I send a troop of leprechauns or goblins to the island to find and secure an entry point, the Fomorians find a new way in." His father frowned. "There is one disturbing bit of information that I haven't relayed. But, as you're here, I'll share it with you now. We've had reports, mainly from the northern counties, of a narcotic that appears to enhance violent tendencies in local Irish populations. There have been reports of increased fighting and property invasion."

Frustration built in Tommy's chest. "Why didn't you tell me this before? The Fomorian has been known to use potions to influence humans. He's not done so in many years. But if he's taken up the practice again, we must be aware and on guard."

"As I recall, the Fomorian used his original potion to change humans into Fomorians. He ended up killing those he injected."

"Until we found a cure." Tommy thought of Eilish. She'd developed the best antidote for the potion used by the Fomorian. He wished she were here with him. If the Fomorian had developed a new concoction to drug the Irish people, her skills could be vital.

"I'll keep you updated as we learn more. You might have your Dr. Higgins in Galway interface with a young doctor one of our allies in Donegal City has been consulting. You've met Esmerelda."

"Yes." Esmerelda was part of the fair folk, working with Tommy to find the Fomorian and send him home. "She runs an herbal shop."

"Correct. She's cultivated a relationship with this doctor. And she's been in contact with another herbalist in the south of Ireland. A woman who lives on a remote island. Somewhere near a place called the Beara Peninsula?" The king raised his eyebrows, questioning, and Tommy nodded.

"I know of it. I'll follow up with Esmerelda."

"None of this answers why you were summoned to your home." The king's voice was troubled.

"If it wasn't you, we have a problem." Tommy glanced at his watch. A quarter past seven. "Few could send a message sealed with your wax symbol and locked with your magic."

"I will investigate." The king's voice shook. "I will not tolerate a spy."

Without warning, Aisling's face flashed into Tommy's head, and the increasing need to get home pressed upon him. He had to move. Get back to the car. "This is wrong. Someone's tricked us. I have to get back."

"I would agree." The king reached out and gripped his son's arm. "It has been a pleasure to see you, Tommy." He paused. "We miss you at home. Your mother in particular." The king cleared his throat. "A visit wouldn't be amiss when you can find the time."

"Of course, Father. I'll plan a trip soon." Tommy patted his father's shoulder. "And we'll stay in touch."

Tommy turned to go, his quick steps taking him to the edge of the hill—and straight into a solid barrier, rough like a brick wall and just as unmovable. He stumbled backward, rubbing his forehead where he'd knocked into the wall.

"What in the hell is going on?"

"What happened?" His father joined him.

"I don't know. It's as if a spell has been placed around the hill."

The king raised his hands and uttered a spell of his own to break any alien curses. The air around them cracked. When they checked, the invisible barrier remained intact.

"Bollocks," Tommy roared. "I have to get back to Galway." He circled the top of the hill, beating against the barrier, hoping for an opening but having no luck.

His father continued to cast spells. Both of them attempted to contact family and friends in the Otherworld. Both tried to enter their home world. Every attempt they made was blocked. Tommy tried to make a call with his mobile phone, but he had no signal. Finally, both sank onto the rocks littering the surface of the hill.

"Whoever did this will be punished." The king glowered. "I will have the spy found and locked away."

"It's a serious breach," Tommy agreed. But he was more concerned for Aisling. And Nuala. His sense of dread, a hollow feeling in his stomach, increased the longer he was stuck. He took a deep breath, willing his racing pulse to slow, when a *ping*, like the sound of a bell on a clear day, startled him to attention. The pinging sound meant he had a message.

From the Druid pen. He pulled the pen from the inner pocket of his jacket and tapped the end of the silver column with the tip of his finger. Shimmering sparks erupted from the end of the pen and a tiny compartment sprang open. Tommy tipped the pen and a thin, rolled scroll slid into his open hand. Unrolling the scroll, Tommy began to read. By the end of the message, his pulse was galloping.

To Tommy:
It's Aisling ...
I need your help,
And a place to hide.
So I can explain,
And make things right.
Everything's wrong.
Bad dreams last night,
Granny's powers ...

The words faded away, an incomplete thought. Had someone interrupted Aisling? He shivered at the notion, and his cold fingers touched the scroll, as if doing so would somehow make the missing words appear. What had she been about to write?

"Bollocks." He replaced the scroll, stood, and strode to the barrier. He kicked at it. Nothing changed. "Fecking shite. I have to get out of here." He pounded on the wall until his hands hurt and he could barely take a breath. He leaned his head against the barrier, his limbs shaking, his thoughts in a whirl. The Druid pen message explained his feeling of foreboding. Aisling and Nuala needed him. And he couldn't get to them.

"I'll kill whoever did this." He swung around to face his father. "Aisling is in trouble. So is Nuala. All of this was done so I couldn't help them."

His father's face was set in grim lines. "We will find the spy, and we will deal with him or her."

"I only hope it's not too late to save my friends."

CHAPTER THIRTY-EIGHT

I stepped from the kitchen door into a wet, murky world. The rain had slowed, but a fine drizzle clung to my jacket and slid in drops from the hood covering my head into my eyes.

I tiptoed past what Tommy had told me was the old gardener's shed where he'd lived when he first arrived in Galway. At the back of the house was Granny's vegetable patch. The loamy smell of earth rose to my nostrils, and I raised my eyes to the upper floor of Granny's house, where she lay in a coma-like state. I'd find her powers. I'd get them back to her and in doing so prove myself to Geraldine. I wasn't going to let my grandmother die.

I took a few steps more and rounded the house, holding close to the stone walls. Once I was past the old oak tree, I was exposed until I reached the middle of the long drive. I surveyed my territory. Maybe I could hang close to the chestnut trees, walk in the shadows. But I had to hurry. The sun would be up soon.

Rooks trumpeted my arrival in the garden, their screeching calls tracking my movements. I hunched in my raincoat against the cold and damp, checking over my shoulder every few steps for signs of Geraldine or Maeve. The trees, the dripping accomplices of the rooks, splattered chilly raindrops onto my head every time a raven-feathered tattletale landed on the uppermost branches to get a better view of my escape.

"Go away." I hissed at the birds, waving my arms, as if the creatures cared a jot about my proclamations.

At the bench, I paused for a moment, peering up at my window and over to Granny's next to mine. No light shone from either room, and my racing heart slowed a fraction at the thought that no one had yet discovered my absence. I'd get to Tommy's, explain what had happened, even the dream about Trevor. Tommy would listen without judgment. He'd help me save Granny and Lorcan if he could.

I stuck close to the stone wall that ran along the driveway to the street, which was hidden behind the line of shrubbery. At the street, I broke into a jog up the hill, desperate to get to Tommy's house before Geraldine realized I was gone. I crossed the busy intersection where Fergus had saved me without incident, adrenaline fueling me through even when another city bus bore toward me. By the time I made it, thoroughly soaked, to Tommy's, my side was locked in a painful stitch and my breathing was ragged.

The house was lit up, as if was waiting for me, welcoming me. I breathed out and my shoulders relaxed. Tommy was up. He'd let me in. He'd listen. I'd tell him everything, and he'd help me.

Tears filled my eyes at the thought, and I headed toward the front door.

Chapter Thirty-Nine

Geraldine entered her attic dreaming space, closed the door, and leaned back against it with a sigh. She needed a break from Maeve's stifled sobs and handwringing and Dr. Higgins's long, pointed looks from under his lowered brows.

She could tell he suspected her of stealing her mother's powers. He was as bad as Mother, always suspecting Geraldine when someone else—in this instance Aisling—was the obvious culprit. Once Geraldine addressed the tribunal and shared what she knew about Aisling's dreams on the night Trevor died and the night her mother's powers were stolen, Aisling's innocence would no longer be assumed. Geraldine was a respected Dreammaster. She would be believed. Life could go back to normal. Or, in fact, better than normal. She smiled, satisfaction and desire pulsing through her veins. She had a call to make.

With a sigh, she pushed from the door and crossed to the fireplace. She snapped her fingers, and the turf laid in the hearth blazed to life. She stroked the crystal swan who guarded the space before pulling her phone from the pocket of her trousers. Selecting a name from her contacts, she pressed the displayed number and waited.

"Well?" A male voice answered, deep and rumbling.

She shivered at his tone, imagining his hands on her body. "It's done."

"And Aisling?"

"In her room. Soon to be thoroughly discredited."

There was a hesitation. "Soon to be? Who believes her now?"

She growled, a soft sound deep in her throat. "The damn doctor has his doubts. I think he suspects me. But he must explain to all and sundry why I would harm my mother, something that will be more difficult once I've made my case against my niece to the Aislingeach Tribunal."

"Indeed, you shall triumph," he purred. "I miss you, my darling."

Her body thrummed. "Should I meet you later?" A sudden need to see him, touch him, filled her. "Once the doctor has left?"

"Is it wise?" he asked. "What about Maeve?"

She gritted her teeth. He was right. She had a part to play. Leaving Mother's side would lead to questions.

"Of course, you're right. I've placed a call to Muirgen to begin a formal report to the Aislingeach Tribunal. She's on her way, but the trip from Inisheer takes a couple of hours. I'll stay here, until Aisling is taken care of. Once I've shared my evidence with Muirgen, she'll have to convene the tribunal. Aisling has no plausible defense." She chuckled as she imagined her niece spluttering her way through the hearing. "She'll be convicted. The case is iron-clad. They'll suppress her powers."

"Excellent," the man said. "That leaves only one person who'll never let this drop. Tommy must be dealt with next." He sighed, seeming almost sad at the thought. But she knew better.

"Yes." Her voice was firm. "With Mother, Aisling, and Tommy out of the way, we can move forward. No impediments. Nothing to stop our plans."

"He can't escape the trap," the man said, his voice jubilant. "The magic is strong, a power he won't know how to defeat."

"Yes." Her pulse quickened. "He and King Finvarra cannot penetrate the barrier. It's time for you to send your men to take care of them."

The air in the room seemed to bristle with energy at her words. Was it the idea of freedom from being what others expected? Or the idea that they could finally be together? Or perhaps both? His thoughts seemed to be in line with hers.

"I was only waiting for your call, my love. Once the job is finished, Tommy is gone, and Aisling is powerless, there'll be nothing in our way. We'll be together," he murmured, and she heard the longing in his voice. "Come to me, my love. Late tonight. I'll send a car. I'm ready for our life together to begin."

"Once I've dealt with Muirgen." Her heart quickened, and a flutter spun deep and low in her belly.

A door slammed somewhere on the floor below where Geraldine stood, and she jumped at the sound.

"She's gone." Maeve's wild voice screamed through the house at such a fever pitch that Geraldine was certain the neighbors could hear her. "Geraldine."

Feet raced down the hall below, and Geraldine heard her bedroom door slam open.

"Geraldine, she's gone. She's escaped."

"Gone?" Geraldine whispered, her body filling with ice.

"What's happening?" asked the man on the other end of the line.

"Aisling's gone." She nearly choked on the words. "Maeve's downstairs yelling about it. An escape."

"Geraldine."

She heard his voice, but she couldn't answer. How had this happened?

"Geraldine, are you up there?" Maeve's strangled voice preceded her up the attic stairs. "Aisling's gone." The housekeeper's voice came nearer.

"I have to go," Geraldine said, slowly lowering the phone.

"Wait, Geraldine," he pleaded. She raised the phone back. "I'll send help."

"She'll go to Tommy."

"And he isn't there," he said, a confidence rising in his words. "But someone else will be. Someone loyal only to you and me."

Fire burned through her. How had she done it? How had one as inept as Aisling escaped? And then she remembered about the unused door in the bathroom, and the fire became an inferno. She'd forgotten. Yet the door was sealed. How had Aisling opened a sealed door? Geraldine gripped the phone so hard she worried it would break in her grasp.

"Tell him to hurt her. Kill her if need be. And tell your other men to hurry. Get to Tommy. Ensure he's dead as well. It's time to finish what we started."

The End...For Now

Aisling's adventures are far from over. The magical danger and suspense continues in The Fae and The Fomorians. Turn the page to find links to both books on Amazon to discover the next challenges Aisling faces.

Happy Reading

KD Pryor

THANK YOU FOR READING

Thank you for reading *The Dreammasters*. I hope you enjoyed the first of Aisling's adventure in Galway. The adventure continues in the next two books, *The Fae* and *The Fomorians*. Be sure to grab them and discover more Celtic magic. Both are available on Amazon!

Authors appreciate your help in spreading the word to other readers, including telling a friend. Reviews help readers find books, so please leave a review on Amazon, GoodReads, or BookBub and thank you for helping spread the word about the Of Gods and Monsters series.

If you want to discover more about what led to Tommy's arrival in Galway and his continued involvement searching for the Fomorian, you can grab the prequel to the series, *The Otherworld Prince* to fill you in. The book is free and is only available to my mailing list subscribers.

Once you join, you'll get updates about my books, new releases, previews of upcoming books, deleted scenes, and tidbits about me. I'll also answer questions about my books and my writing process.

Click the QR Code below to go to my website where you can find links to all my books and the sign-up for my newsletter.

QR Code to KD Pryor Website

You can also find me on Facebook, Instagram, and TikTok.

Glossary and Pronunciation Guide

Aisling: [Ashling] A vision or dream

Aislingeach: [ashling-ach] Dreamer

Caer Ibormeith: [Kyair] Irish Goddess of sleep and dreams.

Daoine Sídhe: [doon-ya shee] inhabitants of the fairy hills or mounds

Éire: [ēr-e] or **Ériu:** [ēr-oo] The island of Ireland and also represented as the goddess of Ireland.

The Fae: [fay] Known by many names including Fair Folk, Fairy Folk, and Aos Sídhe (people of the fairy hills). The terms refer to Otherworldly or supernatural beings. These can include the Púca or Goblins, fairy animals like the Cat Sí, and the Slua Sídhe. The ancient gods and goddesses of the Tuatha Dé Danann are also part of the Fair Folk or The Fae.

Fáilte: [fawl-che] Welcome

Faugh a ballagh: [Fawkh uh Bal-uhkh] Clear the way.

Loughnashade: [Lock na shade] An ancient horn or trumpet discovered in Ireland and believed to be from the 1st century BC. (see below for information)

Mo Ghrá: [moh graw] My love.

Samhain: [sow-n or sowen] The pagan Celtic New Year and the beginning of the gaimos or dark period of the year. Celebrated on November 1 and the preceding night, October 31. The origin of Halloween. Samhain is a liminal time of year when the veil or barriers between the human world and the Otherworld thinned, allowing easier passage between the two.

Sídh and Sídhe (pl): [shee] Refers to the underground realms assigned to the Tuatha Dé Danann accessed by Fairy Hills or Mounds as well as the gods, goddesses, and fair folk living within the realms.

Sídh Meadha or Cnoc Meadha – Knockma Hill, ruled by King Finvarra and Queen Una.

Sláinte: [slawn-che] Health or Cheers.

Slua Sídhe: [Sloo-ah shee] Fairy Host – Craven form of fallen fairies, ghostly in appearance. They feed on the souls of the desperate, despairing human and fairy folk. Do not speak their name out loud. Do not look direction at them.

Tuatha Dé Danann: [too-āh dae donnan] – The People of the Goddess Danu. The ancient gods and goddess of Ireland.

Resources

These are just a few of the many great resources available in books. More information is also available online.

Fairies, A Guide to the Celtic Fair Folk by Morgan Daimler

In Search of Ancient Ireland by Carmel McCaffrey and Leo Eaton

Celtic Mythology edited by Geddes & Grosset

Celtic Myth and Magick, Harnessing the Power of the Gods and Goddesses by Edain McCoy

Early Irish Myths and Sagas from Penguin Classics. Introduction and translation by Jeffrey Gantz.

Ever Ancient Ever New by Dolores Whelan

Celtic Myths and Legends by T.W. Rolleston

Acknowledgements

While a writer often feels alone in the creative process, the truth is many people contribute to the completion of a book. I have amazing support in my writing process, and I am grateful for everyone who cheers me on.

First, thank you to the early beta readers who suffered through the first version of this novel. You know who you are. I appreciate your time and feedback.

Thank you to my editor, C.S. Lakin. You guided me through the re-working of the book and helped me see where to cut, where to add, and how to make the story better. Thank you so much for being not only a superb editor, but a friend and mentor.

Thank you to my family and friends for always championing my writing efforts. To my adult kids, I love and appreciate you and your continued encouragement. Thanks to my parents for believing in me and instilling in me a determination to follow the truth of my heart. Thank you to my sisters in low who willingly read the book and offered feedback. And thanks to all my friends who are waiting patiently for me to get this project finished. To all of you, your love and support are invaluable.

Thank you to my husband, Jim. I don't know what I'd do without you. You plotted with me before dawn when ideas were whirling around in my head after a sleepless night. You read and re-read versions of the book numerous times. You worked on my website, learned all about newsletters, and attended conferences with me. Most of all, you made me laugh and kept me sane through it all. You have the patience of a saint I love you so very much.

I recently decided it was time to update the covers for the full trilogy, and I discovered an amazing and talented designer, Maria Spada. She has created my dream covers for the Of Gods and Monsters series. Maria, you've captured the magic I hope lives within the pages of my books. Thank you so much.

Especially, thank you to my readers. Most of you I don't yet know, but I look forward to getting acquainted. This book is for you.

About the Author

KD Pryor crafts enchanting paranormal fiction where midlife women discover their hidden powers and unexpected destinies. Drawing from her experiences living in Ireland and India, she weaves rich cultural tapestries with threads of Celtic mythology and supernatural elements in her "Of Gods and Monsters" series, including "The Dreammasters," "The Fae," and the "The Fomorians."

A world traveler turned storyteller, KD believes that wisdom and life experience fuel the most powerful magical transformations. This philosophy shines through in her writing, where ordinary women unveil extraordinary abilities and embark on remarkable journeys of self-discovery.

When not crafting tales of supernatural awakening, KD can be found exploring quiet country roads with her husband, attempting (usually unsuccessfully) to conjure sunbeams for her demanding cat Thunder, or dreaming of her next cup of coffee in Galway. Her time living abroad, particularly in Ireland, continues to influence her storytelling, infusing her work with authentic cultural details and mystical elements.

KD remains committed to creating stories that resonate with women who understand that becoming who you're meant to be is a journey that keeps unfolding.